Also by Rebecca Rollins

Angel Between the Worlds (Book 2 of the Angel Series)

Angel in the Mirror

Rebecca Rollins

Cover art by Bill Meuser.

For Mags and the other lost twins and Womb Twin Survivors, may you find peace.

Acknowledgments

I have many dear people to thank. My mother GWS and late father AES were very supportive of my writing throughout my career. My children, DRS-M and RSS-M, are the greatest joys in my life. My dear partner, WPM, you listened as I read chapters aloud and mused with me on my changes over and over. I love you forever. My "Sis-Stars" are all appreciated deeply, as well. The chiropractor/healer/friend who helped me become whole again, GTG, will be eternally in my heart. My friends MJR and LJM, who read final drafts, are also deeply appreciated and loved as well.

Expect the unexpected.

Prologue

Turns out lots of things strike you as hilariously funny when you are in the womb. Especially if you are in the womb with someone else, like your sassy identical twin sister.

As of now, our mom, Faith, was completely unaware that she was carrying twins. This was late 1957 and they didn't use ultrasounds yet. We found it endlessly entertaining to make her hop up and run to the bathroom every fifteen minutes.

"Abe, I do declare, I never had to 'go' this much when I was pregnant with Jack."

"Slap me a nub, Bexs."

"You got it, Mags."

It was clear that I'd be named Rebecca for our dad's mom, and she'd be called Margaret for our mother's mom. Then we'd undoubtedly cart around the late Fifties cutesy nicknames Becky and Maggie. We hoped our names wouldn't be spelled with an "i" at the end, then we'd be foreordained to become cheerleaders in high school and dot the "i"s with those dumb little hearts.

"Yuck, gag me with a spoon."

"Whatever that is..."

Mags didn't know either, but she'd heard it on the radio and thought it sounded cool.

It was also already apparent that Mags would be the ringleader and learn to say bad words first and get us in trouble all the time. But she would also stand up to Jack, who already was turning out to be a bad egg. We'd overhear Mom loudly saying things like, "I've asked you over and over, Jack, *not* to put peanut butter on the cat!" And when she asked him "which way do you want your sandwich cut?" whichever way he said, triangles or rectangles, he would usually reject them and dash the pieces to the floor. It was rapidly becoming obvious that he would be a mean big brother, but with two of us, hopefully we'd have a better chance against him. Hopefully. He was three years old and big for his age, so it was going to be touch and go. He had Mom's brown hair, whereas Mags and I were blonde like Dad. Or we would be when we got hair. At the moment, we were as bald as two tiny bowling balls. We found that funny, too.

"I wish we were as hairy as tennis balls, at least."

"Time will tell. Blondes aren't as likely to have thick hair early on." How I knew that I couldn't say. Perhaps I'd been blonde in a former life.

Mags and I had long discussions about all kinds of stuff as we paddled about in the nice warm water. We talked about family dynamics, how Abe was the king of the castle and Faith the loyal wifey. He was finishing The Great American (Studies) Dissertation on Mark Twain and she was having babies and trying to keep Jack alive. It was an all-American family, except we had not quite achieved the white picket fence as of yet. Instead, we were all crammed into half of a Quonset hut, a kind of metal half-circle bunker that was supposed to have been temporary housing during the last war. Our half measured a whopping ten by twenty feet.

The furniture included a rickety dining table and some mismatched chairs. Dad had a desk piled high with papers and books, which was off limits to Jack (so of course he was absolutely obsessed with tipping over the piles). Mom spent a lot of her time guarding the desk like a soccer goalie. Jack had a toddler bed behind a curtain, Mom and Dad shared a narrow bed which doubled as the sofa. The kitchen consisted of a hot plate, a small frig, sink, and oven, a few open cupboards. A toilet and a shower completed the bathroom. The color scheme was Early Nondescript.

No crib had appeared yet for us, but there really wasn't a spare inch of space left, so Mags and I often wondered where they would put the two of us in a few months. Maybe matching cardboard boxes from the liquor store? Or one big box for the two of us? We were perfectly happy sharing this watery, balmy world of ours, usually cuddled up like spoons. I particularly enjoyed being the Little Spoon, even though Mags, in actuality, was a little smaller than me. I felt so safe, so protected when she literally had my back. It was endless fun to bob around like a couple of ducklings, gleefully annoying Mom.

"It's been fourteen minutes.... One, two, three! Jump on her bladder!" Mags was incorrigible. But I went along with her anyway and we jumped in tandem. Mom leapt up to take yet another pee.

A while back, for quite a few weeks we had made her throw up a lot. All we had to do was imagine what eating spinach was like and she'd heave into the toilet or the kitchen sink or the trashcan. But it didn't work anymore, for some reason. She was back to eating spinach and all sorts of healthy, low-calorie foods. Lettuce was the star of the show. But, truth be told, our only complaint was that sometimes we were kind of hungry as a result. We had heard Dr. Harrison tell Mom sternly that she was *not* allowed to gain weight and she always did what men told her, not just Abe but men in general. Dr. Harrison was a big scary dude, too, with bushy eyebrows that tended toward frowning, so we understood her obedience. However, the good doctor himself was fat, which didn't seem very fair to us.

"Take your own advice, Dr. Fatty McFatty!" Mags shouted but no one outside us heard her. I tried to cover my ears, but my arms weren't long enough, and I wasn't exactly sure where my ears were anyway.

Maybe the cat heard us. She usually came over to sit on Mom's lap when we said something. We already liked her, a calico named Betty or was it Betti? It would take us at least six years to figure out how to spell, so it didn't really matter much. She lay on the sofa and put her head on Mom's little bump, and we could hear and feel her purring, a very soothing vibration. She was clued in that there were two of us and she purred extra hard trying to get that fact through to Mom, but she was oblivious. Betty kneaded Mom's leg through her light blue or pink-striped shirtwaist dress, all of which were all about to be outgrown, though so far Mom had just hitched the waist up higher and higher. During this time, it was considered sort of gross to have a big belly.

"Watch out, Faith, it's gonna happen to you real soon..."

"At least she still smokes cigarettes, that keeps weight down." Even at less than two inches long, I tried to put a positive spin on things.

No one had bothered to forbid that yet, or the glass of whisky that was downed at cocktail hour, 5:30 on the dot, each and every day of our parents' lives. As they sipped, Mom and Dad gamely tried to have conversations while Jack made their lives a living hell, driving his trucks over their feet, sticking foreign objects up his nose, chasing poor Betty with his miniature broom. Why they gave that hyperactive little butthole a weapon of any kind was beyond us.

Every stick was a gun to him. Hell, he'd chew his sandwich halves into the shapes of guns and aim them at Mom during lunch, yelling "Pow, Pow, Bam" at the top of his lungs.

"He's a menace to society, that one."

"We definitely need a plan..."

But right then our machinations were interrupted by an odd whooshing sound.

"What's that?" Mags giant eyes got even bigger.

"I don't know. We've never heard it before." I felt the beginning ripples of fear. Everything had been going along so calmly up until now. This felt ominous.

The horrible sound was getting louder and louder. Mags and I looked at each other in terror and clung as best we could to each other's tiny bodies.

Then the unthinkable happened. Mags started to lose her grip on me and I couldn't hold her anymore either because a strong force of some kind was pulling her away. She was struggling, kicking her legs wildly, pinwheeling her arms.

"Bex!" She cried in anguish. *"Help me!"*

"Mags! Mags! Where are you going?" She was rapidly getting farther away from me and less distinct, fading away before my very eyes. "Don't go! No!" I screamed at the top of my undeveloped lungs. "No, no, no, no, no, no."

"I.... can't.... stay...". She moaned. Her body was becoming transparent and it was terrifying to watch.

"Don't leave me alone, Mags." I was crying and trying in vain to kick my way back to her. "I won't be able to stand it down here without you..."

"I... will... see... you... at... Cotopaxi."

Those were her very last words to me and then she was gone. Disappeared. I was left alone, utterly alone, and absolutely devastated. I had no idea what seeing her at Cotopaxi meant, and I couldn't even imagine the future anyway. Now it was just me. No one would have my back ever again. I wept and wept until I exhausted myself. I kicked and punched in utter frustration.

"Abe, Honey, I felt the baby kick for the first time!"

Chapter 1

"What the HELL? Rebecca! You're actually going to leave me to take care of the *kids* while you and Bhindi run off and do some crazy woo-woo shit? On a school night???" Dan was incredulous, he was livid. His hazel eyes flashed in anger.

Reed's big blue eyes got even rounder and he surreptitiously took Rachel's hand and they quietly crept down the stairs to the playroom.

"Well, you run off anytime you want to ride your precious mountain bike or throw frisbees at trees with your friends!" I retorted. "Yes, for one night you can actually feed the kids and put them to bed. God forbid you make sure they take a bath and brush their teeth. It isn't rocket science, for goodness sake." Lazy fuck.

He was scowling fiercely, practically stamping his foot. I glared right back at him.

"Fine," he spat, "See ya." He turned on his heel and stalked off to the study, where no doubt he'd spend the entire evening staring fixedly at his computer screen.

"They happen to be your kids, too." I called after him. I rarely got in the last word these days or succeeded in putting my foot down about much of anything when it came to him and his behavior. But, fortunately, this time it didn't escalate into a full-scale fight. My mind briefly flashed on the early days of our marriage when he promised things like, "Honey, if you clean up, I'll always cook dinner." Those days were long gone, both the endearments and the kept promises. But he did *know* how to cook so maybe he'd man up for one lousy night. I was determined to escape just this once, even if Reed and Rachel ate cereal for dinner, stayed up too late, and went to bed dirty.

To reassure them, I went down to the playroom where they were cuddled up on the sofa watching SpongeBob SquarePants. Rachel, turning eight, hastily took her thumb out of her mouth when she saw me. Reed, twelve, abruptly stopped chewing on his lower lip.

"Hey, guys. No biggie, but I'm going to a thing tonight with Bhindi. Daddy is going to make dinner and all."

"Daddy? Really?" Reed turned away from the screen to look at me, and though Rachel kept staring at it, I could see her little shoulders tense up.

"Yeah. You know how he used to cook? I'll ask him to make his famous mac and cheese..."

Their little faces lit up. With their thick blonde hair, Rachel's almost eerie light blue eyes and Reed's with a hint of turquoise, they looked like two sweet angels. Dan was handsome, you could give him that, and our children were frankly beautiful, if I did say so myself. Women used to routinely gasp when they saw them in the grocery store as toddlers and go bonkers over them. They'd even ask me if I dyed Reed's hair to get the two lighter blond streaks in it. Yeah, I sit around dyeing my babies' hair, plenty of time for that as a working mother. My heart tightened with love for them, but I felt an answering twinge of sadness at how they had instinctively retreated in case Dan and I got into it. Again. I absolutely hated to fight with him, but I had to defend the kids — but since he would never give in, there was a lot of shouting and we'd end up scaring the kids, so it was pointless. It went round and round. And not in a good way. I had ended up asking my doctor for Prozac last year after a particularly wretched incident in which Dan kicked in a door downstairs. I figured if I padded my head with cotton candy I could keep going until the kids got a little older.

By the same token, I simply had to get out of the house for a couple of hours and look into this women's spirituality group thing that Bhindi had been doing for a while now. She was Reed's teacher at the cool progressive school the kids went to – the one I had gone to in the 70's when it first opened – and Bhindi and I had instantly hit it off. She was plump and smiley, funny and irreverent, adored Reed (who didn't? I had gotten used to mothers calling me the day after he went on a playdate to tell me how adorable he had been). Bhindi had given me the nickname "Bex," which I adored. It made me feel cool, despite being a worn-out, middle-aged, middle-level professor and fulltime Soccer Mom.

That reminded me of how recently Rachel -- sitting in the back seat of the, yes, Volvo 240 station wagon with her friend Rosie -- announced importantly,

"You know, Rosie, I'm really fashionable." She was wearing her signature pink tutu, green tights, and sparkly silver headband.

"I am too! So fashionable!" Rosie, the feisty little thing, was not to be outdone. Her taste ran more to animal prints paired with plaids, and light-up sneakers. Boy's.

"Yes, but my mom…." Rachel paused dramatically and continued in a stage whisper, "she's not fashionable at all." I was trying really, really hard not to laugh. They must think that some kind of a paper cutout was ferrying them around town. A deaf paper cutout. Clearly, they did not think about me at all.

"I know." Gee, thanks, Rosie.

Rachel continued, with wonder in her voice, "But…. she still got herself a man!" In the rear-view mirror I saw them look at each other and shake their little heads in amazement.

I burst out laughing in spite of myself. They hurriedly clammed up and pointedly stared out the windows for the rest of the ride. Oops.

Maybe I did somehow "get a man" without being very "fashionable," but I was not so sure anymore if that had turned out to be such a good thing. Dan and I had had so much fun dating, riding around in his vintage convertible. Even a very nice wedding and honeymoon in Hawaii, where Reed decided to be conceived despite birth control and earned the middle name Dylan, meaning "son of the waves." But over the years, and more and more after Rachel was added to the mix, Dan had taken several major nose-dives, first getting diabetes, then being so pissy at work that he lost his job and had to go out on his own. From doing well-paid psychotherapy he had to resort to psychological testing, the lowest rung in the profession. Now he was so easily angered that me and the kids were tiptoeing around him most of the time. When his blood sugar was somehow perfect, once in a while he'd be nice and funny, like he used to be, een do something fun with the kids. Just often enough to keep us all hoping that the Good Dan would be the one coming through the front door at six. Often to be sadly disappointed.

Meantime, I had been doing well teaching college, somehow writing enough to get tenure -- finishing the last one when pregnant with Rachel, having to wind it up when my belly grew too big for me to reach the computer keys anymore. Doing revisions while breastfeeding her. My good friend Elsa teased me, and bragged on me, that I was the only woman she knew who wrote a book on maternity leave. Like her, I was totally burning the candle at both ends, perhaps the middle too. She had wisely stopped at one child, but spoiled Kitty so rotten that she spent the same amount of time mothering as I did. I mean, she ironed the girl's sheets, for goodness sake. I could barely wash them once in a blue moon, much less sort colors or fold the clean clothes. (Just the other day, Reed had politely requested that I don't buy him white shirts anymore because they all ended up grey. I politely informed him that if he cared that much, then twelve was more than old enough to do his own laundry. He blinked his eyes, but he agreed. "Bless his heart," as they say in the South, meaning "poor thing.")

I suppose it didn't help our marriage that I was succeeding professionally while Dan was struggling. But the kids' school was super-pricey and Dan spent astronomical sums on his beloved stereo system, and everyone had come to love skiing. Not a lot of skiing in Georgia. Life was expensive.

And exhausting. My day planner looked like the London Tube map. Reed's constant soccer and Rachel's modern dance filled any possible spare hours. During their multiple practices and classes I had learned to prepare a lecture and look up once in a while to watch them so I could pretend I had seen every move afterwards. Hell, at the dentist waiting for the novocaine to kick in I was frantically reading for my next class. While waiting for a mammogram, with CNN blaring and the nervous ladies who may or may not have breast cancer loudly chatting away all around me, I had even managed a breakthrough "aha" moment to anchor a difficult article. I carried several changes of clothing in the back of my car, whipping off my blazer and yanking on a sweatshirt while stopped at Atlanta's interminable, ill-timed red lights. I kept an apron in the car because I so often ate lunch as I drove across the wilds of the city, jumping from role to role like a demented frog. My job was not just teaching but museum curating as well. I often thought that I must be stark raving mad to try to keep up with two jobs, two kids, three cats, a horse, ageing parents, a 1925 house, and a shitty husband. Even my brother had been a useless drunk, no help at all. He had left his unhappy life behind a few years ago. Personally, I did not miss him, though I felt guilty and sad to admit it. He had hit me as a kid, shamed me for crying, lorded his age and IQ over me, then taken to LSD at fourteen, drinking continuously. He had been lousy with his only niece and nephew to boot. Sorry, but not sorry, to see him go.

Sometimes my life all swirled together into a perfect storm. Especially if someone in the family got sick, then the whole house of cards threatened to fall down, go boom. Like the time when my mother fell off her horse onto her head and was air-lifted to the hospital. I was in a photo shoot for the museum, which I bagged to rush downtown. My father's increasing dementia meant that he could not be trusted to feed himself without burning down their condo, so I had to take Reed over to stay with him after school and overnight. On top of it all, Rachel came home from school with a 102-degree fever. Thankfully, I had only one course that term and hastily converted it into a discussion rather than the expected lecture, but man. A few days later Mom was fine again so I could get to my conference in Orlando. Dad had obediently done what Reed told him to do (though later he said to Mom that Reed had gotten really bossy and why did *he* have to keep taking care of *Reed*, wasn't the kid old enough not to need babysitting anymore?). Rachel got over her fever and happily my students had no inkling of the backstory on all that sudden discussion time. But still. I often joked with Elsa that you could have it all, but the trouble was you had to have it all at the same time. She heartily agreed.

At least my usual circuit was less than a mile from home to parents' condo to college to the kids' school, otherwise I would have truly drowned. We had moved to Lake Claire from Avondale just to cut off a few minutes of drive time, which for Atlanta had already been short, since the average commute was thirty-five minutes each way and some people drove well over an hour in from Marietta. Over the years since I had lived here, the city had metastasized, Los Angeles-ized, way out of control. Five million angry people and counting. So, keeping my world in the old part of town was crucial and, even so, soccer practices, games, and tournaments tossed us all over the metro area at will. Usually at rush hour, fighting our way to Dunwoody or Vinings, eclipsing dinner time. Rachel had grown to despise soccer, dragged all over hell and gone when she could have been playing with her friends or watching t.v. I had to stock lots of books and games in the car to keep her occupied and break down and feed them from McDonald's.

On the other side of town, in Conyers, my horse Skippy was boarded in a family farm, along with Mom's horse Merlin, the one that pitched her on her head. The drive could be forty-five minutes each way or stretch to over two hours if a truck jack-knifed itself across I-20. But going to the barn was my one treat. I'd play hooky on a given Wednesday morning or a Friday afternoon, sneaking out to ride my much-beloved, 1200-pound ball of joy. He was super sweet and doted on me since I had rescued him several years back. Like a huge orange dog, he followed me around the barn and when I hugged his enormous neck, he ducked his head down to hold me there, hugging back. Fortunately, the kids liked going to the barn on weekends and Rachel had had her last birthday party there, gaining many points with her bevy of giggling girlfriends. Skippy adored all the attention, proudly wearing his paper party hat while five girls brushed him and braided his mane and tail with ribbons. Bomb-proof, he gave great pony rides, once the girls got over how high off the ground they were. He had been a parade horse before I got him, so even a semi-truck tearing past and honking its horn didn't faze him in the least. I called him my therapy and meant it. The funny part was that once when a little rabbit jumped out from behind a bush, we went sideways about thirty feet he was so scared. Wascally Wabbits terrified him, trucks did not.

Tonight, this women's spiritual group event was to take place on the opposite side of town from Conyers, over in Smyrna, but also "OTP," Atlanta slang for "Outside the Perimeter." The Perimeter, aka I-285, was the terrifying drag-race highway that ringed the city but no longer, alas, contained it. It was a given that I'd be late no matter when I started. And the identical strip malls and housing developments were difficult to tell apart, so getting lost was pretty much a foregone conclusion as well.

So, to give myself a fighting chance, I gave up on changing clothes or eating dinner and rushed downstairs. Kissing the kids' heads, I promised I'd tuck them in later. They both turned and looked at me a bit solemnly, effortlessly tripping my ever-present Working Mom Guilt. But I managed to push it away and pasted a fake smile on my face. It was one evening, not the rest of their lives, for God's sake.

"Say hi to Bhindi for me." Reed called out. He loved his teacher just as much as she loved him.

"Will do!"

"Bye, Mommy." Rachel popped up and ran after me up the stairs and I gave her a tight hug in the kitchen. She put her plump little hand in mine as we walked to the front door. "Come home soon, okay?"

"I will, darling. You'll be fine. Remember to brush your teeth for me?"

"Yeah. I hope Daddy doesn't forget the mac and cheese."

"Hey, Dan, your daughter wants your special, super- delicious Daddy mac and cheese!" I called merrily through the closed study door. Maybe flattery would help. He did love his daughter and his son, despite his deplorable fathering skills.

We heard an indistinct mumbling from the other side of the door.

I whispered to Rachel, "If he forgets..." I'll murder him, I thought. "You know how to make a killer pbj, right?"

Rachel rolled her eyes and shrugged, but finally she decided to give me a brave smile and stood by the living room window so she could wave as I backed out the driveway. I waved back enthusiastically and blew extravagant kisses until she was out of sight. Whew. Good kids.

Naturally I had some trouble negotiating the unfamiliar territory OTP, but eventually pulled up outside a cookie-cutter Smyrna townhouse in a cookie-cutter Smyrna subdivision, on a street called "Terrace Lane Trail," or "Terrace Trail Lane," or "Trail Lane Terrace," who knew. Atlanta had sprouted so many streets over the last few years that the new ones had at least three, if not more, names strung together. Downtown it was just "Boulevard," but out here it was "Autumn Park Creek Drive" and such.

Thankfully only about five minutes late, I tentatively knocked on the beige door of number 4078. No answer. They must have started on time... So, after a few more moments to be sure that indeed no one was coming, I gently turned the knob and the door easily opened, revealing acres of beige carpeting trailing down a long hallway. I heard voices further down, so I tiptoed through the shag until I came upon the living room. Furniture, beige, more carpet, beige. Even the poodle dozing in the corner was beige-ish white. But the women holding hands in a circle were very colorful in their jewel-tone flowing outfits, decked out in copious quantities of over-sized New Age jewelry, swirly scarves, and sparkly sandals. Still in my work clothes –art historians notoriously dress in black, so my closet looked like I attended an inordinate number of funerals – I felt like a nun who had suddenly found herself in a flock of harem girls. If harem girls ran to plump and were no longer teenagers. And, from the looks of one couple, liked girls better. Oh well.

As I moved quietly nearer, the two women closest to me silently dropped hands so I could join in. One of them squeezed my hand gently, supportively. I didn't know if I was supposed to squeeze back, so I didn't. This already looked like a game for which I most definitely did not know the rules.

A tiny, birdlike woman was intoning something about Hindu goddesses and Egyptian goddesses and all manner of goddesses that were being invited into the Circle to help us. Do what, I wondered? But her voice was silky, and the words were soothing, and the other ladies were nodding in agreement, eyes reverently closed. My Episcopalian upbringing immediately came to mind, all that praying with eyes closed. On the other hand, in church no one would have dreamt of holding anyone's hand – we were nicknamed "God's Frozen People" for good reason – or talking about multiple gods, much less goddesses. Even poor old Mary never got much play on those interminable Sunday mornings spent doing kneeling and standing calisthenics to please a dead guy on a stick. Embracing shame wholeheartedly as we repeated, ad infinitum, "I am not worthy to gather the crumbs from under His table." Well, fuck that shit. This Circle stuff had to be better than that, unless it were secretly a cult. Ooh, I thought, I do hope it isn't a cult. But darling Bhindi was a smart cookie and not much of a joiner, like me, so I ought to at least give it a chance. As if she could read my mind, at that exact moment Bhindi opened up her eyes and sent me a crinkly smile from her place on the other side of the circle. I winked back.

After the leader lady, whom I had nicknamed "Birdie," invoked a whole other bevy of culture heroines and heroes, from Buffalo Calf Woman to Buddha, on some indecipherable signal everyone sat down on the closest sofa or chair. All at once, one of the women, the only one dressed in beige, suddenly dropped to her knees and crawled across the carpet like a crab. She hauled herself up onto a different chair. I looked around the circle, but no one blinked an eye. Oh no, I wondered, could there be some rule that our heads can't be higher than the leader lady's? Wasn't there some religion or other that believed that or maybe it was when in the presence of the British monarch? I couldn't remember. But I was getting off track here and switched back to listening, the others rapt with attention.

"Birdie" was explaining all sorts of things about her "Mystery School." There were Elements and pagan holy days and dancing and all manner of things to learn. I had vaguely heard of some of them, and though I used to dance, that hadn't been happening ever since the kids came. What she was describing sounded almost, well, fun. And it was meant to empower us as women, evolve our consciousnesses, support our transformations, all kinds of lofty ideals. I had come of age in the feminist era, turning thirteen in 1971, the year the first Ms. Magazine appeared (wish I had kept my original issues). I gleefully threw out my tiny little bras I had recently begged my mother for. So, all the empowering and transforming stuff sounded quite exciting, really. And truly terrifying at the same time.

This program was called the "Sis-Stars." I had always, always longed for a sister, not the shitty brother I was dealt by the Universe. To receive a whole big bunch of sisters at once, what a tantalizing idea. A miracle, actually. I had several wonderful girlfriends, like Elsa at work, and my high-school-onward BFF Hayley, plus my grad-school-onward friend Virginia. But those three didn't have a spiritual bone in their bodies and I was hoping to rediscover some in mine and begin to right my life somehow. It was seriously off course at the moment. Dangerously, in fact.

So, looking around the circle more intently, who were these potential supportive sisters being handed to me on a platter? We introduced ourselves in turn. The woman I had evilly dubbed "Crawling Cathy" was actually named Suzanne and would help facilitate the Circle. This was her home, evidently. But the actual Circle, when formed, would meet at Wisteria's house in Tucker, out past Stone Mountain. Again, OTP but with better trees.

"Birdie" was actually named Wisteria, and said we could try the first weekend and if, somehow, we did not like it, it was free. Good, the Sis-Stars was not a hard sell, pyramid scheme, pre-paying rip off. The weekends, of which there would be about one per month or six weeks, cost 200 bucks each. Hell, group therapy would cost as much or more than that. What was there to lose? I could walk away if it was just too weird.

A particularly large and billowy woman introduced herself as Teddi and said she loved all things Egyptian, as her perhaps slightly too dramatic eyeliner had already implied. She proclaimed herself to be an Aries and proud of it.

The two girls, still holding each other's hands, were Vicky (long hair ending in brilliant pink dye, camo pants, no tits) and Rowan (crew cut, jeans, big tits happily unencumbered by a bra). Very cute.

Then there was a yoga whip-thin, clearly downcast woman, who said her name was, incongruously, Joy. I wondered what sadness she was carrying. But Wisteria had underscored that, besides confidentiality, one of the strongest Circle rules was not to pry or even to comfort the other person when she had to cry. Instead, we all would collectively "hold space," whatever that was. I thought space was, by definition, immaterial. So how the heck did we hold it, I wondered.

Last, but certainly not least, was a gorgeous, café-au-lait skinned woman, Chantilly, originally from Jamaica. Sexy curves undisguised, voluptuous lips painted in bright red, exuberant hair curling all over the place, she was stunning. I wanted to *be* her.

When it finally came my turn to introduce myself, although I routinely lectured to crowds as large as a hundred students, I felt oddly uncomfortable. Being a Soccer Mom and a professor did not seem to be much of an advertisement for becoming a Spiritual Warrioress, so I settled on saying that my Sun Sign was Cancer, the Mother and Moon Child. Then I found myself blurting out that actually I felt pretty lost in my life these days. The others nodded sympathetically, which actually brought a sheen of tears to my eyes. Teddi was blinking in solidarity. Bhindi held both her palms outward toward me, I guessed holding my space or something.

After a short respectful pause, Wisteria stood up and called for the Circle to be closed. The ladies jumped up, grabbed hands, and took lusty deep breaths. I attempted to follow suit. All those forces and deities and fairies and such were released from duty and all the positive energy was exported out into the cosmos, and then there were cookies. Lots of cookies. Homemade cookies. No wonder Sis-Stars had to wear flowing clothes. Having had no dinner, I ate my share too, waistline be damned.

Bhindi chatted with me in the kitchen for a while and then said she had a shitload of grading to finish and needed to run. Just then Suzanne, who had disappeared before the cookies, reappeared lurching awkwardly behind her aluminum walker. OMG, I felt so awful for calling her Crawling Cathy, even silently. She had MS or CP or something! Though I had to admit I was relieved there was no lower-head rule. Geez, get a grip, Rebecca.

It struck me that it was getting late for me too and I was due to tuck in the kids, so I said my goodbyes. Wisteria looked at me kindly and grabbed both my hands in hers and said,

"I would *love* to have you in the Circle. Our first weekend is over Halloween, which is really Samhain, of course." Of course – Sam what? "But absolutely no pressure!" She smiled radiantly and I had a sudden urge to give her a hug. But was that allowed, or would that be invading her space? I decided to just smile enigmatically and slowly pulled my hands back.

Driving home around a slightly less congested 285, I mused about the strange evening. Could I actually get dressed up like them and dance around with reckless abandon? Cry in public without shame? During my childhood, my evil brother had dubbed me "Little Becky Waterworks" and my mother had repeatedly advised me to think about a cow whenever tears threatened. Every detail of a cow, to distract me. My parents had only been caught weeping once, when Kennedy was assassinated, so as a kid I had concluded that crying was officially an

Episcopalian crime, it seemed. Too bad as a Cancer I was prone to such messy and embarrassing emotional outbursts. Now I wanted some good clean emotions back, except for Dan's incessant anger. Would I find out things I didn't really want to about myself and my situation? Was I ready for that? All the questions swirled around my head like bees trapped in a jar.

Well, I had three weeks to decide. I would have to radically rock the family boat to exit one entire weekend a month, though truth be told, the prospect filled me with shivery excitement. Two whole days every month for ME? It seemed too good to be true. Dan would absolutely freak, the kids would have to be accounted for, maybe even bribed, it would all no doubt be uber complicated. All that soccer and dance needed to be covered, but maybe Rosie's mom and Reed's soccer buddies' parents could be enlisted, if I paid them back by toting their kids at other times. Maybe Dan's moods might improve if we had some time away from each other. I know I deserved time away from *his* moods, that's for sure.

Pulling into the driveway, the study light was on and I could see Dan, as predicted, glued to his screen. Loud music was playing, even though Rachel's bedroom was just down the hall beyond the study on the right and on the way to our bedroom further back. Great. And part of his psychological testing work was evaluating Parental Fitness. Somehow I didn't think he recognized the irony in that. His other work was tracking Substance Abuse, of which he had deep and abiding personal experience. Not a speck of irony there, either.

Getting out of the car and walking past the closed study door, through the living room and dining room and back to the kitchen, all in a line to the left, I braced myself for sandwich remains. But I was pleasantly surprised to be greeted by three sticky, cheesy plates, haphazardly left for me to clean up, naturally. Even though I was exhausted, I rinsed them and stuck them in the dishwasher so Dan couldn't hold that against me in the morning. He had not emerged from the study when I had opened the front door and I didn't make a point of going in to say good night or anything. Nor did I want to discuss the Sis-Stars. Yet. So, I visited the kids' rooms, where they were sound asleep and dreaming. When I touched their toothbrushes Rachel's was wet, Reed's was not. Batting five hundred at least. More than I could ever have hoped for.

Chapter 2

While sitting in the breakfast nook the next morning, staring pointedly out the garden window, Dan oh so casually asked me,

"So, how did that woo-woo thing go last night?"

The kids looked up expectantly from munching their cereal.

"Uh, actually it looks really cool. Bunch of interesting women, like a sort of ...a support group. Bhindi and I are going to sign up for the next Circle."

"Huh, and exactly what does that entail? More skipping out on us, I imagine?" His eyes had narrowed dangerously.

"If you choose to look at it like that, then yes. Two weekend days every four to six weeks, nine total meetings." I resolutely refused to look down or act all apologetic, though my heart was beating rapidly. If I wanted empowerment, it started right here. Right damn here.

"Jesus, Rebecca. What am I supposed to do about all the kid's activities???" Reed and Rachel had suspending eating and were looking kind of worried, too. They locked eyes, wary.

"Yeah, Mom. I have soccer!"

"I have dance!"

"Of course, I know that, you guys. Do you think I haven't already thought of a plan? I can get Rosie's mom to do that weekend's dance run and I'll do some of the other weekends for her. Same with soccer, lots of the guys live nearby, and they can pick you up, drop you off, and vice versa for me and their boys the rest of the time. Your friend Sam's mom Jen is usually available for trades. I'll arrange for sleepovers, too, it'll be fun! Daddy won't have to barely lift a finger. I'll be back Saturday nights at home, too." I looked pointedly at Dan – beat that.

"Well, looks like you already decided all this. Thanks a hell of a lot for consulting me." Dan spoke fluent sarcasm.

"I don't recall being asked if you should take up mountain biking and *skip out on us* every weekend either." I sallied back.

"That's different." His chin went up stubbornly.

"How exactly is it different? Do enlighten me." This should be rich.

He bit his lip. No great comeback for that one? I decided it was better for everyone for me to just let it go.

"I think I'll be, well, happier if I do this thing. Like they say, 'if Mama ain't happy, ain't nobody happy.'"

Reed looked at me intently, a little frown appearing in his forehead.

"Mom, are you…. unhappy?" Like it had never crossed his mind that I might not be ecstatic with our life. I guess I kept it nicely hidden, or he repressed all the nasty fighting, or kids just don't think of their parents as actual people. Or all of the above. The cardboard cutout syndrome strikes again.

Rachel was peering at me curiously now, too.

"Mom?" she prompted.

How to answer? I took a deep breath and managed, "I guess there are times when things get to me, like for everybody…"

"Like too much homework?" Reed offered helpfully.

"Yeah. Exactly. I pretty much *always* have too much homework." That was something they might get.

"But you're the teacher!" Rachel looked puzzled. "You give out the homework."

"And then what do I have to do? When I get it all back?" I waited for the other shoe to drop.

The kids looked at each other quizzically. After a long pause, the light dawned in Reed's eyes.

"You have to grade it!" he said triumphantly.

"Bingo! And I have to prepare all the classes. And go to meetings. And put on exhibitions. And write books. And do laundry and cook dinner." With that last item I looked straight at Dan. He quickly looked away.

"I made the damn mac and cheese…" He muttered under his breath.

"And take us to practices and classes?" Praise the Lord, they were getting the picture.

"Wow, Mommy. Don't you get tired sometimes?" Rachel was suddenly all concerned.

"Yep, I do. Most of the time, in fact." Leave it at that. Dangerous territory.

They went back to their cereal, end of discussion.

Dan abruptly got up and said, "Gotta go to work. Daddy works really hard, too, you know."

"Thanks for the mac and cheese last night, Daddy!" Rachel chimed in, right on cue. Daddy's girl up the wazoo.

He looked very pleased with himself, high-fived both the kids, glanced briefly at me, grabbed his briefcase and his insulin kit and dashed out the door.

Reed stood up and came over to me and gave me an unexpected hug. Rachel followed suit. I squeezed them tight.

"Time for school. Last one to the door's a rotten egg!"

And they galloped off to grab their backpacks.

During carpool I thought to myself, that my revelation of joining the Sis-Stars went surprisingly well. I guess this whole turn of events was so astonishing, so out of the blue, that Dan had no ammunition saved up. He was, pure and simple, stumped. And maybe if and when he thinks about it, he'd realize that he can do his own thing during those Sis-Star weekends as long as I have the kids sorted, as the Brits would say. God knows what trouble he might get into, but frankly I found I didn't much care anymore. He could land in the hospital again from another mountain biking accident, for all of me. Run amok with the boys. Whatever. If the kids were accounted for and happy, then he could go hang.

On the way to campus, driving slowly down beautiful Lullwater Road, with its stately homes, vast lawns, and picture-perfect flower gardens, I mused on the first Sis-Star assignment Wisteria had given us at the end of the introductory evening: to start a mesa -- like a pagan altar-- in a special place at home. A place for me and no one else. That was a puzzle. Dan and I shared the bedroom and the study, the playroom had the tv, the dining and living rooms were way too public. Over two thousand square feet of gorgeous 1925 Craftsman Bungalow -- with the original heart-pine moldings and a new, heart-stoppingly expensive yuppie kitchen -- and no nook or cranny available for Mommy?

I ran over the house layout in my mind again, finally alighting on the finished workshop area in the front part of the basement, down the stairs from the kitchen. Hmmmm. It was overrun with Dan's tools, boxes of crap, and bike, acres of kid's art and out-grown clothes, and God knows what else. But it was big, seriously big. Surely I could claim a corner for my mesa somewhere in there. And, moreover, it was high time it got cleared out, organized, and cleaned up. Not that I'd had much time for such tasks, but I'd just have to make the time. I'd do it in bits and pieces. Shove Dan's stuff over further — he'd kill me if I "messed with it." He was pathologically messy and disorganized, but whenever he couldn't find something, he accused me of "messing with his stuff."

The worst time was last spring when he was in full-blown biking mania. On his crazy-pricey bike there was a little metal prong behind the seat where he stuck a stupid plastic troll doll head. Thought it was hilarious. One night I had just fallen into bed and was half asleep when he burst into the bedroom, shook me roughly on the shoulder, and demanded loudly "What did you do with my troll doll?"

"What?"

"My troll doll! It's gone!"

"I didn't touch your precious little dollie. Leave me alone! Fuck, thanks for waking me up since I always have *plenty* of time to sleep these days." Now I was fully awake and really angry.

He stomped off, leaving me to fume, toss and turn, and wonder if he really was worth it after all. His mother had sort of tried to warn me when we were engaged. We had been having lunch together up north and she pronounced, "Dan is difficult, but he's worth it." Huh, not so sure these days, Lila.

Several days later he came home from a ride and the troll head was miraculously back in place.

"Well…. Lookie there. Did the trolls magically return their *god* to you?" I snapped at him when I saw it.

He had the grace to look sheepish.

"Nah. I found it down in the park where I was riding that day."

"Oh, really. Was there anything you wanted to say to me?"

He looked blank.

"Just glad to have it back. What's for supper?" He was innocence personified.

Perhaps a can of sharp nails, I thought to myself. I was damned if I'd beg for an apology. Dan had once told me authoritatively that when you were married you didn't have to say "thanks" or "sorry," because it was understood. Very astute for a psychologist, also super great for marital communication and closeness. Glad we got our monies worth from that Psych PhD of his.

"Well, *thanks* for *not* saying you were *sorry*." I shot back.

He shook his head slightly and looked confused. I guess, every once in a while, my doctorate from Yale trumped his from Georgia State, though I hated to be an academic snob.

By the time I pulled into the parking deck at work I had pinpointed the right side of the workshop as my spot for the mesa. I'd start some clearing out tonight.

"What ya smiling about, R?" Elsa queried when she saw me walking into the museum to use the bathroom. Her office was nearby and she was headed there too. We often ran into each other in the hallway as I was dashing from the Art History building through the museum trying to put out the wildfires blazing in both my jobs.

"E, get this. I had a really cool evening last night. *Away from the family....*" I fairly crowed.

"Away from the family??? How the heck did you manage that? On a school night, no less." She looked bewildered.

"I know, huh. Modern miracle. My friend, you know Reed's teacher, Bhindi, invited me to a women's spiritual group. I just sprang it on Dan at the last minute! He had to cook dinner for the kids and everything!" I preened.

"Damn, girl. And are you actually going to join the group?"

"I am. A weekend every few weeks, for the better part of a year." Just saying it made it seem more real, though it still seemed frankly bizarre. Like I'd up and won the lottery or something.

"Wow. But you know Dan won't be reliable for all the kids' stuff..." We had grouched about our husbands for many an hour over the years of our friendship. Her long-time husband Tom was nice, but totally incompetent at anything she expected him to do. Mostly, he was quite talented at eating ice cream while sitting by the condo pool.

"Of course not. I'm going to invoke the tit-for-tat with other mothers to cover the soccer and dance madness, arrange sleepovers for them, leave meals, the whole bit," I explained.

"OMG. Good for you, R. I'm...well, I'm really jealous. Tom would never be able to man up if I tried that! You sure Dan won't bust a gut over this?"

"He's so dumbfounded he basically doesn't know what to do. Of course he immediately accused me of "skipping out" on the family. Spoiled brat. But then he couldn't even muster a response when I challenged him on his excessive biking as the same as me doing this women's group. It was almost funny to watch him try to think of why his fun time was so different from mine. I even admitted I hadn't necessarily been happy these days. The kids were really astonished and I think I might have gotten through to them a little on how tiring my life made me these days. Of course, Dan had to remind us all about how much he works, too, but the elephant in the room was that he doesn't do shit at home like I do. Rachel gave him kudos for managing to cook them mac and cheese while I was off with Bhindi." I sighed. "Par for the course, huh."

We were washing our hands at the sinks and she looked at me in the mirror with solemn faces.

"But you're doing something! For you! They have to see that as a good thing. Those weekends might be good for everybody." I could tell she was reaching past her own situation, valiantly.

"I agree. I simply have to do it. I just have to or I'll literally go stark raving mad at this point. If it means one less article written, then so be it." I shrugged and dried my hands on a paper towel.

She nodded, suddenly looking pensive.

"Well, back to work, Superwomen!" She pronounced, with fake enthusiasm. "No rest for the weary."

Later, after a long day at work, heaped on a long week, I decided to get the kids early from aftercare, surprise them with movies before pizza for dinner, and start on Project Mesa.

"Hey, Mom! You're early!" Reed was beaming.

"Yep! It's Friday, so what the heck. We'll order pizza and you guys can watch movies, what do you say?"

"I say hooray! Rachel, guess what? Mom's here and it's gonna be movies and pizza night."

Rachel was eagerly running over from playing on the half-buried firetruck in the playground.

"All right!" Her hair was its usual mess, and her clothes were laden with dirt. It must have been a good day in Rachel world.

They piled excitedly into the Volvo and argued about what pizza toppings to order. I said we could do half and half so each could get their favorites. Then it was which movie, again it was impossible to please an eight-year-old girl and a twelve-year-old boy, so I suggested Reed watch "The Matrix" on the tv and Rachel "The Princess Diaries" on my computer. They nodded their agreement.

"Best Friday *ever*," pronounced Reed… "And I did well on my math quiz, just so you know."

"You always do, but good show! Rachel, how did reading go?"

"Good. I'm almost done with the fifth-grade shelf."

"Wow, so you're reading a grade ahead, right?"

"Yes m'am." She didn't do the Southern obsequious m'am, but rather the tongue in cheek version. But she was clearly pleased with herself. Reading had come a little late but now she was gangbusters.

When they were settled with their greasy junk food and respective movies, I changed into ratty clothes to go clean the basement. With a fortifying glass of pinot grigio in hand, I surveyed the disaster area. This was going to be a big chore, but I needed "a room of one's own" of Virginia Woolf's, like I had read about in college. But, as I resolutely approached the workshop I began smelling something nasty coming from Dan's area.

Overturning various and sundry things strewn around the floor, all-to-soon I discovered the culprit and let out an inadvertent shriek. OMG, there was a profoundly dead rat under the lid of a plastic bin, so long dead that it was liquifying into a fetid pool f muck. The smell was horrible. Gaggingly horrible.

At that moment Reed popped into the room.

"What's wrong, Mom? Oh shit, I mean, oh shoot. That is so gross." He took in the slimy grey mass I was staring at and held his nose like I was doing. "I'm outta here!"

"Hey, wait, bring me a plastic bag, some rags, and the Windex, would ya?"

"Oh, all right." He agreed reluctantly. "But for the record, yuck. Double-yuck."

I managed to clean it up without vomiting, but only barely. Now the smell of ammonia had become overpowering and my eyes were burning. Not a great start to a spiritual endeavor, I thought to myself. I retreated upstairs in a hurry.

Another glass of wine to fortify me. Sitting in the nook savoring the relaxing feeling, I had an idea. Somewhere around here I had an old copy of the I Ching, the age-old Chinese divination tool. Maybe I should seek some inspiration to continue my nasty task from there. I dug three coins out of the bottom of my Mom purse to throw. Settling myself on the bed, I decided to ask what I was doing in my life right now. Tossing them six times, and noting down the combinations of heads and tails to determine the straight and broken lines, I looked up what I had drawn. The chart at the front of the book told me it was "Ku, Work on What has been Spoiled. Ku symbolizes the food on the plate which has rotted and become the home of worms." Or rats? "The situation around you is extremely confused and complicated." No shit, Sherlock. "You must work to set things in order – otherwise you will meet defeat. The removal of the decay can lead to success in reversing your fortunes."

Well, I must be on the right track because I was definitely addressing rottenness and making order. My fortunes needed reversing all right. I was encouraged, even though things were pretty darn grim at the moment. And smelly.

Venturing back downstairs, the room was marginally less stinky. I decided to plow on, to resolutely work on what has been spoiled, so as to please good old Confucius and myself in the bargain. Tentatively I searched for other surprises under junk in the rest of the room, but luckily there weren't any more liquifying rodents to be discovered. Whew.

Pushing Dan's abundant crap over, stacking boxes more efficiently, I finally got about ten feet square of blank floor over by the brick wall with the niche in it. In the twenties it was some kind of coal heating mechanism I guessed. I was finally Swiffering the floor when Rachel appeared, her movie evidently over.

"Hey, look at that. It's actually clean." She swung her head from side to side, taking in the empty area. "What are you gonna do in here, Mommy?"

"Well, the Sis-stars, that's the group I'm doing with Bhindi, have this thing where you build a mesa, like an altar but not like ones in church. You put on it anything that you like, that inspires you, things with good energy…" I explained. Not that the kids had gone to church except once or twice with friends' families. They had vehemently agreed that it was boring. Dan was Jewish/atheist and I loathed all things organized religion, so they were pretty much on their own in that department. I hoped that they believed in being good and kind, and respectful of Nature and other cultures, learning from my example. I wanted to be more proactive with them about values, though, as I got more into this pagan stuff. I thought they'd probably like it.

"Cool. I'd like to make a mesa, too. In my room, maybe." Rachel looked interested. "What are you putting on yours?" I saw the I Ching I had laid by the doorway. That would be a good start.

"I don't really know yet, Honey Bunches. It's kind of a process. That book over there has a lot of wisdom in it, so maybe begin with it. First, I had to clean out this area and… well, I found a gross dead animal that I had to get rid of, so I'm just now getting started on the fun part."

"What dead animal?" She was making a sour face.

"You might not want to know…." She did have a lot of Scorpio in her chart, so then again maybe she did.

"A mouse?"

"Bigger."

"A bunny?"

"Yuckier."

"A.... a.... rat?"

I nodded.

"Oh nasty, nasty, nasty. I hate rats. Are there any more?" She looked around hastily, fearing the worst.

"Nope, I've checked. The house is not infested with them, it was just the one, just a fluke. Don't worry. I'll check around more often and now that the basement is getting cleaned up, they won't have any places to hide."

She looked unconvinced, but nodded anyway.

"Good. 'Cuz I don't ever want to see a rat, dead or alive. Ever." Rachel was emphatic.

Just then Reed wandered in.

"Any more disgusting critters, Mom?"

"Nope, all gone. No others lurking about, either, that I can tell." I reassured them both.

"That's good." He looked relieved. "Can we play cards or something? I'm done with my movie and none of my friends can hang out tonight."

"Sure, Sweetums. I'll come up to the nook and we can play cribbage, if you want." We had started a lifetime cribbage tournament, though we never kept score. Reed pretty much always won, anyway. He was super lucky, so much so that it was honestly a bit annoying. But when I was a kid, I always won coin tosses with my brother – my only victories over him. Naturally he stopped agreeing to coin tosses to settle disagreements, so that he couldn't lose to me anymore. Ass. I honestly did not miss the man once bit.

"I'll look around for things to put on my mesa while you guys play cards." Rachel piped up.

"Mesa? What's that?" Reed asked.

"Mom says it's a table-y place where you put stuff you like and have good energetics." Close enough.

"Hmm. What are you thinking of?" I asked her.

"I was thinking about some of those pretty rocks I got at Disney World and some flowers, maybe?"

"Good ideas! Nature is chock full of good energy. You can swipe the flowers from the kitchen and you know where the vases are kept." She skipped off. I was pleased she had glomped onto making a mesa so fast. Perhaps I could take her with me to some of the big pagan ceremonies like Winter Solstice. That would be cool. Girls need all the empowerment they can get, too. Especially when they have fathers like hers. Damn, damn, damn, damn, damn. Push that thought away, fast.

"Let's deal!" I said brightly to Reed.

Chapter 3

All the arrangements to cover the kids' activities over the weekend had been duly accomplished and Dan was basically completely off the hook thanks to Sam's mom Jen and Rosie's mom Alice taking up the slack. Thankfully, Halloween fell on Friday and the first Sis-Stars began the Samhain session the next morning at Wisteria's house.

For their costumes, Reed and Rachel had cooked up a pretty cool idea together: she was going as Little Bo "Creep" and he was the sheep she had apparently stabbed repeatedly in the back. My mom always sewed the children's costumes and she had outdone herself this time, starting with Rachel's innocent pink gingham dress with puffy sleeves and a white collar. The apron was heavily splattered in ketchup blood. For Reed she had devised a fake sheepskin body suit with a huge plastic knife protruding from a clever opening in the back and ketchup trailing from gory wounds littered about his body. The kids had been ecstatic when they tried on the whole ensemble for the first time, giggling as Rachel chased Reed around the living room.

It was basically street theater, but since they would not be likely to trick-or-treat together the whole evening, their explanations would amuse the neighbors as they put two and two together. I stayed home to give out candy to the regular ghosts and goblins, while Dan got on his bike wearing all black, a skeleton mask, and skeletal hands. He was to keep an eye on Rachel and Rosie, who was going as the Wicked Witch of the West (who just happened to wear light-up sneakers). Sam went as a were-wolf. Dan liked to peddle up to groups of trick or treaters and scare the daylights out of them with an evil laugh. He thought it was funny, I thought it was mean.

The five of them came back an hour or so later, breathless with excitement.

"I got gobs of candy, Mommy! Gobs!" Rachel panted and dumped her sack on the living room rug with glee.

"Me, too. Mega gobs!" Rosie did likewise. She and Sam were spending the night tonight as turn-about for their families hosting Rachel and Reed for me Saturday night. I mean, for us. Well, really for Dan.

Reed and Sam made their piles in the dining room and began trading each other for their favorite candies. I asked for an Almond Joy and Reed tossed me one.

"Not too many, kids, or you'll be up all night and get a stomachache." I warned. As if they would listen to me.

Dan piped up amidst the chatter and giggles, saying to me with a grin, "So I went passed this mother and her little girl…"

"Yeah?" I was wary. What had he done now?

"And scared the pants off them. Later the mother saw me making another round and gestured for me to come over to them. She said, please take your mask off and show my daughter you're a person under there. So I did. Then the mom said her daughter also had something to say to you. And the girl said, 'I don't like you.' And they walked off."

"And you think that's funny, I suppose."

"Oh, lighten up, Rebecca. It's Halloween, for God's sake."

"In fact, it's Samhain, the pagan holiday for the living and the dead to communicate."

"Always the professor." He said with a sneer and grabbed a Snickers bar from Rachel's stack.

"Hey, Daddy, that's my favorite." She pouted.

"Mine, too." He snapped and stalked downstairs to watch television, munching on the candy. Since he had diabetes, he should not have eaten the sugar, but his solution was to eat whatever he wanted to, test his blood sugar, and give himself an insulin shot. His thighs looked like they had a bad case of prickly heat.

I wrangled the girls into their pajamas and read them a chapter from The Lion, the Witch, and the Wardrobe, hoping to get them calmed down enough to sleep. The boys had retreated to Reed's room, which was off the playroom, to fight El Diablo on the computer. Dan fell asleep in front of his action movie (what I called a Dick Flick) and I turned off the tv before I turned in so the bang bang would not keep me up.

I was already excited about the upcoming Sis-Star weekend, and a tiny bit nervous, not knowing what to expect. On my way upstairs I visited my mesa where I had begun to put things after the rat incident receded in smell and memory. Besides the I Ching, I had added a statue of Ganesh that I had picked up at a flea market. He was the Hindu elephant-headed god that removed obstacles and I had had an odd experience last spring when chaperoning a fieldtrip to the new Hindu temple in Lilburn. Amidst the OTP strip malls and fast-food chains, the Hindu community had erected a startlingly white, massive, elaborate building out of imported marble. Around the main room were arrayed shrines to the various gods and goddesses, each one in its own little room with a glass front, like so many shop windows. Garishly dressed, painted, and lit, the statues were nevertheless eerily alive looking. At one point I was standing by myself in front of the statue of Ganesh when I heard, clear as a bell, "You are one of us." Looking around at the kids and teachers clustered around other displays, it was apparent that no one had spoken, at least no one physically present. I could have sworn that Ganesh spoke to me. Not sure in what sense was I "one of us," I pondered the possibilities. Had I been Hindu in a former life? Was I a remover of obstacles? A spiritual being too? Anyway, that incident drew me to Ganesh and when I saw that figure on the table full of knick-knacks at Kudzu I snatched it up. Wisteria having emailed the Circle members to bring things for the group mesa, I took it off my mesa to take with me in the morning.

Ganesh would be perfectly appropriate for the idea of Samhain, the day when the "veils" between the worlds were the thinnest. He could remove any obstacles standing between the living and the dead. Wisteria had also mentioned bringing photographs or items that related to someone who had died, to facilitate communication with them. I instantly thought of my wonderful Grandma who had passed away when I was ten, the nice one that I was named after. I had her thimble in my sewing basket, the one she used to hand sew her Double Wedding Ring quilts. The thimble was made of delicate porcelain and painted with little roses, not my style really, but it reminded me of her and the hugs she gave me as a kid. And I decided to bring one of my many photos of Monday, the horse that I had loved for over twenty-five years. Named for the rhyme, Monday's child is fair of face, I got her when I was thirteen and she lasted until she could give pony rides to my kids when they were young. She was a small, scruffy chestnut prone to bucking like a veritable bronco, but I loved her with all my heart and soul. We used to fly over jumps in the fields and she would gallop like a racehorse when I whooped and gave her the slightest kick.

"That horse was a hoot."

The day I had to put her to sleep was in the running for the worst day of my life, that's for sure. At age twenty-eight, she was only able to walk anymore and even that took her breath away. The horrible day that I saw blood running from her nose I called the vet and he gently informed me that meant her liver was failing and "it was time." I was so upset I told him "I'm not ready to hear that!" and hung up on him. As I sobbed my eyes out, Dan -- the nice Dan back then -- called the vet back, apologized for my behavior, and set up the time for giving her the shot the next day. Apparently, the vet told Dan that a lot of people yell at him when he tells them their beloved pet needs to move on.

Forever etched in my memory was the surreal moment when I lead her slowly down to her favorite tree, next to the gaping red dirt hole that had been dug that morning, and kissed her forehead for the last time. The shot instantly and violently buckled her knees and collapsed her to the ground with a thud. I knelt down to hold her head, crying like I had never cried in my life before. Dan sat with us, crying too. Soon the vet put his stethoscope to her chest and quietly stated "She is no longer with us." Oh my God. I felt torn in two. But when I eased myself away from her body and looked at it, she had suddenly become simply a hairy sunken hump of bones. It was not my Monday, my best friend, my happy place, anymore and never would be again. Walking disconsolately back to the gate, eyes and nose streaming, barely seeing anything, an amazing thing happened: the whole herd gathered around me, and they each touched me with their nose. They were saying how sorry they were, how they'd miss crotchety old Monday, that they understood. Dan watched sympathetically and opened the gate when they were done.

Soon other magical things kept coming up around Monday. Reed was six at the time and a few weeks after that awful day we were driving to school when he piped up from the back seat,

"Hey, Mom."

"Yes, Honey?"

"Monday told me she can eat carrots again cuz her teeth grew back." I was startled, to say the least, and almost ran a red light.

"Oh, really? That's, uh, nice." I grasped for a normal voice.

He had nothing more to add, apparently, and went back to reading his comic book.

Another few weeks went by and, again out of the blue, he commented, "Monday's taking a nap."

"Oh yeah?" I could see her in my mind's eye, stretched out in the grass enjoying the sun, and it made me smile.

Some time later he came out with the pronouncement, "Monday has a new owner." In spite of myself, I felt a burst of jealousy, heat spreading throughout my body as if I had just learned that Dan was cheating on me or something.

"Who is that?" I managed to choke out.

"God." He said matter-of-factly, looking placidly out the car window.

"Oh." We didn't talk much about God in our family, but Mom and Dad were devoted church goers, so maybe he had picked it up from them.

I wondered to myself was he really hearing and seeing her, or was he simply trying to make me feel better?

"He sees and hears her."

On a hunch, I finally decided that it was time to go visit her grave and give her soul permission to go on, since every time I was at the stables to visit my barn friends, I still felt her presence so strongly near that tree.

Although I dreaded dredging up the sorrow so directly, I skipped work one morning when I didn't have to teach and drove out to the barn. As I retraced the fateful walk to the tree, I felt the tears come again. Seeing the mound of dirt, already slightly caved in as her body beneath it was collapsing, it hit home. Once more, I knew that was no longer really her, but still her essence was all around. I had looked up a Native American ritual of releasing and I went through the motions, turning to the four directions, making up words as I went along, and finally said out loud as I flung my arms wide, "Monday, I will always love you, but you have to go now." And I yipped the way I always did to make her gallop. There was a palpable moment when she was there and then, the next, her spirit was gone. The tree was just a tree, the dirt was just dirt. I felt very alone, terribly sad all over again, but it felt right at the same time. I didn't have any idea how I had done it, but she was now firmly on the Other Side where she belonged.

After that day, I began to wonder if now that she was truly gone, would Reed's news flashes on Monday dry up? So one day I asked him, oh so casually,

"So, Baby Cakes, have you heard from Monday recently?"

He got a stricken look on his face, almost guilty.

"I've … I've been so busy at school, I haven't had time." He sounded like a grown-up giving an excuse for dropping the ball.

"Oh, Sweetie, that's okay. No biggie." I patted him on his little hand to reassure him. He took so much responsibility for a little boy, it was heartwarming. Or perhaps heartbreaking.

Soon after all that I rescued a new horse, Skippy, who had been abandoned at the barn and desperately needed a Person. I so needed a horse to love again, too. Reed never spoke for or about Monday anymore, making me think that he really had been in touch with her and now she wasn't there for him to talk to since I'd released her soul. He had always been a sensitive child – this wasn't the first time he had astonished us with his otherworldly knowledge -- and he had loved and trusted Monday his whole little life, after all.

So, the photo of Monday and me soaring over a downed tree came with me to Wisteria's, along with Ganesh and the thimble. I hoped against hope that I'd make contact with Grandma and Monday somehow when the veils parted.

I found Wisteria's house easily, a typical split level in a typical neighborhood, but painted a soothing green and surrounded by lovely landscaping. There were little fairy statues hidden in the bushes and around the koi pond in front. The garage door was open, so I figured that was where we were supposed to go in. The driveway was already full of cars and the multi-colored ladies were bustling as they gathered their woo-woo things out of them and disappeared into the garage. In various satchels and bags we all toted food for the potluck lunch -- I had beans and rice to share -- and our mesa items, plus our new journals Wisteria had asked us to buy. I recognized everyone that had been at the introduction evening at Suzanne's, plus a couple of others I had not met yet. Bhindi saw me approach and ran over to hug me and help me with my bundles.

"I am so happy to be in Circle with you, Bex. You won't regret it for a minute, I promise." Her eyes were dancing.

"I'm excited!" I bent over to kiss her on the cheek without dropping anything.

As we passed through the garage I saw that it was packed to the gills with all manner of art supplies, which looked promising. Doing art was another thing that had fallen by the wayside since I got married, had the kids, and started gunning for tenure. I used to do batik, ceramics, printmaking, all sorts of artsy-craftsy stuff. I was getting more thrilled as I thought about all the things I was going to start to do again, like dancing and journaling.

A door at the back of the garage led into a capacious basement room with high windows and comfortable furniture, sofas and easy chairs that looked inviting to plop into, arranged in a circle. I followed Teddi's generous, bright-green-covered behind up the stairs to the kitchen at the back of the house, which looked out on another gorgeous garden full of chrysanthemums in bloom. Very fall. After setting my beans and rice down in the crowded fridge, I poked around to find the dining room and the living room, plus another set of stairs up to three bedrooms and a bathroom. Everything was neat and tidy, spotlessly clean, and traditional without being stuffy. I felt good here.

One by one, the polychrome ladies coalesced in the basement and chose their spots to sit. The mesa was in the middle of the circle, and I placed my things next to the other treasures and photographs. Several women exclaimed over my dainty thimble and the picture of me jumping Monday all those many years back.

Vicky and Rowan were the last to arrive, rushing in five minutes late and causing a stir getting settled. Wisteria waited patiently for them to get ready. Vicky's hair was now green at the ends and she and Rowan were in matching Early Dyke finery. Teddi 's Egyptian-style eyeliner was going great guns and her bangles jingled at every move. Poor Joy was silent, almost not there in her inwardness. Suzanne had her walker in hand and wore in a light blue outfit that made her eyes shine in the exact same shade. Wisteria's tunic was orange and her wide-legged pants brown, going for Fall. The other ladies I did not yet know were equally showy. After introductions, I learned the two new members were Frankie, a banker, and Linda, a massage therapist. Frankie was petite and pretty, Linda tall and willowy. They had been to a different introductory evening that Wisteria had held in September.

I had found something in my closet to wear that was actually not black, a teal skirt and a white blouse with an oversized collar that folded over nicely in front. It wasn't truly flowy enough to compete with the others, but it would have to do for now. I needed to find time to get to a thrift store and stock up on more interesting, wacky clothing. That quote "Beware of enterprises requiring new clothes," or something to that effect, crossed my mind. I disagreed. I needed to change my style, or I just might die of boredom with myself.

Wisteria stood up and we all followed suit, grasping each other's hands in a circle. Our left hands were supposed to be down and our right hands up to move the energy around efficiently, we were told. Several minutes of deep breathing ensued and it felt really good, very calming. I barely had time to breathe in my hectic work and home life, I realized.

Then she led us through a centering exercise in which we imagined our energy starting at the heart chakra, traveling down through our wombs and all the way into the fiery core of the Earth. Then we retrieved the grounded energy, sent it back through the heart and out the crown chakra, boomeranging it up to the very center of the Universe. We did it all over again and I felt the most wonderful energized yet still feeling. There was a collective "aahhh" as all the Sis-Stars felt it, too.

Next it was time to call in that grab-bag of the Other World's gods and goddesses and I hastily added my friend Ganesh into the mix. There were a lot of nods at that choice. Teddi called in Isis and Osiris, Vicky Kali, and Joy whispered "Peace." I was tempted to add "Love, Dove, and Incense," but I refrained, fortunately. Bhindi went with Innana, who was unfamiliar to me -- I'd have to ask her later who exactly was this Innana lady. I had a lot to learn about other traditions, I realized, but Bhindi had been on this path for a long time, plus she taught world religion at the kids' school. She'd fill me in. Or the Internet would, either way.

Wisteria then announced she was going to "speak into" Samhain. There was all this lingo I had to get used to. Myself, I would have said "talk about." As she was speaking eloquently about the living and the dead, I realized I should bring marigolds tomorrow in honor of the Aztec ritual that was called "Farewell to the Flowers" and became the Day of the Dead in Mexico. Marigolds were the last flowers to bloom before the frost, so they naturally marked the turn from light and warm into cold and dark.

I decided to add that cultural tidbit to the conversation, hoping I was not coming across as too much of a "prof." But they all liked the idea of the last flowers of fall, the last vivid yellow life before the death phase of the year. I felt supported. It was a novel sensation.

When asked to talk about our group mesa items, I told them about my beloved Grandma, who let me and Jack help her cook when we visited. There would be flour all over the kitchen, her, and both of us by the time the biscuits were done, but she didn't care. I was her particular darling, having had her three boys and then Jack to contend with. Every visit she'd say, acting surprised, "I have too much change in my purse, you kids go get it and share it." It took me years to understand that before we arrived, she went to the bank and cashed in ten dollars of quarters. In the Sixties, five bucks was like fucking winning the lottery. I mean, my allowance was thirty-five cents a week, come on. I distinctly remembered when Baskin Robbins ice cream cones went from ten to twelve cents, for goodness sake.

After the others talked about, I mean spoke into, their treasures, I brought up Monday and immediately choked up over losing her. But there was sympathy palpably swirling all around me and when I told them about Reed's proclamations about Monday's napping and such, they all laughed in tearful joy. Especially Joy. What was her story, I kept wondering.

Then, in the blink of an eye, it was lunchtime. There was so much super-healthy food to choose from! Kale, and quinoa, and hummus, and chicken salad. It was MY kind of food. We all chatted as we comfortably sat around the big dining room table and the sofas and end tables scattered around the living room.

Full, and a bit sleepy, we re-convened in the basement room. I brought a cup of tea with me to help me wake up. These Circle days were tiring!

"One thing we will always do on our weekends is to dance." Wisteria announced. "I was a ballet dancer back in the day, myself, but ballet was so controlled, so constricted. Plus, you have to be extremely thin." She gestured to her pillowy breasts and full thighs and we all grinned.

"Freeform dancing is better for us to let loose, and at the same time to anchor in our physical selves the spiritual and psychological insights we are having. It reprograms the brain, I believe." She looked around the circle at us.

"So, after we do a visualization and let our lunches settle, we will dance. There is no right or wrong way to dance, obviously, so release all judgment around it. It's about the energy, not the performance."

She began to speak in a rhythmical, soft, persuasive way. I instinctively closed my eyes and breathed deeply, reminding myself that I had always been easily hypnotized. I sincerely hoped I wouldn't bark like a dog or anything. Wisteria enjoined us to imagine our deceased loved ones coming out of the sky and floating down to gather all around us. As if on cue, my mind produced my Grandma in her customary belted dress with the amethyst brooch on the collar. She wafted down and came to sit next to me on the sofa. Her presence was so deeply comforting to me, as it always had been when she was alive. She lovingly patted my hand, leaving it there. Then Monday appeared in the sky and floated her way down to stand in the living room. She ducked her head to have me scratch her behind the ears the way she had always loved. Her fur was silky, the chestnut color vibrant and sparkly. I kissed her nose and stroked its velvety smoothness with the hand that was free. It was heavenly. My two favorite "people" in the whole world, back with me.

Wisteria spoke again, enjoining us to let our loved ones send us a sign, a message, or a vision, of what we needed most right now. It was their gift to us.

I waited to see what would happen. For a while nothing did, but I kept my eyes closed and tried to relax even more. Grandma squeezed my hand once more and faded out. Monday licked my other hand and did the same. Then I looked down and saw the most wondrous thing: out of my, well, my vagina, flew a tiny green and yellow Tinkerbell. Gracefully holding her minute magic wand she turned and, with a snap of her wrist she gestured back to where she had emerged from between my legs and abruptly flew off. Then came another Tinkerbell, and another, and hundreds of tiny Tinkerbells did the same thing, over and over. They were healing me from Reed's birth! I laughed out loud at the joyful and amusing picture they made, zapping my pelvis. I knew I might be disturbing the others, but I couldn't help it. Grandma and Monday had sent me that crazy amazing image, reassuring me that I was whole again, or at least on the mend.

I opened my eyes and saw that most of the others already had, too. Teddi was still "under" and smiling. So was Joy, who was silently weeping. Bhindi winked at me, not knowing why I had been laughing but evidently joining in, I mean "holding space," for whatever it was I had experienced.

When everyone had come to, Wisteria quietly went and turned on the music. It was a lively, cheerful New Age song with lots of bells and wave sounds in the background and we heaved our spiritual butts up out of the chairs and sofas. I felt lightheaded. The music was alluring and the ladies began to move around the room in various ways. Suddenly shy, I wandered out to the kitchen and over to the dining room to dance by myself. I felt as stiff as the damn Tin Man in the Wizard of Oz. So rusty. I had done modern dance all through childhood, then International Folk Dance and disco as a teenager, but it seemed like now I was moving underwater, unsure of my limbs after all these years. In the early years Dan and I had gone dancing at 688, a raunchy club downtown, but that was long gone, both the club and our wanting to go out together and have fun.

Gradually, however, I unkinked some and felt the first stirrings of movement coming back via muscle memory. I decided to make my way back to the basement and join in with the others, though I stayed at the edge of the commotion. I imagined dancing with the Tinkerbells and had to laugh again, which helped loosen me up. The song ended and everyone sighed and smiled, everyone but Joy, that is. But even she was a little more cheerful than usual and I smiled at her specifically in encouragement.

The Circle was soon over for the day and we put away our food dishes, loaded the dishwasher, gathered our belongings, said our goodbyes, and went our separate ways. Our marching orders were to ask for dreams from the Other Side tonight. I stopped by Publix to get some marigolds on the way back home.

Dan was nowhere to be found, the kids at their friends, and so it was me and the cats for the evening, which was refreshingly strange. I ate some spaghetti, watched a movie, and went to bed early.

I dreamt of Monday and me cantering over the fields happily in the sunshine and awoke contented. As I wandered out of the bedroom to get some tea, I saw that Dan was on the living room sofa, probably where he passed out from drinking sometime in the night. He did not stir when I left for the Sunday session.

Chapter 4

Time flew by and of a sudden it was the weekend before Thanksgiving. Dan's mother, Lila, was down from New York for the week, so I was sure the kids were fine with her for a couple of days.

"Ladies, since we are getting ready to feast with gratitude this week in the secular calendar, it is appropriate that this Sis-Stars weekend is dedicated to the Element of Earth. Universally female, the Divine Feminine, the Great Mother, Pachamama, Gaia, she has many names and many faces. The source of all growth, the ground we stand on and draw power from, physically and psychically. She is abundance: soil, rocks, mountains, and beautiful plants of so many varieties. Flowers!" Wisteria gestured to our haphazard Earth mesa, covered with flowers and odd rocks, even a couple of literal pots of dirt. I had brought several of my collection of lucky rocks, the kind with a white stripe all the way through them.

"Obviously I took the name of a flowering vine, myself, to honor Her."

We were arrayed in our beginning-to-be-familiar circle, the ladies resplendent in Earth-themed finery. Yesterday in between work and picking up the kids I had dashed over to Value Village, and I came out with two days' worth of flowery scarves, skirts, and tops. I figured that if the new clothes only set me back $10.56, this new enterprise and its clothing was not so dangerous really. Well, I hoped it wasn't. Dan wasn't noticeably any happier about my venture than the first weekend, but the kids were fine with their sleepover weekend plans, so I tried not to let his sour mood bother me. His barometer was stuck on angry these days, so I might as well please myself, since for all intents and purposes I couldn't seem to please him no matter what I did. I might as well put on my own oxygen mask before helping others, as the flight attendants directed, even if the plane was busy crashing.

"That plane started to crash several years back. Time to bail, if you ask me."

I got a mental picture of a plane hurdling toward the ground at breakneck speed. Time to tell the stranger sitting next to you that you love them.

Wisteria continued, "The Element of Earth is where we are grounded and stable, where we stand in our own power, find our strongest foundations. Roots. I'd like you Sis-Stars to journal on what roots you have put down, what flowers have come up, how stable is your garden, and what else you want to plant in your life going forward."

Poor Joy looked close to tears, but the hard and fast rule was to let people have their emotions and only "speak into" them if they wanted to. Joy didn't speak into much at all.

The others began scribbling madly in their notebooks and I picked mine up to do the same. Well, Reed and Rachel were definitely my flowers, both so beautiful and so different from each other. Reed was some kind of delicate white orchid, while Rachel was something dramatic and fiery, like a flaming orange Bird of Paradise. Maybe I'd pick up one of each type of flower from the Farmer's Market on the way home, to honor them on tomorrow's mesa.

Was the 'garden' stable, though? Not so much. The ground seemed to be shifting perilously underfoot these days. Dan certainly didn't water it or weed it, as it were. My roots were deep with the kids but why should I have to be the only gardener, I wondered resentfully. Many hands make light work, but his hands didn't seem to work anymore, except to stare at his computer screen and listen obsessively to his stereo. He would never tell me how much he spent on that system. I spent my money on the kids....

So, given my situation and how shitty it had all become at home, what *did* I want to "plant"? First, I wanted someone to plant *with* me. Angry Man didn't seem to get that we were supposed to be on the same team. It was struggle, constant struggle. I'd plant the idea of a balanced life. Happiness, bright colors, the breeze in my face. Maybe next spring I'd make time to have an actual garden, work on it with the kids. We'd make it fun, just toss around seeds and watch them grow; anything grew in moist Atlanta if you gave it half a chance. I always thought of the New Yorker cartoon with the desperate man standing outside at the corner of his house and wielding garden shears as the vines threatened to swallow him up, while his wife calls out "Watch out, George, it's coming around again."

Planting a low-stress garden made me think of how Vicky always invoked "Easy Peasy" when we opened the Circle. She had already revealed to the group that on numerous occasions during her childhood her mother had threatened to kill herself if Vicky didn't watch out or do this or stop doing that. "Easy Peasy" her life had not been. My problems seemed minor in the face of that, but there was no winning in the game of comparing pain and suffering. At least she and Rowan seemed very happy together, which was totally inspiring.

"Let's wrap it up, ladies." Wisteria floated to the center of the circle, holding a pack of some kind of cards. "These are a deck of Oracle cards that I made up, my partner designed, and we just got them back from the printer. They chronicle the concepts of all Five Elements – Earth, Air, Water, Fire, and Spirit -- in thirteen cards each. With them we will explore the Element of that weekend, beginning as we have with Earth. I have a set to give each of you. But if you want another, they go for forty bucks." Spirituality had its price. She handed around boxes and everyone "ooh'ed" and "ahh'ed" over how pretty they were. Wisteria's significant other, Mitch, was a designer and had made a killing on some kind of big-eyed dolls. Useful guy.

"You will find that all the cards for Earth are together in a fresh deck, like when you buy a pack of playing cards, but most times you will want to shuffle to mix up all five Elements. Oracle decks are for learning, divination, for asking the Universe for guidance. I think you will discover that they are eerily on point, reflecting where you are in the divine pattern at that moment. They will challenge you, support you, and most of all they will mirror you back to you. So, each weekend we will draw some cards and explore the truths they hold, revealing the messages you specifically need to hear to further your evolution, to fuel your ongoing transformations. Like throwing the I Ching, practices such as pulling seemingly 'random' cards, are based on the premise that so-called "non-linear" experiences and happenings may seem accidental, coincidental, but they are anything but. Like, often I will draw the same card over and over, no matter how much I shuffle the deck. When I figure out and take right action around that concept, then I usually don't get it again for a while, if ever. We think we know everything in our culture and time, that life and time and space play out in a straight line. Quantum physics begs to differ, but that is a topic for a much more advanced Circle."

I was going to interject that Native Americans had figured out Quantum Physics thousands of years back, but I held my tongue. For once.

Wisteria took a deep breath and we all unconsciously followed suit.

"It is best to actively ask a question, to narrow down and focus on what you most need assistance on from the Universe. And if the question is already, hmm, couched in the Element we are exploring, all the better. Like Earth is attuned toward physical structure, not airy thoughts, or unbounded emotions, or fiery actions, right? And don't ask what you should cook for dinner—that's a waste of energy, yours and, more importantly, the cosmos'. Ready to try?"

We chorused "Yes!"

"I suggest you ground yourself, meditate for a bit on your question to give the Universe time to answer it, and then pull four cards. No peeking, either." She smiled encouragingly at each of us in turn.

We all quickly settled down to our task.

"Get your ass outside, Sis."

Immediately I felt a very strong urge to go outside and actually stand barefooted on Mother Earth. I had heard the other ladies talking about being "called" to do or say this or that, and now it seemed like a good word for this pulling sensation. I wanted, no needed, to get more grounded before I could get any messages from Earth. As I was walking out the back door into the verdant yard, I remembered the episode of "Friends" in which hippie-dippie Phoebe heard a mother say to her kid "You're grounded!" and muttered, "As if it's *that* easy."

The grass felt luscious under my feet, since fortunately it was a nice warm fall day. So, I plopped down in the luxuriant grass. The back yard was dreamy. I realized another advantage of thrift store clothing, no worries about ruining it with grass stains.

What to ask Earth? At first my mind was a blank, but I tried to be patient with myself. This was not a test, no wrong answers, or questions, for that matter. In my teaching I had come up with something that was on every test, the ask-yourself-a-question and answer it essay. I graded on both a good question and a good answer, sometimes they did both well, sometimes one half. Here I was in my undergraduate students' shoes (which given the over-privileged student population probably cost way more than this weekend – I mean my fellow professors drive Fords and our students drive Beemers, darn them). But this was still an unfamiliar task, despite my having thrown the Ching for many years. Maybe I'd go back to the garden metaphor — what did I need to understand to grow a better life? Too broad? How should I start to grow a happier life, perhaps? Okay, that seemed like a better question.

Breathing deeply, I pulled out a card from the little stack of thirteen I had extracted from the overall deck. Turning the first card over, it read "Foundations." Hmmm. Dumb ideas flitted across my mind, like should I get the house foundation checked? Should I apply to a foundation for a grant to do research in South America? Both ideas were good ones, come to think of it, but not very profound or suitably spiritual. Quit procrastinating, I ordered myself sharply. More to the point, what "foundations" needed work in my life so I could find more happiness, calm, even some particle of serenity? Should I continue to shoulder the burden of shoring up everybody in the family and patching the gaping cracks, as was my tendency, my comfort zone? Or, on the other hand, should I go ahead and admit that the family was not rooted solidly because Dan and I were profoundly out of love with each other and do something radical about it? That thought absolutely terrified me, so I quickly picked another card.

Oh, shit. "The Power to Stand on Your Own." Out of the frying pan into the fire. Well, I was standing on my own a little already, just by coming to these weekends in spite of the effort it took and the flack I got. But could I really stand in my own power, fully on my own? The immediate thought was, could I stand being divorced? Out there without the safety net of marriage — as full of holes as that net was at the moment, and admittedly had been for years now. My heart was pounding out of my chest just thinking about it.

Move on to the next card. Here I asked a more focused follow-up question of Earth, "when do I have to do something about the situation?" I was amazed when the next card I pulled said "Organic Timing." Talk about timing. I needed to ask Wisteria and the group more about this, but it seemed to tell me, "when the time is right." As if there was no real hurry, whatever it was it would come at the perfect time. "All in good time," as they say. Whew. My heart calmed its frantic beating some. I felt like I was off the hook for now.

Let's see, putting the three in a sequence, I needed to explore my foundations, envision standing on my own, whenever or however. That wasn't so terribly scary after all. Maybe.

For the last card I picked "Gratitude." All this realizing my life was on very shaky ground, my powerlessness was stronger than my power at the moment, and uncertain timing around some pretty profound life changes and... I was supposed to be grateful? These Universe-given cards were damn challenging, just as Wisteria had warned. Was I supposed to be grateful to have to fight my way out the door to come here? Grateful to be sleeping on the couch more and more nights? Grateful Dan was barely acknowledging my existence? Disappearing at will to do God, I mean Goddess, knows what?

But, okay, to be real, I did have good things to feel gratitude for — the kids of course, and especially Reed surviving his birth. Then Rachel's miraculously easy one. I was eternally thankful that I had been able to bring him safely into this world, no matter the sacrifice. I had imagined over and over for the last twelve-plus years that had he died, I would never have gotten over it. Never. How could any woman face that tragedy? But, over the millennia, so many had. What a deeply sad thing to contemplate. Tears sprang to my eyes, and I tried to hold space for all those women.

"Join the club."

To take my mind off of that incredible grief, I thought of how grateful I was to have horses, my darling Monday for twenty-five years and now Skippy. They made me happy to be alive, looking in their warm brown eyes, touching their velvety noses, riding in the wind, feeding them carrots. Hell, I even liked picking out their manure-packed feet and cleaning their stalls, currying their shedding hair in the spring, the whole package. I resolved then and there to get out to the barn more often if I wanted my balanced "garden" life to work. Horses were the epitome of "Easy Peasy," even when they got sick or needed their feet trimmed. Who cared if I wrote one less article? I was doing perfectly fine in my career, so I should take advantage of the open schedule of academia — no time clock to punch or boss to breathe down my neck. The thing was, academics are notorious for being their own worst taskmasters, always having projects hanging over their heads, even in those supposedly free summers. Yeah, right. I had never taken more than two weeks off in summers, maybe another two over Christmas when the kids weren't in school. But if I made up my mind, I could manage to be grateful for the flexibility of my jobs and take more advantage of it. It wasn't like the raises were anything to write home about, even the years you published a book your merit raise might buy you an extra round of groceries per month, not much more.

More gratitude? Cats. I absolutely loved my three little furry feline characters. Monster was the oldest, having adopted Dan and me before we had Reed. An adorable grey tabby kitten who had appeared at the door of our rental house one day so we let him in and he bounced all over the place like manic four-month-old kittens do. I called him a "cute little monster." But the next day some neighbors were going door to door looking for their errant kitten. I told them he had come over on his own, but they summarily scooped him up and said to him, not us,

"Come on home, Monster."

"Is that his name?" I asked in wonder.

"Yes."

"Wow, I called him a cute little monster yesterday!" Dan and I had exchanged looks.

"Well, Monster is ours. We kept the mother's whole litter."

"Ah. Okay. Well, bye Monster..." We actually waved at the little guy.

The next day, like clockwork, Monster was at the back door. He reappeared the next day and the next, until finally the neighbors came over again and admitted, with a synchronized sigh,

"Looks like he's chosen you after all. Take good care of him!" They were clearly angry, but it was the cat's choice, after all was said and done.

And we did.

Then there was K.K. When Reed's six birthday rolled around, at which time his favorite color was orange, he asked for a kitten. Fortunately, cats come in orange. I saw an ad in the newspaper about an orange tabby, three months old, who had been left with some friends when they went on vacation, but the owners never came back. Nice friends.

We went and nabbed him, a ball of orange fluff with a white face, bib, and paws. Melt your heart. He stayed in a closet for a few hours, then he came out bold as anything. Never was he scared of Monster. First long-suffering Monster had taken the kids pretty hard and now was insulted by a whipper snapper cat, too. K.K. -- when asked, Reed said it stood for Kitty Kitty, of course – was a perfectly wonderful and sassy little cat. He came when you called, meowed into the phone if you held it to his face, brought in dead animal presents regularly, and stalked me several times a day for "Kitty Love." I had to sit down and pet him while he drooled in pleasure all over my shirt. It was actually a godsend — he made me take at least two breaks a day. And loved me unconditionally, steadily, like no one ever had in my experience.

When Rachel eventually begged for her own kitten too, I called the vet who happened to have one waiting in a cage on his counter for her forever home. She was tiny, all white except grey ears and a funny face splotch, and the bluest, most crossed eyes you'd ever seen. I joked that she'd never seen anything but her own nose. She was pronounced to be "Snowflake" and whisked home within the hour. She was half-Siamese, per the eyes, and calico, per the splotches which multiplied by the month. Most took on shades of grey, but some had a hint of orange. Eventually she looked like a snowflake in some nasty New York grey slush. Offish, not fond of the boys, lazy as hell, and an avid hunter, she soon deserved the name "Snowball." But she was soft to pet and sometimes graced us with her presence. As my friend Hayley always claimed, "Dollar for dollar, pets are your best entertainment value."

So, I adored all three of them, but then again, I adored all animals. Recently the kids had come up to me after we had taken a walk around the neighborhood and passed some dogs on leashes, as usual. I had sweet talked the dogs as I scratched their heads. Reed shyly asked me after the second or third one,

"Hey, Mom. Could you please not talk to people's dogs on the street? It embarrasses me and Rach."

I thought for a moment and frankly answered, "I appreciate your honesty, Reed, but in fact I really don't think I can stop doing it."

They both looked surprised, but hastily dropped the subject and wandered off, exchanging looks that seemed to say, "Mom's getting pretty weird, huh."

Breaking into my musings on animals and gratitude, Wisteria wafted into the back yard, inviting me to make my way back inside to pull a fifth Earth card, the one that pointed toward the future, along with the entire group.

My fifth card said "Rituals." Hmmm. There were a lot of regular rituals coming up: Thanksgiving, my mother's and Rachel's birthdays that same week, Christmas, New Year's Eve, and my father's birthday, ill-timed on New Year's Day. All he ever got for birthday presents were a pair of socks or maybe the odd new gardening shears during the football game and the naps. He truly did not care, bless his soul.

As I pondered the role of rituals, I was finding it hard to get overly excited about all the secular holiday work, the spending of too much money, the decorating and undecorating. Good old Dan left everything to me, natch, and then he managed to get pissy over his presents. Last Christmas he had opened one from me and immediately tossed it across the room back to me. Glad I caught it so I could return it unbroken. He only wanted more mega-pricey stereo stuff.

But then I thought of the Winter Solstice, a new ritual celebration in my life since joining the Sis-Stars. One so much less tainted by commercialism and Christian overlay. The Winter Solstice and its marking of the longest night was the basis, obviously, of the mid-winter religious rituals all concerned with shining lights in the darkness. Hannukah, Christmas, even Kwanzaa. So, when the opportunity came I asked Wisteria,

"Are there plans for a ceremony on the Solstice?"

"Oh, yes. We always put on a big celebration, down at the First Existentialist Church in Candler Park. This is a great time to talk about that, in fact."

Bhindi piped up, "Last year there were at least a hundred people. It was fabulous! And a yummy potluck, too." She fondly smiled in remembrance. She loved people and she loved food, so she'd be in heaven.

"Yes, it was terrific, always is. Let's brainstorm about this year's one. We won't have a December weekend for this Circle we'll be busy planning the ritual the week before the Solstice to finalize everything. But I would absolutely *love* for any and all of you to participate on the day itself, in whatever way you feel called to do. On the practical side, there is coordinating the food and drink. Setting up the chairs, decorations, props. There are the announcement and the programs to write, design, print, and hand out on the day. But we need to have settled on the theme and the basic order of events to do all that. First, we need to send a "Hold the Date" to the entire pagan community, because we do it on the nearest Saturday night, which this year is the 17th. I always MC it. Then we need performers, mainly to embody the five Elements, though we may want to include other roles, like the Sun and Moon, gods and goddesses, and so on. There is cleanup afterwards, too, everyone's favorite...." She looked around the circle expectantly.

The ladies were silent for a few moments. With my Mars in Aries, I have a tendency to go first and break the ice, so I offered, "Well, I'm a newbie, so I'll volunteer for something practical — how about the potluck coordinator?"

Wisteria seemed delighted with that and wrote it quickly on her pad.

Teddi wanted to do announcements and programs. Vicky and Rowan setup and decorations. Joy asked for clean-up. In the lull after that, Chantilly ventured,

"Seems like now we need to talk the ceremony itself. Maybe, Wisteria, would you speak into the Winter Solstice in general to let us know the possible themes and all?"

"Sure. We know it as the year's shortest day and longest night. As we approach this time of the natural calendar the days are truncated, and the cold nights stretch out before us in a sometimes-depressing way. The darkness is not too terrible here in Atlanta, but still noticeable for sure. However, it is important to keep in mind that in cosmic terms, the solstice actually turns from the darkening and inwardly contemplative part of the year to slowly begin the time when the sun will become dominant. Even in January the days are imperceptibly lengthening. The Sun is masculine, so his awakening and empowering starts the day after the Solstice. Dark begets light. Feminine yields to Masculine. Not in a sexist way, in an Elemental one. So, what we pagans are really celebrating is the *return* of light, action, growing, doing, warmth, love. The delicate, tentative beginning of the promise of spring, which we are celebrating during Imbolc in early February. What does that make you wonderful Sis-Stars imagine for our ritual? Throw out ideas and someone write them down on the big sheet of paper on the easel, please."

Bhindi hopped up obligingly to note our thoughts and intuitions.

"A dance between the Moon and the Sun? He starts out low and tentative then ends up in front or something to show he's coming on stronger? But they are still a pair." Teddi offered.

"The four Elements stand around the edge of the room and Spirit in the center, so the audience will turn to the directions as the Elements call them in?" Chantilly.

"Regeneration and renewal as the overall theme?" Joy.

"The room starts off in darkness, then as things progress more and more lights come on?" Suzanne.

"Start with poems about darkness, inwardness, rest, and its gifts? End with sun poems?" Rowan.

Bhindi was scribbling madly as we called things out. Wisteria looked like she was at a tennis match, trying to keep up. This was fun. Group projects were my favorite kind of teaching, too.

"Ask everyone attending to wear either yellow or black or some of both?" Vicky.

"Make a huge mesa shaped like a mandala to represent the wholeness in the midst of change?" Me.

"Maybe the people being the Elements could begin on their segment of the mandala and make their way toward East and such as they call it in?" Bhindi threw out.

"Wisteria could follow with a lovely speech on the theme, the meaning and experience of moving from dark to light?" Jackie suggested.

"We could do the no lights thing and she begins to speak and then we turn up the lights? That way latecomers wouldn't stumble around in the dark, gives them time to settle..." Frankie offered. Evidently, she knew that pagans were not overly timely folk -- that would be far too conventional.

Wisteria finally held up her hand.

"Fabulous, ladies. We have plenty to work on. Let's go down the list and vote on if we like each idea." We did so.

Renewal as the theme, Element embodiments progressing from the mandala mesa to the room edges to call in the directions, Wisteria's speech beginning in the dark, then the dance between Moon and Sun to follow her words with movement, all these were heartily endorsed. Finding poems, but only if they were really good, maybe read by different members of the audience, was suggested as an action step. But wearing only yellow and black was decided to make us look like a bunch of bumblebees and it was vetoed.

"We need to embody the renewal theme and we usually end with the group dance in a spiral to bring everyone together in the archetypal symbol of the path of life." Bhindi added. Everyone nodded enthusiastically.

"Let's take a break. Good work, my beautiful Sis-Stars." We all preened in her praise.

Several of us needed to pee or stretch or, for Vicky and Rowan, snatch a not-so-secret kiss in the hallway. Lucky girls.

I tried to duck away from their embrace without being seen, to respectfully give them their space to be totally in love, but they unclenched and Rowan casually walked to the kitchen for a snack.

"Sorry." I apologized, following her in for a blood-sugar fix.

"For what? We're always kissing, you simply can't avoid seeing it." Rowan's eyes twinkled at me kindly.

"I wish my husband and I kissed like that anymore. We barely speak. Mostly fight. It sucks." I admitted with a sigh.

"Wow. Shit. That sounds really rough." She was peering at me intently.

"It is. Especially for the kids. He yells at them, too, and then he and I get into it when I call him on it. It's a no-win situation, I'm stuck." I told her as I pulled some leftovers from the frig.

"Well, all I can say is, 'life is too short to put up with that bullshit.'" She looked me straight in the eyes. Sympathetic and challenging in equal measure.

"Easy for her to say, in love and no kids."

Our homework was to think up or create something for the Winter Solstice ritual. We gathered up all our stuff, put away the leftovers, making note of what might be needed to eat well again tomorrow. Hugs were going all around. I still felt a bit self-conscious, but already feeling quite close to these crazy women at the same time.

I found Rowan's eyes on me and went over to give her a hug.

"You can do it. Remember: life is too short. And he sucks big time." She whispered in my ear as she held me tightly. It made me want to cry, but I sucked back the tears.

"Perhaps." I admitted sheepishly.

"I'm holding space for you."

"Thanks. You rock."

"You do, too. Dan's made you forget that."

The next morning, as suggested by Wisteria, I brought a poem I had written last evening. It made me feel self-conscious to read it out loud – I had written poetry since I was a teenager, but only in the privacy of my own room, in my journals. I didn't think they were very good, either. But I was here to be more empowered, so I was going to put myself out there, go out on a limb.

After we went through our routine to ground ourselves and call in spiritual presences, Wisteria asked what we had brought in to share. I hesitantly indicated that I had written something. I felt like I needed to stand up, as if I were teaching, and pulled out my journal where I had penned the final version of the poem. I cleared my throat and began.

"Days like twilight,
nights like ink,
people like animals
retreat to their burrows.

Even the traditional holy days
light candles in the long darkness,
drape the World Trees in sparkles,
and hunker down to wait,
watching the Sun's inch-by-inch progress:
adding minutes to the day,
stealing them from the night.

We who follow the real ancients
also dance for joy,
hand in hand in hand,

to welcome Him back
and thank Her, the moon,
for her constant inconstancy.

It is, at heart,
the cycling, turning, spinning, wheeling
we all celebrate,
whether we know it or not,
and it unites the All."

I nervously waited for a reaction, second-guessing myself that it was a crappy, amateurish piece. But then the Sis-Stars started to clap and they all stood up too. It brought tears to my eyes to get that little ovation. Everyone was smiling.

"Beautiful, Rebecca. Simple but true!" Wisteria praised.

"Let's have you recite it during the ceremony!" Bhindi suggested enthusiastically. "Would you be willing to?"

"I'd be honored to. I talk in front of people for a living, so it should be fine. Thank you, it means a lot..." Wow. Whew. Good. I felt like Sally Fields and her "You like me, you really like me" acceptance speech.

Chapter 5

The end of the semester was always a mad dash to hand in grades as soon as humanly possible and get that magical month off before the next term starts the game all over again. Right in the midst of the holiday season, it was even more brutal to wrestle the Fall semester to the ground.

But thankfully I had finished my grading by the time the meeting to finalize the Winter Solstice ceremony plans came around. I would have to take Rachel with me to the meeting, since school was out and most of the rich people at the kids' school started peeling off for the Caribbean and Europe and such, leaving few of the kids' friends available for playdates. I was sure the Sis-Stars wouldn't mind Rachel's presence. Empowering girls starting at an early age was definitely very important, and Rachel had really gotten into adding to her mesa she was building on the top shelf of her bookcase. Besides the flowers and the pretty rocks, now it had a picture of Tinkerbell laid on a piece of sparkly cloth (I had told her that I had seen Tinkerbell during the first Sis-Stars weekend, but carefully left out the part where she was flying out of my girl parts!).

Rachel was super excited to come with me like a Big Girl, and especially looking forward to seeing Bhindi, whom she idolized, outside of school. She dressed up in all her finery – I might have to dig deep to find my Inner Child, but she was living hers daily – and we set off to walk to the nearby First Existentialist Church. Stopping by The Flying Biscuit to grab muffins and a decaf soy latte for me, we walked down McLendon hand in hand. It was mercifully mild for mid-December and there were lots of ambling couples and mothers with strollers out and about on the sidewalk.

We had left Reed glued to an unprecedented afternoon of video games, no time limits, and he was more than happy to see us go.

Dan was AWOL. I tried not to think about what he was up to.

"Typical. You don't want to know."

"This is so great, Mom. Just us girls!" Rachel swung our clasped hands back and forth to underscore her excitement.

"I know! I've been wanting for you to meet my new friends and Wisteria, the lady that leads the weekends I go to. You'll like Teddi, I bet, and Chantilly. There are two other cool women, Vicky and Rowan. You never know what color hair ends Vicky is going to have next. First they were pink, then green!" I babbled.

"Ooooh. Can I dye my hair ends, too? Purple???"

"We'll see. If you really like Vicky's hair, maybe she'll tell you how she did it." I had no beef with kids and their weird hair – growing up in the Sixties, an inch too much hair on a boy could get him expelled from school. Dyeing hair anything but blonde and blonder was considered heretical. But I identified with the "Hair" generation, still had the album, in fact. Even I had begun to dye mine in the last few years, but it was to cover the incipient grey.

As we approached the stone building, we could see women scurrying around carrying boxes overflowing with decorations, two of them staggering under the weight of a huge painted Moon and Sun.

Rachel squealed with delight.

Some of the billowing ladies turned to see what or who had made that absurdly high-pitched sound. My hearing had suffered since having Rachel.

Bhindi recognized us and came hurrying over.

"What a treat!" She swept my daughter up in a tight hug and spun her around, making Rachel giggle uncontrollably. "So glad you came with your mom!"

"Me, too. Reed says 'hi.'" She was looking at Bhindi with adoration.

"I say 'hi' back." Bhindi grabbed Rachel's hand. "Help me with some stuff?"

They took off.

I went up to Wisteria, "Hey. I hope it's okay I brought my little one, Rachel."

"Of course. The next generation of Sis-Stars is always welcome."

"She has started a mesa in her bedroom!"

"Nice. Can you grab that box over there?"

"Sure. Happy to."

There was chaos for twenty minutes or so. I checked out the kitchen off the main space, since that would be my domain before and after the ceremony. It was a bit tight, but there was a huge frig and industrial-sized bowls and such. I jotted down questions for the meeting, since this was my first time, and I had no idea of the process. How did we make sure we got protein, salad, veggies, and desserts in some kind of balance for a hundred or so people? I had put on a little free-for-all potluck last year and we ended up with *five* rotisserie chickens! It was funny, but not really a great meal.

The group finally settled down in some chairs hastily dragged into a haphazard circle. Rachel sat next to Bhindi, humming to herself happily and swinging her feet.

"All right, let's get going, dear ones. First, let's open a quick Circle so that the Higher Beings can assist in our creative process." Wisteria taking charge.

We all stood up and held hands, with Rachel following along, her eyes shining brightly. Teddi was on her other side and smiled down at Rachel, giving her a big conspiratorial wink.

Wisteria called in the five directions, then others called out names of goddesses and gods, like Bacchus for celebratory abandonment. In a lull, Rachel cleared her throat as if she wanted to speak, too. We all looked at her and I smiled and nodded encouragement. She said in her high, clear voice,

"Tinkerbell, come help us have fun and be sassy."

Everyone breathed out in approval. She looked very pleased with herself. Teddi looked over and caught my eye at the Tinkerbell reference, raising her eyebrows. I shrugged a little.

"Blessed Be." We intoned and sat down, feeling closer, in sync.

"So, who wants to weigh in?"

Each of the coordinators spoke about their parts and we saw a draft of the program. There were a few typos that I gently pointed out. My poem reading was featured somewhere in the early part of the ritual, I was pleased to see.

Then, it was my turn.

"Well, so how does the potluck work? Do I coordinate via email who is bringing what so we get some kind of balance? Or do we let it be a crap shoot?"

Bhindi spoke up, as the only one besides Wisteria who had been at last year's ritual.

"In the email that is going out tomorrow to the whole pagan community we'll ask for RSVP's and what dish they plan to bring. Then if it is getting too full of, say, desserts, you can intervene as the later RSVP's come in. There is always a chance of too little protein or too much sugar, but who really cares? A lot of people don't answer the email but come anyway. Somehow it all works out."

The others nodded. We plan and God, I mean Goddess, laughs.

"And what about plates and silverware?"

"There is room in the budget for paper stuff. Could you go pick up that stuff, and be sure to keep the receipt, so you can be reimbursed? Large plates, small plates, napkins, plastic cups, flatware for 125 people just in case? There are some real ceramic dishes in the First E collection if we do run out. And if we get more than that many RSVP's one of us can run out for more supplies on Friday. We have a love offering box, aka a donation box, that people usually contribute to, as well, to cover the unexpected costs."

"All right! Rachel and I will do our best."

My daughter made a funny face, and everyone laughed indulgently.

"If that is everything, see you all next Saturday. Set up people you be here by two, performers four, potluck five, and ceremony begins at six."

"Real six or pagan six?" Vicky asked irreverently, glancing at Rowan.

"Whichever the Universe decrees!" Wisteria laughed along with the rest of us.

Rachel and I walked companionably home, her bubbling away about how cool it was going to be on Saturday and what we should make for the potluck (mac and cheese figured prominently) and what she was going to wear (watch out, people). The idea of everyone wearing black or yellow had been soundly vetoed, too much like a bunch of bumblebees. I was going to go against my coloring, which was Winter, and pick up some sunny yellow clothes at Value Village. Rachel and I made a plan to stop by there together in the next few days.

Poking my head in Reed's room to hand him one of the Flying Biscuit muffins, he kept his eyes on the screen and his hands flying around, but asked, "How'd it go?"

"Good. Rachel is psyched to be part of it. You're invited too, of course..." I knew that even if he were curious, twelve-year-old boys would find the whole thing weird and embarrassing, I imagined. Especially with his mom and sister in attendance.

"Nah, but thanks." Ever polite.

I kissed him on the head and left his messy, boy room without further motherly comment. It was not actively stinking, at least.

Rachel had made a beeline to room where she was talking loudly on the phone with Rosie, which could go on for hours, so I was uncharacteristically free to do my own thing. I wandered into the workshop where my mesa was hiding behind the screen that I had bought myself to get some privacy. It had grown a lot since the first weekend, overflowing now with pictures and cloths of many colors. I had a pillow to sit on, my Oracle cards, lots of other fun stuff.

As I plunked down on the pillow, I thought to myself that I really needed to wrap Christmas presents while everyone else was occupied, but I also knew I needed to rest.

"Damn straight, Bex."

I thought I had heard something, one of the kids, perhaps? But then it was quiet again. Weird.

Deciding to pull from the deck, I held it and shuffled the cards around as I formulated my question. I hit upon "What is my best guidance through these upcoming months?" As I was moving the cards randomly, one of them fell out on the floor in front of me.

"Wisdom of the Body." Huh. Never had gotten that one.

I knew my body craved rest. Not just right now, but more generally. I couldn't keep up this pace forever. I needed to take more hot baths, eek out more barn time. How I'd love to sit in bed and read a novel! Go shopping in a real store, for me. Nap. I sighed, thinking of a life like that. Maybe when the kids were older? Maybe if I didn't try for Full Professor? I was pretty much assured of that final promotion if I could squeeze out another book, and I yearned to write the one on shamanic visions, a topic which had dominated my research over the last ten years.

My fascination had started that Sunday afternoon in 1993 when I was hosting a speaker at the museum. Reed was three and Rachel hadn't been conceived yet. Dan had still been a somewhat useful partner back then and was babysitting Reed so I could work. I was to bring the speaker, Ed, home for tea with the boys before he had to catch his plane back to Texas. The museum wanted a Mayanist anthropologist this time and I had dug up a guy who specialized in Maya kinship in traditional communities in Guatemala. He'd do.

When we met at the designated lecture hall, he turned out to be a rather forgettable smallish man with blue eyes, unkempt hair, and rumpled clothes. Par for the anthropologist course. We got all the microphones and lights and projector set up and the crowd filed in, the usual blue-haired ladies, eager students who got credit for coming to such talks, a few interested colleagues, some unknowns.

Ed launched into his speech, pointing to those confusing kinship diagrams with the triangles and the squares and lines connecting them all over the place. Blah, blah, blah. I was having trouble keeping my head upright and I saw out of the corner of my eye that the audience was in a similar stupor.

All of a sudden, Ed stopped speaking. Long enough that everyone stirred and I sat up straight and started to worry.

"I don't want to talk about that anymore." He proclaimed.

Oh, no. He was going off subject, maybe off the rails even. But I waited before I did anything rash.

"I have something much more important to tell you good people today."

Here we go. Please, please don't be a born-again Christian.

"I am a bona fide Maya shaman." His voice shook with excitement and the crowd made interested rustling noises. "It has been exactly thirteen years *today* since I made a promise to the shaman in the village where I was doing my doctoral research. It was my challenge not to reveal that I was a shaman for thirteen years and I have faithfully kept it. I was not to tell anyone, not a soul, that I was a Maya day-keeper, a diviner of the future. You see, I had been trained as a shaman myself and this was my, shall we say, graduation test. But when Rebecca invited me to speak on this very day, I knew it was a sign. So here is my story."

I breathed a sigh of relief and could feel the audience behind me moving toward the edges of their seats in anticipation. There were excited murmurings all around.

"Okay. Well, I was down there and going along asking my nosey outsider questions and trying to fit in at the same time. The anthropological paradox. One thing that the townspeople did every morning was to gather in the central swept-dirt area, not fancy enough to call a plaza, and tell their dreams to the shaman, Don José, for interpretation. This was like us reading the newspaper or something. The world of dreams was considered just as real and the waking life, and even more insightful, especially shedding light on the future.

One night I had a crazy dream and so I shared it with the group in my halting Quiché Mayan. It was nighttime in my dream. There was a large oaken table in this cavernous dark room. Sitting around the huge table were skeletons, twelve of them in all, both alive and dead at the same time. I was invited to sit down with them, to complete the important number thirteen. The Maya calendars are too complex to explain right now, but thirteen is a sacred number in general. Anyway, the skeletons were unbelievably wise, and they imparted all their wisdom to me, wordlessly. I felt very humble and also very overwhelmed. When they finished, the ceiling in the room suddenly broke open to reveal that the whole sky, which should have been dark, was a giant star filling the heavens with brilliant radiant light."

The audience let out a "group wooo."

"After I spoke into that dream, the Maya villagers sat silently, rapt, looking back and forth from me to the shaman. Don José nodded his head sagely and intoned 'It is clear that you are called.' I did not know exactly what he meant, although I had a sneaking suspicion. Then, a few weeks later, I came down with a terrible case of dysentery. Everyone in the village had it, but the family I was living with fed me broth and administered herbal cures and I managed to recover before most of the others. After that, the shaman kept looking at me closely, eyes narrowed, watching my every move. Finally, one day when I was finishing up an interview with a tiny, beautiful, demure young woman about her cross-cousins, I felt her stiffen up and looked around me to find the shaman had appeared silently, like a cat, behind me.

'You will come with me.' He commanded.

I immediately agreed. Don José was boss. If I did not please the community's shaman, my dissertation would not happen and I would sink to the bottom of the academic pond like a stone. I would be left as the dreaded ABD – All But Dissertation -- the pond scum of teachers, relegated to making a meager living at a prep school or community college at best." I could see some of the graduate students in the audience shiver.

"So, the Don José said to me, 'My friend. You have learned our language. You have shown respect. And now the spirits of the dead communicate to you and you can overcome disease because they are looking upon you favorably. They have told me, I have divined, that you are to be trained as an apprentice shaman. You will show promise, or you will not, who is to say? But you have been called, twice, and if we ignore this we will be doomed. They have spoken in their way. Do you accept this challenge, to become a *curandero* or even more? A day-keeper? Diviner? Explorer of visions?' *Curandero* is the Spanish name for an herbal curer, the other roles are increasingly powerful ways to intervene in the cosmic balance.

Anyhow, needless to say, I was flabbergasted. I was rendered speechless, rare for an academic. I hemmed and hawed. 'Can I think about it?' I asked him, trying for a way out. I definitely did not want to be a shaman. I wanted to finish my data collection and get my doctorate.

He told me in no uncertain terms, 'There is nothing to *think* about such a calling. It just *is*. You will tell me your answer tomorrow. And, do not forget, my people will follow my direction and if you want them to tell you about their families for your work... I trust you understand me?'

'I do.' I replied. Loud and clear, he was holding my research ransom.

I was in a tough spot. I had gone there with no intention to 'go native,' as they used to say. To veer from my safe doctoral research. To stay up all night on some kind of mind-bending crazy drug. This was not, so not, in my plan. But wrestling sleeplessly all night long with the situation, I realized I had an out. If I did get trained but, in the end, I did not actually cure anyone or accurately divine the future, I would be considered a dud and I could go home and type footnotes. On the other hand, if I refused to be trained, my graduate work was doomed, and I had no other viable, "real world" skills. Maybe I had "other world" skills? I had no idea, but my non-choice choice was clear. I had to try."

The audience exhaled as one. This was good stuff.

"It was hard, I'll freely admit that. It took an extra three years and that got me in some hot water with my program back home. But I convinced my professors that I was onto some very groundbreaking kinship research and they extended my time to degree. I found, to my surprise, that I actually enjoyed the divination and calendrical stuff, it was very detailed and meticulous in a way like kinship mapping. I became quite adept at the whole thing. Finally, Don José pronounced me ready to be initiated. It was a moving ritual and then he challenged me, in front of everyone: 'You may not tell your gringo friends that you have done this momentous thing. For thirteen years.' I was stunned, but I had already devoted three years of my life to this pursuit and the shaman always had the last word. I replied, with as much dignity as I could muster, 'This I will faithfully do.'"

Everyone sighed and spontaneously burst into applause. I was equally thrilled. What a tale, but it was actually true. This was better than all the charts and graphs in the world.

But it had turned out that his story was just the beginning of my extraordinary glimpse into the 'non-linear' world of shamanism that afternoon. His story became my story, in a way.

I drove Ed back to my house, chatting about his talk and Maya divination, a subject that interested me but that I barely understood.

Little Reed came running to the front door, looking like a tiny angel, as usual, in his favorite blue overalls and striped shirt.

"Mommy, you're home! Yay!" He high fived me. "I missed you." He hugged my knees tightly.

"I missed you too, Honey Bunny. This is my friend Ed. He's come to have some tea and snacks before he goes to the airport."

Reed hugged Ed about the knees, too. When he did this to men, his face came right at their crotches. Ed looked a bit surprised, but patted his little blond head absentmindedly.

"Dan, Ed. Ed, Dan. My husband, obviously."

They manned a greeting.

We sat around the dining room table, Reed with a sippy cup of apple juice, the adults with cups of tea.

"So, Ed, what was your lecture about?" Dan asked politely, though I could tell he was prepared to be bored silly by the answer.

Ed and I exchanged a look, which Dan noticed, and he narrowed his eyes.

"Well, I started out on topic. Family organization and terminology among the modern Quiché Maya in Guatemala. But then I switched to something far more interesting."

"Like what?" Dan looked a little bit more attentive. I kept my mouth shut, relishing the upcoming whammy.

"I am a bona fide Maya shaman." Ed looked proud of himself and a little surprised to be saying it for the second time in thirteen long years. He tried unsuccessfully to push his unruly hair out of his eyes.

"No shit. That's amazing." Dan looked at me. "Is that why the look just now?" I nodded. He smiled, no longer jealous. "Tell me more!"

Reed was sucking away on his cup but watching us with his big bright eyes.

"My calling started out with a dream. There were twelve skeletons, but they weren't dead. They invited me to their big table in a dark, oak-lined room. They told me all their wisdom."

"Do you remember what they said?"

"Sadly, no."

"Go on, please." Dan was at the edge of his chair by this time.

But just then Reed started waving his little arm in the air. He had just started daycare and they had taught him to do that to get his turn to speak. He was making little excited noises in his throat at the same time.

"Yes, Reed?"

"And then the top of the room opened to a big, big star!" He pronounced confidently.

I nearly fell out of my chair.

Dan looked confused.

Ed looked complacent.

"That's right, Reed. That's exactly how the dream ended."

"What just happened?" Dan asked querulously.

Then his expression showed that he got what just happened: Reed had either read Ed's mind or tuned into the visual of his prophetic dream somehow. Or both.

Reed looked around, slightly puzzled at the commotion he had caused.

"I like stars. And talking skeletons." He mused, as if that explained everything.

I was thinking really hard. What if Reed were to be called to become a shaman, too? I mean the Tibetans picked out the next Dalai Lama from boys about Reed's age, didn't they?

While Dan was struck dumb, I piped up,

"So, Ed. A question. Reed has always said he dreams a lot about a friendly wolf. She takes care of him and soothes him if he needs it. Told us this as soon as he could talk."

"Ah, nice. Tell me, Reed, what color is your friendly wolf?" Ed was watching Reed intently, as if waiting for a certain answer.

Reed thought for a moment and replied, "She's a gwayish, bwownish wolf." He nodded his head vigorously, "Gwayish. Bwownish."

"Ah." Ed did not elaborate.

"Well, do you have any insight?" I was riveted.

"Obviously it's his animal spirit and to appear to him at such a young age is a great sign. Wolves are wonderful animal selves to have, strong, able to work in the pack and to be alone, either way. But the usual color ones don't necessarily point to a baby shaman. If she were a white wolf, you'd have a candidate on your hands."

I was kind of relieved, to tell the truth. It was enough to have a little Wolf Boy who could read minds, thank you very much. (And, unbeknownst to me at the time, later to talk to the spirits of dead horses.)

Dan and I smiled happily at each other as if to say, "Look what we created."

Reed was munching his crackers and swinging his legs, now bored by the grownup talk and ready to go play.

"Run along, Sweetness." He jumped off his chair and high-tailed it to his room. The sound of vrooming cars and massive crashes ensued.

Ed looked at the two of us and slyly offered,

"You know...... If a shaman is asked to do a divination, he or she cannot refuse..."

Wooo.

"Don Eduardo, will you give us a divination, please?" I obligingly entreated.

"Yes. Okay. So, first I need a sacred cloth of some kind."

I thought a minute and then it dawned on me that my parents had been to the Golden Temple at Amritsar in India and brough back an orange cloth that had been blessed by the Sikh monks there. I ran up to the attic to find it.

"Dan, can you get Ed whatever else he requires?"

"Sure."

When I came back down with the scrap of cloth, they were in the den. Ed was, somewhat reluctantly, clutching a dusty bottle of Triple Sec in one hand.

"He needs a shot of liquor and that's all I could find." Dan explained.

"That stuff must be five years old or more!" I exclaimed.

"It'll do." Ed manfully slugged down a healthy swig of the nasty sweet stuff.

We sat around the coffee table and Ed pulled out of his jacket a small soft bag. It was full of red and black beans, he showed us.

"What would you like to know?" He asked simply.

I took charge. I was not interested in whether the Falcons would win this season. I was interested in the prospects for another child, given how badly Reed's birth had gone and how my body was barely recovered from it even now.

"Will we have another child, will things turn out well, and what will the child be like?"

Ed nodded as if this were just another ordinary question and poured some beans into his hand. He was muttering in Mayan, I could catch a few words here and there from teaching about them. "Balam" was jaguar, for instance. He said that several times.

He counted the beans out on the table in piles of five, making several rows. He began to exclaim and breathe deeply as he went.

52

"Wow." He seemed to inadvertently say out loud.

"Okay. Well. This is quite a reading. You will definitely have a second child. In about a year. And SHE will be, how to say it, a true force of nature. I have never seen so much wind in all my divinations. She'll tear through your lives like a hurricane. And you can never lie to her, because she will know. She will have powers that you don't have, such as to glimpse the future, for example. It might not be the easiest childhood, but she will be truly extraordinary. Like her brother."

Shivers were going up and down my spine. I found myself grinning from ear to ear, and saw that Dan was doing the same.

He grabbed the Triple Sec from the table and took a big swallow, and passed it to me in celebration. I took a little sip.

"Oh, and physically, her birth will be a piece of cake, for both you and her. Your jaguar powers will come to the fore to get you through it."

We whooped, startling Ed and making Reed come running,

"What's wrong, Mommy?" His dear face was scrunched up with worry.

"Nothing at all, Baby Cakes. We're just happy. Ed told us a really nice thing is going to happen soon."

"What? Do I get a present? A puppy?"

"Even better."

Reed looked unconvinced that there could be anything better than a puppy.

"Tell me." He begged.

"It'll be a surprise, when you are four."

Just in case, I didn't want him to expect a little sister, though I had a very strong feeling that Ed was right.

Dan and I gave each other a hug. Then one for Ed, who was looking pleased with his performance, and with finally being able to practice as a diviner after all that time.

"Sorry, but I've got to call the taxi and get moving." Ed looked sad to leave.

"I'll do it." Dan placed the call.

On the way down our steep driveway a few minutes later, Ed leaned over and picked up a rock, slipping it into his pocket.

"It has the energy of my first reading as a true shaman, so I'll treasure it from now on. And it will help me to help others. I'll look forward to getting the baby announcement. She'll be born on an auspicious day, by the way. And be drop-dead beautiful."

It just kept getting better and better. A tear of joy and gratitude slid down my cheek as he waved from his taxi moving down the street.

And, lo and behold, Rachel was born about a year later, on the first day of Hannukah, while I was laughing in joy as she slid out easily. When she latched onto my nipple, though, I nearly hit the roof. Ten minutes old, chomping on it like there was no tomorrow, I knew Ed had predicted her personality to a tee. And the weird thing was as soon as she learned to make word-like sounds, when she was particularly happy, she'd repeat "balam, balam, balam" clear as day.

Both kids liked to tell people that story: "I read a shaman's mind," Reed would brag. "I was predicted by a shaman," Rachel would follow suit. I liked to tell people how her birth helped heal me, in so many ways. And from then on, I kept having those kinds of "spherical" things happen to me – it was a new word for "non-linear" I learned after shamanism invaded my home and my mind that afternoon. "Spherical" encompasses a cyclical worldview, one which values recurring events and does not insist on direct paths through time or space, but is more three-dimensional in its imagery. More dimensions the better, as far as shamanism was concerned.

"I know dats right."

Chapter 6

The Winter Solstice ceremony went off without a hitch. On cue, I stood up and read my poem and again the audience clapped enthusiastically. The potluck was a great success, too, with all sorts of yummy food and just the right amount for the exuberant, colorful, hungry pagan crowd. The get-ups people were wearing were astonishing, full of sparkles and rainbows and suns and moons. Rachel had loved every minute of it and fit right in with her wild outfit. I wore some new sunny Value Village finery, myself. Our little Sis-Stars Circle felt familiar and I relished knowing there were a hundred other women out there, or more, on the same wave length.

Afterwards, pondering the uplifting theme of regeneration and feeling the strengthening of the good light now on its way, I felt a stronger sense of hope.

I got through Christmas. The kids were happy with their presents, Dan was not. Oh, well.

The kids were each going on big trips around New Years. Rosie had invited Rachel to Hawaii, no less. Reed was going with me on a college fieldtrip to Costa Rica. Dan could fend for himself.

Before final packing, I made an appointment to see Dr. Gregg. Always needing a chiropractic "tune-up," I also enjoyed his wry sense of humor. We had known each other for eleven years now, ever since Reed was a little baby and I called him in desperation: I still could barely walk and was in pain at the slightest movement. No one could tell me why. I had no feeling down the inside of my left leg and the muscles around my sacrum would Charley Horse several times a day, leaving me gasping in pain.

When I first met Dr. Gregg in 1991, it had been eight long months since Reed's birth. I had had to tell him what happened during the horrendous childbirth, in hopes that he could provide some insight that other doctors and chiropractors hadn't managed to do. The neurologist had literally poked me with a safety pin to determine exactly where the leg numbness ended. Useful. The obstetrician tried to ignore my symptoms in follow-up visits, no doubt in hopes of avoiding a major lawsuit. They all had fucked up big time.

The first chiropractor had blamed my heavy, thick hair for my back and neck issues. Right. I'd always had a lot of hair, no neck issues. My GP implied I had an emotional block to having a baby. Except I had known that I wanted to have babies since I was age five. Dan was overwhelmed by the new baby and by me sliding into a depression over the whole situation. He changed Reed's diapers and walked him around the block, which I still couldn't do, but seemed totally unable to wrap his mind around doing anything about my condition. I desperately needed Dr. Gregg, or someone, anyone, to diagnose the problem and finally, please, help me heal from whatever it was, too.

Gregg had been matter-of-fact, though when he saw my shuffling movements his eyes had widened imperceptibly. "So, tell me everything, Rebecca. We can figure this thing out together and I *will* make you feel better." He was kindly, plump, short, beginning to grey. On the phone when I called him, he said he had stairs up to his office. When I groaned, he offered "If you can't make it, I will carry you up. The baby, too." That cinched it. He cared, the first one who seemed to.

I launched into my tale of woe. "Okay. So, Reed was late, ten days. No labor in sight, I went to the OB's office and when they ultra-sounded they said there was very little amniotic fluid left and they needed to induce me. We went home, got the suitcase and the car seat and all, and back at the hospital I had settled in, glad that it was finally going to happen. Eight hours of excruciating Pitocin later, there was not one centimeter of dilation. This was midnight, and I'm sure the docs wanted some sleep. The nice midwife had gone off shift, now the abrasive, bossy one was on. They said maybe labor would start up overnight and simply left me in a room. They said Dan had to leave, but instead he hid behind the bed to stay with me, though he was not able to really do anything. I dozed a bit, waking up in a pool of blood. We called the nurse, who suggested I sit on the toilet while she fixed the bed. We waited for the doctor to show up. She checked me and said no progress had taken place overnight, did I want a C-section? I asked if the baby was in trouble, but the monitor said he was not, so I agreed to more Pitocin if I could have an epidural and not feel it. That was produced and I was so grateful I told the doctor administering the epidural that I would kiss his feet. Dilation eventually did commence and a few hours later the bossy midwife told me to push. This was at twenty-four hours with no food, no sleep, much pain, much fear, much blood. And I couldn't feel anything from the waist down, but I attempted to "push" and that went on and on and on and on. It was three hours, I was told afterwards. There was a view of some dark hair, but he couldn't crown, he was stuck. By that time, the baby was beginning to show signs of distress and machines were beeping alarmingly. The midwife said it was "too late" for a C-Section and I just needed to push harder. Finally, with my last ounce of strength I sat forward and pushed straight down. Reed plopped out. He was pale bluish and, like lightning, the team whisked him over to a table out of my line of sight.

I heard them saying 'Reed, get mad! Get mad, Reed.' For what seemed like forever, there was no sound, then finally the loud wail of a breathing baby. They had to suck out the meconium – aka baby shit – he had aspirated and do lots of other things I couldn't see, but he was alive. He was alive! I could not have been happier, or more exhausted either.

Later, they hoisted me into a wheelchair and then into bed, still no feeling below the waist. Handing me the little guy, whose color was moving steadily from blue to pink and he was breathing fine, I was ecstatic. We had both survived. I cuddled him to my breast and he obligingly latched on like a pro. This was going to be fine!

It was, until I got the feeling back in my lower parts and needed to pee. Helping me to my feet, the nurse began to walk me to the bathroom. All of a sudden, I collapsed to the floor, peeing myself, screaming with pain. Reed started yelling too. It was mayhem. Back into bed. What the Hell was that????

Lying still I was fine again. Move and I screamed in agony.

Despite the hefty dose of morphine, I knew I was in major pain when the techs moved me on my side and picked up the sheet to transfer me to the gurney to go get an MRI. The doctor said he couldn't see anything wrong, maybe it was "nerve damage." Turns out he had stopped the MRI just above my pubic bone."

Months and months later, when Dr. Gregg x-rayed me fully, lo and behold there was an inch-wide dark gap of space between the two parts of my symphysis pubis, the part that joined the two halves of the pelvis in front and was only supposed to stretch for giving birth then spring back together. It had evidently ruptured when I pushed straight down, thankfully giving way so that Reed, who had a particularly large head, would live. Pelvis ruptures usually happened in the Third World, not in places like Atlanta, Georgia.

Learning the truth of the situation, I was so shocked on the drive home from that appointment that I ran a red light and nearly killed myself and Reed. Again.

I then made an appointment with a pelvis doctor, who had the nerve to ask me "How much ibuprofen do you think you can take?" Ibuprofen? For a broken pelvis? The other alternative was to be steel plated back together with all sorts of pins and screws. And, by the way, he informed me that I'd almost certainly be incontinent and have no sexual response whatsoever. Yeah, right.

I went back to Gregg. We embarked on month after month of three adjustments a week, shlepping Reed up to Sandy Springs, paying out the nose. Adjustments at first only held for a few hours, then a day, then a couple of days. Progress was made, but it seemed like forever and my bursts of intense pain in the back, where my butt muscles tried to hold me in one piece without much success, continued. But I had found the right person: Gregg did not just crack bones, he gave out supplements, Chinese herbs, and found emotional traumas that were stuck in his patients' bodies. I never knew what might transpire in a given visit. Once my body told him, via applied kinesiology, muscle-testing, that I had been deeply hurt by my grandmother telling me at age fourteen that "For such a homely child, you've turned out okay." Nice. Grandmotherly. Bitch.

"My luck to be named after her, huh. You got the nice one."

Then came a fateful day when it was around the first anniversary of his birth. I was slowly having less pain spasms, but I was also beginning to lose hope. No one but Gregg was helping me. Even my mother had doubted the fact that I couldn't walk – my birth and my brother's had been easily, quick, nothing went wrong.

One of my friends suggested I go to a psychic to see when things would heal all the way. So, I booked an appointment with Sheila – she went by only one name, like Cher – who had originally been a fat hairdresser in Woodstock until she kept reading her clients' minds and opened her wildly popular psychic reading practice. The Georgia Bureau of Investigation consulted her, no less, in Missing Persons cases. So, I walked, slowly, into her office. She stared at me for a long moment.

"Why do you think you cannot have another baby?" Were the first words out of her mouth.

"Bad birth." I answered. Understatement of the decade.

"Well, you were a man in your last life, you forgot how to give birth. Oh, huh, you trained racehorses in Florida for a living." Not much help, actually. "But, you used that masculine power to save the little guy's life, at your own expense, didn't you?"

First, she knew it was a boy. Okay, fifty-fifty chance. But, more importantly, I hadn't thought about the hellish experience in those terms and it sure was better than being an angry, hopeless, confused victim, as I had felt every day since Reed was born. And it was true, I broke myself in half so he would survive, though I did not know it at the time.

"I guess." I admitted, thinking hard about that re-framing of the whole thing.

"No. You did. You and he are in this together, karmically and in all other ways. Not just this life, either. You are a hero not a victim. Though those midwives sucked, and the doctor should have just given you the surgery."

"I see that now, but at the time..."

"No, *other* people should have intervened. Not your fault. Or the sweet baby boy's. He's a shining light, I hope you realize. He definitely wanted to be with you as much as you wanted to be with him this time around."

"Yeah." My main question was the future, when could I walk normally and be out of the shooting pain episodes.

Of course, she read my mind. Duh. "You are very close to being healed. Your friend, the man, is very powerful. He believes. And belief is everything." Dr. Gregg. Whew.

"I'm trying to believe, but I've been through so much it can be hard sometimes to keep up hope."

"Yes, but you are so close. In fact, I see you riding your horse next month." I hadn't said a word about Monday, who was waiting at the barn, apparently as depressed as I was.

"You do!?! That's great."

"And do take care of that near front hoof, the one with the contracted heel. That's going to give her some problems soon. Best to put shoes on her now." What? This woman was amazing. Monday had that very condition, in that exact hoof, but I had obviously been too preoccupied with my problems to address hers.

"Come back and see me, but know that *it is all working out*. There's a divine plan and it is playing out just as it should. Trust me. The little boy is a true light in this world and you did well to keep him here. He has powers, too, by the way." That made me very happy, as did the time the next month when I indeed was able to ride again, a sport not easy on a pelvis in the best of circumstances. Monday and I just walked around the ring slowly, but it felt like heaven to be on her back once more. And I got her shod to help that heel.

It was true, scar tissue had been growing across the "Great Divide" as I called it, and when Gregg x-rayed me the next month there was a faint grey that connected the parts. He said scar tissue is as strong as cartilage, maybe stronger. My sacrum muscles began to calm down, not having to try to hold the pelvis together from behind. Now my neck, which reacted at the other end of the spine, could relax as well. And Reed could have a happier mother. A miracle!

I asked Gregg how he knew it would work out. He looked at me with a twinkle in his eye, "I didn't. I had no clue. But I was damned if I'd give up or let you give up either. We did it, together. YOU did it." We hugged and cried like babies.

Needless to say, I adored Gregg. I ran to him at the slightest provocation. He always put me back together, literally or figuratively speaking. Even all these years later, I still required adjustment every two or three weeks; walking around for thirteen months "sprung" had had its lasting effects. But I was no longer angry or feeling sorry for myself over the whole birth thing. A couple of years after I was in one piece again, Gregg confirmed the shaman's prediction of me having a second child, easily, saying the pelvis would hold and he'd adjust me regularly. The new birth team would be instructed that I absolutely would not push. He also confirmed that my bony opening was an inch larger, so it was likely to be an easy birth the second time. He was right. And a few days after Rachel was born, I was out raking leaves, not in a rented hospital bed crying. Rachel got lots of walks around the block and Reed was very sweet to her, too. When Hayley brought him into the hospital room to meet his sister, his first question was,

"Where is she?" As if I was deliberately hiding his newly minted sister from him.

"Getting her first bath."

When they returned from looking at her through the nursery window, Reed's trusting hand in Hayley's, he had piped up, "Aw, Mommy, she's cute!" A screaming, red, squashed-faced newborn? Okay, I'll take it.

His next question was "Did you miss me?" Hmmm. I was a *bit* preoccupied.

"Of course, my Honey Bunny! I missed you a LOT." The first of many negotiations between two children's needs, not to mention downright lies.

Hayley was beaming and came over to kiss me on my cheek.

"You look like a million bucks!" She enthused. We looked at each other, both thinking of the last birth. But four-year-old Reed was puttering happily around the room, looking at all the interesting equipment but not messing with it. He definitely was living proof that it had been all worth it. Every minute. So was his healthy little sister, even if she were a bit of a barracuda nursing.

Dr. Gregg came to the hospital and adjusted Rachel when she was barely eight hours old. She had flown out of me so fast that her tiny neck was off just a bit. He was so tender with her that it made me tear up.

Ironically, though, Rachel was more of a challenge after she was born that Reed ever had been. I always thought of the two contrasting births and kids' personalities on my way to see Dr. Gregg. They bound us together, inextricably, more than in most patient-doctor relationships, like people who have been through a harrowing experience together feel so close to each other ever afterward. Plus, he routinely adjusted both kids too and they adored him.

"Hi, Gregg." I gave him a quick hug.

"How be you?" He always asked.

"Good. Going to Costa Rica with Reed on Saturday."

"Fun. Just you two?"

"Nope. Reed's tagging along on a college fieldtrip, the culmination of a course I taught with a geology colleague called 'Art and Environment in Costa Rica.' In the fall we studied about the formation of volcanic rock, jadeite, and gold, and we'll go to the museums in San José then tromp around rainforests and craters and caves. It's a blast. This is the second time I've done it. I get lots of points with the administration for cross-disciplinary teaching, too."

I sat on his adjusting table and swung my legs like a little kid.

"So, just a regular adjustment?"

"You tell me!"

He took my pulses, poked my abdomen and gently touched the pubic area from above.

"Hmmm. Something's a little wrong there."

We both knew what "there" meant.

"Yeah. Been a little sore, off and on." What's new.

While pressing on that area, he held his fingers in different positions and stared at the last one, tilting his head in thought.

"Well, it's neuro-emotional. The usual questions for your arm..."

I obediently held up my left arm. This was old hat. In applied kinesiology your arm loses all its normal strength to say "no" to the questions you are being asked. Like if asked to think about Christmas, your arm is strong when the practitioner pushes down on it, but asked to relive a car wreck, you cannot hold that same arm up to save your life. It was totally accepted in psychology and super useful for ferreting out a whole grey area of memories, traumas, and insights that lie in your body's wisdom. "Wisdom of the Body" in living color.

"Money, job, career, or finances?" My arm dropped abruptly, applied kinesiology for "no."

"Everyone you've ever loved?" Duh. My arm was strong as a horse.

"Female?" Arm up, yes.

"Mother?" Arm down.

"Grandmother?" Arm down.

"Aunt, cousin?" Arm down. Arm down.

"Girlfriend?" Arm down.

"Sister?" Arm rock hard. Yes??? What the Hell?

"But, Gregg, you know I don't have a sister!" He nodded, pensive, and looked out the window for a moment.

We ran through the questions again. This time he did not do them out loud, just in his mind. One minute my arm was strong, then weak.

"Sister, again." He looked at me hard.

"What sister, pray tell?"

"All I can say is your body knows you *had* a sister."

When I absorbed his meaning, I immediately burst into noisy tears. It felt true, no other way to explain it. Totally and completely true.

"I had a *sister*?" I sat up and sobbed into his shoulder.

"Yes, you did." He said ever so gently. He let me calm down for a few minutes, holding me loosely.

"And you know what? I did, too. She died in the womb." He said sadly. "Like yours."

"Oh, my God. She died. In the womb." I broke out in fresh crying. "My sister."

"Your twin."

"Are you sure? Does my body know if we were identical or not?"

"Let's see." More gestures and arm testing. Strong, weak.

"Yes, you were identical twins. She resorbed at the beginning of the second trimester."

"Ohhhhhh. That... that breaks my heart." We sat for a moment in silence. "I always *wanted* a sister to make up for my shitty ass brother. But I lost her. We *lost* her."

"It actually, tragically, happened quite a lot in our generation, Rebecca. The first widespread use of ultrasounds, beginning a bit after we were born, showed a surprising number of twins at six weeks but then only a single baby at twenty weeks. Maybe as much as ten percent of all pregnancies...."

"Why? What happened to make that occur?" I was sniffling in my Kleenex, but curious. Gregg knew everything, Western science, Eastern medicine, and who knows what else. Maybe voodoo.

"Well, they aren't too sure. But nowadays if you get pregnant with twins you know it right away and the docs tell you to eat huge amounts of protein and drink gallons of water, and instruct you to gain weight at will. Then the chance of two viable babies surviving is high. And of course the usual no smoking, no drinking. My mother drank like a fish."

"Mine too and she smoked a pack of cigarettes a day. But a couple of years ago, one of my grad students ate and hydrated like crazy and she had two beautiful five-pound twin boys."

"Yep. But, see, our mothers had no idea they were carrying twins and their doctors absolutely forbade them to gain weight. The sad truth is that there were only enough resources for one baby..." He left the nasty implication unsaid.

"You mean you and I hogged all the goodies and our sisters died?!?" I was appalled.

"It was not, I repeat not, our fault. Nor our mothers' – they were doing what they were told. Medicine changes all the time. Plus, the mid-to-late Fifties culture was deeply ashamed of bodily excess. Those tiny waists on the shirtdresses and all. Few women breastfed, it was thought too sexual and animalistic, supposedly, whereas now women pull out a boob in public and nobody gives a crap."

"I did, too. I gained my forty pounds, nursed in public, the whole nine yards. With single babies."

"Yep. Times have changed. Although another wave of twin loss came about with the fertility stuff. With in-vitro fertilization, if too many implanted fertilized eggs 'took' they so-called 'harvested' some out. Same effect. Maybe less painful for the survivor or survivors, maybe not. They weren't meant to be twins or triplets in a spiritual sense, but they still lost the soothing presence of another baby in the womb."

"You mean physically painful?"

"No, psychologically, spiritually, emotionally. We, unfortunately, belong to a group they call 'Womb Twin Survivors' and it comes with a whole set of pretty shitty side effects. Overeating for one." I tried not to look at his belly.

"Depression?" I'd had my share.

"Oh, yeah. Abandonment issues, addiction, a sense of something missing in the back of your mind all the time. Because we were meant to be in this life with our twin. We, how to say it? We feel the loss even though it was so early, maybe even because it was so fundamental."

"Pre-verbal, but still strong, huh?" I mused.

"Perhaps stronger. Our very first bond was irreparably broken. And even if we couldn't talk or even intellectualize anything, we felt emotions, warmth, security, and then it was ripped away from us. That's huge."

I was sitting on the table, slumped, dejected.

"It's so sad, just so sad."

"I know. For me, I have a compulsion to help 'damsels in distress.'" He was on his third marriage to another needy, messed up woman, in fact.

"I certainly qualified as one. And I'll take any love and attention I can get. Even if he's an ass."

"Good old Dan. How is the bastard?"

"Same. No, worse. We barely speak."

"Well, at least you got two beautiful children out of it."

That kind of shocked me to hear, though Gregg and I always spoke honestly and freely. On the heels of learning about my twin and her dying, I was too raw to go there.

"True." I had to admit. I'd cross that bridge after Costa Rica. Maybe.

"My sister was to have been named Teresa. My body knew that, too." He offered.

"Hmm. Can you ask mine about a few names?" I figured if you had twin girls in 1958 one would be named for one grandmother, that was me, Rebecca, and the other for the other, that would be Margaret. So, I thought "Margaret" in my head over and over again, and, sure enough, my arm was as strong as could be.

"That's the one." He affirmed.

"Margaret." At least I was named after the nice one.

"But at that time, you were destined to go by Becky and she'd have been Maggie or something." He suggested.

"I guess." Something felt funny about "Maggie," but I shrugged it off. "Cheerleader names."

"Spelled with an "i"? Dotted by a heart?"

"Obviously." We managed to smile a little. Gallows humor.

"Are you okay to drive home?" As always, he was genuinely concerned for my well-being.

"I'll sit in the waiting room for a bit. Try to absorb this a little more. Then I'll be fine." I hoped.

"You are fine. More than fine." He looked at me with admiration. There'd always been a little spark of attraction between us. I guess some of that was that I was now officially the poster child for 'damsel in distress' and he certainly was the one person in my life so far who believed in me and helped me unconditionally. Except he did cost a lot... Oh, well. We were both married, for better or for worse.

When I got home safely, driving the back roads because 285 seemed too dangerous in my vulnerable state, Dan didn't ask about my chiropractic visit and I was not ready to share something this momentous with him anyway. Now I had more insight into why I chose him in the first place: because he chose me. And seems like maybe I put up with him as he tanked so I would not be abandoned again. Might not have any choice, though, on the latter. "Life is too short" rang in my ears. And I *did* have two beautiful children. *Whose hearts were almost certainly going to be broken.*

Well, my heart broke at three months in utero. I again thanked all the gods and goddesses that Reed made it through his birth. I could process this twin thing – Gregg had given me the name of a support group online — but knew I could never have fully recovered if Reed had died that day. I felt a deep, abiding sadness, nevertheless.

"Mags. You were going to call me Mags. This time around."

Chapter 7

"Oh my God, Mom, I can't believe I get out of a whole week of school! I am beyond psyched!" Reed crowed as he dragged his duffle bag to the front door.

"Well, remember, you have to practice your Spanish every day, keep the science journal on what you're learning about geology and climate and all, just like the college students, and then write a reaction paper for your teachers when you get back home. Not all play!"

"I know, I know. But it's like I'm an honorary college student. That is sooooo cool."

"It's going to be great, no matter what happens!" I could only muster cautiously optimistic.

That was because the last time my geology colleague Ben and I lead this fieldtrip there were several problem students to contend with. (Professors refer to them as "*that* student." The ones that drive you absolutely, bat-shit crazy from Day One of the semester.) There was the pretty girl who had never been abroad and thought that appropriate behavior included refusing to get out of bed during a family homestay and rolling around on the porch kissing a random local while we all waited for a ferry. Not to mention the unmedicated ADHD student who slept the entire time in all her clothes, shoes included, and drenched herself and anyone in her vicinity with bug spray. Oh, and she never once looked up on any of our adventures. Her helicopter father called to check on her even when we were in the most remote places imaginable.

This trip had to be easier, and saner, than that one, didn't it? It would be fun to be with Reed for ten days, anyway.

"Me, too! Me, too!" Rachel was shouting as she tried to close her pink sparkly rollie for her trip to Hawaii. "No school, whoopee!" I came over and managed to jam it shut for her.

"Rosie's mom said you'd have Nature walks and maybe get to swim with dolphins, things that you can tell your class all about when you get back...." I reminded her.

I don't know why I was sweating a few days out of school for them – the uber-rich parents at their school never made excuses for pulling their spoiled-rotten kids out of class to zip off to somewhere exotic at the drop of a hat. Hell, I'd had one of my college students try to get out of a final exam because she just HAD to go on a cruise.... At least this time, *my* kids were gaining some worldly experience, and having fun, like their peers.

On our way past the study, Dan managed to drag his gaze from the fascinating computer screen.

Monster streaked in as we were all preparing to say our goodbyes. The cat dashed behind Dan's chair and pawed at his closet door. Dan absentmindedly opened it for him, but Monster immediately tuned tail and ran away.

"Why is he doing that?" Rachel wondered. Dan shrugged.

"I have no idea. But we'd better get going, kids. You know the Atlanta airport lines…"

"Okay, hey, well, bye everyone. Have fun." Dan tousled the kids' hair and managed to peck me on the cheek.

"I doubt we will be able to call, where we're going." I warned him. In Latin America communication was always dicey anyway. Plus, I was so looking forward to ten Dan-free days that I wasn't actually planning to try.

"Bye, Daddy, I hope you won't be lonely!" Rachel called out.

"See ya, Dad." Reed was halfway to the car already and yelled over his shoulder.

"Don't worry about me. I'll be fine, just me and the cats." I thought he looked a little smug, but when he noticed me looking at him, he quickly rearranged his features to be totally bland. Innocent. As Rasputin, maybe.

"Remember to feed them once in a while…" There were always plenty of squirrels they could catch, not to mention birds, mice, and voles. Maybe the occasional rat, hopefully before it liquefied.

"Tropical breezes, here we come." I wheeled my bag out the front porch door and threw all the suitcases and backpacks into the back of the Volvo.

First dropping Rachel at Rosie's with multiple kisses and hugs, Reed and I proceeded to the airport for our early flight, singing along to Usher, Coldplay, and Green Day on the radio. I felt light and happy for once.

The students were milling around Ben at the Delta counter, handing in their bags and getting their passports checked. Ben's bald head stood out among the long-haired boys and girls in the class. He looked like a kindly grandfather, though from hiking to find rocks his whole life he was in far better shape than anyone else in the group. Reed and I joined the melee. After things got straightened out, I clapped my hands to get the students' attention and introduced Reed, who I could tell secretly liked the attention, though it sort of embarrassed him at the same time. But his friendly smile and shyly raised eyebrows – not to mention the fact that he was the prof's son -- prompted the others murmur their hellos politely.

"He's a paying customer and will participate in everything!" I added, to be sure they didn't think I was abusing my professorial status by bringing him along. "No special treatment!"

One of the guys made it a point to come over and greet Reed personally.

"Hey, man. Glad to have you on board. I'm David." He held out his fist for a dap.

"Thanks, man. Good to meet ya." Reed responded, his chest puffing up a bit, as he matched David's hand motion. "Have you been to Costa Rica before?"

"Nope. First time."

"Apparently I was here when I was about two, but I don't really remember it." They laughed.

David was careful not to meet my adoring gaze as I looked at my son. But his tiny smile acknowledged that he was massing up untold Brownie points with me. Which he was.

"Mom, can I switch seats and sit next to David?"

"Up to him."

"Sure." David's bright blue eyes crinkled when he smiled. Not only was he a good student, but a nice guy to boot. Or a big brown-nose. Maybe both.

Ben began making announcements as we all waited at the gate.

"We will have a buddy system on this fieldtrip." The students groaned as one.

"We know, it may seem infantile... But we needed it the last time we took this fieldtrip."

"Really? Like summer camp?" One of them piped up. The others chuckled.

"Hey, a group of twelve students and two profs is hard to keep together and we are going to be in some challenging places, so suck it up. We're not going to be in Kansas anymore." Ben was firm. Two students looked at each other as if to say "Kansas?"

"Six pairs. I choose to be 'One' and pick Rebecca as my buddy. We might as well go by first names on the trip, just easier. But she and I are still very much in charge..." He made sure he caught each kid's eye in turn.

"I'll be 'Three' and pick Reed." David offered. It would be easy to keep track of Reed, who was already well on his way to full blown hero-worship and probably would never leave David's side, like a pesky little brother.

The others counted off.

"Practice run. When I want to check the group is all present and accounted for, I will clap three times and say 'One.'"

Clap, clap, clap. "One..."

"Two..." "Three..." The kids played along, despite some not-so-hidden eye rolls. Students seem to imagine they exist in their own bubble and that professors are too dim to notice anything they do in there.

"Good. Your parents would kill us if we lost one of you!" That was my personal nightmare, but I would always take the front of any given line and Ben the back, so we should be pretty safe at keeping the chicks together. Hopefully.

They finally called our flight over the painfully loud intercom and all the kids whooped uncontrollably. Reed looked startled that college kids did that too, but he joined the noise happily. Smiling at me, he got in line behind David, slapping his boarding pass repeatedly on his hand in anticipation.

During the four-hour flight Ben and I plotted and planned, going over the itinerary again. Reminding each other of previous restaurants in San José that had been good, and what to reinforce with these students. Dress code, behavior, timeliness, etc.

Ben eventually closed his eyes for a nap, but I felt wide awake. I had a lot on my mind, not just the fieldtrip and its pitfalls, or the deteriorating state of my marriage. I kept going back to what had happened last week at Dr. Gregg's office. How I never knew about "Margaret" until now.

"Mags. Pay some attention, Bex."

What might I have called her, I wondered. Don't twins have their own special language, nicknames, and such? Especially identical ones, which were essentially one person repeated twice or split in two, more accurately? Maybe we even shared the same soul. This was still so new to me, I hadn't gotten over the shock yet. You go along for forty-some years thinking of yourself one way and find out it all was, in some senses, a lie. I guess people who are adopted feel this way when they find out, I mused. Reed's friend Sam was adopted, but he looked so different from his parents that it was immediately obvious, and he knew from very early on. He would have to wait until he's eighteen to meet his biological parents, which must be a super strange thing to anticipate. I felt more empathy for him now that my identity was in question. It was different from his situation, though, since I was still me, my parents were still my parents, but I was supposed to have had a sister, another me.

As identicals, we were to have been in that sort of freakish situation in which other people were confused as to who they were talking to. There had been red-haired identical twin girls in my elementary school class, Mary and Mimi, and to this day I could never remember who was who. One of them now worked at the university, one of them lead a weekend freeform dance group, so they had quite different personalities, but in looks it was a crapshoot. I decided that if Margaret had lived, I would have always insisted on getting a different hairdo from hers, and worn a necklace with my name on it, so as to assert a discernable sense of myself.

But here I was, without that particular problem, but arguably a much worse one: I was alone in this life, left here as half of a whole. I had not found my true "other half" in Dan, either. Were unsuccessful relationships part of this "Womb Twin Survivor" syndrome Dr. Gregg had told me about? To choose so poorly, act from deficit…somehow attract the wrong person, trying for some idyllic version of my twinship, and then take what I could get, no matter how shitty? I was confused by the whole thing. It made the earth seem shaky under my feet, even more so than my family busy falling apart around me.

Suddenly I knew something that helped me feel a little bit better. It jumped into my mind that she would have not called me Becky, but something cool like Becks or even Bex. Hey! That's what Bhindi called me – did she somehow know? I wouldn't put it past her. So, to continue the train of thought, I would not have called my sister Maggie, but something like Becks. Maybe Mag? No, Mags. That's it. Bex and Mags. In a way, knowing our nicknames for each other made me smile. We could still have our special relationship even if it were just in my mind.

"Bingo! Took you long enough."

Stepping out of the plane into the lovely warm, moist air made everyone sigh with pleasure and we all began stripping off our sweaters and jackets like mad. The chaos of the San José airport was nothing compared to the ones in Lima or Bogotá or La Paz, but the kids looked a little taken aback at the men frantically waving taxi signs and lustily yelling at us and each other, the sea of dark-haired children running amok, the vendors rushing en masse toward the passengers like lemmings to the sea. Reed inadvertently edged closer to me, whispering that he needed to go to the bathroom.

Clap…clap…clap… "One!" Ben called out.

Everyone stopped and obediently counted off.

"Okay, *with your buddies*, you can go to the restroom and come *right back here*, no exceptions! Good time to change clothes if you're hot and you have some cooler items in your carry-on."

They had been told to pack that way and would learn their lesson if they had been too "cool" to do so. Ben and I had both traveled the world, him looking at mountains and rocks, me at art and archaeological sites, so we were prepared with those zip-off pants that became shorts and layers ending in sweat-wicking t-shirts. Too bad I had to wear a bra, to be properly professorial. I had warned the girls that they had to watch what they wore, too—Latin American men could be brought to a veritable frenzy by the way American women normally dressed. Even though I secretly called Costa Rica "Latin America for Dummies," you still couldn't show cleavage, a bare midriff, or -- God Forbid – allow a glimpse of a thong above your jeans. You wouldn't survive for five minutes walking down the street the way these girls dressed back home. I had read them the Riot Act on that and on the need for only practical shoes, no heels. Back in Atlanta they may have thought I was crazy to insist on these rules, but already the blondes in our group were causing a minor international stir and we were barely out of Customs. In my time, I had had many a Latino tell me that I had the most beautiful blue eyes in the world as he walked by me in the airport. Now I was too old for that kind of attention, mercifully no competition whatsoever for a gaggle of nineteen-year-old hotties. The boy students, sensing the situation, closed ranks around the girls, who were giggling and batting their eyelashes at the handsome swarthy local guys.

"Remember the hand-out on culturally appropriate behavior, please...." I warned and fortunately the girls took it down a notch or two.

I was more than relieved when everyone came back safely from the bathroom and through the madness we saw a sign that said "Ben Smith." It was held by our bus driver, Ramon Gonzales, and standing next to him was Francisco Gutierrez, our guide for the trip. God bless Costa Rica. In Peru there would have been no chance of actually getting picked up as arranged.

I greeted Ramon and Francisco in Spanish and introduced the group to them. The students nodded politely to the two short, sturdy men while we all piled in the bus, Reed still trailing David like a devoted puppy. Happy chatter filled the bus, as did exclamations, self-fanning, water bottle drinking, and makeup refreshing. Ramon expertly drove the bus, albeit at breakneck speeds, through the dirty, smelly, crowded streets, pulling up outside our hotel with an impressive screech. Some of the students were oblivious, probably the ones who hailed from New York City, while others were wide eyed in shock at Latin American driving habits. To help them cope with the driving, I would have to give them a quick talk on the concept of suspended disbelief. Look the other way was always good advice, too. No seatbelts, of course. I lost a couple of months off my life at every trip south of the border and had once made the major mistake of driving a pickup up the coast of Peru. Never, ever again. I was not suicidal.

"Yet."

After settling in, we had a fun afternoon visiting the San José zoo. We let the students do their own thing, as long as they all met up back at the entrance in an hour and a half with something to tell the group about what they had learned. It wasn't a huge zoo – how much trouble could they get into? I avoided answering my own question.

I wandered around by myself for a while and ended up at the ocelots. Watching them for a while, I noticed their distinctive open, vaguely peanut-shaped spots that were quite different from jaguars' rosettes. The whiteness of their ears, which were pointed like housecats,' and the black stripes going vertically and horizontally from their eyes were also different from their larger cousin, the jaguar. By the same token, though one-tenth the size and weight, they were much like jaguars in their tree-climbing, swimming, and camouflaging abilities. My "aha" moment came: some of the pieces in the museum collection represented ocelots, not jaguars as I had previously assumed. I was thinking that I would tell the students that and when we got back to the museum, I could point out to them which pieces represented which cat. I'd have to change some labels when I got back home, too. This was the kind of realization that made the trip interesting for me, since I had been to Costa Rica numerous times since Reed was a toddler. On the first fieldtrip I had learned useful geological information from Ben, though, and we did more challenging outdoor adventures on these fieldtrips than I did on my own.

Speaking of outdoors, after another day in San José we would take off for parts north, first to climb into – and ideally out of -- a volcanic crater. After that we were going to explore an undeveloped cave and then ride in a boat down the Tempisque River to look at crocodiles, known as caiman down here. Reed was ecstatic about all these plans, needless to say. I said a quick prayer to Ganesh to remove all the myriad obstacles that might be in store for our ragtag group.

"Got your back, too, Bex."

But tomorrow we would take in the three museums: Gold, Jade, and National. None of them was huge, but they were all jam-packed with sparkling, intricate, and fascinating art. The students knew our collection, which was loaded with Costa Rican pieces, but we had very little goldwork and only a modest amount of jade. So, we started with the Gold Museum, located in an opulent downtown bank building. The installation was state-of-the-art, which impressed the students, who, like a lot of Americans, thought of Central America as hopelessly backwards. I had addressed that prejudice head-on in lectures during the semester, but seeing the plexiglass mounts, elegant labels, and perfect lighting drove home my point. They exclaimed over the masterpieces they had seen in class; the small scale and detail of the lost-wax cast jewelry was unfailingly amazing in person. In power-point presentations it was almost impossible to convey the marvelous precision because every tiny imperfection looked huge plastered across the classroom wall.

Everyone's favorite was the necklace with the shaman simultaneously turning into a bird and a crocodile, his body able to swing from the neck and his legs from the torso, due to particularly virtuoso multi-part casting. The display allowed us to see the back where the parts looped together. I made the visit into a review, reminding them of what they had learned in the fall and giving them fodder for their journals. I had them take a break and write so it all would be fresh in their minds. Plus, so much gold could become almost visually overwhelming, tiring in its splendor, and this was the first full day of the trip so we all had to get our "sea legs," as it were.

I stood in front of a case and tried to decide if I could separate ocelots from jaguars in gold. It was probably in the ears, since spots were not included – they were likely taken for granted – and some of the cat-people-bird-reptiles did have more pointed ears than others.

"How is it going, Honey?" I made my way over to see Reed, who was sitting on a bench and writing furiously in the little yellow journal we had handed out to everyone.

"Good, Mom. This gold is amazing. The others know exactly how they made it, but can you explain it to me?"

"Sure, over here there are good diagrams on the wall." Again, state of the art. I walked him through the lost-wax casting process and he studied the diagrams carefully.

A thought dawned on his face, "But they couldn't even see what was happening inside the mold when they were pouring in the melted metal!"

"Spot on. You got the main point, Smart Boy. Faster than some of my students!"

"Aw, Mom, don't call me that. David might hear."

"Sorry. I'm trying to be cool."

"I know. Just try a little harder?" His eyes twinkled with mischief.

"Will do. Now get your sassy butt over to the group. We have a few minutes for the gift shop and we should buy Rachel her trip present if it's not too expensive." I always brought back gifts from my trips. What to get Dan? Ugh. Maybe a t-shirt.

In one of the locked cases I found a little tiny gold pendant that was a miniature reproduction of the three-part shaman and I decided to splurge on it for Rachel. I could always borrow it back to wear when I taught goldwork the next time, I figured.

The next morning, we had to get up at the ungodly hour of 4:30 a.m. to make it to the Volcán Poas and climb down its crater before the park officially opened. Francisco had pulled some major strings to make this happen. At that time of morning my eyes were terminally scratchy, my throat objected strenuously to accepting food – though my fast metabolism demanded it every two or three hours at most – and I was downright cold. But I had to set an example, so I choked down some beans and rice and plantains and hopped on the bus as if I got up this early every day. Reed was the only one who seemed perky. The students all promptly fell back asleep, leaning on each other's shoulders like so many puppies, but my son wanted to chat.

"How amazing is this, Mom? I have always wanted to climb into a volcano. I mean, since I was little."

"I bet. I've never done it, either. And, I was thinking, we should both be fine with the altitude. It's something like think 8,000 feet at the top, but we've been higher skiing out West."

"Jackson Hole is like 10,000 or something. I was fine." He agreed.

"Yeah. Plus, then we climb down, so we aren't even at eight the whole time."

"Piece of cake!" he cried. I hoped so.

"Look at the views, Honey, aren't they stunning?"

"Yep. Do you think they sell Poas t-shirts?"

"Dunno. But Costa Rica's not as capitalistic as some other places."

"Maybe we could print some up when we get home and give them out to the students?"

"Like 'I survived Volcán Poas, Costa Rica, January 4, 2005'? Nice idea. You're so sweet." I had to give him a quick, sideways hug, especially since no one was awake to see me do it. Nevertheless, he squirmed away.

"Mommmmm."

I smiled at him indulgently and closed my eyes for a quick nap.

When we arrived a couple of hours later, everyone was yawning and stretching as they piled out of the bus. The cool air began to wake us up and the students munched on Power Bars and slugged water as instructed. Pulling on windbreakers, we set off over the lip of the crater and saw the magnificent, if slightly daunting, descent awaiting us. The sky was brilliant blue, the clouds picture-perfect fluffy, and the rocks made all sorts of great shapes and shadows. Ben stopped us periodically to point out geological features, especially the fumaroles, the openings that emitted the hot gases from an active volcano.

"Watch out, the steam is hot, over four hundred degrees. It will burn your hand in a split-second." It also smelled like more rotten eggs than you could ever imagine.

"That smell is the sulfur. It's best not to stay too long smelling it directly or you could feel nauseated." No, shit. I was gagging already. I hoped I wouldn't hurl. Some of the students looked pretty green around the gills, too. Reed was fine, predictably.

We clambered down and down and down. David was lending a hand to a girl he seemed to like, Elena, who had been flirting pretty continuously with him since we left Atlanta. She was tall, like him, with long blonde hair, big-boned. Yesterday the students had all been talking at lunch and in a sudden pause in the other conversations Elena had complained, rather loudly, that she was too tall to ever be the Small Spoon when she cuddled. David had gallantly assured her that she could be the Small Spoon and he'd be the Big Spoon if it came to that. The whole group had "awwed" simultaneously, embarrassing them both.

"You were the Small Spoon... even though I was actually quite a bit smaller. Maybe that's why I had to leave."

When we eventually got to the bottom of the crater, Francisco looked around and announced that we could not go back up the way we had come down because new fumaroles had sprung up in the path. The new way up that he pointed to was even steeper and rockier than the descent had been. I felt a little nervous about making it, never a big fan of rock climbing and still not completely confident in my muscle strength since Reed's birth and my recovery. But time to suck it up. I headed to my spot at the beginning of the line, glad that at least I could choose the pace and keep it manageable.

It was definitely hard, but I kept pushing myself until I had to take a break and sit down on a convenient boulder. As I looked down the line to Ben at the end, I saw he was also sitting, but with Elena, and he had his fingers on her wrist. Oh, no. This was not good. David was hovering nearby and after what seemed like forever, the two guys helped Elena to her feet and they all started up the crater again. She might get to be the Little Spoon someday, but she was a big girl and carrying her was not going to be an option if she fainted or something. I started up again myself, willing her to make it.

"I'm helping, no worries."

She seemed to gain some strength and, with David and Ben's help, she made it up to the rim.

"What happened?" I asked Elena, who had sprouted bruises under her eyes and looked like death warmed over.

"Uh. Well, I... I... this happened once before when I was on a mountain.... I guess I don't deal with altitude very well..." She looked ashamed, knowing she should have put that on her medical paperwork for the fieldtrip.

"Okay. That sure would have been good to know..." I said, as much for the benefit of the others who might be hiding important information from us, too.

"I'm sorry. No more surprises, I promise."

"Good. Drink some water and rest on the bus." She nodded, chastened. David took her hand and helped her up the bus steps and she collapsed into the first seat and closed her eyes.

Ben and I exchanged looks. First hurdle cleared. How many more were we due this trip? We shrugged at the same time. As my friend Virginia always said, "Life is a contact sport."

Reed was oblivious to the drama, writing in his little yellow notebook.

"How do you spell 'fumarole' again?" I spelled it for him. "Those were neat. But stinky, huh?"

"Yes, did you feel nauseated at all by the sulfur?"

"Nah. But I am starving. Do we have any snacks or something?"

"We are supposed to stop for a nice lunch in fifteen minutes, if you can hold out."

"I guess...." Growing boy. I slipped him my Power Bar which he snarfed happily. Nothing would ruin his teenage appetite.

The next day we took off further north and west. It was cave day. Another physical challenge for me, but since I had survived yesterday without pulling any muscles, so far, so good.

The cave entrance went straight down. And down. And down.

"How far is it to the bottom?" I asked Francisco nervously.

"About sixty feet. No biggie." Okay....

"Ah." Then I saw him and the two local guides unrolling the ladder, which was only six inches wide, with rungs about a foot apart. Shiny aluminum, no treads for traction. Hmmm....

"Two groups at a time. Rebecca will take you six first." Great. Thanks, Ben. I get to descend into the black hole on a swinging ladder for six stories, first. And I'm not a fan of heights or tight spaces. Deep breaths.

Ben helped me to turn around and get my foot on the first rung. Since I couldn't fit both feet on the same one, with my hiking boots' width, I realized I had to swing the other leg around and reach for the next rung blind. That sent the ladder moving alarmingly side to side. I stopped and took a breath. It did not help matters that everyone was watching me intently from above. Next, I tried a different approach: I took my next leg around the ladder and set my foot, heel first, on the next rung down. Like a ballet move, turned out legs worked best, and I slowly made my way into the abyss without too much trouble from then on.

"Never look down!" I yelled up at the small hole of light above me. "Take your time!"

The cave floor was a mass of mud, and my boots kept slipping and sliding around as I tried to steady the ladder for the next person. One by one I saw my group experiment with the task, to lesser and greater degrees of success. Reed fairly flew down, of course. No fear.

The guide started taking us over the slimy rocks and through absurdly narrow spaces. Soon we were totally covered in mud. There was a final opening, a triangle only barely big enough for my shoulders and hips to wriggle through. I had to force myself to do it, pushing down a surge of claustrophobia, firmly denying myself the luxury of panicking. When all six of my group managed to slink through, even big old David, the guide told us okay, now we turn back. What? It was a dead end and I had to face the Triangle of Death all over again? I started counting in my head to distract myself from the mounting terror I was feeling. The bottom of the ladder now looked inviting in comparison, not to mention that circle of light way up above. But I had to let the students go up first, watching as the ladder got muddier and muddier and muddier. Even Reed struggled to keep his footing when it was his turn.

The last one of the students in my group, Lena, who was a bit plump, took one look at the prospect and turned to me and declared flatly, "I can't do it." My thoughts exactly.

"I bet you can." I looked her straight in the eyes.

"Nope." She looked both stubborn and scared.

I had to get fierce.

"There really is no alternative, Lena. Plus, if *I* can do it, *you* can do it. I'm twice your age. Watch."

I had to steel myself and go ahead and do it, for her as much as for myself.

"I'll catch you if you fall."

I huffed and puffed, slipped and slid, but somehow, like ascending into Heaven, I made it up to the circle of light. Fresh air and sky were delicious. No more caves for me, I decided. I needed some freedom and ease in my life, dammit.

But I was not to get it. The guides were obviously in a terrible mood when I emerged, but I explained about the girl who was afraid, and they tossed a rope down to her. Ben walked her through tying it around her waist. The guides were muttering pointedly about "la gorda" – meaning Fattie -- as they yanked on the rope. Sadly, she was one of the students who understood Spanish, and her face was red with exertion and with embarrassment as she struggled out into the sunshine at long last.

Francisco approached me. Uh, oh. In rapid-fire Spanish he told me that three of the boys in the second group, as they were waiting for their turn, had started harassing the iguanas. It was their mating season and they lumbered silently around in their orange, five-foot-long glory, looking for love. Well, they had come to the wrong place, apparently.

"They threw sticks at them! They chased them all over!" Francisco was irate, stomping around and gesticulating angrily, demonstrating the chasing with sticks. I apologized profusely for them, but I was now furious, too. I hated for the animals to be scared and, almost more, I hated for us to fit the Ugly American stereotype so perfectly.

I whipped around to the three boys, who were standing together and looking distinctly uncomfortable and guilty.

"What in the *world* were you thinking?" They shuffled their feet like so many five-year-old's.

"So, I'm guessing that it was just too damn tempting to harass some innocent animals?" I demanded. "Ben, I say these guys don't get a turn in the cave as punishment." For me, it would have been a reward, but for them it would mean disappointment and humiliation in front of their peers. "And we'll have to tip the guides extra."

"Agreed." Ben's Spanish was limited, but the guide's pantomime had conveyed the story succinctly without words.

I nodded my head toward the bus, which would be very hot and stuffy, and the Three Musketeers reluctantly slouched over to it.

"Write about interspecies respect in your journals, por favor."

"And no chasing the iguanas!" I said loudly to no one in particular. Something I never had imagined having to say, that's for sure. Like when my kids were little and I found myself saying "Yes, you have to wear clothes to school" and such like. "And someone has to clean off the ladder or the last group will be in danger of falling." I was getting into ordering everybody around.

Ben nodded and sacrificed a towel to wipe each rung as he went. That group, being small, was back up more quickly and fortunately without incident.

I whispered to Ben on the way back to the bus, "Maybe this is our last fieldtrip, what do you say?" He didn't answer, but he gave me a sly wink. It was going to be my last one, I thought defiantly. Good thing I had gotten Reed in on this one.

Everyone was muddy, sweaty, disheveled, and out of sorts on the ride back to the rooms. But Elena's bruises from yesterday had faded and when I praised Lena for her bravery, she managed a weak smile. I kept the stink eye on the Three Musketeers and they obediently kept scribbling. They would never forget those poor iguanas.

"Mom, that was amazing! We went through this really tight place and everything. The ladder was fun, like a ride at Six Flags." Reed bubbled. Good old Reed, never a cloud in his sky. I decided to lighten my mood, too, and focus on how we had survived a second incident.

But, bad luck comes in threes, right? A couple of days later we found ourselves getting into a flat-bottomed boat, just big enough for the group. Ben rearranged the students some to get the weight even on both sides. I was once more positioned in front. We were on the Río Tempisque in the Nicoya Peninsula, further west from the cave and the volcano. The ferry had been delayed for four hours, but no students were caught necking locals this time – I kept my eyes peeled. However, several of the girls managed to be caught at a table playing cards with some strange men, complete with a suspicious number of half-drunk beer bottles on the table. One girl immediately slid hers in front of her neighbor, as if we were blind, deaf, and dumb. The university had made us promise to uphold American laws, like the drinking age, but we were not so naïve as to believe these kids didn't party all the time at home, so we looked the other way. However, I did decide to sit with them and learn the card game, which put a notable damper on their enjoyment.

It was another gorgeous sunny day, a little cooler on the water than it had been in the crater or down the cave. Sunblock, hats, long sleeves, bug spray were all in use. David sat next to Elena, to Reed's disappointment.

We putt-putted in a leisurely fashion down the river, which was maybe fifty feet across or so. The trees were thick on the banks, down to where the mud began. After the first bend, we all exclaimed over the number of caiman sunbathing on the banks to either side. They looked to be about six or eight feet long each, all knobby and prehistoric.

"These are Brown Caiman." Francisco explained. "They are smaller than some other crocodiles, like the Black Caiman in Brazil, which can reach over twenty feet in length." We all sucked in our breath at the idea of caiman way more than twice as big as the ones we were seeing. They were threatening looking enough as it was. Then, as we watched with growing horror, a group of them came to life all at once and slithered into the river, heading our way.

"Oh, shit." David inadvertently yelled. "I mean shoot." He amended quickly.

It *was* an "oh shit" moment, though. I realized that seeing caiman was one thing, but *not* seeing them was worse. They could be anywhere under the water!

And, oh shit, oh shit, oh shit, a giant caiman head all of a sudden reared up out of the water on my side of the boat and slapped back down again with an enormous splash. We all screamed. Then the water went smooth again. Everyone looked around frantically to see where the creature had gone, fearing another uprising, but we never caught a glimpse of the behemoth again. Shaky laughter skittered around the boat. Another near miss. With a start, I realized that if everyone on my side of the boat had bolted to the other side, we could have capsized, right on top of our caiman friend. Jesus Christ. Enough, already. Adventure be hanged.

Good old Reed was grinning from ear to ear and saying over and over to no one in particular "Did you see that? Did you see that?"

Elena was clinging to David's arm and shaking her head from side to side in disbelief. The Three Musketeers were laughing a bit too hard, trying to act macho. Apparently, no one peed their pants, that was one thing to be glad about. That would be hard for a college kid to live down.

At that point Francisco allowed as how maybe we should turn back to the dock. There was enthusiastic agreement all around.

I tried for a light tone. "Another day, another adventure!" No one answered.

That night at dinner, Ben and I agreed to let them drink beer if they promised not to tell their parents or their friends or *anyone*, in case it got back to the university administration. Ben's and my asses would be grass if that happened. But I needed a drink, too. I'd let Reed have a sip of mine, so he wouldn't feel left out.

"To surviving the life you lead!" I offered, stealing a Janis Ian song lyric.

"Here! Here!" We all took a big gulp and smiled at one another around the circle.

"So, which 'C' day was most memorable? The crater, the cave, or the caiman visitation?"

Caiman won the vote, hands down.

Chapter 8

Reluctantly back at work on the Spring semester prep and the kids – tanned and healthy -- returned to school, life went on. Memories of the Costa Rica trip surfaced now and then in stark contrast to the cold, grey January weather outside and the prospect of two more months until actual spring.

I found myself staring out the picture window of my office that faced the tall, bare-limbed trees in the Gully, as it was called. There was a creek running through it and some paths that were a nice diversion from a long day at work. Though the room was small, and filled to the brim with books, papers, exhibition plans, kid's pictures, travel photographs and such, the window gave me a restful and often inspiring vista. Today, however, I was not concentrating well, disgruntled to be back from vacation and not looking forward to the upcoming semester. I felt I was stuck in suspended animation and the future did not beckon.

Staring at my left hand, the big ruby of my engagement ring glinting in the dim light, I had an uncontrollable urge to take both my rings off. For the last thirteen years they had never been removed, but now, all of a sudden, they felt uncomfortable. My finger had constricted some around them, since I weighed nothing when we got married and the two births had padded me out a bit over the years. So, I had to lick my finger all around to painstakingly rock them off a little at a time. The air hitting that bare skin was a new, breezy sensation. I slipped them into the center drawer of the desk, so I wouldn't lose them. I knew I'd put them back on when I picked up the kids and went home, but for now, I would see how it felt to be unencumbered, just for a few hours.

"It's almost time, Sis. The airplane is about to hit the ground."

I could have sworn I heard a crashing noise from somewhere outside, but couldn't place it. Probably a truck gathering recycling -- the university was so mad for sustainability that you had to search high and low to find a regular trashcan on campus anymore.

Dawdling at my desk, I thought back to when Reed and I got home and gave out the trip presents. Rachel had been ecstatic over the necklace, Dan had been marginally polite over the "Pura Vida" t-shirt I picked up at the last minute in the airport. It was Costa Rica's catch phrase, equivalent to "Hang Ten" or "Life is Good." It was in Costa Rica, not so much here.

I decided to wander down to chat with Elsa in the museum. In her sadly windowless office, she was talking on the phone and tapping on the computer simultaneously, looking harried as usual. Gesturing me toward her spare chair and tapping on her watch to say "wait a second," she resumed her frantic multi-tasking. I looked at her bookshelf, always happy to see my various books in prime spots. Still burned out from the giant catalogue that came out, along with the second edition of my textbook, both in 2002, I idly wondered when I'd get the chance to write the book that I dearly wanted to about visionary experience, linking ancient effigies to modern shamans' trance insights. There was a grant for next academic year with a deadline coming up after Spring Break, but I could always get started on the proposal now before classes engulfed me. A possible year off to write, just write, was definitely something to look forward to.

Elsa finally wrapped up her call and lifted her fingers from the keyboard.

"Let's escape for a cup of tea?" I offered, trying to lure her away from her exhausting work for a few minutes.

"But I have a meeting in an hour." She was overbooked, as usual.

"So, that gives us a half an hour break then you can get back in time to prep for it." I had to be insistent these days to pry her away from her desk.

"All right. I do need a break." Only for the last ten years or so.

We walked down to one of the two Starbucks located near campus. The faculty and staff frequented one, the students the other. The two populations saw enough of each other during the day and overhearing your profs dissing their students – or vice versa – was to be studiously avoided. Officially, everyone got along. Unofficially, academia is a pretty much a snake pit.

When we sat down with our mugs, Elsa glanced at my hand and did a double-take.

"What happened to your RINGS?" she squealed.

"They're not lost, don't worry." I looked down at my tea.

"Then why aren't you wearing them, if I may ask?" She unconsciously reached out her hand to touch my bare one.

"I bet you know the answer to that." I mumbled.

"Oh, no. This is getting real." She looked very concerned.

"Too real. Elsa, I can't stand it much longer. Ten days away from him was bliss…. And, you mustn't tell anyone…" She shook her head sincerely – it was something we often said to each other when having our heart-to-hearts. "On the fieldtrip there was this boy student who was so nice to this girl student. It made me long for a man to be sweet to me. I was actually jealous of her. He said he'd be the Big Spoon, after she complained that she was too tall to be the Little

Spoon. All the kids went 'awwww.' It was so poignant for me." Embarrassingly, a tear slid down my cheek.

"Oh, Honey. Oh. Geez." After the years of bitching and moaning about our husbands (though hers often sent her flowers and said "I love you" at the end of every phone call), this *was* getting serious. She was stunned, I could tell. But while she would never imagine leaving Tom, despite his faults, she knew Dan was exponentially worse. "Is it past the point of no return?"

"I don't know. Maybe so. It felt so good taking off the rings this morning. But I'm putting them back on before I leave work, for sure. I guess it's sort of like an experiment. Or something. I want freedom and, at the same time, it scares the shit out of me."

"For the kids."

"For the kids."

We looked each other deep in the eyes. Mothering was Number One in both our books. But some things were too much, too far over the line.

I blew my nose on my paper napkin.

She squeezed my hand. Probably some of the old fart profs sipping their hot drinks would think we were gay. At the moment, I could honestly say that I didn't give a crap -- her touch was so very comforting.

"Let me know if there is anything I can do... anything at all." Elsa meant it. She was the kind of friend you can call at two a.m. when you've slipped and broken your ankle and need a ride to the hospital. Over the years we'd exchanged me ferrying her guest lecturer to the hotel for her rescuing me from my car being towed, her driving me to Lasik surgery for me driving her to Piedmont for false alarm labor pains. I knew she would help me if she possibly could. But now we both realized the next chapter would be ugly. Really ugly. My level of dread was through the roof.

"Time's up. Your meeting, my grant proposal." We gulped the rest of our drinks and slowly walked back to campus, deep in thought. With a wordless, tight hug we parted ways to go back to our respective offices.

Gradually, back at my desk, I was able to drag my thoughts to the task at hand. I did love to write, and I was so passionate about the shamanism book that finally I got into gear and drafted a version of the five-page proposal in a couple of hours. The grant was to the university's Humanities Center, and if I got it I would have a whole year with no teaching, no museum, no committees. I wanted it so badly I could taste it. I had paid my dues, producing two catalogues and a textbook so far, and I wanted to get my teeth into a "real" book, an in-depth one, meaty, all my own ideas.

As I was about to straighten up my desk before getting the kids at school, the phone rang. I recognized the number on the screen – it was my colleague in Sociology who was also interested in Latin American shamanism, albeit as part of developing nation theory and such.

"Hey, Mason. How's it going? Getting ready for the Spring semester?"

"Of course, aren't we all? Fun for the kiddies…" He was sounding pretty burnt out himself.

"You'll be going to Ecuador as usual for Spring Break?" He had a long-standing fieldtrip taking his students to see Quito's high-rise buildings, next to the gold-filled colonial churches, around the corner from the Brujos' Market where they sold hallucinogenic cacti. They visited real shamans, too. His students always raved about it afterwards and his picture was in the university rag over and over again.

"You bet. And guess what? This time there's money in the budget to cover a guest professor…"

My heart skipped a beat.

"Are you asking me what I think you are asking me?" I was breathing fast.

"I am. The last time we went, Don Alberto revealed to me that he uses the spirits of boulders to help heal his patients. They are covered with what look to be ancient drawings. Since you do South American antiquity and shamanism, I immediately thought of you."

"OMG. I'd absolutely love that. A dream come true! I need some one-on-one with real shamans for my next book. Maybe you'd write me a recommendation letter for the Hums Center gig next year? I was just drafting out the proposal, but this will make it even better – real encounter with a shaman will boost my chances a lot. It's not due until after Spring Break, so plenty of time." This was fantastic.

"Sure, no problem." He was a nice big guy married to a cute little woman, Sally, and I was excited as could be to go on a trip with them. Gratis, no less.

"Oh, Mason. Thank you so much. From the bottom of my heart. You don't know how much this means to me."

"Well, you owe the class a couple of preparatory lectures before we all go."

"Name the times! I am 'on the bus,' as it were." Kerouak's phrase was well known to our generation. Now the kids said, "I'm down with it" or "count me in" or something like that.

After we hung up, I danced around my minute office like a maniac for a couple of minutes. This offer would help my proposal immensely. I'd never been to Ecuador and going as a guest professor would be easy for me – not like Costa Rica, this time I would have only a few responsibilities and lots of research opportunities.

I called Elsa but her phone was busy, so I left a message. I hated to have dragged her down in the middle of the day with my marital problems and not share some good news to counteract that.

Fortunately, at the last minute I remembered to jam my rings back on my finger, where they felt heavy and constricting.

Still jubilant while carting the kids to the grocery store, letting them buy some uncharacteristic junk food, I kept thinking about another escape to the tropics. And the distinct possibility of a luscious year off to do my favorite part of academia, write, write, write.

Chapter 9

Dan and Reed had left early Friday morning for a boy's ski trip in Colorado, since it was the kids' long weekend Winter Break from school. I promised Rachel a manicure and pedicure and assorted other treats so she wouldn't feel slighted. I felt like we did not have the kind of money for all four of us to go skiing, either.

The Sis-Stars had celebrated Imbolc last weekend, planting actual and metaphorical seeds and setting intentions for the rest of the year. Mine revolved around protection during upheaval and a new life for me and the kids, loosened from Dan's grip.

As I was finishing picking up the house, I was thinking about how the other day I had listened to a message on the answering machine that lived on Dan's desk, and it had me wondering. It was Lisa, a lawyer and a flake even under the best of circumstances. She was the mother of an on-again off-again friend of Rachel's, named Veritas, who was always being left alone or not getting picked up from school and I was often called in for the rescue.

On the tape Lisa was stammering a little, asking Dan when "that thing" they had talked about would be ready. Huh. It sounded like when teenagers talk about drugs and think they're being cryptic when instead they might as well have been shouting "I'm buying illegal drugs" from the rooftops.

Monster was sitting next to me, watching me intently. As I pondered this new wrinkle in the shit show of my life, he pulled his closet maneuver again. Scratching at the door, I opened it, he ran away.

Then it clicked. I started rooting around inside Dan's closet, digging among the chaos of office supplies, old psychology reports, dead pens, crumpled up papers. I almost gave up, but finally my hand touched a ziplock bag, back in the far corner of the lowermost shelf, well hidden. Not well hidden enough, though.

White powder. Full. Heavy.

So that's what the cat was doing— trying to warn me about the white stuff in his closet. That motherfucker.

"Go, Monster. Fuck Dan."

My heart sank and my body got hot all over. Lisa wanted her cocaine, apparently. I hoped it wasn't meth, which I had never seen, but I had heard was worse. Then I panicked, realizing the baggie now had my fingerprints on it. I ran into Rachel's bathroom and wiped the baggie down, then held it wrapped in a piece of tissue. She was busy playing with her Barbie, but I turned my body away from her to shield what I was doing. How to explain to an eight-year-old that her daddy was a big, fat, lying drug dealer?

Holding the baggie, I had another jolting thought: if a policeman came in for some reason right now or any time, they would take our kids away, my kids away. If a fire broke out or Dan played his music too loud late at night and the neighbors complained...I had to destroy the evidence, right now. But wait, I should take a picture of it or get a witness and then flush it? But wait, maybe there was more in the house. I was freaking out big time, my heart pounding out of my chest. For now, I would put it back where it had been and start over, come up with some kind of a plan.

But first I decided to make myself a cup of tea and try to think straight. Episcopalians would make tea when the world was imploding or aliens had finally landed. I guess my roots were showing under the pagan veneer after all.

Sitting in the breakfast nook, staring out the window, it started to hit me. Hard. I began to shake uncontrollably, spilling tea on the table. I set my mug down and started to cry, quietly so Rachel didn't hear.

This was it. This was undeniable. My husband was dealing drugs, probably taking a lot of his own wares himself too, with no heed to his family, the risks, the unfathomable consequences. It was how he drove – as if the laws of physics did not apply to him, as if there weren't other lives on the line, whether perfect strangers or his own children, never mind his wife. I looked down at my hand and licked my ring finger, easing the ruby off and stuffing it in a drawer in the Butler's Pantry. If Rachel noticed, I'd say the stone was loose and I needed to get it fixed. Oh, the lies that were floating around this house and would only get worse as the shit hit the fan.

But first and foremost, I had to know how bad it was and I had to destroy the drugs to keep my children safe. So, although my shaking had only barely subsided, I made myself get up from the table, pour my now-cold tea down the sink, and check in on Rachel. I had to keep her occupied so I could search the whole place up, down, and sideways. And it was a big house.

"Wanna watch a movie on my computer, Honey Bunches?"

"Sure! What a fun day! Later we'll go do our nails, too, right?" She had Barbie in her swimsuit pretending to swim across the bedclothes.

'Yes m'am." That would be surreal. Choosing what color toenails to get when the sky was falling. Reading old copies of Vogue about how to keep the spark in your marriage. The spark was about to be a bonfire in mine – and not in a good way.

Rachel gave me a kiss on the cheek in appreciation for the unexpected bonus of a movie. It might be my last kiss from her for quite a while, as I was under no illusions that I'd come out as the heroine in this saga. Dan used all his psychological prowess to deny, prevaricate, throw up smoke and mirrors, blame, manipulate, and, his ace in the hole, get viciously angry. It was going to be heinous.

Well, he was certainly in the wrong here, no doubt about that. But it was Saturday, not the best day to find a divorce lawyer. It occurred to me that I should document the drugs I found, and get a witness to back me up, and then destroy them before anything unmentionable happened.

I started in the bedroom. His bedside table. Little twists of aluminum foil revealed several shapes of blue pills. White pills. I scooped all of them out and put them on the bed, my stomach in a painful knot. Next, his closet, another hellhole of wadded up clothes and other crap. Deep in the morass I felt a large metal canister, covered in duct tape. Stuffed to the brim with pot. Okay.

And two prescription bottles, with the name of a Puerto Rican pharmacy, dated May of last year, 180 quantity each of Hydrocodone. About maybe half gone. Wow. Dealing in narcotics, cocaine, and pot, plus miscellaneous God knows what. Maybe good old Lisa had a bad back or something. Right. Maybe most of our friends, well that would be Dan's friends really, relied on him for their guilty little pleasures. Maybe I was totally screwed.

Oh, God. There was a rushing in my ears as I closed the bedroom door so Rachel wouldn't accidentally see the pile that was forming.

I had to get backup. Who could I call? The first person nearby and reliable was my old BFF's big brother, who was also a friend now that we were adults. Dennis would be perfect. He used to take stuff, but long ago swore off it. He'd recognize things that I didn't. And, he was a strong guy who would act as a credible witness in court if it came to that.

Court?? Oh, my Jesus. We'd be plastered all over the fucking local news! The kids would be humiliated in front of all their friends! My job could be on the line. He would be jailed, I'd get no child support. I'd have to sell the house. His children would talk to their father on the phone through the Plexiglas during Sunday afternoon visiting hours.

We would be ruined. Completely ruined. No more fancy private school. I wasn't even a good waitress, to boot.

I slumped down on the bed, absolutely and totally drained and dejected. But there was almost certainly more to be found and to fully protect the kids I had to find it all. So, I grabbed the flashlight out of my bedside drawer and carefully looked in every place I could think of, every dark corner, every nook and cranny. There was another large stash of pot in the extra freezer downstairs, plus several pipes and a bong amongst his basement mess. Finally, I had to stop because her movie would be over soon, and we were going to Subway and then getting our nails done.

But first I'd make a quick call to Dennis, to see if he could "accidentally" drop over ASAP so he could see this shit and help me destroy it, maybe he'd even cart it off in a trash bag for me.

"Oh, R. Oh. I'm so sorry. Of course, I'll come right over. Five minutes."

I stalled Rachel by getting her to pick up her dirty clothes off the floor, a monumental task.

Soon Dennis tapped on the front door. I let him in and gestured for him to follow me to the bedroom.

"Hi, Rach!" He called out as he passed her bedroom.

"Hi, Uncle Dennis!" She adored him. "Whatcha doing here?" She came to the door of her room to give him a hug.

"Just getting something from your mom." Upbeat.

"What?"

"Uh, a…. book…. that she thought I would like." He was a quick study.

"Okay, but we're going out soon." Rachel warned sternly.

"It'll just take a minute!" He tousled her hair affectionately. I gestured for him to follow me.

His eyes widened at the pile on the bed.

"Damn."

"It was hidden all over the house." I still had trouble processing this. I had been living in a drug den and had had no clue. What the fuck. Under my very nose. Well, 'fraid, Danny Boy, that little secret was out now.

He immediately formulated a plan. "Let's take pictures on our phones. I'll be in one of the shots and you in another to show our presence. Then get me a garbage bag and I'll take it away."

"There's a dumpster by the Flying Biscuit." I suggested.

"Good call. Plenty of hippies around here to blame for drugs in the dumpster, or to steal them. Get me a towel so I don't leave prints anywhere? I wouldn't want to go down with Dan's ship." Like I was about to do.

He made short work of the gruesome task and I remembered to hand him the book I had been reading. It happened to be a romance, to add another bizarre twist to this day from hell.

"Oooh, I haven't read this one." He trilled, as if he were gay.

"Ha. Ha. But, really, thanks. I mean it. You are my savior."

"No problem. I am so very sorry for this." He took my hand and squeezed it. I leaned in for a brotherly hug and got one.

"R, do you know a good lawyer?"

"No, but I'll ask around on Monday. The guys don't get back 'til Monday evening. Half the kids' friends' parents are divorced already, surely one of them can steer me in the right direction." Like Lisa, both divorced and a lawyer? Right, I don't think I'd be talking to her anytime soon. Or ever again. A family lawyer buying drugs from a psychologist, one who specialized in parental fitness and substance abuse cases. Nice.

"Mom! Ready? Did Uncle Dennis get his book?"

"Almost and yes. Just a sec." As unreal as it remained, at least now that I was sure they couldn't take the kids away and I felt a tiny bit better. But first, I desperately needed a glug of wine to calm my nerves. I tossed down a glass like a cowboy with a shot of whiskey in a bad Western and grabbed my coat.

"Let's go, Baby Girl!" I tried, semi-successfully, for lighthearted. More lies.

As my feet soaked in the hot water and Rachel babbled away about something, my mind was revolving like hamster on a wheel. Should I have put the drugs somewhere off the premises instead? But then I could have been caught and it would've been me in jail not him. No, I covered my ass as best I could at the time. I hoped.

I decided I would call Virginia the minute I got home. She was, as always, had my back and if I tried to get through the next few days alone, I'd lose it. Not only was she super smart and could be totally ruthless, but, more importantly, she disliked Dan with a passion. Most of my friends did, come to think of it. Though she had never married, she had had an over-twenty-year relationship and their breakup had been pretty ugly. Plus, she had plenty of disposable income so I knew she'd loan me enough for the lawyer's retainer, as loathe as I was to ask her for money. I had vowed when she sold her company for many, many millions that I would not be one of the gold diggers that masqueraded as a friend. But, at the same time, I was damned if I'd be one of those women that was stuck in an abusive situation because of a lack of money, either. One kid in Reed's class lived in the family home with his mother, his father and his father's girlfriend— no one could afford to buy the other out and they were upside down on the mortgage. The wife was slowly going insane, she said, and I believed her.

Virginia, bless her, booked the next flight and would arrive by ten pm tonight. I pretended it was a surprise I had planned for Rachel, who loved her "Auntie V" dearly. Virginia had been known to take the kids for wild joy rides in her golf cart when we visited her in Florida and she had a huge-ass swimming pool and hot tub. Auntie V was officially fun.

After settling Rachel in bed with the promise that she'd see Auntie V for breakfast, as I was anxiously awaiting ten o'clock to come around, the phone rang.

"Hello."

"Hey." It was Dan.

"What's up?" I was filled with white hot hatred for him at that moment and sorely wished I could blast him with the truth, but that would be way stupid. I had to play my charades close to my chest, not show them.

"Uh, well. Yesterday, you see…"

"What? Spit it out!" I demanded.

"Reed fell and broke his wrist…"

"WHAT??? And you tell me NOW?"

Silence.

"Are you on your way home, I hope?"

Silence.

"You're just going to stay. You're going to keep skiing??? While he watches tv? You asshole."

I hung up on him. I turned off my phone, but I doubted he would try to call back. I'd check it once in a while to see if Virginia had called to tell me she'd be late or whatever.

Let's review. Drug dealing. Dangerously selfish parenting – what if Reed slipped on the ice going to eat dinner? He was in major growth spurt! No cast? No x-rays? Probably some ace bandage or something. Oh, man. I was on the internet in a flash, researching divorce lawyers with the best ratings and the meanest looking faces. I was spitting mad.

"Taking you DOWN." I kept muttering. "Not hurting MY children, Asshole."

Virginia was a sight for sore eyes, wafting in wearing her designer clothes and her uber-expensive haircut, pulling her Italian leather suitcase.

The whole mess poured out of me, as we downed glass after glass of the extremely fancy champagne she had brought.

"Champagne? Is this a celebration?" I had asked glumly when she pulled it out of her voluminous Prada handbag.

"Yes, indeed it is." She was very insistent. "No matter how dark it seems right now, you'll find that it is actually the first step toward freedom from That Man. In fact, I am not using his name ever again. Unless I call him three shades of a son of a bitch. Or Asshole, Motherfucker, or Spawn of Satan. Maybe He Who Shall Remain Nameless. I haven't decided which." She gave a sardonic laugh and took another hefty swig.

"We need a plan of attack." I suggested.

"Did you find some likely candidates for the lawyer?"

"Yes, there's a guy with a face like a bulldog and five out of five stars, Henry Gilder. He's expensive, but he comes highly recommended."

"You know I'll write the check for him and you can pay me back whenever." She looked at me straight in the eyes.

"I hated to ask, but thank you. Thank you from the bottom of my heart."

"What are friends for?"

"Times like this?"

"Times like this. So, you'll call him first thing Monday. Tomorrow we should look in Asshole's computer, there may be more incriminating stuff in there."

"He has been obsessively staring at the screen for months now, come to think of it." Could this possibly get worse, I wondered morosely.

"I bet he has. God knows what's lurking on there." I shuttered to think.

"I cannot take any more today. It's been just about the worst day of my life, to tell you the truth. The walls are falling down all around me. And the kids. How can they ever cope with this?"

"Cross that bridge. You four cannot stay together, no matter what he pulls. Now, where am I sleeping?"

"My bed. I'll take the couch. I've been sleeping there a lot."

"Let's change the sheets so I won't get His cooties, please."

"Already did."

I managed to conk out from the wine and slept until about six am, when I jerked awake and in a rush all the horror hit me with a crash. I tried to will myself back to sleep, but all I did was thrash around, worrying, crying, raging, moaning.

"Mommy, you woke me up!" Rachel was indignant. As if she had never woken ME up in her life. Parenting is decidedly not fair.

"I'm sorry, Lovie. I had a bad dream."

"Is Auntie V here yet?"

"Still sleeping, but she'll be up soon. Let's make us some pancakes for breakfast, shall we? You can mix."

"Super dee dooper!"

As we were finishing the batter, Virginia wandered sleepily into the kitchen. Rachel squealed and practically knocked her over with her ferocious hug.

"We're having PANCAKES, Auntie V! And I mixed them all by myself." She crowed and did a little happy dance.

"Aren't you the smartest girl ever?" Virginia praised. "I'm extra hungry for YOUR pancakes, Baby Darling." Rachel beamed.

Virginia and I caught eyes. Let her be happy for two more days.

Rachel wanted all of V's attention, so I went surreptitiously to Dan's computer and booted it up. When I tried the usual password, M1onster, nothing happened. Tried it again. Same. Damn him, he'd changed it and I had no clue what else it might be. We had always shared passwords, but I should have figured those days of trust and openness were dead and gone.

I had a flash: Geek Squad. I'd call them and make up some kind of excuse. They worked 24/7/365 and I easily made an appointment for one pm. I said I'd explain the problem when they got there. And when I had figured out a good story, with Virginia's help.

I pried V out of Rachel's clutches after lunch, saying that she and I had an important computer problem to solve for Virginia's work. As if Virginia were not a computer whiz herself and as if I could have ever fixed a computer problem, but Rachel didn't have to know her mother's distinct lack of technological prowess.

The lanky, greasy-haired young man at the door introduced himself as Freddy and shuffled in.

"What's going on?" he asked, in a bored voice.

Virginia had come up with the tale of a husband who was all the way in a remote part of China on a business trip and had emailed for me to send him some document on his computer. But he must have forgotten I did not know his new password and now he wasn't answering his emails.

Freddy looked at me, then at Virginia, shrugged as if to say "Yeah, right," but nevertheless he obligingly plunked himself down on Dan's chair. It took maybe ten minutes, and he wrote down the password on a scrap of paper. Virginia and I waited impatiently at my desk.

"Interesting. What do you suppose your husband means by 'God of Gods'?"

"Wow. I don't know. Maybe it's a video game or something." My stomach was lurching and I had to turn away. "But, anyway, thanks so very much. What do I owe you?"

"Fifty."

After he was paid and drove off, Virginia and I were free to wipe the bland looks from our faces and exclaim about his password.

"I think it's the coke talking. That makes people grandiose. Think they are gods." Virginia offered.

"In their own minds. Jesus, what a load of fucking crap. What next?" I moaned.

"Let's see what old God of Gods has waiting for us on his desktop." Virginia looked perversely excited by the prospect. "This oughta be good."

She was a PC person, and I had always been a Mac one, so she took over the mouse and scooted around his C drive and whatever.

"Nothing obvious. Yet." She commented.

"Try email?"

She tapped several keys. Then she drew in her breath sharply.

"Oh, Rebecca." Her voice was serious.

"What is it? A list of his drug clients?"

"Way, way worse."

I waited, frozen.

She swiveled the screen toward me and there, in living color, I saw the picture of a lithe, small-breasted woman/girl in her panties with a big old cock in her mouth.

"No." My mind would not accept this final blow. Not teen porn. No.

Virginia had sagged against the back of the desk chair, her head in her hands. I closed my eyes, wishing I were dead. Or, better yet, that he was.

"If I had a gun and he were here now, I swear I would shoot him, first in the balls then in the head. You know I would." I said almost defiantly, daring her to disagree.

She nodded her head. "I'd help pull the trigger. And bury the body."

"Too bad we'd get caught if we did."

"Shame. It would be so satisfying."

"Well, since we can't kill the bastard, I'll make a complete copy of his hard drive, emails, everything. That and the drugs should do the trick. For blackmail, if nothing else." Virginia sat up and snatched a blank disk from a pile in the closet and began furiously tapping away. I sat and stared, unseeing, at the wall and tried not to think at all, but I couldn't keep all this at bay.

Rachel skipped into the study. "Are you guys done yet? I want to play Clue with Auntie V and you, Mommy." Great, a who-killed-whom game, perfect choice for my mood.

"Okay, Sweetie. Here we come. You get it set up on the dining room table? I'll get some snacks." Mommy had to cope, no matter what. There was nothing left to do for today, anyway, except to digest this latest pile of steaming shit Dan had thought he had hidden from me. Did he want me to find it? Was he too much of a coward to say he wanted out of our marriage? Did he think he'd get away with it? Assume I was a numbskull? I had to admit that I felt like one at this point. An angry, murderous, terrified, heartsick numbskull. A soon-to-be divorced one at that. But there was a hell of a fight and nothing short of the destruction of my children's whole universe to go through along the way. Yeehaw.

"Locks to change. Put that on the list." Virginia piped up as she ejected the second disk and handed it to me. "I'll keep one of the copies just in case. And send me the drug pile pics, too, while you're at it." Every new step pushed me further into the abyss. Kicking him out of the house, handing him the divorce papers, what to tell the kids?

We played Clue, twice. We ate dinner and made inane small talk. Rachel got Virginia to read her the required bedtime story and then, at last, we were alone again. More wine.

"Oh, R. Even I didn't think it would be THIS bad." And V had a good imagination.

"Me neither. Not in a million years. I mean, I knew we were desperately unhappy. Barely speaking. He was AWOL a lot. But two crimes, like actual go-to-jail crimes, and then poor Reed's wrist. Oh, geez. I have to make a doctor's appointment for Tuesday, too. I just pray he hasn't done irreparable damage to that arm. What the hell kind of a father just GOES ON SKIING?"

"A truly shitty one. Dangerously shitty, in fact. Playing fast and loose with other people's lives, people he supposedly loves."

"Not my definition of love."

"No. No sane person's."

"Tomorrow's going to suck. We still need a plan for the airport. The surprise factor of handing him the papers in public. Not in the living room, in case he gets violent. I wouldn't put it past him. But the kids need to be diverted from seeing the handoff in any case."

"I'll whisk them off for muffins."

"Good idea. But for now, I'm totally beat. I need sleep."

Me, too. You're doing the right thing, R, just remember that."

"I'll try."

Monday went by in a blur, Virginia taking Rachel to the mall while I got the locksmith and went to the lawyer's office. He tut-tutted, sympathized, and dashed off the paperwork post haste. He eagerly took the check for five grand that V had written. Ambulance chaser. But beggars can't be choosers and he assured me of a good outcome, fast and to my advantage. The only worrisome thing he said was that things can backfire when drugs are involved. People may think I was taking them also, his word against mine. And if the girls in those emails were a day over eighteen, no case there either.

"But Dan doesn't have to know either of those things, now does he?" Henry smiled viciously, nearly smacking his misshapen lips. "So, we scare the pants off him. Did you save any of the actual drugs, by any chance? They could come in handy if he calls our bluff."

My first thought was "no" but then I remembered that, in the heat of the moment, I had never gone back to retrieve that white powder baggie in the closet.

"I have one baggie of white stuff, cocaine or maybe meth."

"Ah, good. Bury it in the garden for now and bring it to me on Wednesday. We'll meet again to see how he reacted and such. Hammer out our strategy."

"Okay. Will do." What a fun prospect. And, lo and behold, I remembered that Wednesday was Valentine's Day. How special that I'd get to bring my husband's illegal drugs to my divorce lawyer's office on fucking Valentine's Day. I'd be willing to bet good money that Hallmark didn't make a card for that. Come to think of it, maybe I'd start a line of "Happy Divorce" cards for the major holidays. "Merry Christmas without your kids!" And mugs that said, "You owe me the child support, asshole!" with a happy face. T-shirts that read "I'm the world's worst dad." I could make millions.

Eventually, gallows humor aside, it was time to go to the airport. My stomach was heavy with dread, my head ached, I felt nauseated. Virginia drove.

The boys came up the escalator and both broke into smiles to see Rachel and Auntie V standing there with me. Dan was very surprised, and looked at me quizzically, but he went along with the story of a surprise visit from my old friend. Virginia hustled the kids off, calling back "Getting my favorite kiddos a treat!" and waving her hand cheerfully.

I pulled Dan out of the crowd, and held out the thick, white envelope which he instinctively took.

I leaned in and viciously whispered, "I know you're selling drugs and I know about the teen porno all over your computer. Those are the divorce papers. Oh, and the locks have been changed." I started to stalk off to meet V at the car.

"Wait, Rebecca. Wait!" He wailed as he trailed after me.

"What? What? You think I'd stay married to a criminal? Much less to a father who keeps on skiing and lets his son hang? You disgust me. I hate your guts. I'm telling the kids about the drugs. Find somewhere else to stay tonight." I hissed and took off at a fast clip.

He was crying. The big bully. Sobbing in the Delta baggage claim. Fuck him.

"I'll do my part with the kids." He squeezed out. No apologies, no "take me back," no "But I love you." Not that any of that bullshit would do a thing at this late date.

"When you cross the line of someone with Mars in Aries, you better watch out. My lawyer will be in touch." And I was out the door.

When the kids got to the car, they looked around.

"Where's Dad? Where's our baggage?" Reed asked, his expression puzzled. He was cradling his left hand, swathed in an ace bandage, which made me have a jolt of fear.

"He's got the baggage. He's got something important to attend to." That was the best I could do. I could see the kids looking at each other, afraid to ask more. Rachel began to cry.

"But I want to see Daddy! He just got home." She protested through her tears.

"You'll see him, Honey." Virginia took over. I was numb.

And half an hour later, we did see him, sitting on the front step with his head hung down, ski bags and luggage strewn around his feet.

"It's my house, too." He said belligerently. "You can't keep me out."

"What's happening? Daddy? Mommy?" Rachel was terrified. Reed was looking around wildly.

I was afraid of what Dan might do if I tried to get past him and into the house while keeping him out. He was strong and he had stopped crying, a sure sign that a tsunami of anger was on the horizon.

Virginia nodded at me, thinking the same thing. We had a plan if he got violent, we could call 911 now that the house was clean of drugs. Domestic violence could be added to his list of charges and no risk of me losing the kids. Virginia was trained in self-defense and strong as an ox. It was a calculated risk. Also having it out on the front lawn was not a good option for anyone, especially the kids.

So, I whisked past him and unlocked the door with the new keys.

"Mommy!" Rachel wailed as she and Reed ran inside. Virginia next, Dan last.

"Sit down everyone." Virginia planted herself between me on the couch and Dan in the chair opposite. She looked spring loaded. Rachel immediately jumped on Dan's lap. Reed sat down as far away from me on the sofa as humanly possible. This was already going south.

"Your father has been acting irresponsibly. He let you, Reed, sit in the motel room with a broken bone so he could ski. And while you boys were gone, I found drugs, illegal drugs, hidden all over the house. His drugs, not mine." I jabbed a finger at Dan, who hugged Rachel closer. She clung to him. Reed looked stunned.

"No, Daddy wouldn't do that!" Rachel objected. "He wouldn't!"

"Did he come home to take care of Reed?" I challenged her. She looked away.

"I saw the drugs, too." Virginia lied smoothly. She had seen the baggie of coke and pictures of the rest.

Dan jumped up so fast he nearly dumped Rachel on the ground and ran down the hall to the bedroom, no doubt to check on his stash. Which was gone.

He stormed back into the living room. "You tossed my favorite pipe, too?" He was incensed.

Reed knew what that meant and stole a look at me, the light of understanding dawning in his big, frightened eyes. He got it, at least for now, that the drug accusation was true. For a split second, I felt triumphant that Daddy was such a druggie that he gave himself away with that irate question. When the shock wore off, maybe Rachel would forgive Bad Mommy for accusing Poor Daddy of doing bad things.

Virginia was recording this epic conversation on her cell phone, just in case of catching revealing comments like those. I had verified with Henry that this was legal — he said it was, as long as the person recording was part of the conversation.

Reed jumped up and ran downstairs to his room. I followed him. When I got to his room, he was curled up in a fetal position on his bed, crying his eyes out, clutching his broken wrist.

"Oh, Honey. I'm so, so sorry. So, so sorry. If I could change this, you know I would. But your father is breaking the law and we could all have been punished. Really punished. So, I had to do this. For you, for Rachel, for me."

"What about Dad? Where is he going to go?" He sat up with fear in his red-rimmed eyes.

"Tonight, he can stay here and tomorrow he can find a friend to stay with. Maybe Jimmy will take him in or something." His problem, I thought to myself.

"I hate this. I hate both of you." He stormed and turned his face to the wall.

"I know it's a terrible shock." I said weakly, feeling as guilty as if I were the one selling drugs and looking at disgusting porno.

"No, Mom. It's not. I've been wondering when I'd hear 'we're getting a divorce' for years now. The other kids have told me their stories. The fighting, the silence. The LIES." He spat out. "Please leave me alone."

"Tomorrow we have a doctor's appointment at ten to fix your arm."

"Whatever."

Back upstairs, Virginia had Rachel on her lap, trying to soothe her tears. It wasn't working very well. Dan had evidently locked himself in the study, the sound of the banging computer keys loud and clear. He must be madly erasing stuff, clueless about what I had hidden in my underwear drawer and what was now buried under the dead plants in the back garden. My little Imbolc seeds, huh. I'd rather have sowed razor blades or taken V up on the shooting and burying the body scenario. No such luck. No luck at all, as the Dead sang.

Rachel finally cried herself to sleep and I laid her under the covers, weeping myself for the trauma just inflicted on her innocent little self. But probably she had some inkling, like Reed, down deeper maybe. As the shaman had predicted before her birth, she saw through lies. She KNEW things. For several weeks before 9/11 she had been upset, not sleeping, telling us that "bad things" were going to happen. The night after the Twin Towers fell, she slept like a baby again. For her, it was over.

Enmeshed in my personal 9/11, I dragged myself back to the living room and Virginia.

She handed me her phone set on the recording, to show me it had turned out. Loud and clear, he'd confessed that he'd lost his favorite pipe, bless his heart. She also looked at me and showed me her speed dial list. Number one was a very famous woman, no less.

"What? You know her?"

Virginia nodded.

"I had my finger on speed dial the whole time. She is going through a hellish divorce, too, and if I called her, she was to immediately call the Atlanta police. On *her* speed dial." V looked pleased with herself.

"Geez. That's unbelievable." I knew she had friends in high places, but this was amazing.

"Think. If he had gone ballistic and I had had to call 911 myself then Dan would have had time to exit the scene of the crime before the police arrived."

"Oh, right. I cannot thank you enough."

"Just pin his sorry ass to the wall and I'll be perfectly happy to have been part of it. It felt a little like the adrenalin rush in the boardroom when I got to fire some overbearing, mansplaining man."

I did not have that experience, and for me the adrenalin was awful, not exhilarating. But she had come through with flying colors, so I couldn't complain.

"Bet he stays up all night, trying to cover said ass. Where do we sleep?" I wondered.

"We'll share your bed. He can have the couch. We'll lock the door and have the cell phones at the ready."

"Sure he won't kidnap the kids or something?" I was suddenly petrified.

She thought for a minute, then her eyes lit up.

"Have an old baby monitor or two lying around?"

"I think so. Good idea. We'll put one in each bedroom. I'll barely sleep anyway, with him still on the premises like this."

And I did only manage to catch a few hours of fitful sleep. But finally, eventually, it was morning.

The kids were safe and sound, and I whisked them out to Waffle House for a big breakfast that none of us felt like eating. They were silent, Reed sullen, Rachel hiccuping once in a while from all her crying. Virginia had stayed back at the house to make sure He packed his bags and left before the rest of us got back from the orthopedist, not taking anything he shouldn't.

"You are one lucky young man!" The tall, thin doctor announced as he held up Reed's x-rays. "His wrist is indeed broken — in two places, right near the growth plates, no less — but thankfully the bones had not shifted. Not sure why they didn't, without a cast, but there you are. You dodged a major bullet. If they had moved, you might never have had the same length arms." Reed looked as horrified as I felt. Rachel clung to my hand, not quite understanding but knowing the tension in the room meant something bad.

"Don't feel lucky." Reed muttered defiantly under his breath, but fortunately the doctor was talking to the nurse about the cast production process and didn't hear. All of a sudden, I felt numb again, desperately tired, longing to be home without Dan there, no matter how wretched it was for the kids.

Virginia called my cell as we waited for the cast to set.

"Coast is clear. Said he was going to Jimmy's."

"Whew. That's good news." Rachel looked at me questioningly. "Glad you fed the cats."

"Huh? Oh, little pitchers, I guess."

"Yep."

"Look, R, I'm going to take off now if it's okay. I think things are under some semblance of control now."

"You've been absolutely incredible. I can't begin to know how to thank you."

"No need. Kick his butt, help the kids understand, call me whenever."

"Bye, I love you."

"Love you, too. Go Team!" It had been our catch phrase for over twenty years since we met on the Amtrak train platform in New Haven during grad school.

"Go team." I whispered, drawing Rachel closer beside me.

Chapter 10

I found myself standing in the overly empty and terminally quiet kitchen. It was the first weekend that the kids were with their father over at Jimmy's house. It was also the first time I could remember being alone in the house for two whole days. Long days.

I looked out the garden window for a while, then I turned to the sink, hoping for dirty dishes to give me something to do. When I saw there were none, I swung back toward the front of the house. Then I looked out the back deck window for a while.

This has got to stop, I said to myself firmly. Turning in circles like a dog chasing its tail, only not nearly as entertaining.

Okay. Think. I have friends, right? And I could go shopping for spring teaching clothes. Upon further reflection, I could do some Sis-Stars exercises at my mesa. Obviously, I always have work to do, plenty of work. Anything was better than moping, worrying, regretting, second-guessing myself. Dreading the rest of the divorce process, watching the kids trying to cope. Me trying to cope. I needed distraction from all that, and pronto.

So first I called Elsa to see if we could have lunch, but naturally she was busy at the museum doing a kid's workshop today. She tentatively agreed to us having lunch tomorrow at Chai Pani, our favorite Indian street food restaurant in Decatur. Then I called Hayley who said she was free today, predictably (she lived on a modest trust fund and barely worked). We agreed on the Raging Burrito, where possibly it might be warm enough to sit on the patio. I loved the giant Mona Lisa mural looking down on us and the sounds of the multi-colored-hair kids rattling around on their skateboards in the parking lot past the brick wall. Maybe we could browse the trendy shops afterwards in case I could afford something slightly off-beat for work.

Okay, now I'm getting somewhere, I encouraged myself.

Besides a little fun, it would be nice for a change actually to be prepared for my teaching and museum work ahead of time, a luxury I rarely enjoyed since having the kids. Work was so hard to keep up with, much less get ahead of, these days. I had to answer to so many people: the general public from ages three upward in museum programs, all my undergraduates and graduate students, the administration, my department, not to mention other colleagues' students who would email me all the questions their profs couldn't answer. On top of all that were my least favorite: random people claiming to have priceless "Aztec" art for me to appraise or at least authenticate for them for free using blurry photographs. They were rarely happy after talking to me, since I could not set a money value on anything because it was a conflict of interest for me as a curator. Plus, almost every piece they showed me was a fake, and if it weren't, they had just broken international law by acquiring it (oops!). It was true that I was, as Hayley put it, being nibbled to death by ducks. Oh, yes, and on top of all that I had to write brilliant scholarly articles and books, not to mention hundreds of exhibition labels.

I had learned to put the pedal to the metal during the day, rarely eating lunch anywhere but at my desk, so I could pick up the kids as early as possible. Thank the Goddess they were extroverted and loved daycare, then aftercare. But soon Reed would be too old for aftercare, but still too young to drive, so my time would be under even more pressure. Whoopee.

So, when in doubt, work. Merit raises in academia were meagre, but any more money for the next few years would be a blessing. I strode to my desk, passing the now deliciously bare desk that He used to use. I made sure to have fresh flowers on it, to change the energy. It was actually heavenly to come in the door after work and have none of Dan's moods to put up with, no wondering where he might be or what dangerous thing he might be doing. What variety of white powder might be lurking in his closet.

Now that the drugs were cleaned out of it, Monster could care less about the closet – he hadn't gone to the door since I had buried the baggie before the great Valentine's Day drug caper. I had assured him that he could live as long as any cat on the planet, with extra treats in gratitude for his trying to alert me to the danger. Like most felines, he had looked at me levelly and then proceeded to lick his butt, back leg hoisted gracefully in the air. As if to say, "my work here is done."

The trees were beginning to bud outside my window, and I admired them as my computer booted up and made little pinging noises indicating a shitload of emails landing out of cyberspace. If I delved into them, though, I'd be playing that mall game "whack a mole" and more would magically appear as I killed off the others. I'd never get my own work done, so instead I reread my proposal for my next book to get myself going. It sounded good, I only found one typo.

The subject of shamanic visions endlessly fascinated me, even more so now that I recognized an ability in myself to open up to visions without much prompting, as with the Tinkerbells and such. There was obviously a propensity in some people to See and there were whole cultures that valued it above all else, saw the truth nestled in the unconscious mind, what Carl Jung so aptly had called the "collective unconscious." The images that bubbled up were unexpected and yet perfectly encapsulated what was going on. Like all those Tinkerbells in my girl parts made light of the birth trauma, healed it, defied it to bring me down, got me out of victim mode and into "who cares, it's done." And they made me laugh.

Then again, last week I had gone to get my teeth cleaned, everybody's favorite thing to do. As the woman was painfully scraping away with her metal torture instruments, I desperately wanted to dissociate a little from the situation. Guess who appeared? Lots of tiny Tinkerbells, sitting on my various teeth, crossing their tiny legs and petulantly filing their nails, patently ignoring the scratchy sounds and intermittent splashes of water. I was so amused watching them and their bitchy antics that I forgot about the hands all up in my mouth and the imminent, unexpected moments of pain until, suddenly, it was over. Bravo, ladies. Thanks!

My cell phone rang out into the silence. The kids???

"Hi, Mom." Reed's voice was small.

"Hi, Honey Bunny. Are you guys okay?" I wanted to jump through the phone and yank them back to me.

"Yeah. I guess... Jimmy made a big breakfast for everyone." Okay, they weren't hungry at least.

"Good. He's a good cook." And takes care of his kids better than your father does. Despite the late-night cocaine "adventures."

"And Dad and me and Rach are going biking in Piedmont Park later."

"Cool. Any timing on that? You'll need to come by the house and grab your bikes..."

"Uh. Well, I dunno." Dan did not do schedules.

"Okay, Sweetie. I'm having lunch with Auntie Hayley." This was a totally new concept—Mom doing stuff on her own. "If you haven't gotten here by around 11:30, I'll put the bikes and helmets on the front porch when I leave?"

"Nice. Okay. So, wanna talk to Rachel?"

"Of course. Love you. So.... sorry...all this...." I trailed off.

"Rachel?" He yelled. "Mom's on the phone." Incoherent muttering in the background.

"Um. She's busy playing with Eva." Jimmy's daughter.

"Oh. Okay, tell her I send her a kiss. And you, too. Should we eat fried green tomatoes at the Biscuit when you get home tomorrow night?"

"Yeah." He paused. "I miss you, Mom."

"I miss you, too, so much. We will get through this, I promise. It totally sucks though." I had to be honest. There had been too much pretending, too many heads in the firmly buried in the sand.

"I know, Mom. I mean I kinda understand. But, well, not really." His voice faded. "Bye." And he hung up.

Take a knife and rip all my innards out. Without anesthesia.

"They'll survive, you'll see."

Trying unsuccessfully to feel nothing, I sat at my desk for a very long time.

Finally, I roused myself and looked at the clock. It was already 11, so I should get the bikes up on the porch for the kids. Dan had already taken his precious mountain bike with him to Jimmy's that first day.

I wrestled the bikes up from the basement and decided to put a little goodie bag in each basket. I found some fruit and cheesy crackers and juice boxes. No doubt Dan would take offense at this, but he always did, no matter what. The king of No Win.

I was combing my hair and putting on my shoes when I heard his car pull up out front.

I dashed to the porch.

"Mommy!" Rachel nearly bowled me over with her hug.

"Mom." Reed allowed me to squeeze him for a second.

Dan stayed in the car, thank goodness, staring fixedly forward.

"Oh, look, a picnic!" Rachel was excited. "Any candy?"

"You get plenty of sugar, silly."

"I suppose. Well, we gotta go." Rachel glanced at the car.

They wheeled the bikes over to the bike rack on the back and Reed lifted them into place.

"See you tomorrow! Have fun! Love you!" I called, as gaily as i could.

"Love you too." They chorused, not too grudgingly.

I smiled but the tears welled up in my eyes as soon as they were out of sight. Of course, Dan was driving too fast down the suburban street. I sent a little prayer to my friend Ganesh.

Then I roused myself to get into my car and drove sedately to Decatur, miraculously managing to find a parking spot on Church Street.

Hayley was already in the restaurant, perched on a tall chair in the front dining room near the bar. She was tall, her thick hair graying, wearing her customary jeans and a bulky sweater.

"Hi, Darling. How *are* you?" She had concern in her big blue eyes.

"It's rough. Really rough. First weekend without them. I don't know what to do with myself. I mean I was turning around and around the kitchen this morning. Pitiful."

"No, not pitiful, predictable. I mean you haven't had a minute to call your own in years and years, no wonder it feels strange. Good thing we have each other!" She was being perky, which was nice. We'd been friends since high school and knew each other inside and out. Our families were similar, liberal and activist, and our mothers had worked together at the Poverty Rights Office helping advocate for poor people in the Seventies.

"Let's talk about anything but the situation at home, shall we?" I pleaded.

"Better living through denial!" Kind of Hayley's overall philosophy of life.

"Better living through beer!" I joked, ordering my favorite Sweetwater 420 on tap.

"What are you going to get to eat?" Hayley had always had a love-hate relationship with food. Right now it was love, but at one time years back I was within an inch of frog marching her to the hospital because her anorexia was spiraling out of control. I was living with her at the time and saw her OCD behaviors up close and personal. One apple would last her three days. And she had seventeen — count 'em, seventeen — toothbrushes, too. One day I screwed up my courage to ask her why so many and she said she brushed her teeth three times a day, with different toothpastes and brushes. Then those six had to be completely dry, so she had another six for the next day. The other five were spares. The girl was a bundle of nerves, but one of the sweetest people on earth. It wasn't her fault that her parents made no bones about her being an "accident" making her appearance long after the first four kids, or that Ruby, the mean black nanny, had essentially raised her because her mother was too tired. Hayley had spent a lot of her childhood hiding from Ruby in the linen closet.

"I think the fish tacos with the cilantro lime salad dressing."

"I'll get my usual burrito."

"Sounds like a plan."

We chatted as we snarfed our lunches and I had another beer for good measure. Maybe I'd actually take a nap this afternoon, the ultimate luxury.

"Do you want to walk around with me to the shops? I think I should treat myself to something new to wear for teaching this spring."

"Sure. That'd be fun."

We wandered around and I flipped through dresses and jackets until I found the perfect thing – a teal and black loose blazer that would go with everything I owned. I owned a lot of teal and black. Hayley picked out a pair of earrings for herself.

"Hey, thanks for this. I needed a friend today." I squeezed her hand as I unlocked my car.

"Silver lining? More time for us to do stuff." She kissed me on the cheek.

"Yeah. Look on the bright side, huh." Not too much of a bright side, but it was something.

I did take a lovely long nap but when I woke up, I was momentarily disoriented. Why was the house so quiet? Where were the kids? Oh, yeah. I remembered it all with a sinking feeling, the whole surrealistic turn my life had taken. Drug dealing, porno watching, bones breaking, locks changing, children crying, nasty lawyers fighting, the whole nine yards. I would give anything for none of that to have happened, none of it to be happening still. My eye teeth, whatever they were. A few months off my life. All my jewelry.

What were those five stages of grieving again? Denial, anger, bargaining, depression, acceptance. My feelings were a great big stew of everything except acceptance. I wanted it all to go away, I still fantasized about Dan's premature death, I had just been bargaining with my life span and my jewelry, I felt hopeless, round and round and round.

But for now, I could make up next week's power points to distract myself from it all. Then maybe I'd watch tv. Try on my new jacket. Write in my journal.

Or, hey, it came to me – this was the first Saturday of the month, which means there was a fire circle down at the Land Trust. The neighborhood hippies gathered around a bonfire and let loose until all hours of the night. I had wanted to go there for a long time, but kids' bedtimes always took precedence. Silver lining? I had the properly improper clothes now, thanks to the Sis-Stars, and I wasn't too shy to dance anymore. If it sucked, I'd just walk the couple of blocks home and be none the worse for it.

My spirits rose in spite of myself. Get that work done and then have some fun. What a concept.

When I walked to the edge of the circle around the raging bonfire a few hours later, I literally could not believe my eyes. It was Dean, gorgeous as ever, across the bonfire from me, gulping a beer and idly swaying from side to side. Thirty years later, he was still sex on a stick. Maybe with a bit of a middle-aged belly, but close enough. Same blue eyes, dark swath of hair, same swag. Some of my ruder college girlfriends used to claim, "some guys just walk like they have a big dick." And Dean, believe me, was one of those.

I waited for a minute or so to see if he still recognized me, too. Thinking back all those years, we had dated for a New York minute when I was fifteen and he was seventeen. Experience wise, he was way, way out of my league. When I told him I wouldn't have sex with him, he dumped me. I mean, I was still a virgin. And on our first date a guy friend of his thought we might come in for a threesome. Okay, yes, it was the Seventies, but still.

His eyes idly trailed over into my direction. Wait for it.... Snap. It hit him. That slow, molten, Elvis-like smile crept over his face. I started toward him, he started toward me. I mean, really, cue the romantic music, someone.

"Becky."

"I go by Rebecca now."

"Rebecca." The way he said it made me weak in the knees. "Still beautiful."

"Still handsome..."

"Dance?"

"I thought you'd never ask." It was on.

"I've seen you around the neighborhood, you know." He was hypnotizing me with his eyes.

"You have?" How weird. We'd been there for years.

"I live right across from the Biscuit. We're neighbors...."

"No shit. I guess I've been in my mother cocoon. Now my divorce cocoon. More like, what-the-Hell-do-I-do-now quandary."

"I've seen your kids. They're both gorgeous, like their Mom. But who's your husband?"

"A steaming pile of shit."

"Okay..."

"This is my first night out alone in years and years."

"Been there. My sons are just leaving the nest to go to college. Twins... Their mother left me with them when they were three."

"Shit. Wow." The twins part had me floored.

"I was kind of a shit to you back then, wasn't I?" He looked beguilingly at me from under those crazy long lashes of his.

I thought about it for a moment as we flirted shamelessly with our bodies.

"Well, we were bad timing, I'd say. You were seventeen going on thirty, I was fifteen going on fifteen. Your, uh, shall we say, 'bisexual' friend was way too much for me, let's just leave it at that." I guess that made him bi, too, come to think of it. Okay, well, if you were as beautiful a Scorpio as he was, it was no wonder the whole world wanted to jump your bones.

"But, see, I really am sorry. I was a prick."

Hmmmmm. He'd shown me said body part briefly back when we were teenagers. It scared the shit out of me at the time, but now...

"Can I walk you home? It's starting to rain..." He offered softly.

"Perfect."

We fell in step as if thirty years were nothing.

And we kissed like thirty years were nothing, too.

"Call me?" He pleaded and rattled off his number, which was only a few digits off mine.

"Yes."

Chapter 11

Dean was like a breath of fresh air in my life. He blew through my fog and melted it away. We saw each other when the kids were with Him only. And I had gone so far as to check with Henry that me being with Dean wouldn't mess up the divorce – he assured me that Dan's crimes were real, and this was small potatoes. But I still kept my two lives apart, mostly so the kids could begin to get used to the new normal without anything else being thrown in their faces.

"You deserve a little fun."

The thought popped into my head -- I deserve some fun in my life. And some hot sex to boot. Dean was amazing in that department and I felt like we were teenagers again.

"So, fill me in on the last thirty years, Gorgeous." Dean and I were sitting in the twilight on the back deck as spring had decided to come around finally in early March. The light scents of the first flowers were wafting in the air, which was soft and breezy. I felt grand. No one had called me Gorgeous for years. It flashed into my mind the time Dan had refused to go to a fancy Buckhead dinner party at the last minute and then when I dressed up and asked him how I looked, he replied that I looked like shit. This was a whole new world.

"That's a tall order. Where to begin?"

"The beginning. Meaning after I so rudely dumped you, for which I sincerely apologize at this late date once again. I really do. I was a prick, and you were a baby, I should have been more sensitive."

"You ran with a wild crowd, at least by my standards. Are you still friends with that guy that wanted us both to, uh, 'play' that night?"

"Nope. He died of an overdose a few years later." Dean was matter of fact about it.

"Oh, that's horrible. What a blow." I was appalled.

"Play with fire, get burned. He was out of control and seemed bent on destroying himself. I loved the guy, but I couldn't save him..."

"And you? What's up with you and drugs these days?" I tried for casual. But I did not want to fall down the same rabbit hole as I had with Dan.

"Clean. For a while now. Some pot and some beer, but nothing major."

"Cool. So, hmmm, me at sixteen. I did a lot of international folk dancing and horseback riding and art, did well in school, got into the University of Michigan. Lived in Mexico between high school and college, finished undergrad in three years."

"Whiz kid. I did two years at State, but it wasn't my thing, so I went into carpentry and played music on the side. I'd sometimes play with Thermos G., my brother's band."

"Your whole family is so musical." I admired that since I could not read a note, much less hold one.

"What happened next?"

"Moved to Boston with my college boyfriend. Who had been the Teaching Assistant in one of my Anthro classes, so twelve years older than me. He got a job teaching at Tufts. I worked nine to five for a year and hated every minute of it, so I applied to grad school."

"Where?" This was the part when men usually got kinda silent.

"Yale."

"Damn, girl. Good for you. Your whole family is so brainy."

"Yeah. Lotsa faculty brats often follow in their daddy's footsteps. Beats regular work, hands down, though it is not easy, like people think. That saying 'those who can't do, teach' is really insulting. Try it sometime, you'll see."

"I believe you. My sibs, Brad and Mary, both teach and they complain a lot."

"You will recall that your big brother Brad was my high school social studies teacher ..." We exchanged looks. That had not ended well, as he was caught screwing one of his girl students and was summarily sacked. Even in the Seventies there were a *few* boundaries, after all.

"So, go on, Miss Smarty Pants..."

"Grad school was super hard, long, and scary, but I made it through and ended up back at 'the local institution' like my dad. Either I have very little imagination, or I liked my upbringing, because I work where he did, drive a Volvo like my parents did, live within a mile or so of where I grew up, and I even have a chestnut horse like I did for so long. But this one, Skippy, is a gelding and Monday was a mare."

"Nothing wrong with staying put. No one in my family has moved away from Atlanta, though most of us cannot afford, or stand, Buckhead anymore." Theirs was an 'old' Atlanta family, well off, stable. Five kids, all of whom had gone hippie on their parents' Republican asses in one way or another.

"So, I write books, curate, teach, mother, juggle like mad. Now, finally, I'm getting out of this wretched marriage. It is heartbreaking for the kids, but I figure that to live with parents who hate each other would be worse. Not to mention what might have happened if the authorities found out what their dad was up to." I had filled Dean in on most of the gory details already, but I didn't want this affair to be about my soon-to-be ex. He'd used up enough of my life and caused enough pain to last for years to come.

"The gift that keeps giving..."

Dean offered, "I think I told you that eighteen years ago my girlfriend at the time accidentally got pregnant, with twins, but by the time they turned three she told me she had had enough. Not a natural mother, like you. So, she bailed. Never looked back. It was all up to me."

"That totally sucks. How did you manage?" Dean was not automatically reliable and steady, at least when I had known him first. Party had been his middle name.

"Not well, especially at first. My sister Mary helped some, fortunately. She's a good egg. One of the boys got into trouble and I sent him to a strict school in Alabama for a couple of years, which my parents paid for. Now the twins are both graduating from Grady and in the fall are on to UGA. I am done. I mean, you are not really ever done with your kids, but they are just about outta the nest at least." He looked relieved.

"Mine have a few more years to go..." Which did not bode well for this affair to turn permanent, I had to admit. He did not reply. I was well aware that this was the definition of a rebound relationship, fueled by the romantic twist of dating in midlife someone you had dated as a teenager.

"Show him your poem. Go ahead."

"I wrote a poem about, uh, this whatever it is we are doing." I finished lamely. Not knowing exactly why I brought that up in the first place.

"Really? Do I want to read it?" He looked a little apprehensive.

"Up to you. It's pretty nice, I think, though I don't claim to be a poet really."

"Okay. I'm game."

"I can read it out loud to you if we go inside where I can see. I don't have it memorized yet."

I surprised myself for being so bold, but he was a musician and creative with his hands so he might appreciate a poem. More than some other people I knew. And the Sis-Stars had liked my solstice one, so what the hell.

"Here goes. It's called 'Contours'..." I cleared my throat.

"So, she drops off those near-flown kids at school,
as always predictable,
fortyish, like him,
complete with graying parts
and disconcerting crinkles appearing daily here and there.

All newly scabbed from major extractions
husbands, wives flying off everywhere,
replaced by frenzied mounds of expensive documents
hovering in drawers
that vouch for those relentless years in water-torture marriages
no longer, oh thank god, thank god, germane.
Many duties remain, yes,
but longer just sadly, strangely dutiful.

Patently not trundling off to work,
as one might think,
or tending to the this and that of who needs what,
instead she hurries, thrumming,
into his run-down garden
past unnoticed slouching tables
(first having checked the rearview mirror in hopes to find
the teenage face he kissed in lifetimes lost --
it hides behind the years donated to causes
grown unfathomably mean,
it requires drawing on,
but still she smiles to think that he too,
melted somewhat himself,
will mostly choose the beauty among the years accrued).

She truly bounds the stairs
while he, lightly smiling in response,
watches over his father's reading glasses
until he finally scoops her up
and up
and up he fills her even now,
far deeper than when they looked the part
and thought that parts of bodies mattered
but the contours of the soul did not."

I waited, feeling self-conscious.

"I like it. The 'my father's reading glasses' part especially, it brings the teenagers and middle age together in a cool way. But now I'll have to fix up my yard furniture..."

"No, you don't. It went unnoticed."

"Yeah, in the poem, but the *poet* noticed them herself."

"Point taken. But it's only a poem, not taking your inventory or anything."

"Understood. You know, you're good at so many things, R, it's kind of daunting."

"You have the power of two, girl."

I had the desire to tell him about Mags, but enough had already been packed into this evening for us to digest. My twin story might be too much for him, in fact.

"Dean, I've had a great time with you, but I'm getting tired and I have to teach tomorrow. Can we call it a night?"

He kissed me thoroughly in answer, winked, and stepped out the front door.

"Kids this weekend?"

"Yep. My next free night is Tuesday."

"See ya then, Gorgeous." My heart felt lighter than in years and years. No matter what this turned into, it was good for me in the present. What did people say? "He might not be Mr. Right, but he's Mr. Right Now."

Mr. Right Now knew I was watching him lope down the street and waved his hand without looking back, the confident bastard.

Chapter 12

Spring break was coming up soon for me, always a welcome change from the relentless teaching grind. And this one was going to be really different – off to Ecuador, for the first time. I had heard it was a beautiful place, like Peru but lusher, with equally dramatic peaks, the western edge of the Amazon rainforest, and the famous indigenous crafts market of Otavalo. Plus, we were scheduled to meet with two different shamans, one highland and one lowland, and that was the biggest draw for me. And I liked Mason, though I did not know him that well, and his wife Sally, who were old hat at this fieldtrip: a well-worn path for them and I could just go along for the ride. Since the last Costa Rica jaunt, I was over being responsible for a hoard of terminally irresponsible American undergraduates let loose to wreck havoc on an unsuspecting Latin America. No more dealing with reckless iguana chasing for me, thank you very much. The students' antics would be Mason's problems, not mine.

My lectures for his class had gone over well, I thought, and I had tried to describe to the students the challenging idea of our linear thinking versus the indigenous "spherical" worldview. Not only did repeated phenomena take precedence, but there were no coincidences, everything was alive, sentient and meaningful. Whatever happened was interpretable in spiritual terms rather than via chemistry or "common sense" (actually the most culturally determined way of thinking – one person's "common sense" was another person's "irrationality" and vice versa). And time does not necessarily go in one direction, either. There are many ways of knowing things. Providing an example from my own life, I had described the time when three-year-old Reed knew how that shaman's dream ended, not so they would "believe" me necessarily, but so they would have to try to accept and respect my experience as part of another way of being than the one they had almost certainly been taught. On the other hand, it was a sure bet that many of them had gone through something that Western science could not "explain," too. According to respected researchers like Michael Winkelman, at least forty percent of people report having seen a ghost, or known the future, or something along that vein.

Mason had added his insight that when science incorporated the "Placebo Effect" it was nailing its coffin shut. Just because they had a name for "mind over matter," it did not make it explainable along the line of equations and such. Then they tried attributing cures to increased levels of immunity from believing in something or someone, but how was that explainable in the world of measuring and treating symptoms and extracting body parts and all the things that Western medicine was good at? Sure, I'd want my burst appendix removed, but what if I had a premonition that it was going to happen a week before? Would the doctor check me out?

The key, both for me and for Mason, a Presbyterian-raised social scientist well-versed in statistics and theories, was the potential complementarity of the two systems. That was what he sought to teach in this class about religion and science in the so-called "Third World." Treatments by the shamans we were going to consult were reimburse-able by insurance in Ecuador, that's how interlocked the two ways of thinking were. I had read an article about an

Ecuadorian doctor who consulted a shaman when he got sick and a shaman who routinely sent his clients to doctors for antibiotics. This class, and especially this fieldtrip, were liable to blow the students' minds, if they were lucky and openminded to begin with. I was quite prepared to have mine blown, too. Looking forward to it.

This was my weekend with the kids, thankfully, and He had moved out his boatloads of crap from the basement and the infected closets last week. After letting him in the door, I had left him to it, retreating to my office on campus, after carefully taking all my heirloom jewelry, computer stuff, and the kids' childhood memorabilia with me in the car. I would not have put it past him to snitch something and then lie about it to my face. There had been so very many lies. I could imagine him resentfully unhooking the world's most overpriced stereo system, no doubt stomping around in a fit of pique the whole time. Somehow, he managed to be angry at me all the time still, despite what he had been doing and not doing for months and months.

My lawyer was gleeful when he told me about calling Dan and mentioning the baggie of white powder that he was keeping in his evidence drawer. He said he had Dan nearly in tears, asking what terms I wanted as if I could have them for the asking. Henry had gotten Dan to agree to the two most important issues: me keeping the house and my retirement (it was amazing that I had been the major breadwinner for most of our relationship, but he could have snatched half of my hard-earned pension money). Money was a deal breaker for me, since I was under no illusions that he would keep up with his share of the kids' financial needs. Henry said Dan had already talked about putting in the clause that his money would be cut off as soon as they graduated from high school. Even though Dan's father had paid for his entire education, including graduate school, and bought him a car. Such a cliché... the man ejaculates and that seems to be the extent of his responsibilities, according to him, anyway.

But Henry said I should give in on that clause so as to preserve the bigger issues like the house and pension. Plus, he reported that Dan insisted on seeing the kids every Wednesday and every other weekend, too. Those arrangements both sucked, we would be tossing them back and forth like ping pong balls for years, but I agreed with Henry that the big-ticket items were more important there too. I had to be able to support myself and the kids. I could always sell the house and downsize and with a decent pension I didn't have to work until I was eighty. But I told Henry to refuse joint custody, taking the option that my opinion where they were concerned took precedence, on the grounds that he had been willing to let Reed have a shriveled arm for life, the police put our children in foster care, and nameless girls be sexually exploited so he could wank off.

Henry mentioned another clause Dan was gunning for -- whether either of us could move out of Atlanta until both kids were eighteen. That one was a little dicey. What if I got the job offer of my life, like the curator of the Americas at the Denver Art Museum or something like that? What if, by some extraordinary streak of luck, Dan decided to move away and leave us the HELL ALONE? Henry said he'd talk to the other lawyer, who frankly sounded like she'd been stuck with a hopeless case and just wanted it over with quickly. Join the old club, lady.

I simply wanted out, too, and fast. Even if Dean were a flash in the pan, like the last time we tried to date three decades ago, I needed closure on my marriage. Why prolong the torture for all of us? There would be no teary reunions here, people. He could go fuck himself and anyone else stupid enough to agree. I'd already overheard the kids talking about some lady he was bringing around, some insurance agent's assistant they didn't particularly like. Go for it, asshole. Knock yourself out.

So, it was Sunday morning and I had packed most of what I'd need for Ecuador the day before. I had world-class rain boots, 100% DEET bug spray, all sorts of hand sanitizer, the whole travel-in-Latin-America nine yards. My arms were still sore from the shots that were required when you went into the rainforest. It was always a little disconcerting when the nurse holding the yellow fever needle smiled and warned that the shot could, possibly, kill me. Great. Travel in South America was not for the faint of heart.

My bulky blue duffle was full and my passport was up to date and ensconced in the leather holder I always wore around my neck. Happily, my mother and my ex-mother-in-law (almost) would split childcare duties, five days each. Lila was going to fly down from New York and everything. Even she realized that her third son, her baby, was still a baby. I had no beef with her, an attractively ageing hippie hairdresser. When we had gotten engaged, she and I had gone out to lunch and she had admitted to me that Dan was "difficult," but she said he was still worth it. She got the first part right and I should have realized that any mother that admits her child is a problem should be heeded. My bad. At least I had gotten two wonderful, beautiful kids out of the deal.

Rachel wandered into my bedroom as I was gradually waking up and looking at the newly minted green leaves on the tall trees in the backyard. This neighborhood still had a lot of the big trees Atlanta was known for, gorgeous in the spring and summer but deadly during winter ice storms. The ice-laden trees tended to fall down, go boom.

"Hey, Mommy." She was clutching her purple teddy bear Princess tightly to her skinny little chest. "Are you awake?"

"Of course, Honey Bunches. Come cuddle?"

She jumped into bed with her usual abandon and snuggled under the covers with me.

"What are we going to do today, Mommy?" she asked.

"Well, I thought maybe you and I would go to Home Depot and help pick out a new color of paint for this room..." I needed a change and could not afford a new bed, but a couple of gallons of paint would go a long way toward wiping away the bedroom's memories, I sincerely hoped.

"Ooooh. That would be fun." Rachel was practically an artistic prodigy at this point, having learned to paint a close-up at age five, convincing shadows at seven, and slightly disturbing portraits of "the face of the sea" just recently. Her art teachers had pulled me aside on more than one occasion to praise her talent, skills, insight, color sense, imagination.

"What about a nice light green?" I suggested, drawing her warm squirming body closer to mine. Babies were stuck to you like glue, but as they grew up the physical closeness waned dramatically. I'd take what I could get from an eight-year-old.

Rachel thought for a while. Her answer surprised and warmed me to the heart.

"You know, Mommy...I've been thinking... Maybe... it's better this way." Her voice was muffled a bit under the covers, but I heard her loud and clear. "You... get to do what you want... and so does Daddy." The last was barely a whisper. From the mouths of babes.

I was floored. It took me a minute to answer – it felt like an important answer, in both our lives.

"I think you are right, Baby Girl. Absolutely right." Her insight was profound. Would she and I gone off easily to get a perfect paint color if Dan had been his grumpy, foot-dragging, hateful self? With him, everything had become an ordeal, drama to the max. It was a paint color, for goodness sake. But it was way much more. It was freedom.

"How about we eat at Waffle House on the way!?!"

"Oh, yeah. You rock!" She jumped out of bed to get dressed, skipping to her room.

I left Reed a note, knowing he'd likely sleep until we got back, teen style.

"I'm looking forward to seeing Nana, but I don't really want you to leave." She mentioned as we waited at the Home Depot desk for the perfect shade of green paint, aptly named Serenity, to be mixed.

"I know, Darling. But this is part of my work, going places in South America and teaching at home and down there. I want to learn more things for my next book and when I write it, I will make a little more money for us to live on."

"Yeah. And I'll get another present!" She fingered her gold necklace from Costa Rica fondly.

"You bet! There is the second-biggest market for arts and crafts in Latin America, called Otavalo. I will buy a lot of presents there, I'm sure."

"Oooh. Take lots of pictures?"

"Of course."

The paint was done.

"Home? See how it looks on the walls?" I asked.

"Home." she agreed solemnly. "Princess is missing me." Her purple teddy was very sensitive.

The green was fabulous. Soothing, different, new. I'd get new bedding to go with it and save up for a new mattress to get rid of Mr. Toxic's energy completely. Dean's enthusiastic presence had masked a lot of it, but he only stayed over every other Saturday night. We were still having fun, but I wasn't sure he was It. If I admitted it to myself, my life had been so turned upside down that I should not avoid leaping headlong into something, or someone, else. What I really needed was to catch up to myself, the new and improved me, thanks to the Sis-Stars mostly. They had held a shitload of space for me these last few months, that's for sure.

But Dean agreeably took me to the airport in his ageing car, impressing and embarrassing the students by planting on me a breath-taking kiss goodbye, and then we were off.

I sat with Mason and Sally at the gate, going over the itinerary and when they'd want me to talk. It was hard to know, though, because the shamans were deeply spherical spiritualists and Western timing and planning flew out the window at the drop of a hat. Sally told me that they never knew exactly which day Don Alberto, the lowland shaman, would appear in the frontier town of Tena. He always did, though. They said that he was such a revered healer and visionary that the Ecuadorian government had given him 10,000 acres of the Amazon rainforest for his work in perpetuity.

Last month it had been bizarre to try to formulate the questions I was going to ask the two shamans, to comply with Federal regulations that monitored researchers' behavior towards their subjects. Back in the bad old days, as part of an experiment some psychologists would do stuff like tell people they were dying and other heinous things. As a result, now all of us who worked with live "subjects" had to jump through multiple hoops, even art historians who were not exactly abusing their interviewees. For my part, the whole thing was ridiculous. I was supposed to read this long statement to the shamans and get them to sign it – if I did that, I imagined that they would refuse to talk to me on the grounds that me and my whole world were as bat shit crazy as they had always been told. And then I was supposed to share my list of inquiries in the *order* I was going to ask them – another absurdity. So, if I started with the obvious, 'How did you become called to be a shaman?' then what, based on his unknown answer? Linear thinking crashing into its opposite, just like a replay of the Spanish invasions only with words. In the end I just scribbled some nonsense on the forms and then filed them away under "Pointless." I was not going to comply, I'd put an "X" as their signatures and call it a day.

That exercise made me think of a teaching point for the students: the importance of asking questions that the person can answer, according to his or her way of thinking. I was imagining that because everything was considered sentient in shamanism -- trees, rocks, flowers -- there could be some relevant questions on the spirits of what we were seeing in Nature and how the shaman interacted with them. Probing the plants' spiritual essences as experienced during trance made sense, asking the Latin names for those same plants did not. Some kids might have a hard time not judging belief in Plant Spirits as "primitive," but I had drummed into them the logic of shamanic visionary spirituality and banished such words as "primitive," "superstitious," "imaginary," and "the natives" from their vocabularies. I would be caught smack in the middle of the contrasting worldviews, as my Spanish was good enough to help the guide translate the shamans' spherical words and I could try to further interpret things to the linear-minded students in English, though the prospect was tiring. I was going to try to take notes, too. So much for spring "break." Same as "summers off" for academics, what a laugh. But, hey, I had an all-expenses paid trip to a beautiful place and access to some exciting insights, why should I complain? And ten days free of the nightmare of divorce, though I'd miss the kids and no doubt worry about them. Rachel especially missed me when I was gone, writing me plaintive letters and drawing pictures of her crying. Ouch.

Despite the unknowns, the trip was well orchestrated: first we had a day and a half in Quito, which was a bustling city with well-dressed businessmen and women rubbing elbows with indigenous people carrying towering cloth-wrapped burdens on their heads. The snow-covered peaks that sprang up in all directions loomed over the city majestically and the sky was that piercing shade of what I called "Andean blue." Sky blue on crack. The colonial churches were gilded with the melted-down antiquities that the Spanish stole from the inhabitants – both impressive and painful to contemplate. The colorful stucco buildings lined cobblestoned plazas. Sadly, we did not have room in the schedule to visit the world-renowned museums, but this trip was not about art per se.

After that, we travelled north to the Otavalo market, which was indeed overwhelming -- endless stalls bursting with bright weavings, dangly earrings, odd items made from coconut leaves. I nabbed a sort of woven coconut briefcase for myself and a purse made from a halved coconut for Rachel. Somehow, they had even attached a zipper between the two parts! Such wonderful mishmash of cultures. I ladened myself down with five-dollar pair of tie-dyed pants, a woven jacket for my mother, and a miniature guitar for Reed, complete with handwoven case. The students were amazed at how much I accumulated in two hours, but I told them I did my Christmas and birthday shopping when I came to South America. Plus, I always packed an empty nylon garment bag for my spoils.

Then we were ready to go little further north to consult Shaman One, the highland one, which was really three: grandfather, son, and grandson. I couldn't wait.

Chapter 13

Our bus bumped over the cobblestones in a tiny hilltop town just north of Otavalo and came to a jolting stop outside a modest stucco compound, replete with mangy chickens pecking the dirt, skinny dogs snuffling in the garbage, and run-down walls topped with a crazy quilt of aluminum roofing pieces. The lively conversation that had been going among the students ground to an abrupt halt, as everyone realized we were about to climb out of our American bubble into the unknown.

A handsome, slight teenage boy popped out of a doorway excitedly. He was decked out in a traditional highland woven poncho, a lowland circlet of feathers around his head, and numerous jangling necklaces, atop half-outgrown, navy-blue polyester pants. And those ubiquitous sandals made from old car tires.

"Hola. Me llamo Teo, pero Mateo is mi nombre en realidad." "Hello, I am called Theo though my real name is Matthew." "Eso es mi padre, Nicolas," he introduced his dad as Nicolas. They stood to each side of the doorway and grandly beckoned us into one of the crumbling buildings as if we were visiting royalty and this was their palace.

The students exchanged curious to mildly apprehensive glances as we filed into a dark room with built-in benches ranged around three walls. Another giant step outside of Kansas. On the end wall stood a large table, covered with candles, rocks, statues, flowers, cigarettes, and perfume bottles, among other things. A true shaman's mesa, just like I had taught them about. On the wall behind it hung a large painting of a Plains Indians man in full war bonnet regalia astride a paint horse with a circle drawn around its eye. Next to it was a shrine to Jesus, with the requisite dripping blood so beloved in Latin American Catholicism. Not only I was truly excited for my first real shamanic reading, but their power objects perfectly illustrated the concept of syncretism – the blending of cultures and religions – so prevalent in the indigenous Americas.

I could see the students looking around uncertainly as they took their seats.

Another, much older shaman, wearing the same multi-cultural get-up, had joined us and taken up his apparently rightful central position behind the mesa.

"Eso es mi abuelito, el también se llama Mateo." "This is my grandfather, also named Matthew," provided Teo. "Don Mateo."

Jessica whispered to me, "Why is *Jesus* here?" Primo teaching moment.

"Shall I ask?"

I asked in English for the benefit of the kids, "The students were wondering why you have a shrine to Jesus on the wall?" "Los estudiantes quisieron saber porque está Jesus aquí?"

The three shamans looked somewhat confused by the question, but Don Nicolas rallied first. He patiently explained, as I translated, that Jesus had been introduced many years ago as a powerful spirit, he had defeated many other spirits of the Inka, so it would be crazy to ignore him. He came back from the dead, like so many shamans did, and conducted miraculous healings! Jesus lived in the desert without food or drink, and he changed water into wine. Of course, he was invoked. Don Nicolas added something in his native language, probably Quichua for "duh."

I continued in English, for the benefit of the students, "The blending of religions, especially under political duress, was a response to trying to keep your culture alive when foreigners came and told you that everything you believed and did was wrong, even punishable by death. So, time to hide the power of the waterfall behind Jesus, tell people that it was God who told you to imbibe hallucinogenic brews. It was a familiar dance of Colonialism, submission and subversion, and shamanism was a particularly adaptable system since it dealt in experiences, not books, and victory over disease and discontent, in whatever crazy form the information came. The magic inherent in Catholicism was a great foil for that of shamanism." I mean Santa Teresa and her visionary orgasm by Bernini? Come on. The girl was about to need a cigarette. But I left that part out.

The shamans had no idea what I was saying, but they stood waiting patiently, acknowledging I was an esteemed "profesora," though not as esteemed as a shaman.

When I got quiet, as one, the kids turned their attention to the mesa. Don Nicolas had set a row of white candles set across the front edge and he gestured for a brave person to come up first to be diagnosed. When none of the students reacted, I eagerly made my way to the chair. I loved going first and I did not want Don Nicolas to think we were unappreciative of what he was doing.

He had me blow on the first unlit candle and then he lit it with a Bic lighter and stared at me fixedly through the flame for a long minute. I felt a bit like a bug on a slide.

Finally, he pronounced gravely, "Usted lleva la tristeza de todas las mujeres." "You are carrying the sadness of all women." Some of the students who understood Spanish gasped. My reading was a pretty private thing, so I did not elect to translate for the rest of the group.

Shit. That could not be good. All women? Really? Why? Why me?

He invited me to return to my perch on the bench. Don Nicolas was on to the next person, Jessica. She burst into tears after hearing her prognosis. The others shifted uncomfortably, and Jason hopped up and ran out of the room. No one said this was going to be a walk in the park, but maybe I should have warned them more carefully. No, let them get the real shamanic experience, which is not necessarily pleasant. Welcome to a different world.

One by one, they heard their readings, to which some had no reaction, others strong ones. As I tried not to hear their personal business, I sat pondering my reading about "the sadness of all women." All of a sudden, a lovely young woman in traditional dress walked in the room from the outside and came directly over and sat down next to me. She leaned over and whispered in my ear, "Me llamo Margarita, como tu hermana." "My name is Margaret, like your sister." It was my turn to burst into tears. She hugged me until I calmed down, then she smiled dreamily, stood up, and wafted out of the room as quietly as she had entered it. As I tried to recover, I wondered if I had dreamt that interaction somehow, though I knew for certain that I was wide awake.

"Actually, you're finally waking up."

What the hell. Mags and the sadness of all women swirled around my head for a while.

But before I had too much time to think, we were asked to get ready for the cleansing and uplifting parts of the ceremony. Don Nicolas came over to me and explained in a low voice that for healing purposes it would be ideal if everyone could take off all their clothes now. This was a new wrinkle. My first thought was if we did and the kids told their parents there'd almost certainly be hell to pay. My second was that I would not particularly like to bare myself to the students or to Mason and I imagined the others would feel similarly. My third was that it would be fucking chilly in the buff up here at ten thousand feet plus. I finally replied that American students were not accustomed to taking off their clothes in public, but maybe we could all just wear our underwear? He reluctantly agreed, though his look said he thought we were crazy. Come to the doctor and not want to strip? Americans, what babies.

Everyone looked shocked when I told them, Mason and Sally included. The students stared fixedly at each other, at the ground, anywhere except at their profs. But to their credit, they obediently began to peel off their nice warm sweatshirts and pants. I took myself to the darkest corner and followed suit. Thank God I had worn a decent bra.

The shamans maneuvered us into rows and started patting us down with their scratchy dried leaf bundles. Then they lit cigarettes from the mesa and blew the smoke on the tops of our heads. Then they took mouthfuls of cheap perfume and literally spit them on us. It was cold, sticky, and bizarre, but fortunately no one laughed. We were all in too much shock, I guess. Then the most amazing thing of all began: the two older shamans lit another set of the white candles and gulped mouthfuls of grain alcohol and blew across the flame. They created hot, orange-yellow fireballs that flew toward each person's face, stopping just before singeing it. It was wild and, frankly, took quite a bit of pluck to stand there without flinching. I was proud of the kids when they seemed to take it in stride. Almost.

Back behind the back row, where I was attempting to make myself invisible, Teo was practicing his fire-balling. His technique was not yet as advanced as his elders -- he blew the candle out each time he made a fireball -- so his mother, Rosa, handed him a new lit candle for each person. But he made them nonetheless and no one got burned, thankfully. Another thing to hopefully not explain to the parents? Teo, though diminutive, seemed to be around Reed's age, and I felt all maternal toward the budding teenage apprentice shaman. I thought of Reed incessantly playing his video games to defeat the Devil, with all their violence and adrenaline rush, versus Teo learning to blow fire at people's faces to cleanse them of malevolent energy. Playing with fire in two very separate, yet weirdly allied, worlds.

When nothing else strange ensued, shivering and uncomfortable, we struggled back into our clothes. We were each given one of those brightly colored hand-knit hats with the ear flaps to wear for a full day. They would protect our fontanels which had been cleaned with the leaves and the tobacco, but were vulnerable, like newborns, Don Nicolas explained.

Finally, safe to look at each other again, we saw ourselves bedraggled, relieved, and a bit silly in our hats and shiny perfumed faces. We smelled strongly and not necessarily in a good way.

We paid our money (not always true for a shamanic exchange, but we did not have proper items to barter with, like chickens or food) and gave our profuse thanks to the family. I asked after Margarita, and was told "Ella no está," "she isn't here." I began to wonder in what sense she wasn't here, once more seriously considering that I might have imagined her.

Jason was found standing outside the bus, looking pensively down at the incredible valley spread out below the town. Mason went over and they had an intense-looking talk as everyone got back into their seats.

On the drive at first the kids were silent, perhaps in disbelief of what we all had just experienced. I let them steep in it, feel the shock they might feel over their uncanny diagnoses or stripping down and having perfume spit on them, not to mention balls of fire that stopped just short of their over-privileged American noses.

After a bit Mason piped up, "Anyone want to comment? Reactions?"

Nervous laughter broke out all over the bus.

"It was frickin' amazing!" Rob yelled from the back. A ragged cheer rang out.

"The fire scared the crap out of me." A girl named Jenny offered.

"I want a nice hot shower." Tyler was frank. Others heartily agreed. "But how exactly I do that with my hat on has yet to be revealed." Giggles.

Jessica shared, "I have a question. How in the world did Don Nicolas know about my mother being sick? But he told me for sure she was getting better. I am so happy, so, so, happy, no matter how he knew."

"Shamans see across time and space," I challenged, "according to them. What do you think now?"

There was a respectful silence. These things take time.

"But why did we have to strip like that?" A shy girl named Ann asked. "I don't think I'll tell my parents that part. They're really religious, I mean Christian, and they'd be really upset. It was hard enough for me to convince them that I could take this course and not become an instrument of Satan."

Mason took the cue. "We were being as respectful as we could of *their* beliefs that our healing would be absorbed better without intervening layers of clothing. Of course, it's all your own decisions, but let me, uh, *encourage* you to follow Ann's lead and keep the details to ourselves? Let's just say the college might not allow another fieldtrip to come down here..." There were general murmurs of understanding, agreement. Whew. Way to cover our asses, Mason.

"So, more interpretation of the ritual? Applying what you've learned in class about shamanism?" I was here to teach -- as well as to have my head busted open and my soul ripped apart at the seams.

"Maybe blowing on the candle was for us to like, I dunno, put ourselves into it? Breathing on things seems to happen a lot in shamanism." Rob offered.

"Yes, good, you're right that breath is a form of life force. Practically speaking, of course we all have to breath constantly to be alive. But more relevant to the spherical worldview is that breath is something that comes from inside then goes outside, first hidden then becoming revealed. We also draw in breath and let it out again repeatedly, cyclically, round and round. Breathing joins the species and it is quite intimate to share breath." Some tittering reminded me these were hormone-soaked teenagers. "What other types of breathing did we experience?"

"The stinky perfume was kinda like breathing on us. Only wetter..." Jessica shivered at the memory. "But that was, according to them, to uplift us with sweetness."

"Don't a lot of shamans believe that spirits love anything that smells sweet? Like it was how to communicate to them without words? In class we talked about the ancient art in the museum that made sounds as another way of spiritual interaction. Interacting with spirits can't be like regular life, right?" Rob offered.

"Yes. Good. How about the smoke?" I prompted.

"Cleansing? Especially the fontanel where the spiritual energy, uh, goes in and out? But to us cigarettes are not for cleaning, they are the opposite, so it's weird." Jessica mused.

"And there weren't cigarettes in olden times, were there?" Ann wondered.

My turn. "Well, in a way there were. Maya art shows smoking gods and many South American indigenous cultures use tobacco as a mildly mind-altering substance. The so-called 'peace pipe' in North America was a ritual for all guests. It turned out, as we all know, that some of the 'guests' were actually enemies: the Europeans who stole their land and killed them and their livelihoods for hundreds of years. But in this case the important thing is that all Native Americans smoke pure tobacco, *Nicotiana rustica* in Latin, which has no additives and is much stronger than a regular cigarette. Also, in traditional settings it was not used addictively, only ceremonially. Like the coca plant was and still is sacred and the cocaine that is chemically derived from it is not. I have a whole lecture on it!" The students groaned, only half joking.

"Any other observations, guys?" Mason cut in.

After a pause, a small voice offered, "I...dunno why, but I feel so much better after that. I don't know why a bunch of leaves, some fire, and candles did anything, but it meant something to me." Ann admitted. Her shy voice held wonder. That was a lot for a Christian girl to concede.

More respectful silence.

"Thank you for sharing that. It meant something to me, too." I wasn't ready to go further into my personal life and its winding paths, but I wanted to support her for making herself vulnerable. We all had put things on the line, standing there in our skivvies and getting spit on and dodging fire balls.

I leaned over to ask Mason in a low voice about Jason, the one who had left partway through.

He whispered back, "He had a strong reaction and was pretty freaked out. He told me as he was looking at the valley and the mountains beyond, he had a vision of them all exploding and collapsing, like the Apocalypse. He was still shaking as we spoke. I'll check in with him in a bit. Maybe the next shaman, Don Alberto, can see if he needs some help to resolve that visionary insight or personal one, whatever it might be."

"We want them to give this experience a try, but surely don't want to mess with their mental health too much." I offered. We both went quiet, thinking about how once you dip your toes in shamanic waters, there can be no turning back. As my afternoon with the gringo shaman Ed had proved to me without the shadow of a doubt many years back.

"The blue pill or the red pill?" Mason asked ironically. Scenes from the Matrix flashed in my mind.

"How about the yellow one?" I joked.

"There is no yellow one." Sally leaned over and gravely joined the conversation. She was a naturally quiet person, but 'still waters' and all that. I was growing to like her a lot.

"Come to think of it, a shamanic interpretation of The Matrix would make a good term paper," mused Mason, ever the teacher.

"We could get them to write about that in their journaling, I suppose. But keeping them in the here and now is better. We have enough levels of reality mashed up together to contend with, if you ask me." They both gave me enigmatic looks, but nodded in unison.

Mason added, "Today made me remember my first brush with all this. A few years back Don Alberto had told me that he saw a woman in white bending down in front of me, shining a flashlight on the dark path ahead. I told him that my cousin Amy, who was a nurse and like a sister to me, had recently passed away in my arms and he said she was my guardian angel now. Still brings tears to my eyes." He and Sally both wiped their eyes. His admission made me think of sharing Mags with them, but I wanted to see what else would happen with Don Alberto before I went there with anyone. We were off to the jungle tomorrow, so I didn't have too long to wait.

"I'm going to check on Jason." Mason announced.

"Good idea." Sally and I chimed.

Chapter 14

Though it was sweltering as we descended from the highlands, the air conditioning having stopped working in the bus, everyone still dutifully wore their rainbow hats. I thought that was touching – even if they thought the whole thing was a farce, the students were being respectful anyway. I had taken a bath yesterday instead of a shower to honor the ritual protection instructions, so my hair remained uncomfortably sticky under my orange and green hat. But I did believe in what shamans do and say, especially after Margarita tuned into my sister. Or whatever that was...

After a number of hours bouncing around on the world's worst roads – and I'd been on some pretty bad roads in my time, but Ecuador beat 'em all, hands down – we finally got to the scrubby little town of Tena. The not-picturesque, smelly, dangerous frontier town that was the last stop before the Amazonian rainforest took over, stretching mile after mile all the way to the other edge of the continent. As we drove through Tena, the excitement level in the bus was growing audibly -- our next adventure was upon us.

After we left the outskirts of town, the clouds gathered darkly and it started to rain. The fieldtrip was always at this time in March because usually the rainy season was conveniently over by our Spring Break. Apparently, this year the jungle had not gotten the memo. The road was rapidly turning into a sea of mud, the bus slipping and sliding around rather disconcertingly, eliciting gasps from all of us.

Miguel Garcia, the driver, unexpectedly stopped the bus just before a small river that had, if his surprised expression was any indication, recently flooded the road ahead. The brown water was churning, racing by, angry.

Much shocked staring at the situation ensued. Much consternation. Apparently, we were still several miles from our intended destination, but the bus had just been rendered useless. This was not good. What could we do? Go back to Tena with our tails between our legs? What about meeting Don Alberto? Everyone piled out of the bus to get some air and was instantly soaked from the pelting rain.

Our guide, Juan Antonio, took off on foot back the way we had come.

Eventually he returned with some men, one of which was riding a skinny little white horse with a tiny bay foal following her mother closely.

It turned out that these men would lend us their mare for money, and she would swim the river with one person at a time perched precariously on her rump. Oh, okay, no problem. Jesus H. Christ.

I took a deep breath. Since I was more familiar with horses, I volunteered to be first and tried to show the students how to mount and not plop down heavily on the poor mare's kidneys. I clasped my arms around the wiry man riding her, and off we plunged into the raging water. The little foal jumped in after her mommy, the valiant little thing. My boots were instantly overcome by water. I was thoroughly soaked now, inside and out.

I hoped that the students and big old Mason could deal with this new challenge. And the horses, too. When I slid off on the other side of the torrent and the mare was catching her breath, the foal shaking off some of the water, I decided to give her a treat. I pulled a granola bar from my sopping pocket, broke off a little piece, and held it under her nose. She obligingly smelled it but looked confused and ultimately elected not to take a bite. Back into the water again, she came back with Jason, who looked shell-shocked but triumphant as he slipped off her rump beside me. I tried again to treat the mare and this time her eyes visibly lit up and she cautiously nibbled the granola bar piece from my palm. I bet she had never had a sweet before in her miserable life.

"High five!" Smack. He sent two thumbs up back to the others waiting their turns. Ann looked visibly frightened, but some of the others sent their thumbs up across the churning water.

When the horse delivered poor Ann, I gave her a pat on the arm and received a shaky smile in return. Gradually as the rest of our party gathered, streaming water, I fed the mare both of my bars. It was all the thanks she was liable to get, poor thing. The little foal was exhausted and lay down for a rest in the road. Her mother sniffed her tenderly and licked her ear. Horses.

Mason was the last to arrive, shaking his nearly bald head with a dramatic flourish.

"Is my hair perfect?" He asked me in a mincing voice.

"Not a hair out of place!" I joked, hoping to help lighten the mood of the group, which was getting glum after the adrenalin wore off from the strangest introduction to horseback riding ever.

We had to take turns pulling each other's boots off to empty them of water, and the suction made that virtually impossible. Hugging a tree for dear life worked the best. I noticed that Rob did not have any socks on. Oh, man, he was going to be in a world of pain walking in wet rubber boots that way. But there was nothing to be done about it — our stuff was officially now stranded across the river and God knows when we'd see our dry clothes again.

"Vámonos, pues!" "Okay, let's get going!" Juan Antonio enjoined us like an upbeat camp counsellor.

And so we walked. We walked. We emptied our boots. And then we walked some more. Rob began to limp. We got thoroughly chilled and the rain did not let up for one single minute.

"Let's sing something!" I suggested desperately. This was greeted by a chorus of loud groans. Cool college students definitely did *not* break into song. They had probably never even seen "Oklahoma."

"Let's not and say we did!" Jessica offered and she got cheers instead of jeers.

And so, we kept on walking. Even with socks, my heels were rubbing painfully, and I couldn't imagine how poor Rob was making it. Well, no one had much of a choice, when it came right down to it.

After what seemed like eons, a small, dirty cinder block building came into view around a bend. Then another and another. Civilization, or what had to answer as such.

We passed a leaning, rotting wooden sign that was crudely hand painted with the name "Bajo Ila." This village's apparent claim to fame was that it was located "Below Mt. Ila." Slowly a few curious, dark-haired people began poking their heads out of the doors of the tiny, wretched structures. Then one man came out to openly peruse the parade of wet gringos that had somehow appeared out of the rain.

Juan Antonio took over and we all tried to look inconspicuous – yeah, right – as he hopefully negotiated our rescue. After what seemed like forever, he came back to the group with a smile.

"We're in luck, my good people. These nice folks have an empty building that we can pitch our tents in for tonight! And they said they can catch tilapia in the river over there and make us some rice, too. We can have lunch, even if there is nothing for dinner, unfortunately. Of course, we are paying them for this." Relief washed over everyone's face simultaneously. "They even have a fire going over there to help warm us up! Please practice your Spanish, at least say 'muchas gracias.'"

I was the first to go over and thank the man profusely and he gravely nodded his head. Small, dark, thin, he had on jeans and a t-shirt that read "Wild Girls of the West... We kiss and tell. The Mangy Moose, Jackson Hole, Wyoming." There was a big lipstick kiss on the back. Okay.... So, *this* was where those clothes we donate to the Salvation Army end up, I concluded. (It reminded me of how once in Peru I had passed up buying an orange and white t-shirt that proclaimed to represent "Harvard State University." I had always regretted it, but at the time I was a starving grad student and ten bucks was too pricey for me. It would have gone over well at Yale, that's for sure, locked as the two schools were in a perennial fight to be Number One.)

Trooping over to the fire and pulling off the boots one more time, we steamed under the open-sided roof. The fire would not make a dent in drying off our socks, but we draped them around it anyway. Warm and wet beat cold and wet any day. I tried not to stare at Rob's poor hamburger feet and prayed to Ganesh for us to get our stuff from the bus. I asked Juan Antonio about the prospects for that and he said the men with the horse were going to do their best. It would be a long night if they didn't make it. I felt like the invading Whiteys with their big, plump bodies, carrying way too many things, and lacking in the necessary survival skills.

The little kids of the village were shyly ogling us with their beautiful big brown eyes. Sally was giving out some candy she apparently had stored in her pockets. They solemnly accepted the plastic wrapped peppermints and compared their wonders with each other. It didn't look like they knew what candy was exactly.

We were slightly warmer and a tad more comfortable, but absolutely starving by the time the women had cooked up the whole tilapias that the men had miraculously just caught for each of us. Mounds of plain white rice looked amazing, too, even with no butter or salt. I passed the hand sanitizer around under the table, so we might have a fighting chance of not getting sick. I had pretty much always gotten ill when travelling in South America, the runs came with the territory. But having made the students take off most of their clothes in front of each other and get bombarded with various substances, then ride a swimming horse over a fast-running river, and rub their feet raw walking untold miles in the rain, I could try to save them from the fate of Montezuma's Revenge. Or, down here, I guess it would be Huayna Capac's Revenge, I suppose. The last Inka ruler himself died of smallpox, or perhaps the measles, before the Spanish even made it all the way to South America. He would want his revenge too, for sure.

We tucked in, knowing there was to be no real dinner. I had given up my dinner to the mare. Oh well, she was hungry most of the time, I was not. Probably none of the kids had ever been hungry before this, either. We wouldn't exactly starve, though it might be uncomfortable.

The man we had thanked was the self-appointed mayor, Gustavo Martínez, and he proudly showed us around the town after we ate. Not a hell of a lot to see, maybe ten or twelve tiny houses made of cinder blocks and topped with tin. Plenty of mud. There was a schoolhouse, though. We went in and found...a whole lot of nothing. It was completely bare. No chairs, no desks, no books, no paper, no educational posters on the walls. I tried to hide my shock. Gustavo proudly remarked that the teacher, Luisa Alvarez, came every other week to teach the children. Wow. Damn. What would she do with no materials, I wondered. It was evidently still an oral culture, as in ancient times.

When I looked around that pitiful space, I realized that we owed all these nice people big time and a great idea flooded into my head. I announced to Gustavo that I would do my best to come back here and bring the children school supplies, even though I lived really, really, really far from here. He looked both pleased and politely skeptical – Whitey made shit tons of promises they didn't keep. Like the over four hundred treaties that were broken with the Native Americans in the United States. Indigenous people came by their suspicions honestly.

The tents and some of the bags did manage to get to us later that afternoon. At least tonight there would be tents out of the rain and borrowed dry clothes. And band-aids for feet. Dry clothes felt incredibly good, even though we were sitting on the bare concrete floor of our bunker and would be sleeping on it all too soon.

Jessica pulled a pack of Uno cards out of her bag like a magician.

"No singing? Still?" I joked.

"NO." We all laughed.

Very soon it was dark – like clockwork near the Equator the days were twelve hours of light, twelve of dark. 6:15 a.m. to 6:15 p.m. Even at that early hour, we were all tired enough to crawl into our tents and settle down under our light blankets. It was quiet soon enough, no flashlights or books to read. Sharing tents was definitely an awkward feeling. I had gotten Jessica in the tent lottery and we were studiously turned back-to-back. Another university no-no breached — "sleeping" with your students. Oh, well, the rules were down the proverbial tubes at this point. It was not my best night of sleep -- I was afraid that I'd roll over and touch Jessica inadvertently, plus my stomach rumbled insistently -- but I got through it somehow. As I lay awake in the pitch-black dark I thought of my kids, all warm and cozy in their beds, full tummies from their grandmother's delicious meals. Bedtime stories, television, cars, cell phones, streetlamps. They'd be surprised to know that their mother was at this moment huddled up with a student named Jessica and wearing her t-shirt, on the edge of the world's largest rainforest. "We plan, God laughs," as my soon-to-be-ex-mother-in-law Lila always said.

Yawning and stretching, the group eventually all came alive with the morning light. Now what? No one wanted to ask it out loud.

Then there was a sudden commotion outside and we all struggled out of the tents and into our still-wet boots. Nice feeling.

Mason, Sally, Juan Antonio, and Gustavo were in a loose huddle around another group of men.

"Don Alberto ha llegado!" "Don Alberto has arrived!" Juan Antonio announced jubilantly.

I immediately went over to greet him and to ask him how he had made it to us in all this rain. Oh, that's right, take my own advice and ask him a question he could answer. He was a goddamn shaman, a little rain or a flooded-out river or two wouldn't faze him in the least. I changed it to how happy I was to see he him, how honored. His black eyes sparkled in his handsome wide-cheeked face.

He said he had known that we were here in Bajo Ila, but he had had to ford several rivers to get down to us. Join the club. But while we were already muddy, he looked perfectly dry and clean in his khakis and used car tire sandals. So did the other younger men that he introduced as some of his many sons: Wilson, Manfred, and Chuck. Ecuadorians loved American names; we had met a Herman and a Winslow in a restaurant in Quito a few days back.

The sons dutifully helped us tear down the tents and efficiently strapped them onto their shoulders in bulky bundles. Two new horses had materialized out of nowhere and were loaded up with some bags. The mare I was told was mine to ride was a skinny chestnut and the boney grey stallion was for Mason, in honor of our being the esteemed professors. Mason looked ludicrous on the tiny horse, but he grinned and saluted like a general, getting his sought-after laugh. My saddle was a piece of carved wood, but I took off my outer shirt to pad it a little under my butt. We headed out and began the climb up Mt. Ila.

My little mare could clamber over small boulders, up absurd inclines, and through deep masses of mud. It was a rough ride, but I had to admire her. I wished I had another granola bar for her, too although my poor empty stomach protested. My blood sugar was definitely rock bottom at this point, but I had to ignore the light-headed feeling I had. Suck it up, Bwana.

The ride went on and on, hour after hour. The poor students were slipping and sliding in the mud, while the shaman and his sons continued to remain spotless. That was magic in itself, I mused. But also, the American kids were oblivious to the instructions to walk on the *edges* of the path. Live and learn, in the classroom of the Amazon.

At one point I was on the trail a bit ahead of Mason and his feisty little stallion. Suddenly my heart hit my boots when I heard a series of crashing, crackling sounds that could only mean that the two of them had fallen off the path and down the tree-covered slope. I turned my horse around and dashed back, only to find Mason on his feet, laughing, and the stallion struggling to his, shaking his head like a cartoon character seeing stars.

"Don't ever do that to me again!" I scolded, "I just lost months off my life."

"Well, I'm fine and so is this little guy, but maybe I'll walk beside him for a while." Mason said sheepishly.

"That would be good for all concerned." I replied. "I couldn't exactly carry you the rest of the way if you had a broken ankle or something." My heart rate was gradually slowing down.

"Good thing Sally wasn't here to witness that little maneuver, she'd kick your big old ass." Having seen each other in next-to-no clothes and made it through that river, we felt close enough for me to tease him a bit.

"Keep it a secret?" He pleaded. Sally was petite, skinny, but it was clear to see that she wore the pants in the family.

"Okay..." I pretended to agree reluctantly.

I was literally about to faint from hunger and fatigue when finally, finally we arrived at the top of Ila and saw a welcome sight: a newly minted wooden platform that had been built for our tents to keep us all slightly above all the Amazonian creepy crawlies. Nearby I noticed one of the carved boulders that had brought me this far away from home. But I was way too exhausted to go look at it.

Most of the rest of Don Alberto's family was there, his tiny wife Constantina, plus two of his various daughters, Rosa and Lucia. I was expecting them to have names like Gretchen and Eloise, if the boys' names were any indication, but the rules seemed to be different for naming girls. They had eleven kids altogether, but to look at Constantina's flat stomach, you'd never know it. She effortlessly toted a toddler on one hip while she dished out beans, rice, and plantains for the tired gringo hoard.

I gobbled my lunch with no care for manners. There was almost nothing said until we all cleaned our plates. I would have licked mine clean if I hadn't supposedly been an authority figure.

Now that we had conquered the Mountain of Mud, as the students had deemed Mt. Ila, and my blood sugar had been revived, I figured that I would feel good. Instead, I felt worse than on the ride. I was all churned up inside, half dizzy, shivery despite the moist jungle heat. In case I was getting badly sick, I took myself over to where my tent had been set up and climbed inside. The blanket felt good over me, despite the fact that it was extra hot and airless inside the tent. I wanted to hide under it and disappear. My head was spinning. I began to shake and cry.

I heard a rustling outside my tent, and managed to peek my head out. It was good old Jessica.

"Jess." I called out weakly. "Jess."

She heard and rushed over, looking scared when she saw my face.

"Are you all right?"

"No, I don't think I am. Could you get Juan Antonio over?"

"Sure."

His kind face appeared in my tent door slit a few moments later.

"What is wrong, Profesora?"

"I don't know." I wailed. "I feel horrible."

"Fever? Chills?"

"Not really. It's hard to explain, but I need help."

His face retreated from view as he promised, "I'll get Don Alberto."

I lay there, feeling like one of those ice walls that slide into the sea in slow motion in those Nature shows. Like I was truly falling apart at the seams.

"I'm a good mother!" incongruously popped out of my mouth when Juan Antonio returned.

He looked confused but rallied with "I'm…. sure you are… but right now Don Alberto needs to see you. He said he knows what's going on."

"I hope so." I whispered.

Juan Antonio helped me clamber out of the tent and I clung to his arm as we walked past the other tents and off the platform. The students had sensed drama and melted away, which was good because tears were uncontrollably running down my face and I was panting in a decidedly not-authority-figure manner.

Don Alberto took one look at me and pronounced "Mal aire." "Bad air," meaning a malevolent spirit invasion.

Juan Antonio unceremoniously plunked me down on the sawn-off stump that served as a chair near the kitchen tent and discretely disappeared.

The shaman slowly and deliberately did the usual shaman-y things: the leaf bundle tapping, the cigarette smoke on the fontanel, some guttural chanting in Quichua. As soon as he began his ministrations I felt twice as good as the minute before. My tears dried up and I took some deep, shuddery breaths. The change in my body and mind was profound, unmistakable, undeniable.

After a long pause, he explained, "This is just a tiny cure, only half. In the daytime you cannot defeat a 'mal aire' completely."

"I do feel a lot better. Thank you very much, Don Alberto."

"Of course, but still tonight you must drink The Medicine." Uh oh. I knew what medicine he was referring to: ayahuasca. A frighteningly powerful hallucinogen and not exactly on the university's list of things that professors on fieldtrips should be knocking back. It wasn't the slightest bit illegal down here, but we were supposed to be obeying U.S. laws. Plenty of anthropologists had tried all manner of "medicines," even writing openly about their experiences, but the same did not really apply to art historians.

I tried to tell him these things, but he only agreed, reluctantly, to give me a small dose and make sure it was too dark for anyone else to see. The darkness was easily achieved hundreds of miles from an electric light, though without a candle burning the students might get spooked. But they knew that Don Alberto was going to take ayahuasca in order to do their lowland-style readings, so they would probably not question the lack of light. Visionary states make your eyes dilate really widely, so shamanic ceremonies were typically done at night in as close to utter darkness as possible. The first shamans we had visited had been the exception to the rule with their no-medicine, daytime practice. It was good for the students to see the range of practitioners and approaches, on a continuum from more European influenced to less so. There was no "pure" shamanism; it was adaptable in the extreme, hence its continued existence. Yet the shamans of the Amazonian rainforest were about as "traditional" as they come.

I thought Don Alberto was finished with my mini cure, but then he imperiously called for Constantina to bring him a glass of water and an egg. She silently glided out of the kitchen tent, handed them over, and went back to cleaning up after lunch with her daughters, toddler still glued to her hip.

Don Alberto informed me that he needed to consult the good spirits as to exactly why I had taken in a bad one. He carefully broke the egg into the water and watched the white and yellow drips form, turning the glass from side to side. I was reminded of a doctor scrutinizing an x-ray, recognizing deep meaning in the inscrutable dark and light areas. After he had stared into the glass for a good long while, he nodded as if he were responding to someone. He eventually spoke out loud, with authority,

"Yes, it is the rock that opened you up, the sacred one over there. It is a very powerful spirit, but it is a little unpredictable, too. You are sensitive to rocks, they hear you, they recognize a kindred soul. Almost all stones are alive – unless too much, uh, contaminating energy has killed them -- and they want to help us in curing old ills." In spite of my Christian upbringing and all, I was honored that the rocks liked me. Well, some of them, I guessed.

He turned to look right into my eyes,

"Usted lleva la tristeza de todas las mujeres." "You are carrying the sadness of all women."

What? Again?

"Do you know the Tamarindo family? Near Otavalo?" I cried out. "Don Nicolas told me the exact same thing three days ago!" I exclaimed.

"I hear he is a very powerful shaman, but I do not know him personally. Or his father and his son, little Teo."

I'll be damned. A burning candle or a dripping egg and they came up with the same fucking diagnosis, word for word.

"But, Don Alberto, what does this mean? Why do I carry it? What is the sadness of all women anyway?"

"The spirit of the egg told me that you are ready to understand it all out now. That is why the rock gave you a 'mal aire' to show that you have, how do you say, old business to take care of. Your soul is heavy because you are here alone this time. Rest this afternoon by yourself and you will finally heal. Then you will eat only fresh bananas for dinner and later take The Medicine. Only then will you be whole, cured, happy."

I was suddenly very tired, and the tent seemed inviting, a little island of my own. I had no idea what was going to happen that afternoon, maybe I'd just take a nice nap, but I was willing to try to get to the bottom of this "sadness of all women" shit.

Mason, Sally, and most of the students were down by the stream, splashing and laughing. You'd think they'd be exhausted after that hike, which it turns out had taken six hours. You'd think they'd be tired of being wet. But kids are resilient and college ones seem to have boundless energy. Rob was playing Uno with Ann at the makeshift plank dining table. I assumed that Juan Antonio would let everyone know that I was feeling better, just resting.

I gratefully collapsed on top of the blanket and idly watched the shifting shadows of the rainforest canopy as they played on my blue nylon walls. However, oddly, I did not feel sleepy at all anymore. But I let my mind drift and it started to do what it did during Sis-Stars weekends.... See things.

In vivid colors, I saw a beautiful green valley and rolling hills, almost like the old Jolly Green Giant commercials from when I was a kid. I enjoyed how peaceful and lovely it was for a while, relishing the puffy white clouds in the blue-blue sky. Then I noticed a strange thing: a little tiny tornado of wiry energy, almost like a drawing of a spiral turning very quickly around and around, going clockwise. In whatever scale I was seeing, which was unclear, possibly irrelevant, I felt as if it was about as tall as my knees. I could also feel that it was deeply unhappy. Trapped, frustrated, and hopeless.

"Who are you?" I telepathically asked the tornado.

A moment later I heard, "Your sister."

"Oh. Oh. Mags!" I was stunned.

I looked up at the sky for a second and there had appeared a huge shape, an oval, also as if drawn on it. I instantly knew it was "The Hole in the Sky" that souls are meant to move through to the Other Side when they died.

OMG, my sister needed to move on! She had been stuck here, in some kind of limbo, all this time? But how could *I* help to get her through The Hole in the Sky and be where she was supposed to be?

As I was pondering this conundrum, I watched as Don Alberto casually walked into the valley, stage right, took my hand and, somehow, the tornado's as well. The three of us began walking up the sky, easily, as if there were a staircase but there patently wasn't one. At the top, we simultaneously let go of her and she popped through the hole in a wink. She changed from unhappy to ecstatic as she started spinning counterclockwise. Wondrously, Mags expanded and expanded until she was not really gone, but everywhere. Beyond.

Euphoria spread over me in waves. The joy was more than I could ever remember feeling in my entire life. It surpassed even the happiness when Reed survived his birth, when Rachel slid out of me, when I got my doctorate, tenure, accolades. It was the most fabulous revelation: Mags was on the Other Side. For my whole life, she had been caught Here, held by our twindom, or by me unconsciously holding her back from really leaving me alone. Like Monday stuck in her tree until I released her. I wasn't sure how I had done it, but the contentment and the absolute rightness of her soul going forward was immensely clear. Don Alberto and I proceeded to descend the sky, return to the valley floor, and Don Alberto silently exited the scene, stage left.

Now when I looked all around me, I saw that the valley was filled with many more tiny tornados, hundreds, thousands, an infinity of them. All unhappily spinning clockwise. Oh, my Goddess. How could I help all *these* souls through The Hole in the Sky, too? It was overwhelming.

I sat myself down on the brilliant green grass to figure out what was happening. My sister had died and gotten stuck here, so it made sense that all these other tornados must be other babies or fetuses that the same thing had tragically happened to. Losing a sister or a daughter, a son, whatever – *that* was the sadness of all women! A miscarriage, an abortion, a still birth, SIDS, twin resorption, they were tragically part of so very many women's lives from time immemorial. And I, well, my soul I guess, had taken on their, no, *our* burden. But now I was being shown what to do, how to help everyone proceed as they so vehemently needed to, to reach the Beyond and finally capture ultimate happiness, resolution. I must be able to help shed "the sadness of all women" because I seemingly had powers to cross the realms, with a shaman's help at least. This was news to me, but I wasn't shocked. My role, too, seemed so right, as if I had agency, as if I could do something for all the babies. It struck me as a wonderful privilege, and I felt profoundly grateful, both for myself and for all the other stuck souls.

So, in my vision, I began running around frantically trying to gather up all the tornados, but to no avail. They slipped through my fingers like water. But, once more, in came Don Alberto. He was carrying, bizarrely, my grandmother's best porcelain thimble, the one she used to make her quilts by hand, the one I had put on the group mesa for Samhain months back. I saw that indeed, it had the little pink rosebuds painted on it, exactly as the real thing on my mesa did. As Don Alberto walked around, he effortlessly scooped up the tornado souls and popped them into the thimble. They all fit. Okay....

Again taking my hand, we ascended the sky, and he released the tornados and they swarmed out of the thimble like a million bees. As we watched them change the direction of their spinning, I was overcome by elation, a thousand-fold version of what I felt when we freed Mags. Their new-found release from this heavy, earthly plane surged through my soul, uplifting me incredibly. I looked down at myself and I saw that angel wings had sprouted from between my shoulder blades. They were marvelous, soft, white, and absolutely strong. This time, Don Alberto simply vanished and so I spread my wings to fly and float down to the valley floor. It was a glorious sensation that I never wanted to end. I envied Mags and the other babies if they had these angel wings now, as I was sure they did. When I landed, sadly I felt the wings melt away. But I was so happy I felt as if I were still flying, as if my feet did not touch the ground at all.

Gradually I emerged from the vision and came to, sitting up in the tent, tears of joy washing down my cheeks.

I was so ecstatic that I had to share it with someone, and I wrenched open the tent flap just in time to see Mason walking nervously toward my tent. God knows what he thought he would find — was his colleague having a nervous breakdown? Sick as a dog?

I hopped up and held my arms out wide, clasping him in a fierce bear hug.

"Mason!"

"Yes?" He wasn't quite sure about the hug. Presbyterians were not big huggers.

"Guess what? Guess what? I'm not responsible for all the lost babies anymore!" I was exultant.

He patted me gingerly on the back, managing "Uh, that must be... uh, quite a relief for you." Poor thing, he was totally mystified but at that moment I simply couldn't explain. I staggered back to my tent and left him standing there, awkwardly, sweetly. It occurred to me that I should have married a man like him. But I was stuck in linear time, desperately ridding myself of Dan. Sigh.

To my surprise, as soon as I lay back down in my blue nylon oasis, the vision resumed right away. Second reel.

Back in the valley, I was riveted by seeing a little red airplane flying around the sky, just under the Hole. It was a small, plastic plane, like an oversized child's toy, but inside it, his knees bent up around his ears, was my darling Reed. He was so joyful, doing loop-de-loops and Figure Eights with happy abandon. It felt to me as if he were spreading every ounce of the happiness he felt, invisibly infusing the world with the delight of being alive. He laughed and waved at me, and I waved back, filled to the brim with my love for him and his love for the world at large. Then I looked around and noticed my sweet little Rachel, sitting very still in the Lotus Position on the top of one of the green, green hills. I knew, I just knew, that she was embodying pure Peace, that she was anchoring it through her body into Mother Nature. She felt like a very strong conduit, like she was ultimately grounded, for the good of all. My precious babies.

As both of their destinies were revealed to me, I felt so proud and moved to be their mother, to acknowledge their personal essences, to see that they were giving to the world and how they would prosper. The moving of stuck souls, on the one hand, and witnessing the paths of living ones, on the other, felt like it formed a balanced picture. A perfect sphere.

While all this was going on, Ann had won Uno, Jason had found a giant millipede, I knew everything that had been happening around me all afternoon. *I had not been asleep.* I had not had any Medicine yet, either. But I finally understood "the sadness of all women" and I had torn that heavy mantle off my shoulders and summarily tossed it away. Reed had lived, Rachel had lived, I had lived. We had things to do for this world, for the Beyond, for each other, for ourselves. I could be what I had only read about in passing in my studies of shamanism – a psychopomp, a soul-mover. Who knew? With a shaman's help, it seemed, but still.

I finally was done being in my tent and I emerged into the dappled sunshine, steamy air, and company of people (who actually were there). I stretched, drank some tepid water, and wandered over to the kitchen area.

Don Alberto glanced at me and commented,

"So, now you know."

"Yes. Thank you."

"We moved them all, didn't we?" He was intently watching me out of the corner of his eye.

"Yes. They all thank you." I spread my arms wide, to encompass so many rescued souls, including my own.

So, he *had* been "there" in my visions in some way, shape, or form. Things had gotten so bizarre so fast in the past few days that I accepted this without a problem. Now just get me through taking The Medicine and try to process all this madness, possibly for, I dunno, the rest of my life?

During my dinner of three small bananas, freshly picked from nearby wild banana trees, I found that I felt I existed in a completely other space from the rest of the group. The students chattered like monkeys about the upcoming ceremony, among all sorts of late-adolescent concerns, but I felt irrevocably distant from them, looking at the group as if from a great distance. I glanced over at Sally and Saw something that I felt I had to tell her.

I wasn't sure I should invade her head like this, but I felt compelled to tell her in a low voice, "Your mother loved you, in her own crazy way, you know."

Sally looked like she had swallowed a bag of nails.

"She never said so...." Her face became so sad.

"But she meant to. She was just very limited, uh, emotionally." I had a mental picture of an older woman sitting in an armchair, wringing her hands and staring blankly out a window.

"How do you know all this?" Sally murmured wonderingly.

"I have no idea. But I had just spent all afternoon traveling the cosmos and learning life-changing truths, so I guess my mind feels very open at the moment. I hope I didn't offend you or cross the line."

"No, no. Just surprised me, I guess. I should be used to this overturning of life when we come down here, shouldn't I?"

"Seems so. I'd have to say that, actually, my world has been righted. For the first time ever."

She looked at me curiously, and I could see a light dawning.

"Does it have to do with what you told Mason about all the lost babies?"

"Yeah. It's a long story."

She lowered her voice even further.

"I wasn't going to tell anyone, but, well. We couldn't have children, me and Mason. And we wanted them very badly. So many failed attempts..." Her voice cracked, heartbroken at the memory.

I reached over to take her hand in mine. "I am so, so sorry. That must be the worst. I know from loss, myself."

"I figured."

"We can talk more on the bus back, maybe?"

"I'd like that." We smiled wanly at each other and went back to consuming our meals.

Soon enough, like a curtain dropping darkness fell and the preparations for the ceremony ensued. The sons bustled about, producing a jar of disgusting-looking brown sludge, which Don Alberto downed with practiced alacrity. He did this several times a week, apparently. There was one candle lit at the end of the table and all the students and profs were gathered around, waiting expectantly to see what happened next.

Slowly, the shaman shifted into a different gear. After a few minutes, he waved one hand rather drunkenly at Wilson, who obediently blew out the candle. I felt a hand under the table handing me a cool tin cup. Here goes nothing, I thought to myself as I silently let the bitter, slimy, brew slide down my throat. Nasty stuff. I sincerely hoped I wouldn't heave in public.

Don Alberto was making the rounds with the students, as my mind was losing its moorings slightly. When he made his way to me, he mumbled something at me that I didn't understand, maybe it was in Quichua, maybe Spanish. Soon, at another gesture from his dad -- how he saw it was now unclear in the inky night -- Wilson came over and offered me his arm. I had a little trouble standing up, but he helped me gently but firmly, and the others were preoccupied with their readings and watching Don Alberto in his entranced state.

Wilson tucked me into my tent, wished me "buena suerte," "Good Luck," and retreated as silently as a cat. The monkeys howled, the insects chattered, the birds called to each other in many different voices, and it was as if each animal were talking directly to me. Loudly.

I lay back on my blanket and floated and floated and floated. Little pinpricks of lights seemed to go on and off all around me, like so many energetic fireflies. The dark was as warm and comforting as I had ever felt in my life; it sensually enveloped me. Then I had a strong feeling that just "over there somewhere" awaited a huge black jaguar, keeping watch but remaining elusive. He conveyed to me that he would visit me again when I was ready. I knew I had to honor him and that I would get a chance to, somehow, when I came back with the village's school supplies.

I barely slept and several times had to rush outside because The Medicine went right through me, but when it got light in the morning, I felt incredibly good. Euphoric. Clean and light and sparkly. My emotional body was in ecstatic purity, my soul was revived.

We had to hike back down and hope that the bus was back in Bajo Ila to get us this time. Everyone at breakfast was babbling excitedly.

"I feel great!" Jason exulted. "Wilson cured my stomach with a touch."

"I do too." Others chimed in.

"And why might you all feel so good today?" I queried. Did they *still* think this shamanism thing was a bunch of baloney?

"I think we all just got cured." Jessica said it with a touch of reverent surprise in her voice.

I left it at that. I had learned long ago that the best teaching was gently guiding, not telling.

Before we left the camp, I went over to thank Don Alberto once again. I handed him one hundred dollars, which he slipped into his shorts pocket. If I'd had chickens, I could have paid him in them, but I was fresh out of chickens at the moment.

"Doña Rebeca." He was standing very straight and his face was even more serious than usual. "The stones tell me you must return to see me and them, again, soon. They know you will honor your connection with them. They helped me heal you, and you heal yourself, and all those others. We can keep in touch, I have email. Or I can just ask the rocks." It was a pact, a spiritual exchange, to him. To me, I knew that I simply must bring the kids of Bajo Ila school supplies to fill their pitiful empty classroom. If I could possibly help it, I would not be just any old using, abusing Whitey. Those tilapias saved our lives, and I wasn't one to slight traditional people and ignore their hospitality like a Colonialist, like an invader, like someone who slavishly worshipped the Almighty Dollar over all else. I felt sure that the university would help me – changing the world was in its mission statement, after all. If they didn't, I'd make it back here anyway, come Hell or high water. Damn it.

All of us fairly bounded down the mountain, even running out of water halfway through, but no one even cared. We were cured!

The bus, blessedly, was waiting patiently in the pitiful, welcome little town. We exchanged effusive greetings and thanked the townspeople and beautiful children over and over again and finally we boarded the bus and were off once more. Even being in a vehicle felt odd, after all that had transpired up on Ila. My eyelids became very heavy after just a few minutes ride and I fell dead asleep as we jolted back to Tena.

"Good work, Bex. I am in Heaven. My wings fit perfectly, too."

Chapter 15

Water weekend. My favorite, being a Cancerian, a Moon Child. I relied on that Sun in Cancer because it was my only water amongst the wildfires constantly burning through me. It made my kids the most precious thing to me, made my dearest hope to have a lovely family, and made me mourn for how my family was ominously approaching what the kids called an "epic fail." This emotional Sis-Stars weekend would be good for me, since I would be forced to feel the feelings, much as I so, so did not want to.

In my closet I had plenty of blueish and greenish clothes – it was my best color, made my eyes look extra-blue – so dressing up for Water was no problem. Looking in the mirror, I laughed to see that I too had become one of those flowy women. As I admired myself shamelessly, however, my clothes seemed to take on a life of their own, though, moving around more than usual. It was that damn mirror thing all over again. Shimmering, but more noticeable than it used to be.

"Look. Look. Pay attention. I'm right behind you!"

Could there possibly be someone behind me? Maybe Rachel had crept up and was swishing my clothes to mess with me? Nope. She was in her room singing at the top of her lungs to Kelly Clarkson's "Breakaway."

Okay. I needed to pull it together, grab my potluck and mesa contributions, and get my flowy butt on the road to Wisteria's or I'd be late. The kids had a rare day off from their activities and, when asked if they wanted me to arrange stuff for them, they both wanted to stay home and watch tv, play video games, take it easy. I had cooked a nice chicken stew last night that they could eat whenever. They said they were getting used to these weekends and they were fine to stay by themselves. I hoped they were right, and they were getting old enough that I had to let them grow up. Letting go was super hard for a Cancer mother to do, granted, but it was all the more important to be a *good* mother and let them try their wings. I kept my cell phone turned on, despite the Sis-Star prohibition to do so.

"Water. We start in our mother's womb, floating in the amniotic sea, so we are creatures of water in our earliest, pre-verbal memory. If you could capture that in words or in a drawing, what would it be like?" The perfect prompt.

Me and Mags, nested together, happily floating, instantly sprung to my mind.

Wisteria gestured to the pile of paper and colored pencils in front of her and we all dove for our share.

I drew two big-headed blobs spooned perfectly, yin and yin. Mags was the Big Spoon, I was the Little Spoon. Her nub of an arm was around me and I felt so safe, so connected. Perfect. It made me tear up to think of what happened next, how she was ripped away from me and how I became alone, so alone. Bhindi was watching me from across the circle, knowing what was going on for me. I began to weep in earnest and others murmured their sympathy but stayed put as instructed. Respecting me by letting me have my emotions was even more important on Water weekend. I knew crying was a release and necessary – I hadn't really mourned the loss of my twin yet. It was such a huge and unexpected revelation, but then I had rushed off to Costa Rica (and, come to think of it, no wonder David's Big Spoon declaration had touched me so deeply), and then went right back to work. These Sis-Stars weekends were my best, almost my only, time to process my life -- just surviving it day to day was usually enough challenge.

All of a sudden, I felt like I urgently needed to write about it, too, so I grabbed my journal and went off to a corner of the room for some privacy. Random phrases flew into my head... Slap me a nub... Laughter... the reassuring pounding of our mother's heartbeat... I basked in those feelings for quite a while. I didn't want them to end.

But they did. Her arm loosened, we lost contact between my shoulder blades, she struggled wildly. A horrible sucking sound and she was gone. Lost. Missing. I thrashed around looking for her, feeling for her familiar warmth. From somewhere outside, our mother placed her hand on her belly and exclaimed,

"Abe, I feel the baby moving for the first time!"

There were muffled but excited murmurs on the outside, yet I was frantic, kicking my tiny feet and waving my arms in panic. Eventually I exhausted myself and lapsed into a troubled sleep. When I woke up for a moment I was disoriented, but when I reached for my sister she still wasn't there. I felt myself crying soundlessly.

Then I was actually crying, not so soundlessly either, making my journal damp and my nose run. Someone sympathetically pressed a tissue into my hand.

I remembered that we were allowed to ask others for comfort, just not barge in with it. I got up and went over to where Bhindi was drawing and waited quietly for her attention. Soon she looked up and I held out my hands to her, unable to speak. She got up and we went to my corner hand in hand. I sat down and she instinctively sat behind me, wrapping me in her pillowy body and strong arms. It was Heaven and Hell at the same time, comfort and sadness in equal measure. We sat for a long time like that, gently rocking.

After lunch Wisteria asked if anyone wanted to speak into their womb experience. Everyone swiveled their eyes in my direction, and I nodded. No one else had cried all morning like I had and, though I was under no pressure to reveal the reason, I wanted to share it with people who would understand or at least believe me. I knew there was no "proof" of my sister's existence, in a medical sense, and that most people would assume I was making it up and being dramatic. Even delusional. But these women would get it

I explained about my visit to Dr. Gregg, how my body knew that I had had a twin sister, the timing of her demise, how this morning I had tapped into the details and the devastating feeling of losing Mags. Quite a few of the women were wiping their eyes by the time I finished.

I turned to Bhindi and officially thanked her for holding me, just like I had been held by Mags before she left. The parallel was not lost on anyone, especially Bhindi. I also told the group how my family had shamed me for crying as a kid, so letting go like I did was important in healing that conditioning. I declared myself forever done with being "Little Becky Waterworks," not because I wouldn't cry but because I *would*, and I'd claim it as a good thing to do, not a terminal weakness and an embarrassment.

"Such is the power of understanding how Water works – no pun intended -- in our lives, ladies." Wisteria proclaimed. "Moving water literally, as in crying, washes away the pain, the stuck emotions, the soul decay caused by pushing feelings *down*, not getting them *out*. Buried feelings never die. Sadness, loss, disappointment, and anger that were never acknowledged cannot be released. It takes effort and it's not particularly pleasant, like cleaning house, but if you don't wash your emotions clean periodically you will feel and look like a filthy house. I have a visualization that I use to keep my feelings sparkling, see-through, and streaming, the three 'S's.' Please close your eyes and take three deep breaths."

We did as we were instructed.

"Now, concentrate on the area called the perineum, between your vagina and your anus. This is where your original eight cells still exist. Since that area is where you began as a feeling being, it is also your emotional core. Imagine you can unplug it and have access to your emotional body inside your physical one. However you feel it or see it is fine. Explore what it is like in there – do you see brown or blackish sediment? Twisted places? Slow-moving, sluggish water?" She paused so we could look around up in there.

I was utterly absorbed by the slimy state of my emotional body, disgusted by it actually. It reminded me unpleasantly of the rat I had come across rotting away in the basement.

"Now it is up to you to cleanse anything like that out – spray, hose, sponge, whatever. Let the old water run out your eight cells, give it to Mother Earth who can transmute anything. Keep at it until there is no more stuck energy."

I industriously scrubbed and expelled, each round getting a little better. I saw myself using a toilet brush and a garden hose to wash the large globs of muck off the walls of my feeling self. It was quite cathartic. One final rinse.

"If you are ready, then fill up your emotional realm with sparkling, see-through, streaming water. A bubbling brook, a rushing river, waves in the ocean, even a swimming pool. Whatever image you get that is absolutely squeaky clean. Revel in it for as long as you want, then when you are ready, plug yourself back up."

It felt wonderful and all around me the Sis-Stars were sighing with pleasure, too.

"Now step aside and look at the muck you got rid of. A lot? A little? What was stuck in there? As you recognize anger toward a parent or sadness around a loss, or whatever it was you needed to pass out of your emotional realm, watch it be absorbed into the Earth."

A huge pile of sadness around Mags. Some anger at being abandoned. Beaucoup fear of the future – more sadness and anger at Dan.

"Acknowledge confidently and even sternly that you have no need to carry that around anymore. It is not YOU, it was taken on by you. I repeat, those feelings are not YOU, they were taken on by you, and have been kept around for too long. We are not taught how to achieve emotional health in our culture, we are apt to have been told that feelings are unacceptable, especially those of girls and women. But now we can take charge and slough off what no longer serves us. The Earth will take our stale, unnecessary feelings and make them into fertilizer for positive things, new growth, progress, unhampered by all that sludge. Then next Sis-Stars weekend we will celebrate Imbolc, the early spring holy day that begins the season of new life, acknowledging the seeds hidden beneath the snow."

New growth in the spring reminded me of Chauncey Gardener's naïve, hopeful observations by the brilliant Peter Sellars in his last movie, "Being There."

"The emotional cleansing that we just did will help us to start anew, just as spring comes out of winter. The fertilizer of past negative emotions, crystal clear water of positive ones, and intention to evolve are a powerful combination in the soul as in the ground, figuratively as well as literally."

Even though my eyes were still puffy and hot from all that crying, I felt a surge of hope.

"Let's take a break, ladies."

As we were waiting for a turn in the bathroom, Vicky asked me if she could give me a hug for all my hard work and for Mags. I agreed. As I absorbed the hug, paradoxically I felt the lack of Mags' touch acutely, somewhere deep inside. It had been in there for so long, the feeling of aloneness, disconnect, something missing, and now I had an explanation.

"It's weird, Rowan. I've always craved love and touch, especially by a woman, but I am not attracted to them."

Rowan smiled gently, "Like me."

"Yeah. Now I see that I was denied a close sisterhood from the womb onwards. Sleeping with a woman would be like incest to me, since what I want is my sister's total but platonic love. I so want that level of closeness again, but am stuck with men. One man in particular...." I trailed off.

"How is that going, if I may ask?"

"Horribly. A huge void. We barely speak anymore. I feel the end coming like a storm on the horizon, but I am heartbroken over what it will do to Reed and Rachel. Sometimes I wish their dad would die in a car wreck or something and spare us what's coming next. I want to put it off and I want it to be over with, in equal measure."

"Just remember, you are very strong, Reb, or shall I say Bex? I am sure that Mags is here with you and she will help you get through it and so will us Sis-Stars and your other friends. You have support all around you, you only need to ask." Rowan spoke with quiet conviction and squeezed my arm. I smiled at her and nodded agreement.

"Next!" Teddi trumpeted, sailing out of the bathroom.

I took my turn, studiously avoiding looking in the mirror, not wanting to see my puffy, blotchy face and equally afraid that it would shimmer again.

"Coward."

"Now. Let's let Water speak to us individually during a meditation. It is simple but powerful. After taking your cleansing breaths, tap into your sparkling emotional waters."

As I let myself relax and envision my rejuvenated inner self, I saw the image of a perfect, placid lake on a beautiful day. It was like Lake Lanier, but without the rednecks, motorboats, or floating beer cans. Vast waters lapped at the shore, families of ducks paddled around, it was idyllic. Such calm, such beauty.

Sitting on the lakeshore, I looked down into the water and gradually my reflection seemed to grow wings, great, magnificent white wings. It was incredible, the feeling of that grace and strength coming from between my shoulder blades. I admired them, turning this way and that to see them from different angles. Then, to my astonishment, when I turned left, my reflection turned right. I tried it again, and once more the other me diverged.

151

"Come on, Bex. You can figure this out."

I closed my eyes to see if the effect would still be there when I looked into the water again, and there it was. What in the world was going on? I felt like I was losing it, my reality literally shifting. Then it snapped into place: I was not seeing myself, I was seeing Mags. She was there, in the water, in mirrors, wherever I thought I saw only me, I was seeing double. Twin vision. Only she was not "here" – she was "there," wherever "there" was. Maybe somewhere in between. Oh, God was she trapped between the realms? I had heard of that, souls that did not want to die and stayed around as "ghosts." What a horrible fate! Had our little fetal selves refused to let her leave in some way? Our souls too entwined to let go?

This was so shocking that I forced myself out of the vision and looked around the room, blinking and shaking my head. The others were still deep in their watery meditations and Wisteria had left the room. All of a sudden, I felt claustrophobic and needed to go outside for some fresh air. There was a creek at the bottom of Wisteria's lot and I wandered down to it. I did not try looking into the water, and it was rushing along anyway, but it was soothing to watch it flow past. I did ask it what was now a burning question: could I do anything to help Mags in any way? Help myself? This was such a new feeling for me. First to learn about her existence, then her death, now not sure about either or both. I fervently asked Water for enlightenment – to lighten my burdens, show me the truth of the situation, if there were one.

In my head I heard,

"Coto…"

Coto? What or who is Coto? Some goddess I had never heard of? I needed to ask the Sis-Stars if they recognized that word, so I leapt up and hurried back up the path to the house. The group was milling about, snacking and chatting casually.

Wisteria gave me a quizzical look and I nodded, going over to her.

"Can I ask you a question?"

"Of course, Dear One."

"Does 'Coto' mean anything to you, like is it the name of a goddess or something?"

She thought for a moment. "Not that I know of. Why?"

"In my vision just now I saw myself as a winged being, looking into a lake and seeing another me, but when I moved right, my reflection moved left, and so on."

Wisteria took in a surprised breath,

"Mags?"

"Mags."

"Oh, Rebecca, that is so wonderful!" She enthused, giving me a fierce hug.

"Yes, but... I've always had this odd effect when looking into a mirror, like a shimmer, and now it is getting clearer that she is somehow *in* the mirror, it's not just my reflection, it's, it's both of us at once. That's the best I can explain it. And it's pretty much freaking me out, to be honest."

"I can understand that. It's nothing I've ever heard of, but of course I believe you. And where does this 'Coto' come in?"

"I'm not sure, but right after I figured out that the angel in the water was her, and by extension, so was the angel in the mirror, I went outside and I heard that word in my head. Clearly. Except it could also be 'go to?'"

"Or both? Go to Coto... Well, Water is very wise, and she will reveal to you what to do, where to go, when the time is right." Wisteria sounded certain.

"I hope so. It is puzzling. Strange. But also exciting... like again my body knows the truth, but my mind still has to catch up..."

"Remember that Innana goes to the Underworld and returns, so do Persephone and Ishtar, it is an archetypal journey, not just for heroes but for heroines, too. You are on the exact right path, no matter how it seems to be out-picturing. We are all here to hold space for your spiritual quest and your understanding of your unique journey. It sure is a unique one, if I may say."

Multiple votes of sisterly confidence and two seminal visions in one day. I was exhausted.

Chapter 16

"Air. Thoughts. We tend to let our thoughts rule us, but it should be the other way around." Wisteria was holding forth ensconced in her comfortable armchair, looking like a pagan queen in her throne. "We need to control our thoughts because *energy always follows thought*. So, if you think something negative, you draw that negativity to you. Think something positive and you are more likely to get it, that's the law of attraction in a nutshell. It isn't totally woo woo, either. If you go into an interview saying to yourself, 'I'll never get this job,' then you will project inadequacy, self-doubt, and defeatism – lo and behold, no job offer. However, if you do the opposite, expect to succeed, you convince yourself and others that it is so. Maybe the job is already filled, and you don't actually get it, and yet you made such a good impression that when another job comes up you are recommended as a good candidate. As I said, energy, positive or negative, follows thought."

"Good reason to believe in Heaven. Besides, it's real."

"The real key is to *co-create*, meaning you create your world in concert with letting the Universe, the source of all energy, help you achieve your goals. Many people have lost sight of what *they* have to do to make their dreams come true – you don't just say "I want to win the lottery," or as Janis Joplin sang, "Lord, won't you buy me a Mercedes Benz." You cannot just sit back and expect it to come straight to you. The Universe is not one giant McDonald's, let's just say. In our interview example, you still need to dress nicely, do your homework on the company, write a follow-up note, all those actions are part of the mix.

Say you want to manifest more prosperity, there are concrete steps you can take, including working harder, changing jobs, or getting another degree. So, ask yourself what you really want, make sure it is attainable, and put your positive thoughts and actions behind it. We will do Fire soon and fill in the right action piece of the puzzle.

Oh, and there is our old friend "Organic Timing" from Earth, remember? Saying 'I will make $50,000 by tomorrow' is very unlikely to work. I wouldn't rule it out, exactly, but co-creating is more of a gradual process most of the time.

For now, we will explore Air, the realm of thought and focus. Today we will concentrate on setting good intentions, upholding high-energy ideals and goals, which are Air because they are insistent, consistent thoughts, ideas, and concepts. You must have your thoughts straight before you can manifest them."

Wisteria looked around the circle at each of us in turn.

"So, my sweet ladies, here is the question for today: what do you want most of anything you can imagine? Let yourself answer it in any way or in many ways. Listen to your inner self and to the clues in the world around you, the answers are all present if you pay attention. You could journal, dance, make a collage, take a walk, sit in the corner with your eyes closed, whatever. Keep in mind that usually Air works best with words, so try to end up with a written answer to the question. We will reconvene for lunch, so our first baby goal is to have a way to convey your desire to the group by then. If anyone needs more time, we can always take more time in the afternoon. If anyone gets done earlier, then just sit with your intention, bask in it. Feel what it feels like to have that desire fulfilled. *Act as if it already is.* That brings the right kind of energy to it, a feeling of success that breeds success."

Inspired, we each went our separate ways. I was drawn out into the balmy spring weather, not having allergies -- if you did, Atlanta's spring and fall pollen counts would just about kill you. The backyard azaleas were blooming in several gorgeous shades of pink and scarlet, the grass was green and lush, and the sky was startlingly blue. I claimed the hammock to figure out my intention.

Could my intention be to never leave the hammock? No, I wish. But just having that thought made me wonder if "rest" would be a good intention. Relax. Kick back. How to do that during divorce proceedings, working two jobs, having an affair, and raising two kids that were suffering, angry, and confused, I wondered. Not going to happen. But there was something to the concept, nonetheless. Be kind to myself, perhaps? Find balance? Stop pleasing everyone else first... One tiny silver lining to this whole shitshow was that the weekends without the kids I had some more time to myself, despite missing them and worrying about how their dad was treating them pretty much the entire time. But He seemed to be trying to be a father, providing them bike riding and frisbee throwing, sometimes a movie on his weekends.

During those weekends I could be a little less scheduled up for a couple of days, catch up with my life, myself. I wanted to, what, I guess give myself back to myself. Those words popped into my head. Give myself back to myself. Get back to myself. But not back to the past me, rather to a new self, a much healthier one. Part of that process was accepting how far off course we had all gotten and beginning to move back into the center, the fulcrum, an authentic life built on truths, however painful they might be. Still, I had to contend with Dan, his anger, his irresponsible behavior, how he'd bully me, the kids, be wildly unpredictable, just like before only worse even. He continued to intimidate me, frustrate me, and piss me off every time we interacted. The shit was, I figured it would go on for years and years. Yoked to an asshole.

Trying to shake that unproductive, negative train of thought – could I manifest being free of him altogether?? -- I decided to take a walk, let ideas percolate. I went back down to the creek where I had gotten insight before. Today the water was calmer, lazily moving by, taking a leaf or a twig on a leisurely ride downstream. The creek mirrored my desire for calm, quiet, beauty, harmony. Don't push the river, I thought. Go with the flow. Lots of wisdom in water.

I sat down on the bed of prickly pine needles and idly tossed one in the water. Watching it drift off I thought to myself, letting go might be the key to less stress, more compassion for myself, and some escape from this no-win situation I was in. My mind was jumping around to why the hell did I manifest the present this way in the first place? Of course, it was not just me, Dan had made a major contribution to the current misery, he was the mastermind of it as far as I was concerned. But, of course, blame is a dead-end game and resentment only hurts the one who is resenting. I knew these things mentally, intellectually, in Air, but not so much in the water of my emotions. With Dan very much still being himself, and anything I did he would manipulate to increase the kids' unhappiness, letting go seemed almost impossible. I had tried for so long to accommodate, to mediate, to tiptoe around, when pushed to the limit to fight, lose, and ultimately to retreat. Wash, rinse, repeat. I'd even medicated myself for the last couple of years so I wouldn't care as deeply or fight so readily. But could I have done things differently or gotten out earlier? Then the divorce limbo for the kids would have gone on even longer. It was a vicious circle and I felt as trapped as a fat, juicy fly in a spiderweb.

"The only way to win the game is not to play the game."

What was that? I thought I heard someone talking. About a game or something.

"The only way to win the game is not to play the game."

I did hear something, an indistinct voice like from the far end of a tunnel.

"THE ONLY WAY TO WIN THE GAME IS NOT TO PLAY THE GAME!"

The only way to win the game is not to play the game! I heard it. Wow.

"Is it you, Mags?" I said out loud for some reason.

"YES. YES, IT'S ME. MAGS."

It *was* her! It was Mags and I heard her, I actually heard her! This was very exciting. The stream must be some kind of a magical communication place. Like an Inka *huaca*, a sacred place that the worlds can reach each other more easily, where the ancestors can speak though visions and help the living. A lot of Inka *huacas* were springs and lagoons, too.

Then I wondered why I was hearing her now.... Was it because I helped her soul pass on last month in Ecuador? Must be it.

"Got it in one. Catching on quicker, aren't ya now?"

Catch. Quick. What was she saying?

"Catching on quicker."

Ah, she said I'm catching on quicker. I was hearing her better and better, if I kind of dug deeper inside, was extra still and focused. Air governed focus and I was listening as hard as I possibly could.

"Are you happy, Mags? Now that you're through the hole in the sky?" I was desperate to know.

"Oh, yes. It's pure, unadulterated bliss up here. But I'm so glad we can finally talk. So, get this! I have one 'free pass' to come back into materiality and see you, touch you! Isn't that wonderful?"

"In the flesh? Really?" OMG. This was mind-blowing news. First I could hear her and now I'd be able to see her too?

"Yes, but only for a little while. And only in one place."

"Where???" I was dying to hear.

"That's the catch. They say that I cannot tell you where, you have to work it out on your own. Think of something that has puzzled you recently... And there's another caveat: when you do remember correctly and we get to meet, then our connection may well be broken forever. If we choose not to take that risk, we'll always be able to hear each other, now that you have conquered your doubt and fear."

"Oh, shit. If we meet and then lose touch, will I remember you or will all this be erased?" Who made up these rules anyway? They sucked. Big time.

"I don't know. They won't say."

"Who ARE 'They' anyway?"

"They won't say. But They run things. Everyone knows that."

"Gotcha. So the rules are beyond any of our control. Like basically everything else."

I stopped myself. Hey, that was purely negative thinking and I did not want to draw any more shit into my life, thank you very much.

My mind was awhirl. The positives? I might have a chance to meet her. And I might remember her, or not -- at the moment it was unclear which was the better alternative. Remember losing her forever? Was it really "better to have loved and lost than never to have loved at all"? Jury was out on that one, in my opinion. There was the sure thing, leaving our relationship as it was now, being able to 'talk' in a manner of speaking. It was a bit disrupting to carry on long dialogues with your twin who is a spirit, all the while standing still and not being functionally present in this realm. Not easy to drive carpool or give lectures while tapping into another plane of existence, I would imagine. But the connection with Mags was amazing, after all this time and what had happened in my life since I had learned of her existence, or, I guess, her existences, which seemed to change a lot. But, thinking it through, I just had to see her in the flesh, no matter what the consequences might turn out to be. Mars in Aries strikes again.

"I want to try to meet, if you do." I sent it out there to wherever out there was.

There was a long pause, and I was afraid I had lost her.

"Okay. I really want to, too. I knew we'd agree. I'd so love to have a body again, even for a few minutes, and especially so that I can feel you and see you in the flesh. I miss all that up here. Someday when you come through the hole in the sky, we'll be together, but in this non-material form of being. This may be our one chance for physical contact."

"So that is true? We meet our loved ones again in 'heaven'?"

"Yep. True as a moose, as an old friend of yours used to say."

"OMG." I suddenly had another burning question for her. "Can you see Monday????" My heart leapt out of my chest at the thought.

"Clear as day. She's whinnying, 'bring carrots when you come.' Her teeth grew back."

Oh. This just got better and better. That's what Reed had said about her teeth when Monday's soul was still hanging around for him to talk to! So, when I die, I would see my favorite horse and my beloved Grandma, too. All the cats and dogs that had passed during my childhood. I had always wanted to believe in that ultimate reunion in Heaven – but simply was not willing to take on Hell as a package deal. Now I felt convinced that the Afterlife was real, I had a reliable informant!

I had so, so much to think about. And I realized, an intention to finalize. I had not the first clue how much linear time had elapsed.

"Hey, Mags. Any insight into a good intention for me?" Was it cheating to consult the dead on these matters? I really didn't give a shit. She was basically me, anyway.

"*Something about the power to stand on your own? That was a really good card you drew back in Earth weekend.*"

"So you've spied on the Sis-Stars from up there?" I wondered if I could tease a spirit.

"*Of course! You and me, the whole lost twin situation, it seems to create some of its own rules. I and the other guardian angels who were multiples need to reunite more intensely than most. In short, I have full access to your life. Man, sometimes it's been a rough ride, that's for sure. You've been through the old ringer a few times. But Reed and Rachel are clearly Beings of Light, that's why you got to see their destinies right after you experienced yours as a psychopomp and set my soul free. Up here there are the people who lost life-long loves, they get some special dispensation to help the one left behind, but at least they had their lengthy earth time together. We separated souls have an appropriately double task: to get the lost one processed well, like we did in Ecuador, and then try to heal the survivor as best we can, which I suppose is why we get to meet once if we so choose. Anyway, all that to say that I was given full access to your life soon after I died...*"

"Wow. That's a lot to take in. Now I get to believe in Guardian Angels, too. This is amazing. But have you been able to, like, I don't know, help me from the Beyond any?"

"Bex, come on. Why do you think Reed survived his birth? Monday lived for twenty-eight years? You got your plum job? I did what I could, I gave things a push here and there. But Dan has been too strong even for me, sorry 'bout that. Sometimes karma just has to come around to bite you in the butt. He's such a piece of work that his poor Guardian Angel gets overtime."

"I wish They would abandon him as a lost cause. Maybe you could suggest it?"

"Sadly, it doesn't work that way. Like innocent until proven guilty, everybody who is currently living gets a buddy that's passed on, maybe more than one. And none of us up here can interfere with any of the other living-dead relationships. Though, as I said, us multiples have precedence because we're trying to find another part of our very soul that got separated — we are open to a being or beings that are truly, profoundly elsewhere. Only our resolution will allow our soul to fulfill its unique purpose, one that has taken lifetimes and lifetimes to approach. It's hard to explain. We have to reunite the two parts of one soul or something is left undone for our entire soul line, our evolution gets stuck. That's why it's so great that we are going to meet on the physical plane, it's gonna help both parts of us a whole lot."

"I do hope so. Now, according to Their damn rules, I have to figure out the 'where' part."

"Don't worry. You are partly there already and very soon another piece will fall into place."

"Okay. I'll do my best."

"You always do. Even when you should give up…"

"Thanks, Sis." My head was reeling.

As I entered the kitchen, I found everyone eating already and realized I had not managed to pull together my intention, what with talking to Mags for the first time in my life and all. Learning how it all really works behind the cosmic scene and other minor details.

So instead of chatting away with my friend-sisters, I took my plate overflowing with healthy foods and retrieved my journal. As I went past Bhindi on the way to my favorite corner, she must have noticed the huge grin on my face because she gave me a thumb's up. With my hands full, all I could do was nod and whisper, "I'll tell everyone in sharing, but it's mind-blowing!" She clapped her hands and went on eating her tabouleh salad.

Eating and writing, I wrestled with my inner questions. How could I somehow unite my past and my new sense of self, find my sea legs in this turbulent ocean, fully heal and move on? Tall order. Balance between the old and new? What about the stress, the need for rest? Being nice to myself? Mags' advice to stand on my own was almost ironic since that was what I'd been forced to do without her help -- oh wait, but now I knew she'd been my wing-woman all along! That made me smile even more... I needed a spectacular angel figure for my mesa, note to self. And a mirror. After this morning's revelations, I was so giddy with excitement and plans that it was really hard to concentrate.

I tried several different phrasings for manifesting all those things. Just as the others were making their way to the basement for the afternoon session, I finished writing up an intention statement that I thought might do the trick.

We sat back down in our comfortable circle after lunch, the ladies sighing and arranging their rainbow of skirts.

"How did it go, my friends?" Wisteria was perky and curious, as always.

People looked around at each other and finally Bhindi raised her hand to go first.

One by one, we all went. No one commented one way or another on the content of each intention, that was off limits, but we nodded in support of each individual offering.

My turn came and I read my journal entry.

"I intend to actively help the Universe to balance my past, give me peace in the present, and move into the new me, able to stand comfortably on my own, step by step, with confidence, compassion, and acceptance."

It felt right.

"Nice."

"Thanks." Oops, I said it out loud. But the Sis-Stars seemed to take it as aimed at them, or the Universe. Whatever. I had stated what I wanted and intended to get, one way or another.

Chapter 17

With a growing sense of excitement, I clicked open the email that said it was from the Humanities Center, hopefully with news on my proposal to write the shamanic visions book next academic year. Mason had written me a glowing recommendation, conveniently avoiding altogether the subject of pushing dead babies from one side of the universe to the other. That was best kept under the table – although academia was supposedly open-minded, in fact no weird personal experiences were to be acknowledged. I walked a very thin line as it was, writing about trance experience and all. I had been turned down already once by the Hums Center a few years back, and one reviewer had said that I was arguing that the ancients were "all high on acid." Wrong on all counts: very few people ever became shamans, visions were not seen as recreational but sacred, and LSD was created in a lab in Switzerland in 1938. I was desperately hoping they had found some more enlightened reviewers this time around.

Basically, all I needed to see was either "Congratulations" or "Unfortunately." I was almost afraid to look but when I did, it was "Congratulations"! Hooray! I did a little happy dance in my tiny office. A whole year to write! On my favorite subject, to boot.

I practically skipped down to Elsa's office to share the good news. She'd be happy for me, even though it would make doing museum programs in the Americas collection harder for her since I was not allowed to work on anything but my book – as if they had to twist my arm.

I waved the printed-out email under her nose and placed it on the desk where she was typing and talking on the phone at the same time. When she said goodbye and hit send, she looked down at the email. One word and she squealed!

"You got it! Oh, Rebecca, this is so, so great. Congratulations, my dear, you richly deserve it. Finally, someone understands your work."

I beamed. More happy dance ensued. She giggled at me prancing around in my high heels.

"Well, the only thing is you can't get me to do anything in the museum that whole nine months. I will have an office in the Hums Center building and an unlisted telephone number." I warned.

She nodded philosophically. "That's what your grad students are for, filling in for you. It's a big year for African art, anyway."

"The department can't get me either, which is the best part. And no college or university service. I will be a free woman, so to speak."

"You lucky thing. I'll still be chained to this desk." She sighed deeply.

"But maybe we can eat lunch more often, maybe? Meet at Saba's for salads…" I suggested, as part of Operation Enjoy Life. And drag my workaholic friend away for some breaks. Her mean father had once called her, the last of seven kids, "useless" and she had spent the rest of her life trying to prove him wrong. She worked more than anyone else in the museum, maybe the world.

"Possibly…" Her eyes were inexorably drawn back to her computer screen overrun with emails, documents, PowerPoints.

"Okay, well, gotta fly! I need to thank Mason for his help. Ttyl, Sweetie." My time was over.

"Bye. Glad for you." Her mind was already elsewhere, Bless her heart.

When I told him the good news, Mason was super pumped, too. Plus, he told me that he knew of a university fund that might be able to add a few thou to my departmental research and travel money. It might be enough to get me back to Ecuador over the summer to work more with Don Alberto and the rock spirits. More good fodder for the book. Mason had mentioned in his letter for me that a very important lowland Quichua shaman had expressly invited me back, which was a rare honor. He left out the talking rocks and all. Mason was sure that the school supplies would be a deciding factor, too. The university's mission statement was to "create, preserve, teach and apply knowledge *in the service of humanity.*" My plan to research indigenous knowledge, while giving back by supporting Western education and making international ties, was like shooting fish in a barrel. Tilapia, I should say.

Applying for that funding definitely was worth a shot, especially because I did sincerely look forward to giving the school supplies to the Bajo Ila kids as promised. I looked up the funds website and checked with the departmental office manager to verify how much money I had left in my account. If I used all my departmental money plus got another two grand then I could hire Juan Antonio and Miguel again, take a photographer and maybe Sally, too. I filled out the forms, attaching the Hums acceptance letter and emailed Mason to ask that he forward his recommendation letter to these people for good measure. I even uploaded a photograph of Don Alberto gesticulating to the students and myself while perched atop the sacred rock near the camp. Hell, I'd go all in and add a picture of the empty schoolroom and the adorable local kids with their soulful brown eyes, just to cinch the deal.

My kids would have to put up with me going on one more trip, then I'd settle down for at least a year, busy working on the book, revisions, and all that. And with only writing on my docket, I'd have more time for and with them. Reed could walk home from school, because he would be too old for aftercare by then, and I'd get Rachel from aftercare fairly early so he wouldn't be home alone for too long. He'd probably lap up the independence. I hoped he wouldn't get into too much trouble at home alone for a bit. But I'd run it past Reed's friends' parents so they would be aware that if their kids came home with him, they'd be unsupervised for a couple of hours. Oh yeah, and I was supposed to tell their father what the kids would be doing. Joy unbounded.

Well, time enough for that when I heard about the next trip money situation. Those could be His two weeks with them for the summer, maybe. Or one of them, and the other for July 4th up north with Nana and the cousins. Hopefully the divorce would be final by then and those visitation rules would be in force. Henry said we were very close to wrapping up the wording.

I kept rereading my intention statement that I had written on a piece of paper and put in my purse. This grant for next year seemed like a pretty good example of co-creation – part Mason's fieldtrip invitation for spring break, part my years of previous scholarly efforts, plus asking a rich university for some of its money and giving it back to indigenous people. Call me Robin Hood. And, as a personal bonus, I might receive more visionary help around Mags and me. I was still on a wonderful high from that day in the rainforest!

"Me, too!"

"Hi, Sis! How goes it?"

"Same old, same old. Bliss 24/7/365, as you Materials say."

I had to smile. But I was kind of jealous too, with all I had on my plate down here in the physical plane.

Like if I got that extra money then I needed to organize the school supplies donation project quickly. The kids' school had a volunteer club and I'd propose it for that. Everyone could buy supplies from a master list, I'd get large ziplock bags, the American kids could write letters and include a photo of themselves, decorate the bags and stuff them. I'd bring back photos of the Bajo Ila children getting their bags and me giving the teacher the larger items like posters, textbooks, etc. It would be so cool to go back there bearing a shitload of gifts. I should figure out a way to raise some money to flat out give the teacher, too, for her to help broaden their horizons.

Indeed, the opportunity for money raising came along naturally. Some "Buckhead Betty" types had asked me to talk to a group of them that were celebrating one member's fiftieth birthday by taking a girls' trip to Peru. If I could talk and show them pretty things, they'd have me for their fancy catered lunch. Whoopee. I dutifully showed up at noon to find that the Betty's, in their requisite Chanel suits and Hermès scarves, had started in on the champagne a while back and were whooping it up with genteel laughter. One of them glimpsed me hovering in the doorway of the museum's boardroom and waved her hand imperiously.

"Hello, Dahling. We have a slight change of plans. We'll eat and then you give your talk afterwards. Come back in an hour."

Excuse me? No lunch for me? The hired help? Cool my heels while they get drunk? I was royally pissed as I went to buy myself a sandwich in the café upstairs. While I waited for it to be made, I resolved that they would pay, but how? Aha, the lightbulb soon appeared over my head: they would donate beaucoup money to the Bajo Ila cause! I dashed back to my office to print out some photos of the fabulous munchkins. They could absolutely suck money out of Scrooge himself. No one could resist those gorgeous creatures.

Perched outside the boardroom nibbling on my sandwich and plotting my revenge, Benni, the director of the museum, walked by in her art historical tunic and well-coifed hair.

"I thought you were in there having 'Ladies Lunch'?" She was puzzled.

"Well, they decided to let the hired help eat separately and come back when it was *convenient* for them." I said sarcastically. "Not paying me a dime, either..." Sucking up to rich people was my least favorite part of museum work, plus I was not very good at it, truth be told. I thought that art and culture were more important than money grubbing and social climbing.

"Well, I'll just see about that!" She huffed indignantly and opened the door abruptly.

I heard vague mumblings, a moment of quiet, then Benni popped back out with a triumphant smile on her face.

"You can give your talk now. I read them the riot act about pushing a renowned specialist and curator around like she was dirt. There's lotsa champagne for you, to boot. Knock 'em dead."

"Thanks, Benni. I plan to."

They were shame-faced and pink from drink and embarrassment, clucking over me like so many over-dressed, over cosmetically enhanced hens. I whipped through my talk, which I had nicknamed to myself "Peru for Dummies," and then launched into my sales pitch and passed around the Bajo Ila photos, to a chorus of "aww's"... The Betty's totally fell over themselves to contribute, competing to throw their twenties, fifties, and hundreds into the serving bowl I had nipped from the staff kitchen. Ha. I flounced out with a wan smile and three hundred bucks in my hand. My evil plan was working!

Later that week I found out that, yes, I had been granted the extra two grand to go back to Ecuador. Yay! It was all falling into place, as if the Universe were finally smiling on me. Maybe because I was indeed standing in my power? Was getting the hang of this co-creation stuff?

With Mason's help, I quickly set up the trip arrangements. Sally said she could go when her grading was done and graduation was over, so in early June. David, the nice kid from the Costa Rica trip, Mr. Big Spoon, was a talented photographer and he was graduating so he wouldn't technically be my student. He was an intrepid traveler as well. He was ecstatic to get the trip and some money to boot.

"What does that make you think, Bex?"

"About what?" I was confused.

"You getting to go back to Ecuador? How quickly they forget... Perhaps meeting someone special?"

"Oh, of course. Sorry, Mags. It has been a whirlwind."

"Funny choice of words."

"A bunch of whirlwinds, then." Our little in-joke. Or was that twin joke? A cosmic joke? Who knew, who cared.

"Think about it. In your head you heard a word that was unfamiliar once..."

"Will do. However, at the moment I simply must go grocery shopping." Juggle, juggle, juggle. This cosmos hopping could get tiring sometimes... The kids loved crab legs as a special treat and

I had a lot to celebrate in getting the money for the next trip. Reed and Rachel might be a little upset about all the travel I was doing, so I'd get them some ice cream for dessert. Bribe away, the divorcing/divorced parent's shuffle.

On the drive up to the Publix, I wracked my brains to remember all that Mags and I had talked about since I started sensing or hearing her. Fortunately, I had written everything down in my journal so maybe tonight I could reread those entries. Another note to self.

The kids enjoyed the special food and didn't guilt trip me too very much about a second Ecuador trip. As we were sitting there snarfing our bowls of Rocky Road, I spontaneously decided to tell them about my visions of each of them that I had experienced during the first Ecuador trip. Not letting them in on Mags yet, though; regular life was surreal enough right now.

"Hey, guys. I haven't had a chance to tell you about something really cool that happened to me in Ecuador." I ventured.

They swiveled their heads in my direction as they spooned up their dessert.

"So, we were in the Amazon rainforest, right? And we had visited this shaman, a healer, named Don Alberto. Don means 'Sir' in Spanish, to show how important he is."

The kids were losing interest already. Blah, blah, blah. Professor parent. I knew the syndrome well myself, come to think of it. My father had conducted dinnertime lectures my entire childhood...

"Anyway, so, I felt kind of sick and he told me that a spirit had gotten into me." I watched to see how they were going to take that little bombshell.

"What kind of a spirit?" Reed was frowning at the idea. "The Devil?"

"I'm not big believer in 'The Devil," Honey Bunches, as you know. But when Don Alberto did certain things, like blow smoke at my head and tap me all over with a bundle of special leaves, I actually felt much better."

"That's weird." Reed was shaking his head in disbelief.

"Yeah, kinda. But he told me to go back to my tent for the afternoon and said that I'd see things that I needed to see."

"I'd take a nap if I felt sick." Rachel offered.

"That's a good idea. But actually I didn't sleep. As Don Alberto predicted, I really did see things. It was like a movie. And two of the things I saw were you guys."

Now they were paying attention. Their spoons were suspended in midair, in fact.

"Reed, I saw you riding in a little red airplane round and round in the sky, having a wonderful time and spreading joy, like invisible fairy dust, all over the world."

"Wow. That sounds like fun." He agreed and finished his bite of ice cream.

"And Rachel, there you were sitting on top of a hill in the Lotus Position." I turned to her.

"Like this?" She hopped off her seat and took up the pose on the floor, quick as a wink.

"Exactly. You were sending peace down from the sky, through your body, and into the earth."

"I like that!" she exclaimed. They both smiled and she licked her spoon.

"Mom. Geez, I'm Joy and Rach is Peace. No pressure there." Reed rolled his eyes, but I could see he was secretly pleased.

"It made me very happy to see you guys doing good for yourselves and for the world." Especially since joy and peace had decidedly *not* been in abundance as of late. But I was busy manifesting them, in spite of that pesky Organic Timing thing...

"Hey, maybe I could take a yoga class, Mom." Rachel was buzzing.

"Okay. Maybe Reed wants flying lessons?" I joked.

He darted a look at me to see if I was pulling his leg.

"I would, but I think I'm still too young." He joked back.

"Afraid so...." I ruffled his hair fondly. "Learn to drive a car first, probably."

Since Sam and Rosie were coming over soon for sleepovers, I got the kids to help me clean up the dinner dishes and then listened with half an ear to the ensuing girl-noise – high pitched – and boy-noise – low-pitched -- for the rest of the evening. I got out my journal and flipped to the parts about me in the womb with Mags during Water weekend. There was something at the back of my mind that I had not understood and maybe it would make sense now. It must be the name of a place, since that was the only clue I had to go on.

Here it was. "Coto" or "go to" or both, I had written. It had appeared in my head just as Mags' voice was first getting through to me.

Maybe the computer would help, since I did not know any place called "Coto" offhand. Turns out there were some places with that name in Brazil, and it was a type of tree bark in Bolivia, so apparently it was vaguely South American. That was promising.

Since so much had happened in Ecuador, especially moving Mags' soul onwards, maybe there was a Coto there? When I put in both "Coto" and "Ecuador," I was soon rewarded with numerous photos of a stunning volcano called "Cotopaxi." Wow. I eagerly read about the tallest active volcano in Ecuador, at over 19,000 feet. The blurb said it was considered feminine by the indigenous peoples and that she had a husband volcano and a lover mountain and their antics at night were like the juiciest gossip from a soap opera. The lover could transform and be either a man or a woman, adding to the drama. Cotopaxi *must* be it, a female sacred mountain with a sassy energy, remarkable beauty, and wild stories to tell. A challenge to climb, often shrouded in clouds, Cotopaxi was legendary to locals, hikers, and tourists alike. I could tell she would be a Mags kind of place, for sure. Beautiful, challenging, sexy.

I hastily dashed off an email to Juan Antonio and told him to factor in a day trip to Cotopaxi as part of my June research. He knew gringos well enough not to ask why. As a skilled mountaineer who had climbed Cotopaxi many times, he wrote that he'd love to take me there. I said we had to arrange for the photographer and Sally to stay in Quito, though, because this was a "personal" day for me. Again, no questions asked. Bigger tip that way.

"Mags? Did I get the right answer?"

"Oh, yeah. You done good, figuring it out. You arrive there and I will find you. I'm over the moon."

"You *are* over the moon, huh."

"Good point. It's absolutely great up here, over the moon, and the stars, and the planets. But I still want that bit of time in a physical container, together. We need it."

"It will be a dream come true. The biggest miracle of all."

I heard some rather louder than usual noises from downstairs, so I trotted to the top of the stairs and yelled down,

"Everything okay?"

Rumble, rumble, rumble.

"What?"

Rumble, rumble.

"I'm coming down there!" I warned them.

The boys were in the midst of an epic pillow fight and several eviscerated pillows had sprayed their contents all over the furniture, the floors, and the walls.

Sam had a big white feather stuck in his glossy black hair and grinned impudently at me. Reed was panting and laughing so hard he was holding his stomach.

"Good luck cleaning all this up." Was all I said. "Anyone hungry?" Duh. They were teenage boys.

"Can we order a pizza? Please?" Reed waited breathlessly for the answer.

"Half cheese, half pepperoni?" I suggested both kids' favorites.

"Yay, Mom!" In spite of himself, he ran over and gave me a quick hug. Then he remembered he was a big boy and shuffled off, muttering "Yeah. Good. Thanks."

The girls ate the cheese-only part and then I hustled them off to bed. It would be an hour or so before they settled down, but they had to start sometime, or they'd be up all night. And I would, too, mother-hen-style.

I had to take one more look at the pictures of Cotopaxi before I turned in. I printed one out and taped it to the wall next to my computer. It would keep me going until I made it there.

Chapter 18

It was Fire weekend, and the room was alight with red, yellow, and orange caftans, harem pants, tunics, and scarves. We looked like we might break into wild belly dancing or something.

Wisteria clapped her hands for attention after we called in the directions and all the usual deities.

"Since Fire is the realm of action, this time we will start out by dancing, long and hard. The only instruction is to keep in mind the intention you came up with in Air weekend, and the movement will anchor it in your body. But other than that, let go. Letting go is a Fire concept, too. So, dance!" Wisteria had picked some wild music for us. I was more than ready to let loose myself. And six planets in fire signs made this Element right in my comfort zone.

Chaos ensued, but it was joyful and exhilarating. I kept repeating to myself, "I intend to actively help the Universe to balance my past, give me peace in the present, and move into the new me, able to stand comfortably on my own, step by step, with confidence, compassion, and acceptance." Each time I said it, I liked it more.

With Fire, the "move into the new me" part was especially relevant, since balance was mostly Water, and peace was Air, so the transformations I sought were Fire to the max. Bring them on.

We all twirled and spun and waved our arms around like veritable madwomen. We clapped and stomped and laughed out loud. It was like a pop-up party at 10 a.m. Saturday morning and without the booze. Who needed booze? This was much more fun.

Eventually the song played itself out, and we were all leaning over, panting, and holding our sides. Even Joy was smiling, and I went over to see if she would accept a hug from me. I held out my arms welcomingly and she shyly stepped into them. No words were exchanged, but I had a thought fly into my head: somehow she too belonged to the "sadness of all women" club. I just knew, deep down, that that was her story, in some form or another. But I had to wait for her to speak into it and not invade her process -- I could only tell my truth and see if and how it might resonate with her. During Air weekend it turned out Wisteria had us booked solid and I had not had time to catch everyone up on my Ecuador visions and how I was able to speak to Mags now that she was where she was supposed to be in the cosmos. And I needed to announce my plans to return to see her at Cotopaxi! There was a lot.

After lunch my opportunity came up, as I was hoping it would. We were exploring Fire as transformational: take air and earth in the form of wood and you make fire, which would devour the wood, warm the air, and leave fertile ashes for the earth. Water would safely put it out, making the five Elements complete, under the ever-present guidance of Spirit. In the process, some things were destroyed and others were left behind in a different form. Change as the only constant... I had embodied that like hell these last months.

Wisteria talked at length and eloquently about the transformation from caterpillar to butterfly, how it moved through a completely liquid state and all the cells took on new roles. It was absolutely amazing to really think of it, a totally magical and beautiful process. For tomorrow's group mesa I decided I'd bring in my painting of the butterfly/owl/jaguar/woman that I had bought from a Peruvian shaman that had visited my class. We had gone down into the Gully behind my building and had a ceremony to heal the creek waters and Don José had brought a roll of paintings to show the students and hopefully to sell. I had not been able to resist this one: everything in the painting was morphing into something else, like the big blue butterfly contained the white owl and was part of the jaguar's head all at the same time. I never tired of looking at it and always found something new in its wild colors and sinuous shapes. I'd grab it from my office after the afternoon session. It was a mesa in itself.

But for now, Wisteria invited Sis-Stars to talk about what was transforming in our lives. Perfect prompt for me.

I tried not to go first, but I was just so eager. Teddi beat me to it, but I jumped in second.

The telling took a while, though I tried not to hog the spotlight for too long or make it into an impromptu lecture. Put a quarter in my back and I talked for either fifty or seventy-five minutes, the two lengths of classes at the university.

The ladies were suitably amazed and gasped at proper intervals. They laughed over the thimble full of souls and appreciated my seeing the kids' destinies laid out so clearly. I mean, who wouldn't like to know that someone had Joy and someone had Peace down pat? I got to the Cotopaxi realization and then to my plans to return to Ecuador and getting the grant for a year off to write. They spontaneously clapped when I was done. I took a mock bow.

"Good manifesting, Rebecca! That's co-creation, Sis-Stars. You put in your effort and let the universe do its thing and change will happen, seemingly quickly and easily. But remember, Rebecca had studied a lot, had not been defeated by all that has been going on elsewhere in her life, and kept her purpose strong. She put in the legwork over Spring Break and now can reap the benefits."

I felt happy and proud. Listening to the others I was glad for them, too, as they chronicled their changes inside and out. Teddi was changing careers, Rowan and Vicky were planning to hand-fast (pagan for marry), Bhindi was finally moving into a house with her son, Chantilly had a new man in her life...

Joy had been typically quiet, but when everyone else had finished and Wisteria looked her way to see if she would put her voice in, Joy looked up and nodded as if convincing herself that it was okay.

"Um." She looked lost as to how to go on. We waited, as we had been trained to do. We held space.

"Uh." She tried again. "I have something to say. It's related to what Rebecca spoke into, actually. If that's okay?" She looked at me to be sure.

"Of course. Please go on." I smiled encouragingly, fairly sure of what I was about to hear.

"I had a baby. Once. He was...." She was fighting with herself, trying not to cry. We waited quietly, sadly.

"... born dead. Stillborn, they call it. He was all blue and everything."

Sympathetic noises played all around the circle. Several women pulled tissues from the well-used box to dab their eyes.

"I was only nineteen and having a baby would have stopped me from finishing college and going on with the life I'd planned, but still I wanted him very badly. I was going to name him Oliver...." She trailed off.

I felt so, so sorry for her. Bhindi was blinking her eyes furiously.

"I guess that was a transformative event for me, but not in a good way. I lost a lot of my will to live when he died inside me. I have had a really hard time getting it back. But hearing Rebecca speak of the souls being moved on and now being happy, well, it sorta helps. Not that I won't always miss him, but thinking he is in a good place is.... comforting."

"May I add something to my check in?" I asked gently.

Joy nodded her head.

"When I talked with Mags during Air, she said that it was true, 'Heaven' is where you see all your loved ones who have already passed on. She said my horse Monday was right near her – in whatever sense nearness was in that realm. That made me so happy. The church version of Heaven seemed weird to me as a kid, all the old-man-sitting-on-a-cloud stuff was way too improbable. But now I believe Mags. She is there, wherever there is, so she should know."

Joy looked pensive. "I want to think that he's in Heaven, but I'm not sure. Catholics think he's in Purgatory. But that's made up, as far as I can see. Yet, believing in a better place, or maybe state of being, might help me re-frame losing Oliver a little. Like you reframed almost losing Reed into saving him."

Bhindi was obviously itching to talk. "May I jump in here?" She asked.

"Sure." Both Joy and I agreed.

"Well, I'm not sure how many of you know this, but my son was born extremely premature. He nearly died several times at the beginning. It broke up his father's and my marriage: his dad couldn't take the emotional roller coaster and I had to use all my power to will Justin to stay on this earth with me. So, I guess, my story falls somewhere in between your two's, but along the same lines – life and death with babies. Every day I thank all the spirits in the firmament that Justin did survive, but I never can quite forget the feeling of losing him, almost, over and over. It makes his life even more precious, though it derailed mine in some pretty profound ways. I still haven't found a good man to this day. But I would never blame Justin for a nano-second."

"I can't blame Reed for my pelvis breaking, either. It kept him here." I added.

The room was silent, no doubt thinking of how little Oliver did not make it, how unfair, how profound were the risks of motherhood and the strength it took from the beginning. I felt glad that my experience could be met by that of other women and respected, shared, and hopefully changed into something more positive. Transmuted, like alchemy, turning base metal into gold.

I knew Bhindi was a marvelous mother to Justin, who was a student at the kids' school, in between their two ages, and he had been a source of great joy to her despite the price she paid. Ditto Reed. Sometime I might suggest to Joy that we send love to Oliver's soul even though he wasn't here, like Mags. Maybe someday she could talk to him or see him... it was happening to me, so what the heck. Linear experience was a distant memory these days.

"Good work, Fire ladies. Let's put our transformations into some artistic expression. I'll put on another song for whomever wants to dance some more. Art supplies in the garage, you know the drill. We've grounded ideas physically by dancing, now take an hour or so to ground the changes in material form. That harkens back to Earth and makes things real, present, palpable, which is opposite to Fire but therefore they are complementary."

It seemed like a no-brainer for me to render my vision of the tornadoes, the hole in the sky, and the kids in a combination painting and collage. I was super inspired by the morning and enjoyed clipping pictures from magazines and drawing on and around them, combining them. The little red plane was especially fun to put together out of a mosaic of reds, and I even took the photos of the kids I carried in my wallet out and cut their heads into silhouettes and pasted them on the plane and the yogini on the hill. The whirlwinds were easy to render in black pencil, but to show them switching direction, I came up with a trail of them, turning right under the hole in the sky and further on turning left. Creative freedom. Telescoping events into one scene. I was so engrossed that Bhindi had to touch my shoulder to get my attention when it was time to share.

Joy had made a very touching tribute to Oliver -- she was a good artist that hadn't shown all her cards before. It was pastels amorphously overlapping one another. This was a big step for her, making herself vulnerable this way and finding nice soothing colors for her baby boy.

Bhindi was artistic, too, and had also conveyed Justin's fight for life in an abstract way, slashing black through areas of bright colors to convey the death and life struggle he, they, had gone through after his birth.

My collage was dutifully "oohed" and "ahhed" over, now that they knew the whole story. I said to the group that I had told my kids about my visions of them, too, which they thought was very cool. I revealed that the idea of being a "psychopomp" was a bit daunting for me, but that I could wait and explore it more when I was back down in Ecuador with Don Alberto. My vision had told me that alone I was clueless as to how to move souls, but with a powerful shaman, and a man, I could hold the Feminine energy for that super-transforming experience. And the joy that suffused me when the souls were released was the reward for me personally, not only that feeling of elation but knowing I was truly helping resolve pain and stuck energy in some real, if surreal, way. I was still getting used to the fact that I had a minor calling, even, to heal. I certainly embodied the wounded healer...losing Mags had helped propel me in this new direction, probably. Since I could feel the unique pain of losing a twin, and then almost a son, I could assist other mothers, sisters, and babies in their struggles.

But I had to find my equilibrium with all this mind-blowing stuff, and still carry on with life and the divorce. I still hated with all my heart and soul handing Reed and Rachel to Him, knowing they weren't going to get as good parenting those times, but I had to just accept my being trapped in the non-decision I had been handed.

In the last round of negotiation between the lawyers, Dan's had said he wanted to strike the clause that neither parent could move out of Atlanta. He also requested to add some weeks of child visitation with the kids no matter where he was living. That was a little discomfiting for me, sounding like he was going to bail, but to tell the truth I would be just as happy to be acknowledged as their single mom instead of continuing in this horrible limbo. So, I asked Henry to make sure that child support would still be in force, even internationally, and that I had veto power if he moved somewhere that I deemed dangerous for the kids to visit. You never knew with Dan, he was a risk-taker at heart. But we had eventually gotten the wording to my liking and I was ready to sign on the dotted line.

Finally, yesterday I had gotten the call from Henry.

"Good news!" He crowed. Though with Henry it was more of a croak.

"What? Are we DONE?" I crossed my fingers.

"We are. You can come sign anytime. 'He' already has." Henry sounded jubilant. He loved squeezing the bad guys. And I'm sure he loved the money he made, billing out at $300 an hour as he did. But Virginia's loan had saved my ass and I could already hand back half of it as soon as the ink dried. I planned to refinance the house and send her the difference in the new and old mortgage payments every month.

"I'll be there first thing Monday morning. I am so thankful. Then how long do we have to wait?" I was breathless with anticipation.

"That's not exactly clear. The judge has to review it and set a date for you to appear in front of him or her. Could be a month, maybe less."

"And did I hear right that Dan doesn't have to appear?" I was hopeful.

"Nope." He answered promptly. "You were the one who divorced him, so it's on you. The usual 'irreconcilable differences' is the plea. If we're lucky it takes only fifteen minutes, depending on the number of cases on the docket and how quickly the judge goes through them."

"That is great. You know that I'm off to Ecuador the first week in June for ten days, so I hope it will be over by then. If the date is scheduled during that week, am I allowed to put it off?"

"Yes, you can postpone one time without being held in contempt of court, but you'll have to show a clerk your paid-for plane tickets."

I was super excited. Things were coming together finally!

I would add the divorce news to Sis-Star check-in tomorrow morning, I had talked plenty already for today.

As the day drew to a close, Wisteria assigned us an evening-to-night task, the first time we'd had "homework."

"To truly change, something has to die in order to leave room for new things to happen or start to step into being. Death begets life, life includes deaths, necessary endings." Didn't I know it...

"What needs to go so as to leave room for the new desires you are manifesting now? The old ways of being, people, beliefs, anything that no longer serves who you are now and want to be in the future. It's quite simple, in fact. If you take a completely full suitcase on a trip, there is no room to buy something new and bring it home." That hit home with these very clothes-oriented women, who exchanged mock horrified glances and giggled at themselves. And, of course, there was the double meaning of baggage. I was definitely not dragging old Dan around like a bag of dirty clothes anymore. As a matter of fact, lately my dreams had been frustratingly full of packing and having too much stuff and trying to move out of the wrong house and find a new one. Not rocket science to see that my unconscious was well aware that I had a monumental task of changing myself, my surroundings, my whole life. Hopefully I could nudge that process along a bit with tonight's task.

"Please, dear ones, you must not go out tonight or answer the phone, nothing, so that you can put yourselves deliberately 'between the worlds.' Eat some dinner, put on something black, and work at your mesa on what needs to die. A burning ritual is best – writing things you are dying to and then burning them with focused intention, use your Air skills. You can say out loud something like 'I hereby release fear, anger, a person, a memory, whatever, and clear it from my field completely.' After you run out of things to burn – and make sure the actual fire is out, please, sometimes Fire weekend can get out of control, one Sis-Star had a bad kitchen fire a few years back on Fire day one... Anyway, when you go to sleep, ask the Universe for dreams to solidify what you burned, and to tell you more. Then when you wake up, write down any downloads you got immediately." Downloads meant dreams, visions, aha moments in the Sis-Star lingo.

"And gather for tomorrow's session good symbols of what you want to 'live to.' What you've made room for in yourself, your life, your experience, your suitcase as it were. We will together perform that part of the cycle, the calling in of the new. Just be extra careful as you drive in tomorrow morning because you will still be in between the worlds."

She made it sound like a piece of cake. But I had made no plans for the evening – oddly Dean hadn't called for a few days -- and would be more than happy to turn off my phone for a few hours. I hesitated, though, about what if the kids needed something. I hated not to answer if they called me, so I decided I'd fudge our instructions a bit and leave the "do not disturb" setting on, but with my "favorites" able to get through. That way I could give myself over to this process more easily without worrying.

I followed the guidelines and burned numerous things from my life: Dan, self-doubt, the sadness of all women once more for good measure, fear of the financial and emotional future, a few other minor things. As I searched myself for more to let go off, I came upon a feeling that Dean might be drawing away from me as my divorce became realer. He had told me outright that he was sick of raising kids. So, even though the sex was a draw, I decided to let go of any dependence on him in my new life going forward. If I were to lower my stress, which was absolutely necessary or I might pop, I had to simplify my life some, keep my eyes on the prize. I was going back to Ecuador a free woman and then I'd be busy writing next year. Healthier for me to concentrate on myself, the kids, emphasize Air thought and focus for writing the book. So, I burned the dependence on any man and felt uplifted as the ashes piled up. I took them and buried them in the back garden, to give back to Earth through Fire.

Dead exhausted, I fell into bed. My new mattress was comfy, I still loved the green walls, and after asking for illuminating dreams, especially about how Dean figured in my world, I fell instantly to sleep.

And there he was, handsome as ever, standing on my front porch in my dream. He had a beer in one hand, a lit joint in the other, and was squinting through the smoke, swaying slightly on his feet. As I watched, he simply turned, opened the screen door, and walked away, without a backward glance. I called "Dean," but he didn't answer. I looked down and at my feet Monster was looking up at me with his green eyes, switching his tail back and forth with little snaps. He meowed up at me once and stalked off.

I jotted down the dream on my pad I kept next to the bed for this purpose. No mystery there. Dean was another Dan – I hadn't noticed the similarity in the names until now. Duh. And Monster's insight cinched it, once again.

It seemed obvious that I had something unpleasant to do later today. If there was time after today's session and before the kids got back home, I'd drop by Dean's and get it over with. In my new life I did not need to make the same mistakes or keep going down a familiar dead-end road. What was that saying? The definition of craziness is doing the same things and expecting different outcomes. I needed much better than that, for me and for the kids.

The other day Reed had told me conspiratorially that Insurance Office Girlfriend was history, but Dan had someone else on the line. He was obviously *not* keeping his love life nicely separated from them. Since he had no boundaries whatsoever, why would this be a surprise to me? Well, I could still be the good parent and they'd have one out of two at least. Me, I'd give men a nice long rest -- no man was better than a bad one. Work on my own self for a change, as per my intention.

I went around the house before I left, gathering things for today's ceremony of bringing in the new me. A photo of me literally standing on my own, a mirror to show I could look in them without fear now that Mags was coming closer and didn't have to hide in the between of a reflection anymore. I tore a photo of me and Dean in half. Breaking up with him would be a big step that would solidify the ritual of letting go and opening up. I dressed all in green, to symbolize my new life as being a traffic light stuck on "go."

Remembering Wisteria's advice, I was extra careful as I drove to Stone Mountain, lumbering along in the Volvo. It had been acting up recently, declining to start easily, and I was going to take it into the shop this week. The last of the 240's, it had plenty of miles on it and, like most Volvos, the interior was falling apart. I couldn't afford to be marooned somewhere if it broke down, particularly out at the barn twenty miles away.

But she got me there and we had a great day embracing life. It recaptured some of what I had felt after moving all those souls. Fire was fun. It would have to propel me past letting Dean down, then I could rest.

I parked in front of the Biscuit and crossed the street to his house. He was on the little front porch, full of rusty furniture and the screens choked almost opaque with ivy. Dean did not do upkeep, I realized, and that was another strike against him, since Dan did not either. Just like in my dream, he was holding a beer and had several empties strewn about his chair, one spilled in a big yeasty puddle that was seeping into his dirty Converse high tops. He held out a joint to me. Well, I guess some dreams come true, not necessarily the pleasant ones.

"Hi." He slurred. "Did we have plans?" His eyes were red rimmed and his hair unattractively greasy. I was already wondering what I had seen in him.

"No. I just wanted to stop by after my workshop for a minute before Reed and Rachel get back." I was stalling.

"How are the little brats, anyway?" He almost sneered.

That totally pissed me off. He could go back to his old ways, but he didn't need to insult my children. Now I felt empowered by the anger and was totally sure that anyone who called my kids brats was history.

"Dean, it's over."

"Oh." He took a puff, then a slug. "Well, it was fun. Again."

I decided not to comment on the rerun aspect of our encounters over the years. History had neatly repeated itself – we were together briefly, I realized he was still too wild for me, and that was that. He certainly was not broken up over breaking up. I felt good about my decision and wondered at how my subconscious had figured out that he was back to drugs, sex, and rock 'n roll. I might miss the epic sex, but I would not be a whore to it. Surely there were other generously proportioned dicks out there, maybe some belonging to nice men? What a thought. So I haughtily turned on my heel and drove home around the block feeling altogether lighter, quite relieved really. I mentally washed my hands of the whole thing.

I hugged the kids hard when they bounded up to the door, chattering about the movie they'd just gone to with Daddy. We were going to eat supper, do homework, take baths, read books, and go to bed, in the nice routine I had come to treasure now that it was not an every-night thing anymore. I was grateful that they both seemed happier, happy enough. Seeing them since I broke it off with Dean, I was doubly glad not to be desperately hanging onto a man who might not be any nicer to them than their own father was. That would just add salt to the wounds of the divorce, which was bad enough as it was. I had been forced to rip us all up from the roots for reasons beyond my control, but I could take responsibility for creating a better family somehow from the ruins, a better half of a family at least. Kind of a Fire death and rebirth, come to think of it.

"Guess what?" Rachel was hopping from leg to leg as if she had to pee.

"Do you have to pee?" I asked, even though at her age that had been her responsibility for years now.

"No." She gave me a withering look. "I'm excited."

"I can see that. How come, Baby Girl?"

"Daddy's going to take us to Costa Rica while you are in Ecuador. His new girlfriend has a place there!" She squealed. "Now Reed's not the only one who gets to go there. I do, too." She pointed to herself and jumped up and down a couple more times for good measure.

"Oh, wow. That's..." I was having a hard time finishing my reply.

"It's gonna be great." Reed offered. "He showed us pictures and the house is right on the beach and everything! There are macaws in the garden, too!"

"That sounds like fun. I'm really happy for you." I infused a modicum of enthusiasm into my voice as best I could. Now I understood that divorce clause better. He was planning to leave the country, I bet, and he had a meal ticket, a new gravy train to ride. And his recent rather suddenly agreeing to the divorce wrapping up began to make more sense, too. He wanted out in a major way, apparently he didn't think rebound relationships were any problem, he was horny after years of boring married sex, it was all falling into place. I'd be just as happy seeing him go, with whatever woman would have him. Maybe she'd feed the kids once in a while, if we were all lucky. Even Costa Rica was a good choice in my book -- it was a safe place, no standing army, all sorts of politically correct things like universal literacy and one-third of the land in national parks.

I searched myself for any jealousy, but there wasn't a drop of it to be found. I didn't want him, she could have him, she'd find out soon enough. He could be very charming at the beginning, as I well knew, it just didn't last when responsibilities reared their ugly heads. He could be the world's premier beach bum and gold digger for all of me. If they did not make any babies – God forbid – it might even work. There was something in it for the kids, too, nice vacations. Maybe Little Miss Thing would lure him away for good with her tropical beach house and we'd all be spared some of the drama. Fire was really changing things up, I thought. Good endings, hopeful beginnings, here I come.

Chapter 19

It was now May and we had finally come to Spirit weekend. It would encompass Beltane and, Sunday afternoon, we'd have our "graduation" ritual, and the Circle would be complete. All five Elements had been explored, at least on a beginner level, though Wisteria ran four levels of Circles, so I could continue next year and onwards. I was seriously considering it, knowing it was better than all the therapy in the world for me. Even when I got to see Mags, it would only be for a little while, and I'd still need my spiritual Sis-Stars in this realm. Virginia, Elsa, and Hayley did not know me as well as these women did – love them as I did, my old friends were not as spiritually oriented as I had become.

"Let's go back to our decks for inspiration, as we did in the early weekends of this Circle. Go ahead and each pick four from the Spirit thirteen. Some concepts we may have already touched on, but since this process is spherical rather than linear, the ideas come around in different guises naturally. Pick the four, then choose which one you want to start with, and we will dance between each card choice." Wisteria was ethereal, decked out in yards of pastel pink finery. Even though I pretty much hated the color pink, I had reluctantly picked up a final outfit at Value Village for today, but for our graduation, I also nabbed some wacky clothes in my signature sky blue. It was already feeling bittersweet, a last weekend with this exact group – future Circles would have some new members and not all of us might go on in the process.

I held the Spirit cards I had extracted from the overall deck already, anticipating this move. First came "Divine Feminine." Ahhh.

I easily identified with "Divine Feminine," expressed through The Goddess, all goddesses, mothers, nurturers. It was the main archetype for Cancerians like me. And through all this I had begun to find my way back to that core, taking baby steps to value the female in all her daily and holy aspects, in her power. And for me specifically, the sadness of all women was transforming into resolution, healing, and moving forward. I genuinely felt I was helping right the cosmos when loss comes pounding at the door for so many women.

We danced, smiles on our faces, familiar with each other and the process of grounding a concept in our bodies and uplifting our souls.

Bhindi held up her card, "Uplifting," in fact. I flashed her my "Divine Feminine" and she did the thumbs up as she twirled past.

Next was "Purpose of your Life." Well, obviously to nurture my children and to help souls move on, like I just thought. And to write about all this and more, popped into my head. That gave me a frisson of excitement, the idea of not just doing academic writing – oh, how I despised footnotes and bibliography – but more creative stuff. Like more poetry, even a novel. That would be fun, albeit out of my comfort zone.

Dancing to the next song, I felt called to make a lot of motions in toward me, and out from me, in equal measure. Hold the kids close and release them, welcome in intuition then push the souls on, write as the ideas come in and lob them back out to the world. It felt fantastic, fluid.

Then I got "Active/Receptive." A bigger perspective on the last one – doing and being, balanced, but dynamic. The rest I needed, the actions that needing taking, could I pull that off? To model the back and forth, I rested and caught my breath for part of the song but jumped to my feet to dance wildly for the rest of it.

Finally, came "Creativity." My favorite! What I very much wanted in my life. More of it, less stress along for the ride. I'd take Rachel pottery painting, see if Reed wanted to take an art class... Wait a minute, though, I stopped short. What about *my* creativity, not everybody else's? I should be the one to take up painting or ceramics, maybe get back into making batiks, like I enjoyed doing so much in high school. Now that Dan's shit was out of MY house, I could set up an art area next to my mesa in the basement. The kids could participate, of course, but it would be mainly for me to play around in, especially between Sis-Star Circles when I had weekends free.

So I danced with exuberance to an even larger room of my own. Space for all of me. I remembered how after the first meeting of this Circle I had desperately carved out a few feet of floor space and had no clue what I wanted on my mesa, whereas now I had an overflowing area of meaningful things and the rest of a huge room to do with as I pleased. Coming home was a breeze these days, the house calm and harmonious without You Know Who around. I danced for my Air freedom, Earth power to stand on my own, Fire transformation, and Water emotions turning positive and clear. Putting it all together, Spirit. Realizing how far I had come in the last few months, I felt proud of myself that I was beginning to construct a new life, amongst or despite the hurt, worry, anxiety, and doubt.

"You are doing great, Sis. So great. And we have only a few weeks to go until Cotopaxi!"

"I know. Absolutely cannot wait." I spoke in my mind, despite knowing the ladies would be okay with my talking to a ghost in their presence. They'd probably know who it was I was talking to.

We had a good afternoon going over Beltane as a holiday of fertility and sex, which made me think once or twice about not having that with Dean anymore. But it was a good decision and I really had not missed him much at all. I went home tired, as usual, but also exhilarated, lighter than I had felt in months and months.

Sunday was splendid. The weather, the mood of the group, Wisteria's excitement to move us up and out, all conspired to make a very happy vibe indeed.

We set up a threshold to symbolically step out of the Circle and into being full-fledged, Level One Sis-Stars. Wisteria had a trellis that we erected and decorated until it was groaning under the weight of the ribbons, flowers, swags of cloth, and such. We made flower headbands under Teddi's tutelage and arranged the feast for afterward.

One task before we started the ceremony itself was for each of us to write on a strip of paper a phrase or encouraging comment on each other person. We placed them in baskets with our names on them, as a gift to be read aloud during the ritual.

They were easy to write. For Bhindi, "You are so powerful, my lovely friend." For Teddi, "Love the sass. You go, Aries girl." For Joy, "Here for you." For Rowan, "You made all the difference." "Beautiful in all ways" for Chantilly. "Mom has no power over you anymore" for Vicky. "Keep on dancing" for Suzanne.

We were all busy primping like crazy, excited as school kids before getting out for the summer. We had statements and actions, like lighting candles, all planned out.

Looking around at all the colorfully clad ladies, and down at myself, we were all just beautiful in our silly, mishmash ways. We had all worked so hard, cried and laughed, learned a lot. What would I have done without them, without all this? I couldn't even imagine.

Wisteria was watching me as I absorbed the moment. She smiled to herself and turned away to arrange more flowers on the mesa, which was already overflowing with them. Our mother bird was seeing her chicks hop out of the nest and try their wings.

Later, when I walked through the threshold I felt truly reborn. Supported in my evolution and released to go on to bigger and better things.

The strips of paper in my basket were so moving: "You have done it and you can do it, love," "We've seen you soar," "You have so many options," "Keep loving YOU," and "We are truly Sis-Stars."

"So are we. See you soon."

"See you, Mags. Don't be late!" I joked aloud.

"Not a concept where I am."

Wisteria knew I was hearing my sister and she blew me a kiss.

Chapter 20

The semester was in its last throes, like one of those long, overacted cowboy death scenes, it seemed to take its time writhing around and being dramatic until the end. I finally wrestled all the final projects to the ground and handed in my grades. It was not my most stellar semester of teaching, but considering what had gone on, I had survived. Reed and Rachel still had three weeks of school left, then they would be whisked away to Costa Rica, and I would return to Ecuador. I was looking forward to it with all my heart and soul. I just knew I'd see Mags and I couldn't believe how lucky I was, how much I yearned to hug her. It was my first thought in the morning, my last thought at night.

But I had to concentrate on the present, even if teaching were over for a few months there was much to do. I had an undergraduate student graduating with Honors and there was a ceremony for that, plus two graduate students who had finished their dissertations and I would put the hood – the very Medieval symbol of receiving academia's highest degree -- over their heads. There was the unpleasant task of filling out my annual report on the new automated website that was super convoluted. My always-ongoing museum work needed to be somewhat under control so I could take next academic year off without guilt. I had to prep for the Ecuador trip, which was more on my shoulders than the Spring Break fieldtrip had been. The kids had to buckle down for last push of school and get ready for their trip, too. I had to get a cat sitter, clean out the frig, there were a thousand details on my list.

Best of all, however, Henry had given me the date for court, and by some miracle it was the Friday before I left on Saturday morning for Quito. Could not have been better timing. Thank you, Ganesh. Reed had a musical performance that evening – he played the cello, effortlessly I might add -- and we would all go, pretending to be a family one last time. Ain't we got fun?

Then after the trips, there'd be the Summer Solstice celebrations, my birthday, and starting on the book I'd always wanted to write. Lots of things to look forward to. Some down time I hoped, but time to write was a rare and precious gift and the kids had some camps set up so I could get started gradually in July and August. We could lounge by the neighborhood pool in the heat of the late afternoon and have a pretty good summer all in all. Although I was certainly still raw, still hated the back and forth of the kids with Dan, once in a while still missed Dean a tad, nevertheless I felt like I could hobble along anyway, lick my wounds. And in the fall, I'd start the second Circle, I had already decided.

I realized I wanted to do the next level of Sis-Stars when I had a dream the other week, after our final meeting. That evening I had watched a nature show on Dusky dolphins that live off the shores of Argentina. I had found their dark brown markings strikingly beautiful. When I fell asleep, I found myself dreaming of swimming with them in the bay, easily, playfully, happily. They drew me further and further down with them, until I started feeling that I did not have enough air to go any deeper. Just as I was about to tell them this, I saw that the expected sandy bottom of the bay was, in fact, the surface of another ocean. It reflected the shifting light and beckoned to me with its mysterious depths. But I communicated, telepathically, with the pod that I would need to return to explore that other ocean when I had more air in my lungs. They reluctantly agreed and we surfaced together with a dolphin flourish.

When I woke up, I marveled at the visual of the sea beneath the sea. It was a clear sign, from myself to myself, if nothing else, that I needed to dive deeper and join the second Circle. I needed to work more with Air and Water, my thoughts and feelings, symbolized by breathing under water, until I was as free and as agile as the Duskies. As happy and risk-taking and connected as they were. It was as clear as the water in the dream that my process was not over, it was just reaching a whole new level.

Admittedly and blessedly, my days were less hectic with classes over, and the graduation rigamarole went well. The kids aced their tests and waited impatiently for school to be over already. There was the end-of-the-season soccer team dinner and Reed got "Best Defense" which made him and me and Rachel very proud. Dan elected to bypass the party. Fine by me, but not so fine with Reed. Nothing I could do about it except make a congratulations cake for him to pig out on with his buddies the next day.

Finally, I was ready for the trip, had the kids' stuff together, arranged the cat sitter, asked my mom to come by and water the plants and check for mail once in a while, wiped out the empty frig, backed up my computer, and changed my outgoing message. The boxes were all ticked.

At last it came to the Friday itself, the day "it" would become official. I dressed nicely so as not to piss off the judge at the last minute, met Henry in the lobby, and chatted as we waited on the long, hard benches outside the courtroom while the wheels of "justice" turned ever so slowly. At last, our group was called. My case came up around twenty minutes into the docket and was perfectly straightforward. The stern man in the black robes asked rote questions, I answered submissively. Henry stolidly stood beside me. Bang went the gavel, and it was over. Thirteen years of marriage, a couple of years dating before that, all wadded up and thrown in the trash in a few short minutes.

Outside the courtroom door, Henry turned to me and asked,

"So, how do you feel?" He looked expectant, like he was fishing for a compliment.

"Good…. in a really bad sort of way." I answered honestly.

He nodded at the wisdom in that. I didn't envy him orchestrating the sad demise of marriages and families all day every day. Even if they had stopped working years ago, even if they had best be put out of their misery, still it was sad.

Suddenly, I felt all empty inside. What should I do with myself until Reed's performance? I wandered over to the Raging Burrito, which was just catty corner from the Decatur courthouse, and ordered myself a Sweetwater 420. The television was blaring with fast-paced soccer, the bartender had an orange mohawk, other at-loose-ends Friday afternooners were sharing the bar with me. I had a second beer. That would be dinner. And help me through the awkwardness of the evening.

The performance was terminally painful, Rachel sitting between me and her father like a little uncomfortable buffer. As soon as we had all dutifully clapped and stuffed down some dry cookies in the school lobby, I wanted out of there.

"You were great, Honey." I praised Reed, who played second cello very competently without a lick of practicing.

"Thanks, Mom. Are you off soon?" He was inhaling a brownie.

"Yep, first thing tomorrow. You guys leave Sunday, right?" I had put their suitcases in my car to transfer tonight since no one but me had the new keys to the house anymore. Ha!

"Yeah." Reed was still elated from performing. Rachel was bored with another of her big brother's events, but enjoying the sugar buzz.

"Okay, we only have to say goodbye for a couple of weeks. Not long. You have lots and lots of fun in Costa Rica, promise?" I was determined to be upbeat, trying to disguise my eagerness to fly away myself. "Remember sunscreen and bug repellent?"

Dan looked daggers at me, but the kids nodded affably. Mom was being Mom.

After Reed got their bags out of my car and put them on the trunk of Dan's, I came back in for a moment.

"Bye, my darlings." And I hugged them both fiercely.

"Bye, Mom." Reed was upbeat still.

"Bye, Mommy." Rachel was less so, but not despondent. Her friend Rosie caught her eye and Rachel ran over to talk to her.

I took that cue to back away and turned as they got swallowed up in the milling crowd of proud parents and loud kids.

As I walked to my car, more than ever I craved the quiet, majesty, and otherness of the rainforest, not this precious crowd of private school posers and snobs. I wanted reality, however challenging it might be. I was almost sure that Don Alberto would ask, no tell, me to take the real amount of Medicine and I was nervous about that, truth be told. But cross that bridge. Hopefully we could cross that river first, since I definitely did not relish a repeat of March. I would be loaded down with several extra duffle bags full of the school supplies and I wanted them to get to the Bajo Ila schoolchildren, not be drowned in unexpectedly raging waters. But Ecuador was Ecuador, a place where control was elusive, if not downright illusory. I absolutely had to go, though, to repay the debt to the townspeople of Bajo Ila, to hug my sister for the last time, to reach the culmination of this crazy, fantastic, painful, surreal year.

I slept deeply.

Chapter 21

Sally, David, and I met at the airport early. David had graduated last week and was hefting a fancy camera. Sally was happy to go back to Ecuador so soon and I was glad to have the chance to get to know her better. We chatted as we waited for the flight to be called, while David napped nearby, cradling his Nikon protectively on his lap. I never could sleep in an airport, not much on a plane either, so I was drinking tea and munching on a muffin, while Sally relished her coffee and Danish.

I had checked three huge duffle bags full of school supplies and had the Buckhead Bettys' cash safely in my passport holder. No jewelry – I had already pawned my ruby ring and my hands felt gloriously unencumbered. I kept wiggling my fingers to feel the new sensation.

I was catching Sally up on my crazy life. She was happily married to Mason but very sympathetic and suitably aghast at Dan's doings that lead to all this upheaval.

"How have you been holding it together?" She asked me, "The job, your kids..." She always looked wistful when mentioning children.

"I'm not really sure. I guess I had no choice. Yes, I mean, I have tenure so I can't be fired unless I sell grades or sexually harass my students, but still, one wants to do a decent job. Bad course evaluations don't help when they hand out those huge raises..."

She guffawed. "Yeah, right." She was a lecturer, so she had to get good evaluations to keep her job at all and her raises were even more pitiful than mine. But my grant was picking up her expenses for this trip, like Mason had for me in March, so we were kind of even now.

"So, I think we should deliver the school supplies to Bajo Ila first off, not to drag all that around more than we have to." I suggested.

"I agree. You did an amazing job pulling that together. I especially love the Buckhead Betty fundraising, too." We chuckled at that petty revenge.

"I'd love to see them staggering around Machu Picchu in their designer heels and all."

"Probably wearing white head to toe. Like the Brits in India."

"'Oh, no. I got a smudge on my Prada bag.'" Sally imitated a strong Southern accent.

"More like, 'Oh, no. They just stole my Prada bag.'" I added. "I tried to warn them not to carry purses or flash their giant diamond rings around, but they were too drunk on Veuve Clicquot to pay me any attention."

"Serves them right. Peru is no walk in the park, even if you are rich. The wealthy are more of a target anyway." Sally was rueful. With her frizzy blonde hair, light skin, and blue eyes, she was a quintessential gringa, like me, but rich we were not. And we never wore white in Latin America, that's for sure. But still it was dangerous.

"You know, the first time I went there was in 1981 and it was really rough back then. No toilet paper anywhere, only one-way tickets to places because it was too chaotic to guarantee when a bus or a plane would return to get you anywhere. I got stuck in Huancayo for three days, trying to get to Cusco overland, and that was one nasty town. My boyfriend and I had to give up and go back to Lima on the bus and wait for a plane. And we were mugged too. Good thing he was six-two."

Sally nodded, knowingly. "We all have stories to tell, huh. Mason and I have gotten into some tight spots ourselves over the years."

"Riding that plucky little horse across the river right up there?" I wondered.

"That was, let's just say, exciting, shall we?" We smiled at the memory. After we got back, the students had made up t-shirts that said, "I survived the Wall of Mud in Ecuador, Spring Break, 2005" and given both of us one. This time around, I was hoping for dry weather and a smidge of luck. Of course, mainly I couldn't wait to meet Mags at Cotopaxi. I was sure Don Alberto already knew all about that without being told in conventional ways. I'd bet "his" rocks had told the rocks on Cotopaxi to expect matching visitors from different cosmic realms.

"So, after the visit to Bajo Ila, I want to go to see more sacred carved rocks with Don Alberto, hopefully without absorbing any more 'mal aires.' I have an article in mind, about the continuities between the Inka and the modern traditional Andeans, specifically beliefs that rocks are alive and actively help shamans to cure. What do you think of the title 'Using the Past to Heal the Present' with some sort of subtitle?"

"Sounds great. Did you have to do another set of stupid paperwork to talk to Don Alberto again?"

"No, I just sent a note that I was going back for more answers to the same questions. Although I am not really. I mean, I never followed up on his comment that the one rock with all the spirals helped him talk to visionaries in Africa, for goodness sake. I just wrote it down in my notebook and didn't have time to think about it until I got home and then it struck me as bizarre and fascinating. I want to ask him how he *knows* they are in Africa and what they consult about, if that's what they're doing."

"He says surprising things, even after all these years of the fieldtrip. Hell, we just heard about the rocks last year!" Sally shook her head slightly.

"Definitely you guys' long relationship with him has paved the way for my research, and I am very grateful to you and Mason, I hope you know."

"Of course, our pleasure. One of the perks of what we do is getting to know our colleagues better when they come on the trip." We smiled shyly at each other.

"So, one more thing. When we're done with Don Alberto, I'm going to go on a day trip by myself with Juan Antonio. You guys can have some free time in Quito." I didn't especially want to share my reasons and though Sally looked at me curiously, she nodded and politely didn't ask what I was going to be up to.

The flight went by quickly and we landed once again in the Quito airport, this time being mobbed by porters wanting to help with all the luggage. Good old Juan Antonio was waiting for us outside Customs and Baggage Claim, a sight for sore eyes.

"You made it! And look at all this — is it all for the children's school?" He was upbeat as usual. The university was certainly bolstering his tourist business these days.

"It is. And I have three hundred dollars in cash for the teacher to spend however she wants to! On the kids of course." I felt very proud to be back, fulfilling my promise so quickly. Something in my life was going well, at least.

"I've told Don Alberto that we're coming to Bajo Ila the day after tomorrow and they've planned a whole big ceremony for us."

"Oh, wow. That sounds wonderful. I'll have to practice a speech!" Maybe write it down and run it by Juan Antonio. I could speak Spanish better than I could write it but if I got nervous, I'd lose all my verb tenses, guaranteed.

We hoisted the heavy bags into the minivan, thank goodness David was a big strapping guy, and set off to the hotel for the night. Same accommodations as before, and the city was as beautiful as I remembered, with the glorious mountains in the near distance and the almost painfully blue sky above. A delicious meal and some quick shopping for the required trip gifts for Reed and Rachel followed. For him, I found a chess set that pitted the Spanish against the Inka, the "knights" riding horses or on llamas, which was also funny because you can't ride llamas. They lie down and refuse to get up if there is much more than eighty or a hundred pounds on their backs. For her, I figured a pretty embroidered summer dress would be good. No need to struggle for a gift for Him this time, either. Hooray! The three of them would be on the plane to San José tomorrow, along with Rich Girlfriend. Please Ganesh, keep the kids safe, I prayed silently.

The road to Tena had not improved one iota since the last time and we bumped along for hours and hours in the smothering heat. The town was dustier and no less depressing than last time. After a crummy dinner and a restless sleep in a lumpy bed, we started out for Bajo Ila first thing. The river that raged last time had kindly retreated to being a gently flowing creek and we sailed through the water as Sally and I cheered. David enthusiastically snapped photos the whole way. He was planning to propose a little exhibition of trip photos for the university's library gallery – it was another part of the grant that the university had evidently liked.

"Maybe we'd call the show 'Giving Back'? To highlight the school supplies?" I asked David.

"Sounds good." David was terminally laid back, his long blond hair straggling into his bright blue eyes.

We pulled up a little way outside of town and this time the people poured out of the houses to greet us. Don Alberto stood calmly by the side of the road with several of his sons, Constantina, and a couple of miscellaneous daughters clustered around him. He never smiled, but gravely bowed his head in acknowledgment of our repeat visit.

The little kids were all dressed in their khaki and white school uniforms and lined up to shyly offer us their hands as they must have been told was what gringos did. But no one had told them that they were supposed to squeeze our hands, so it felt to us like grasping a little limp fish every time. I was glad to feel my hand sanitizer safely nestled in the pocket of my pants, to be brought to bear at the earliest moment. Bajo Ila did not look like much of a toilet paper kind of a place.

We approached Don Alberto and paid our respects. I told him about the school supplies we had brought, and he sent his sons back to the van to heft the duffle bags over to the schoolroom. They carried them like they were feathers, not seventy pounds each. Constantina kissed me and Sally on the cheek, smiling broadly when she saw how much we had brought for the children. She introduced these daughters as Camila, Antonia, and Marta. They shared their father's broad, high cheekbones and their mother's wiry build.

The motley crowd of townspeople seemed to have swelled to about fifty people, so some had to be from another town in for the grand occasion. I fervently hoped we had enough of the ziplock bags ofp aper and pencils to go around. Gustavo formally ushered us into the school building where some mismatched chairs had been wrangled from somewhere and, surprisingly, a boom box was plugged into probably the only electrical outlet in town. The teacher was waiting at the front of the room, and grasped our hands warmly in greeting, introducing herself as Luisa Alvarez. She too wore khaki and white, a rather bizarre choice for a terminally muddy or dusty jungle town, but obviously government-mandated nonetheless.

I was gestured to the center seat like royalty and the proceedings began as we fanned ourselves vigorously with our hands. Luisa took over and announced there were seventeen items on the agenda. My heart sank a little at that number – there would be no lunch for a long, long time. First the students were performing, then we'd have speeches, the presentation of the school supplies, then lunch, dancing, and a game of futbol. Dancing! In rubber boots and zip-off jungle pants in the million-degree heat? Jeez, we'd be here 'til dark!

The tiny little children went first, doing a simple dance in a circle and clapping their hands. It was incredibly cute. Then a slightly older group of girls came in, astonishingly decked out in coconut shell bras over their white t-shirts and grass skirts over their regular skirts. It was hard for me to keep a straight face. I dared not look at David or Sally for fear we would fall out. How Polynesian costumes had gotten over here was a mystery, but it seemed like when white people came to visit brown people it was what was expected. Colonialism lives on in strange ways.

Then a boy recited a poem in which he said that when his mother said she loved him, her eyes were as blue as the sky, more racism that made me feel very uncomfortable. I didn't want to be "Bwana" but here I was, travelling to exotic places, doing charity work, and dashing back to my uber comfortable life far, far away. Oh well. If the rainboot fits... And some kids get to learn something potentially useful in making their ways in the world they were born into..

More songs and dances ensued until finally they had performed themselves out. We clapped hard and long for their brave efforts. David must have taken a hundred photos.

Now Don Alberto rose deliberately and began a long speech in Quichua. I had no idea what he said, naturally, but sat attentively watching and listening as if I did. Then Juan Antonio nudged me, and I stood up to give my speech, which he had helped me flesh out to be as long-winded and flowery as possible, since that was de rigeur with Spanish. I tried for maximum drama in retelling the story of how we were saved by the town, how I promised them I would return with school supplies, and how we had retraced our steps to be here today and to present them with said school supplies. David was still furiously snapping away. I could tell by all the nodding that my tale was hitting the spot. Then I ceremoniously pulled out the envelope of cash that I had commandeered from Atlanta's well-heeled ladies and handed it to Luisa. She did not act surprised, oddly, and casually laid it on an empty shelf on the wall. My Western paranoia kicked in, the feeling that it wasn't safe out in the open like that, but then I reprimanded myself – the money was a gift and how it was handled was not my business. Plus, these people were so kind and generous, I couldn't imagine anyone stealing it from their own children.

Finally, it was lunch time. I squirted my hands under the table as before, passing the hand sanitizer to Sally and David in turn. We had the tilapia and rice again, a huge pile of food to be consumed in the oppressive heat and humidity. No sooner had we shoved as much as humanly possible in our mouths, but it was now time to dance. Ugh.

Gustavo turned on the boom box and some tinny, jangly music poured out into the echoing schoolroom. None of the townspeople watched us dance, which seemed strange, but whatever. I clumped around with Gustavo in my sweaty rubber boots, careful not to move my hips provocatively or look him in the eye. Then it was Sally's turn to dance with him and I with Juan Antonio, David with Gustavo's wife Maria Cristina, and so on and so on for what seemed like an eternity. I couldn't remember a time when I sweated more profusely and I had spent many a summer in Atlanta, aka Hotlanta. (There was a bumper sticker you'd see around the city that read "Hell, it's not the heat it's the humidity.") After we performed all the mathematically possible combinations, mercifully we were allowed to stop. I plopped down in a chair to rest and fan my no doubt bright red face.

At that point the locals seemed to be pretty much done with us, and they gathered in ragged groups outside to drink massive quantities of manioc chicha and play soccer in the dusty field. I had warned Juan Antonio that in Peru I had once tried chicha, which was made out of corn chewed up and spit into water, allowed to ferment, and drunk about five minutes before it rotted completely. Here they fermented manioc instead and this version smelled and looked just like sour milk. Since I had nearly puked from one mouthful of corn chicha, I knew manioc would not go down any better, or, more specifically, it would surely come back up. Although I was supposed to be a good anthropologist and "man" up, throwing up would not accomplish the comradery that was the point of sharing drinks in the Andes. Although really getting drunk off your ass was also the point of sharing drinks in the Andes. So, I asked Juan Antonio if he could please explain to them that I was allergic to manioc and get me out of that pickle. Since gringos were well known to be bat-shit crazy, it probably didn't surprise anyone and they guzzled away the rest of the afternoon, Don Alberto and his whole entourage becoming glassy eyed and wobbly on their feet along with everyone else.

I was getting very tired, bored, and still uncomfortably hot by this time and I whispered to Juan Antonio that we really needed to be getting going, since dark would fall pretty soon, and we were still quite far from town.

He had a word with Don Alberto, and suddenly we were whisked back into the schoolroom for some more dancing. Oh, lord. Clump, clump, clump. Change partners. Clump some more.

I found myself near Luisa who was dancing with poor David, who looked a bit the worse for wear since he had tried the chicha, and I caught her eye. I asked her in my best school-girl Spanish what her plans were for the cash. What I heard as her answer was "going on vacation." Shit. I asked Juan Antonio who clarified with her that she meant "go on a field trip" with the kids to the town of Baños, where hot springs abounded and there was a neon light shining on the church tower. They literally had never left this godforsaken place in their lives and for them, Baños would be like Disney World. Whew. I felt even happier that I had wrested the money from those rich bitches. I supposed I would have to tell the Betty's what good their money did, if only to encourage them to support the museum in the future. But I knew they'd just pat themselves on their collective backs for their generosity and have some more champagne. Plus, I'd wait and see if they made it back from Peru after all. I figured the odds were about even money on that score.

Finally, we corralled the empty duffle bags, touched everyone's flacid little hands again, bowed and thanked endlessly and eventually managed to extricate ourselves. Sometime during the day Juan Antonio had moved the minivan farther from Bajo Ila for some reason, so there was a bit of a walk left to do.

I actually felt enormously happy as we meandered down the road. David was in front, then Constantina, and the rest of us followed along in a rag-tag group. There was some chicha-induced stumbling, but we carefully ignored that as par for the course.

All of a sudden, out of the blue, Constantina screamed bloody murder and yanked David's arm, pulling him abruptly backwards with surprising strength. She was minute and he large, but like a mouse pulling an elephant he was reversed several feet in record time.

Then the rest of the group all started pointing, yelling, and running backwards, too. It looked like someone had rewound the video tape.

"Culebra!" Don Alberto shouted as he ran. "Snake!"

And, boy howdy, was it a snake. It was an enormous snake. Stick straight, bright green on top and acid yellow below, at least six feet long and not altogether pleased to nearly have been trodden upon. Hissing, puffing up around her triangular head, weaving back and forth menacingly, she was mad as hell and it was absolutely terrifying. Constantina had broken out in a sweat, it was running down her face like in one of those old Airplane movies, and she was laughing hysterically out of fear. This was not good. Nothing should have freaked a mother of eleven and the wife of a prominent shaman like that.

Regrouping, the now only half-drunk men decided to try to scare the snake off the path by tossing stones at her. We figured it was a her, a mother protecting her young in a nest somewhere off the path but nearby. The sons hefted rocks at her, which only served to make her madder and madder. My heart was pounding out of my chest at this point. What if she didn't ever cede the path to us? We couldn't stay out here in the dark, that's for sure.

It seemed like forever, but, at last, one of the rocks connected and she slithered off into the jungle noiselessly.

As one, we peeled past, running like the devil was chasing us, which she might have been for all we knew. No looking back. A few more yards and we dropped down to a fast walk, huffing and puffing.

I was afraid to ask, but I had to know just how venomous that snake was. Don Alberto informed us that if she had bitten David, he would have died in half an hour without the anti-venom. And we were an hour away from a hospital. He admitted he had no power against such a culebra as her.

I got shivers and chills up and down my body. Poor David was visibly in shock – he definitely would have been the one bitten if Constantina had not spotted the snake and pulled him out of danger the way she did.

I asked Juan Antonio if he knew what type of snake it was and after consulting Don Alberto for a few moments, he replied,

"I think you would call it in English an 'Emerald Viper.'"

"Oh, shit." Sally and David and I chorused, looking at each other, aghast.

David gulped, but to his credit he managed a weak joke.

"My parents would have killed me if I had died down here." Rueful smile, brush hair from eyes.

"And me." I added. "And I wouldn't have blamed them one bit."

"Well, hopefully I still have eight more lives left." He was taking it awfully well, whereas I was getting more and more upset and shaky the more I thought about how close that call really was. Sally was rendered completely speechless, trudging along watching every step of the path extra carefully.

At last, there was the minivan and we jumped in and made it back to Tena just before nightfall, not saying a word.

I thought to ask David if he had gotten photos of the snake and he showed me a number of them, bringing back the horror in living color all over again.

"It'll play well in the exhibition, at least. We'll look like brave adventurers instead of scared shitless academics." I offered. "But then your parents will know how close you came…" I couldn't finish the sentence, it was too awful to contemplate.

I decided over a nice cold beer that evening at a wretched Tena dive bar that this would be my last foray to the Amazon. There were only so many bullets you could dodge. Little did I know that the gun remained fully loaded.

Chapter 22

Don Alberto had sent his son Chuck into Tena to lead us to another of his camps, this one on the banks of the Río Blanco. This camp was luxurious by Amazonian standards, with three wooden buildings, one actual bathroom, and a raised deck. The rainforest was close in all around the little encampment, greener than green, pulsing with the shrieks of howler monkeys and macaws, crawling with oversized bugs. Sally and I shared one of the buildings, which had walls going most of the way to the roof, but openings all around the top to allow for air circulation. We merited the only bathroom and wooden twin beds with light scratchy blankets on top and flat, elderly pillows, no sheets. The weather was warm and humid, but not too hot under the rainforest canopy, so we'd be fairly comfortable. David and Juan Antonio had the second building and the family was packed into the third, hammocks draped everywhere for sleeping. Winston had already taken a hammock when he preceded us to the encampment.

We were lounging on the deck, which had built-in benches around the perimeter. Everyone was a bit drowsy, having gotten up early to get all the way here from Tena. The minivan had to stop several miles from here because the rainforest got too dense and there wasn't a road anymore. But it was mercifully not raining, since it was the dry season, so the walk had been easy.

For the past few days we had been based in Tena but traipsing around the countryside on day trips to visit the boulders and hear their stories. One was a nice rock, known as the Mother of All Frogs, because it had outlines of them etched all over its smooth, grey surface. We had chalked in the lines to make the carvings visible and David took copious photos as Don Alberto told us her tale.

Though he always spoke to us in his somewhat broken Spanish, he began her account with the traditional Quichua phrase "Ñawpa pacha" which meant "in the old days, long, long ago" like our "once upon a time." As in so many folktales, there was a terrible flood. The frogs, led by the Mother of All Frogs, knew to swim upriver to where there would be higher and drier land, but the (unutterably stupid) humans did not. So the frogs very kindly showed them how to build balsa wood boats. The humans managed to do so and to climb on them, but then they didn't have any paddles. By this time the waters had risen alarmingly, so the frogs sighed and said they would tow the boats for the hopelessly inept people. They all got to higher ground safely. Then the poor humans whined that they were hungry. The Mother of All Frogs spun around, reached into her belly and produced corn, telling them they could pop it. But we don't have any fire, they complained, so she spun around again and out came a burning stick. Having done all she could for the useless, pathetic people, she jumped straight up in the air and came down as this rock, covered with all her baby frogs. It was such a cool tale, I'd retell it in my article. And my students would get a kick out of it, as would Mason's when Sally told it to him.

Another carved boulder we visited was a stern father figure, keeping shamans on their diets or punishing them if they lapsed. Its spirit had once sucked Don Alberto down into the Underworld, where he had a different wife and family, lived in an unfamiliar village. His "this world" family hadn't seen hide nor hair of him for three months, though to him he was only gone for a few days in the other world.

One rock near Tena was called the Shaman Rock, but he had told us that the spirit was gone from it. It was too close to town and the energy was wrong, so the spirit had abandoned it a while back. But, Don Alberto explained, people still came to it to be cured. That was startling, but when we asked him why, he told us that the people who *believed* in its powers still got healed. OMG, shamanism includes the "placebo effect"! I'd have to tell Mason and it would confirm all he thought about how the placebo effect undermined Western science at its very core. This was classic. Worlds collide.

Yet another boulder had female figures all over it and Don Alberto used it to help with fertility, either too little of it or, as in the case of his eleven children, enough already. He explained that when he took the Medicine, he had to see one of the enigmatic hooked lines either right side up to encourage pregnancy, or upside down to prevent it. Constantina had begged him to do the latter and she had finally stopped getting pregnant as a result, according to him.

"The stones have advised me...." Don Alberto intoned and we all roused from our stupor to listen to what the rocks had to say now.

He took a moment in silence.

"We must all take the Medicine. Full dose. Tonight." He was adamant. "I cannot let you know all about the rock spirits without you meeting them in *their* world. If you are to write things down and have other people read what you write, then you must know what you are talking about. As you know, ayahuasca is the key that opens the Portal." His face was even more serious than usual.

It was just as I had suspected, I had to do it or break Don Alberto's trust and defy his explicit directions. His argument made some sense, too, my book would be somewhat hypothetical unless I had had a version of the experience that was its subject. My article and the book were basically being held ransom. David looked startled but nodded his agreement to the plan. Sally quietly nodded too. David was young and his generation quite familiar with drugs, but I didn't know if Sally had imbibed any on her many trips here. It was not polite to ask. Don't ask, don't tell basically.

"We understand. We look forward to it. Thank the rocks for their wisdom, please." I gave a little bow of respect, despite my misgivings. The first time had been fine, but that had only been a half dose.

He tipped his head back at me and strode purposefully off into the jungle, taking Winston to help him pick a good vine and harvest some of the leaves that made the vine work. We call the vine *Banisteriopsis caapi* and its partner *Psychotria viridis*. From among the untold thousands of plant species in the Amazon how the indigenous cultures had long ago figured out those two catalyzed each other was a mystery. Well, it was a mystery to us, the shamans all said that the plants told them directly. I always had my students read *The Cosmic Serpent* by Jeremy Narby which was based on believing the shamans about things like that – it would always blow their minds as it had mine the first time that I had read it. By now, to me it was old hat, having experienced so many spherical moments in the last year.

The rest of the afternoon I felt some trepidation about taking a full dose of the Medicine, but I knew that you had to go into these experiences with a positive attitude. I knew and trusted Don Alberto so that was a good start, and the small amount I had taken on the last trip had kept me feeling great for weeks afterwards. Plus, there was that black jaguar who was waiting for me to come back and meet him. I would concentrate on all those things and hope for the best. In the back of my mind, on the other hand, I knew that even Western medicines affected me strongly and not predictably. Oh, well, no turning back now. Suck it up.

We knew there would be no more food for us today, but we were given a little juice during the afternoon and tried to nap so we could stay up late.

"Are you really okay with this? You don't have to do it on my account." I asked David when we were back on the deck as evening fell, like clockwork, at 6:15. I felt almost like one of his parents, tasked with keeping him safe – humongous, deadly Emerald Vipers notwithstanding – and here we were planning to take an electric can opener to our heads together. Much less on the university's dime. Was in some bizarre contest to see just how many of its rules I could break in one year? At least David was not my student anymore, he was over twenty-one, he could make his own decisions.

"I'm super curious about it, so this is cool with me. Reading about it just isn't the same as doing it. And I'll keep it to myself, not to worry." He smiled and his dazzling blue eyes flashed in a beam of sunlight that had penetrated the canopy.

"And you?" I turned to Sally.

She smiled conspiratorially but answered readily, "I'm excited. Bring it on."

Okay, well, here goes nothing, then.

"You can do it. I'll protect you."

I silently thanked Mags for her support.

After a while Winston appeared with four cups of the nasty brown liquid, which was not any better going down than it had been the first time. It made us all cough and gag. There were puke buckets nearby, just in case. And lemon wedges close to hand on the railing of the deck to help clear the bitter taste from our mouths. Of course, Don Alberto did not need such things anymore and he threw his Medicine back in one practiced gulp.

I knew that the onset of ayahuasca visions were often heralded by hearing a buzzing sound, like a swarm of angry bees. I sat and awaited the spiritual bees' arrival, feeling my heart knock around in my chest in nervousness. What I gradually heard instead was like a freight train going a hundred miles an hour, coming straight towards me. Oh, shit. Oh, shit. Oh, shit, I thought, and it all started crashing down on me.

I looked over at the others and their heads were lolled to one side and their eyes closed. I shut my eyes, too. Another thing that I had read about visions was that you are in a state of dual consciousness, both Here and Not-Here at the same time, so if you look at this world it will be overlaid with the other realms and it gets even more confusing. Closed-eye seeing lets you concentrate on the visions on their own. Seeing better than you ever had with your eyes shut tight was another wonderful shamanic paradox.

And soon I was Seeing like crazy. Like crazy crazy. Images flashed by at breakneck speed, I felt I was on a wild rollercoaster ride up and down, round and round. It went on for what seemed like an eternity. At one point I did lean over and contribute to the bucket, which was most unpleasant. Winston put a lemon wedge to my lips after I puked. He was the helper tonight, holding space for all of us.

Then I saw the whole sky become the most beautiful butterfly, stretched from horizon to horizon, wafting her enormous wings back and forth. Her loving protection filled me to the brim. At the same time as I was watching her above me, she was encompassing me, I was safe wrapped in her colorful wings. It was ecstatic.

But then a deep grumbling male voice started speaking to me, in slow motion, like a really scary horror movie. Like Vincent Price on steroids. I hated that. He kept calling me "Becky" in that drawn-out ominous tone as if I had done something terribly wrong. I tried to say, "please stop," but found I could not speak. That made me panic, knowing I could not ask for help. Winston must have sensed my discomfort because he came over and put another lemon wedge up to my lips and patted my shoulder. That helped me to understand I was still here, somewhere in my body, and it calmed me down some.

But soon panic coursed through me again when I found I was no longer able to move any part of my body either. I began to chant to myself "I'm almost okay" over and over, knowing I wouldn't believe myself if I said I *was* okay. Because I wasn't, not even close. NOT OKAY.

But just before I thought I'd lose it completely, the scene in my head again changed dramatically. I was seeing the night sky, twinkling with a million stars, black as pitch. As I enjoyed the view, a piece of the sky seemed to peel back, open up, in the shape of a mandorla, a body halo like the one around the Virgin of Guadalupe. Inside it brilliant light, daylight times ten, was shining out. At that moment, I understood that the night was just a veil, a thin layer of darkness obscuring the perfect light of the universe. My glimpse of the truth of the matter made me happy to the depths of my soul. And I had the abiding sense that the human-shaped light was another female protector, actually the Virgin of Guadalupe who had revealed herself to Juan Diego in 1531 and promised to help defend the Indians against the Spanish. But the female-shaped opening in the sky was also, somehow, "me." I had the profound realization that I was the light in the darkness. And I was part of a universe of light, each star was another little rent in the black curtain of the night. I felt flooded, overflowing with hope and wisdom.

Then in my visions, out of nowhere came the black jaguar, stepping onto the deck as if he owned it. Even though it was coal black dark I could see him clearly, black on black on black. But, surprisingly, he was completely emaciated and his coat was dull. He told me, wordlessly, that he was very hungry and piteously pleaded with me to feed him. I felt no fear of him at all, only deeply sorry for his condition and magically I fed him some meat. He was very grateful, then abruptly disappeared. I looked around and noticed there was his mate and their three cubs nearby on the ground. They too were in bad shape, asked me to feed them, and I did. Sending me glorious love and gratitude they winked out like the male had moments before. Or hours before, it was hard to tell. I felt extremely blessed to have Seen them and especially to have helped them. Even in my state I remembered that jaguars don't have triplets in "reality." Well, in this one they did.

"The cubs are you and your kids, silly."

The roller coaster continued on and on after that for an eternity but eventually I felt Winston pull me to my feet to help me walk back to our room. I was like a baby taking her first steps, but he encouraged me, propped me up, and somehow we made it there. I collapsed on my bed and he pulled the cover over me, like a loving parent would a sleepy child. I tried to thank him, but nothing came out of my mouth. I heard him say "de nada," "you're welcome," and then, thankfully, I passed into a heavy sleep.

Sometime near dawn I awakened to the feeling that someone was pressing lightly down on one of my feet, maybe to wake me up? But why would someone wake me up, I wondered, confused. Then I opened my eyes and made out a dark, vaguely triangular shape that was sitting on the blanket. Instinctively I kicked that foot up and whatever it was fell with a plop onto the floor. Grabbing my flashlight from under the pillow, I shined it on.... a very large vampire bat. It had the body shape, long rat-like tail, and held its wings out to the side for balance as it walked, like a drunken Charlie Chaplin, all around the perimeter of the room. I watched in horror as it scuttled lightning fast up the wall and flew out the opening under the roof. Shit. Why I didn't scream, I don't know. Sally slept peacefully in her bed throughout the whole thing. Deep breaths, Rebecca, deep breaths.

I barely made it to the bathroom before all the ayahuasca exited my body in various odorific ways. I sat on the toilet, shaky and weak. How was I going to clean all this up, when I felt like an over-stretched rubber band? After I rested some more, I managed to peel my disgusting clothes off and take a shower, rinsing the clothes in with me. The floor was another matter, but I half-heartedly mopped it with the wet clothes and rinsed them in the shower again. I would just throw them all away. They would contaminate everything else I had with me before I could get to an actual washing machine. So I stuffed them in the trashcan and staggered back to bed, begging the Universe for no more surprise animal visitations, in one plane of existence or another.

Of course, when we all emerged later that day, Don Alberto loved the bat letting me see and feel it. Bats were now one of my spirit helpers, he announced with a rare, fleeting smile. My mind was full of the specter of giant rabies shots to the belly if the bat had bitten me, not yet seeing it quite as such a blessing. I was running smack into my Western worldview that wild animals were dangerous, in the flesh, even if the five black jaguars in my vision had been benign. When I recounted the butterfly, the light behind the darkness, and the jaguars, Don Alberto was visibly impressed. I omitted the bad parts, still feeling shell-shocked by the ominous voice and the roller coaster ride from hell. But I still felt like Teacher's Pet.

"I knew the rocks were right. You were given much wisdom on the Other Side. The bat also confirms this. Now you can write as an authority, not as a, how you say, passer-by. It is good." He declared with a brisk nod.

We celebrated by sharing a lukewarm beer, which threatened to make me heave again, but I choked it down manfully so as to be culturally correct this time. At least it wasn't chicha.

He told us tomorrow was a day off from rocks and visions, and we would go take a nice swim in a waterhole. Whew. That should be a relief.

Or not....

We paddled in two dugout canoes up the river a ways, clambered out and started hiking, our clingy nylon bathing suits smotheringly hot beneath our clothes. We passed one inviting-looking waterhole, bubbling away, but Don Alberto shook his head vehemently for some reason and we silently kept slogging on. At last, we came to a second one, nice and calm and inviting. He nodded and we gratefully stripped off our sweaty clothes and stepped onto the rocks conveniently protruding from the oasis of cool water.

Although I had so looked forward to the nice dip, suddenly I felt very weird about actually getting into it. I hesitated on my rocky perch while the others splashed around happily. Okay,

I'd get in and cool down, then get right back out, I decided. I did so, but a near-panic feeling came over me just before I hauled myself back up onto my rock. Gradually the others did the same and we all sighed with the pleasure of being wet all over, cool for a few precious minutes.

On the tromp back to the canoes, we carried our clothes to preserve the feeling for a few minutes more, wearing just our big rubber boots and bathing suits. I'd seen Sally in her underwear the last time we were in Ecuador getting fireballs blown at us, so it was no big deal. I averted my eyes from David's incipient beer belly as best I could.

As we scrambled back into the boats, Don Alberto commented casually,

"I bet the anaconda that is usually in the first waterhole was in the second one today. The first one was too turbulent for him."

Anaconda? A motherfucking anaconda? Right below our legs??? Oh, my Jesus. First the world's most poisonous snake, then a mondo vampire bat, and now a goddamned anaconda???? I instantly wanted to be home in my own house, in my own bed, with no animals more threatening than three lazy, spoiled house cats to contend with. Now. Yesterday.

David, Sally, and I shook our heads in disbelief at one another. Three close calls. Three flirtations with death. Enough already.

As soon as we got back to camp I told Juan Antonio we had to get back to Quito tomorrow and it was hastily arranged, though Don Alberto couldn't understand the urgency. Well, he lived in the jungle and took ayahuasca several times a week – that was his life, but I finally got it through my thick skull that it was not mine. No matter how much it interested me, no matter how much I respected him and his world, it still was not mine. All I had to do was get to Cotopaxi and see what or who was there and then I would hightail it home, back to my children. What if something catastrophic had happened to me down here? The thought made me go cold. My motherless children would be raised as hellions on a beach in Costa Rica and major in surfing and smoking pot.

I had a lot of trouble sleeping that night, with bats and snakes and deep voices calling me "Becky" swirling all around my head. Around three a.m. maybe, I realized that I'd much rather teach about dangerous jungle animals and extraordinary visions than confront them directly, thank you very much. These would make great stories for my shamanism and art classes (minus the profs snarfing ayahuasca), and to impress my friends with how macho I could be, but it was simple: I really didn't want to be this macho anymore. My Mars in Aries had had itself a workout and now I wanted to be back being a gentle homebody Cancer, please, Universe. Even if this was Mags protecting me, none of the animals actually killing anybody, I was taking way too many risks. As much as I longed to be with her, I was certainly not ready to join her permanently on the Other Side, watching helplessly as my children floundered.

When we said our goodbyes and thank you's to Don Alberto, he wished us well on the rest of the trip and then astounded me by adding, "Say hello to your sister for me." Par for the damn course. The others looked confused but kept their mouths shut.

Sally, David, and I tried to begin processing everything on the ride back to the big city. They had received some pretty heavy visions, too, and the snake and the anaconda freaked them out as much as it did me. Hearing about the bat was sobering to them, too. We managed to laugh a little, after a while, but it was weak and not very heartfelt. It had been way too overwhelming.

The jungle gave way to town and town to city the noisy traffic and lit-up restaurants and overall bustle of Quito a jarring juxtaposition of worlds. However, a truly cold beer and a nice cool shower felt positively amazing back at the hotel.

And tomorrow beckoned.

Chapter 23

I was beyond excited when Juan Antonio picked me up to set out for the day trip to Cotopaxi, only about thirty miles south of Quito. David and Sally were going to sightsee around the city together, visit churches and museums, maybe shop, eat out. I envied them a day without having to brave the god-awful roads, but I knew my jostled kidneys were going to be worth it, at least I hoped so. If everything worked out, each lurching pothole would bring me closer to seeing, and feeling, my sister, my twin, for the very first time in my conscious life. Probably the last time, too, but right now I wouldn't think about the bargain we had made with Them, perhaps more like a pact with the devil. But there'd be plenty of time to find out whether we'd be able to still communicate after this or if today would be my first, last, and only contact with her. Either way, I was determined to savor it.

"Are you on your way yet?" I heard like a shout in my head.

"Yes!"

I forgot and said it out loud. Juan Antonio said,

"Yes, what?"

"Uh." I couldn't think of anything, my mind was a total blank.

He glanced over at me with that patient look on his face, no doubt reserved for the antics of us pesky gringos.

"Just remembering something nice." I left it at that, lame as it was.

As we drove along, the scenery was simply amazing. Horses and cows stood hip deep in the tall, ultra-green grass, munching away without making so much as a dent in the dense, overflowing foliage. Outrageously bright red and orange flowers dipped and drooped over the walls around the houses where women were hanging out the wash to dry and children were noisily chasing each other around. Men were pushing wheelbarrows or standing around chatting and smoking cigarettes. Our minivan was noted by the locals but made no great splash. They were obviously used to tourists being shepherded around by guides and taking pictures of them and their world as if we were on safari or gawking at caged animals in the zoo or something.

In fact, I had borrowed David's Nikon for the day, though I was getting spectacular nature shots and was not going to try to photograph Mags. If all the ghost stories were true, her image would not register anyway. Come to think of it, if it did, it would simply look like I had coerced someone into taking a photo of me. The linear world of photography and the "real" world should not attempt to coexist, anyway. They were just different, complementary, outside and inside, not really occupying the same space. But the mountain was going to be spectacular and the landscape on the way there was changing minute by minute as we gained altitude. The exuberant foliage was gradually giving way to shorter grass and then drier, higher land, in various shades of brown and eventually dotted with large boulders. Juan Antonio pointed out to me the wiry, skinny wild ponies that inhabited these moonscape highlands. Even from a distance, our car scared them into galloping away and hiding behind the boulders, ears flicking back and forth in fear.

"It's remarkable that they can find enough to eat up here to survive." I commented.

"They sometimes wander down lower for the grass," Juan Antonio explained, "and of course no one ever bothers them." The boys on the Costa Rica fieldtrip heedlessly harassing the iguanas came painfully to mind. Americans. Sometimes I was ashamed to be one of them.

"This is the most amazing country. So much wildness, so much beauty." I mused.

"That it is." He smiled broadly. Being an inveterate hiker and climber, he was visibly more and more content the higher toward the sky we climbed. His unusual dark green eyes sparkled – he was more Euro than Indigenous. "I come up here a lot. It is such a long climb to the peak that you have to start from base camp at midnight to begin the ascent if you hope to make it back down before dark the next day. It's safer to go upwards at night than downwards, too." That made sense, but I had no desire to climb that high.

"And the summit is what, 19,000 feet?" I asked.

"And a bit more. We will be lucky if we can see the top, it's usually covered in clouds. When the massive ice cliff peeks out and the sun reflects off it, they say that Cotopaxi is flirting."

"I just love how the whole landscape is chock full of different personalities. The kind rocks and the strict ones, the female mountains, that will all go into my article when I get back home."

"I'd like to read it. You seem to understand the Andes more than most gringos do. They just want to take photos to show they were tough enough to travel here. And to capture 'the natives' in their natural environment and show their friends their spoils." He twisted his mouth in an ironic expression.

"Thanks, Juan Antonio, that really means a lot. Partly, it's my job to try to grasp the Andean way of being and thinking, because it interests me so much. But really it also makes more sense to me personally than molecules and atoms, much less Jesus hanging on the cross." I was on my way to meeting my dead twin sister angel, after all, so atoms staying in one place and Jesus dying for my sins seemed absurdly irrelevant. But that would be TMI and Juan Antonio, though deeply sympathetic to shamanism, himself was a lapsed Catholic who had been to college in the States, hence his perfect English and worldly ways. But still, maybe I shouldn't have mentioned JC in such a flippant way. However, he nodded in agreement, so it seemed I had not managed to offend him.

We wound our way through windswept landscape, climbing gradually but steadily. I was beginning to feel a little out of breath from the altitude.

"How many feet up are we now, you think?" I queried.

"About 14,000. The base camp is at 15,250 and we're getting close." The peak was indeed lost in the clouds, as he had predicted, but there was still a chance she'd "flirt" with us. The lower slopes of the volcano were enormous. I hoped today would not be the day she erupted -- I had a date to keep with an angel.

Higher, higher, higher. Even just sitting stock still in the car I felt quite light-headed. Being this excited, too, didn't help. I had to concentrate on breathing in and out, in and out. In Peru once I had ridden the highest regular-gauge railroad in the world at 16,210 feet and had had this same feeling. Even the Peruvian passengers were passing out and throwing up, but I was fine if I just breathed. The strangest feeling at high altitude was that all the other bodily functions turn off so the lungs can work overtime to grab the measly amount of oxygen in the air. It was like when you hadn't consciously been listening to the refrigerator's hum but then it turns off, and the lack of that noise becomes noticeable. That day and now again, I felt like my inner workings had halted, even though I would not have said I was actively feeling myself digesting before that.

Finally, we arrived at the base camp, which was a battered, once-blue concrete building and an outhouse with a wonky wooden door. A few hearty souls were wandering around, but, according to Juan Antonio, the serious climbers were still descending from last night's ascent, so the others were likely just curious tourists like me. No doubt "eco-tourists," the bread and butter of Juan Antonio's business. Yet I was not just here simply to look around or brag that I had been on the slopes of Cotopaxi.

"I know this is odd, Juan Antonio, but I'd like about an hour to myself up here. I'll meet you back at the car, okay?"

He nodded politely and briskly headed off to the building. The altitude was nothing to him and he probably had friends to catch up with.

I hefted myself out of the car, slowly, still making sure to breathe consciously. My legs felt a bit shaky underneath me, and yet very heavy, but I managed to walk, bit by bit, away from the camp. I came upon a large, conveniently placed boulder that would shelter me from the view of the buildings and plunked myself down with my back against the massive rock. My heart was pounding so hard I could hear it in my ears. When would she come? What would seeing her be like? What if she never did? My mind was whirling, and I kept glancing left and right, back and forth, looking for her. What if this was all a mistake? Or my overactive imagination? Or a trick? I'd be so disappointed if that were true. I'd be devastated.

Then I noticed that the wind had suddenly picked up, blowing from behind the rock, around it, and past me. Funny, there hadn't been a wind before. Shamans claimed that sudden winds were spirits visiting, so maybe this was her?

I waited, finding myself holding my breath. But that made me nearly faint, so I went back to steady breathing.

"Bex." I didn't just hear it in my mind, I heard it with my ears.

And there she was, materializing suddenly right in front of me. Not three feet away. Me, Not Me. She had the same features, the same hair, size, shape, posture, everything. My mirror. I had the crazy thought that she was shorter than I had expected, but then I knew I must be shorter than I think of myself as being, since we were a matched set, as it were.

She smiled broadly, lighting up her face, and reached out both her hands entreatingly toward me.

"Mags." It came out as a strangled sob. "Mags."

I struggled up from my sitting position but had to place a hand on the rock's face so I wouldn't collapse at the knees. She was right in front of me. I found myself mesmerized, but at the same time feared that if I tried to touch her, she'd be incorporeal and my hands would go right through her. Or, worse yet, that she'd disappear.

"You can touch me. I'm real for a little while!" She was exuberant. "I can actually feel my body!"

We both began to cry.

"I've missed you so. Even when I didn't know about you, I missed you." I wailed. Tentatively I touched her hands with mine. She was solid. She was real. That made me cry even harder.

"I've been watching you your whole life, you know..." she sobbed as she squeezed my hands tightly, "Every moment. And I've tried so hard to help you, but we can't make choices for you. This was your life to be on your own. Without my being your backup. And it was mine to watch and wait. And hope. You had to come to believe more and more that reality is, well, malleable, or, what was the word you used?"

"Spherical." My nose was running, my eyes were puffing up, but I didn't care. I held her hands so tightly it hurt.

"Yeah. I like that. It comes close to what I experience up, out, wherever it is I have been. There is really no way to convey it in words."

She was staring at me with my own eyes. It was overwhelming, frankly. Mind blowing. Ecstatic. Absurd.

"Can I hug you, is that all right with Them?" I pleaded.

"Come here, you big dummy." She held her arms wide and I stepped into them. It was like nothing I had ever felt before. I was home. I was whole.

We stood together for a long, long time. Everything in our bodies exactly matched, breasts, hips, feet. It was a mirror without the mirror, nothing between the two of us, the one of us, us.

Finally, reluctantly, we parted.

"I need to sit down. This altitude is hard on a body." I admitted.

She grinned. "I love it, it's all so wonderfully solid. The earth, the rocks, the horses, they are incredible. I wish I could stay forever! Never leave you again."

"Oh, so do I, Mags, oh my God, so do I." The thought of losing her again was a sudden stab of agony.

"We have to catch up, quick. Even though I saw your life unfold, I have so much to say to you. And you must tell me everything, too. First, do you remember us in Mom's womb?" she asked hopefully.

"I tuned into it during that Sis-Stars weekend, but it wasn't fully clear."

"Well, maybe it was better not to have remembered it blow by blow as I do. We were having fun at first, laughing at being twins, at Mom and Dad, brother Jack, by the way, who never made it to where I've been, for what that's worth. I think he has a lot more lifetimes to serve. Not much of a fast learner, that boy. I hated that you were stuck with him and I wasn't there to run interference."

"That's for sure. He was a horrible big brother." I shrugged. Water under the bridge.

"Well, you and me, we had a saying, 'Slap me a nub!' and we'd crack up so hard we'd pee more amniotic fluid..." She was smiling at the memory. I was trying to take it all in, but it was a lot, definitely an overload. My mind was positively reeling.

"Then what?" I didn't really want to hear the rest, but I had to know.

"Oh, Bex, then it was terrible. Simply awful. One minute we were bobbing around in the nice warm waters and I was behind you being the Big Spoon, and the next minute an insanely powerful force was dragging me away from you, sucking me away forever."

"Oh, Mags. It was horrendous for me, but even worse for you." There was that Big Spoon thing again, confirmed.

"It certainly wasn't a competition, so no wagering." She kidded. "Anyway, living mortal life can be a bitch, as you well know. Watching you struggle and suffer was no picnic -- damn that man by the way, damn him straight to Hell. Really, really mean. But you're right that I knew for all this time about us being separated and that you were spared that knowledge, at least until recently. Though I know you felt the lack, just didn't have words to put to it." She looked at me so sympathetically that I began to weep again.

"Very true." I choked out, "Apparently, there are quite a few of us so-called 'Womb Twin Survivors' around. They, I mean we, have some pretty notable psychological problems in common. There's even a website."

"Yeah, I know. I told you that those of us who died in the womb have been all around me up here, all of us trying our best to connect to our twins, much less the poor triplets and multiples that got 'harvested.' They are a train wreck. We lucked out, if you can believe it."

"I so want to do something for the survivors like me. You saw that Gregg is one, too, right? That he's the one who clued me in?"

"Sure. But your body told him, only he had to know how to read the signals. He definitely is a godsend."

"What a wild ride, huh?"

"So, the kids. My nephew and niece. Do they know about us yet? I haven't heard that conversation...." She was looking at me levelly.

"No, Mags. I haven't told them yet. I mean it is pretty heavy stuff, right? And Reed first has to learn about the whole story of his birth and all. I have no idea how to tell him about it without him blaming himself, he's such a sensitive kid. They both are, for that matter. But more importantly, right now and for the foreseeable future the divorce has trumped everything else in their lives, our lives. Rachel's only eight after all, poor baby. I am at a loss, so much has been lost."

"And also gained, my darling sister. Reframe, reframe, reframe. Their dad is not going to get them taken away by the police because of the drugs riddling the house anymore. You have kept the house, your pension, and, best of all, you did not drag everyone through the local news circus. They have one very good parent. You have seen their destinies and they rock. They rock. Happiness and Peace? I mean, come on. You raised a Dalai Lama and a Ghandi, girl, in spite of Major Mr. Asshole. Hell, you are Wonder Woman and Bat Girl all rolled into one!"

I tried to absorb all that. Red, white, and blue over black leather? It boggled the mind.

Thinking hard for a moment, I replied, "I think *you* had a lot to do with it, actually, Mags. Sometimes I felt like I had the energy of two people. Which I have definitely needed. But sometimes I think I could sleep for months if I had the chance."

"That brings me to another thing. I must order you to take this summer off from work, Sis. I forbid you to darken the doors of the museum or the department. I mean it!" She stamped her foot for emphasis. And stomped it again, looking delighted at the solid feeling of her body hitting the earth.

"Yes, M'am!" The idea of taking it easy made my insides melt. Yeah, I should sit the fuck around. Go swimming with the kids. Read junky novels. Paradise.

"What else, in case our time is short. What do you REALLY want to know about the afterlife?" She leaned toward me provocatively. Damn. This was nutso, but what an opportunity.

"Let's see. You told me it was true that all our loved ones would meet us, right?"

"Absolutely."

"Is it always warm and sunny? You can eat whatever you want and not gain weight? Is there constant singing?"

"Whoa, one question at a time! So, warm and sunny are physical sensations, but since I can see the sun right now and it is fabulous, I guess it is 'sunny' up there. Anything that you see as positive here, it is in spades up there. There are no bodies, though, so eating and weight are irrelevant, fortunately. We have no idea why that's so important to you Materials. Singing? Sing something for me so I can figure out if that applies in any way?"

"I am a terrible singer, but here goes..." I tried the first stanza of "Amazing Grace," squeakily. When pestered, one of my musical cousins had once described my singing voice as "shrill."

Mag's face lit up and she did a little happy twirl. And another, for good measure.

"Oh, yeah. That's it. We 'sing' all the time. It helps absolutely everything. You Physicals should do it more often. But, uh, maybe you should take lessons or something, 'cuz I think we angels do it a hell of a lot better than you do. Some of you people seem to get together in certain fancy buildings, wearing special clothes, and sing once a week, don't you?"

"Churches, synagogues, temples. Yes, they do. Never did much for me."

"But you dance around with those plump ladies in their silly clothes every month or so, don't you? I like those weekends, they really help you a lot."

"Yeah. The Sis-Stars have done me a word of good in the last few months."

"It was one of my proudest minor interventions to have Bhindi nudge you into it, Bex. She hears us angels loud and clear."

"That's so cool. I suspected as much. I'll be sure to tell her when I get home."

"Okay, in case I disappear soon, there's one thing I have to tell you. No, two. First Bhindi has to do something for both of us. I know you and Don Alberto pushed me through the hole in the sky, and I am forever grateful for that. But, there is, how can I put it, a piece..." She paused, catching her breath and sighing heavily.

"What? What? A piece..." I was desperate to know.

"Okay. A piece of me, not really physically there, but still there. Between your shoulder blades. It's where we spooned. It's like, like, a spiritual molted snakeskin of me. That's what the babies that get starved out of existence in the womb turn into, little wispy, paper-like fetuses stuck to their twin, okay? The doctor saw me, what was left of me that is, but he didn't tell Mom, because back then it was deemed far too weird. No one wanted to upset Mom or Dad with that, so they just... well, they peeled me off and threw me away."

"Oh, Mags. Oh, my God. *The doctor threw you in the trash?*"

"Yeah. That was the times. All the dead twins and multiples ended up in the garbage." We stared at each other in horror. No names for them, no funerals, no headstones, no nothing. Trash. They were not even known to their own families. They were treated as if they had never really existed at all.

"And later I was pushed out into the bright lights and the cold and the dryness. Alone. So alone." I countered.

"Yeah. No one the wiser, except the doctor and the nurses. And they had more babies to help birth that day, like every day, so they had no time to grieve me even if they had somehow wanted to."

I had to sit there for a long time, trying to absorb all this. My heart hurt. My brain hurt. My soul hurt.

"There's one more thing, Bex, that I have to tell you..."

"Okay. Hit me." I tried for some humor, though I was in shock to my core.

"A guy. There's going to be a guy. I know, you probably hate all men right about now, I understand. But it's not Him. He's not perfect, by any means, but he is very, very important in how you proceed from now on. Very important."

"Okay...." I felt deeply skeptical. But Mags was adamant that this was information I needed so I had to trust her.

"He's Native American. Kinda' short and sorta' fat, sorry. But he will do what Don Alberto did with you and all the tornado souls, if you get my drift. Go with him, learn. It's a big part of your fate. It won't last forever, but still, please watch for him and try. That's all I'm allowed to say."

All of a sudden, her face turned a noticeably paler shade. Her body started to lose its color, its solidity, too. She slowly faded out before my very eyes, though I could tell she was trying to stay with all her might.

"No, don't go!" I cried out instinctively.

"I love you, Bex." She managed to blurt out before she disappeared altogether.

"I love you, Mags." I said to the wind.

And I was profoundly and utterly alone. Again.

Chapter 24

The kids exploded out of their dad's car the minute it pulled up with a screech outside my house. My house! I still loved the sound of that.

"Mom!!!" Reed flung his arms wide.

"Mommy!!!" Rachel wiggled all over, her hair flying.

They both rushed over and hugged me at the same time, and it felt like heaven, only made physical, as Mags would say.

"We have so much to tell you!" Reed was still flailing his arms around and Rachel was hopping up and down in her excitement.

"I want to hear it all, but let's get your stuff out of the car first, okay?" And get Dan off my property. I had a vague glimpse of The Girlfriend in the passenger seat, both of them staring fixedly ahead, patently ignoring me. Fine with me. I ignored them back. But she looked tacky, trashy, in her overly dyed blonde hair and copious makeup. Ha.

The kids ran quickly back to the car, Dan popped the trunk, and they hurriedly fished out their roller bags and overflowing backpacks. He tooted his horn once and drove off. The kids didn't even notice.

"Guess what? Guess what? Guess what?" They were falling over themselves with news as they clambered onto the front porch and dragged their luggage into the living room.

They hastily dumped all their stuff by the door and plopped down on the sofa in unison. They were wearing new flip-flops and silly sunglasses on their heads, their hair was a hot mess, they sported golden-brown tans, and their florescent orange and green t-shirts had palm trees and beach umbrellas sprinkled all over them in gawdy profusion.

"My goodness, what? Tell me!" I was caught up in their fervor, though a little apprehensive about the news, since they had been with their father for two weeks, after all. There was no telling....

"Dad's moving to Costa Rica!" Reed crowed and pumped his fist in the air. Rachel giggled with delight and kicked her heels against the sofa as I had asked her specifically *not* to do perhaps, oh, a thousand times.

Wow. "Really? When?" This could be just the thing I was hoping and praying for – Dan thousands and thousands of miles away.

"Uh. This summer sometime." Rachel shrugged her shoulders offhandedly, as if that wasn't the point, Mom. "Isn't that cool! He says that we can go visit him whenever we're not in school." There went my holidays with them. No, wait, I'd fight for my every other Christmas, tooth and nail. And alternate Thanksgivings, too, dammit.

"And guess what else?" There was more? Jeez.

"Okay, what?" I was mentally flinching.

"He and Tiffany got married on the beach last week." Her name would be Tiffany. Married?

"What? They got married? They barely know each other." I blurted out. Truly I was struggling to process all this. The ink was barely dry on the divorce papers, for goodness sake, and he was already re-married? To a Tiffany? The hair and makeup made more and more sense. Where he had met this Tiffany, I was afraid to ask.

"They had some old hippie dude marry them. In their bathing suits. We wore ours, too." They exchanged wondrous looks. Dan could be counted on to do shit like that, and the kids apparently now got a hoot from it. I, however, did not.

"Well. Isn't that…. Something." I was trying to be calm and look neutral but interested. They were so excited they didn't notice my not gushing more.

"Tiffany has a house down there, in a town called Montezuma. That's where we stayed. It had a pool and everything!" I had heard of Montezuma, full to the brim with ex-pats, hippies, and druggies, which was to be expected for Dan to end up there.

"I wonder what he is going to do for *work* down there…" I offered. The kids looked startled, obviously they had not thought that far ahead. Nor had their dad, apparently, who was slightly *less* mature than his children as usual.

"Dunno." They did not look worried. Money was for grown-ups to produce, like living ATM's. Not their problem. But it was going to be, the more I thought about it. And mine too.

As the news began to percolate through my brain, I realized it was going to be a very mixed blessing. Yes, he'd be far away but possibly my child support would go down the tubes, although I had made sure with Henry that Dan would still be held responsible if he moved away. But would I have to fly to Montezuma, Costa Rica, to wrest the money out of him? No matter what, his income would decrease — it was the age-old ploy of deadbeat dads the world over to reduce their income and even quit their jobs so they didn't have to pay as much for their unlucky progeny. Plus, it would be very hard to determine what his income really was, he'd always cheated on his taxes even in the U.S. I'd call Henry tomorrow and ask about the relations between this country and Costa Rica on enforcing child support and reporting income.

We might have to forge another agreement, which filled me with dread. And I'd have to pay Henry's exorbitant fees per an hour to find out... Great. Now I was getting worried.

Then another bad thought hit me: unpredictable, lower, or no child support meant I would have to sell this house. Refinancing would not cut it anymore. The mortgage was pretty steep, over two grand a month, and we did not need all that space anymore. A three-and-two would suit the three of us just fine, not this four-and-three behemoth, much as I loved the house and the neighborhood. How would the kids react to that, I worried.

My mind was working overtime and I was not even hearing the kids' chatter consciously. More ideas came. If I bought a house in Decatur, I'd still be close to the campus and the kids would have a decent public school to go to when the money for their current private school ran out, as it was going to do all too soon. Another thing for the kids to blame me for, no doubt, because that's how Dan would spin it. I could hear him telling them, "Your mom didn't have to sell the house. And your grandparents are rich, they could have kept on paying for the good school." Not that my parents hadn't sunk a hundred thousand dollars for each kid into an education trust, only to see it eaten in half in 2001. Dan thought everyone should be as reckless a spendthrift as he was, and that my family's money meant he was somehow magically off the hook. Easy to spend other people's cash, huh Asshole? The debt he had gotten us into was revealed during the divorce proceedings to have entered six figures and I had had to swallow some of it to buy my freedom. Drugs as well as stereos and ski trips must have upped that debt, now that I thought about it. But I hadn't even known about half of it. Another fucking lie.

I remembered how that fateful weekend in February when I found out about all his nefarious doings I had called the bank and wheedled them into lowering our home equity credit line so Dan wouldn't run it up to the max the minute I served him the divorce papers. I was lucky enough to talk to a woman on the other end of the phone and I laid my problem at her feet, woman to woman. I should have had Dan's signature to change the credit limit, but she miraculously felt sorry enough for me that she evidently was able to bend the rules. Anyway, the money hemorrhaging phase of life was officially over, at least for me. And I needed to show the kids how to be responsible with money and pretty much everything else, including not marrying someone you barely knew. Selling the house and going to public school would make that crystal clear, for better or worse. I could eventually tell them about the debt their father had so wantonly engineered. The trouble was, the bastard always landed on his feet, now that he was gold digging Tiffany and squandering his job to move to Hippieville and drink multiple margaritas watching the sun set.

The upshot of all these worrisome thoughts was that although, yes, I was super happy he was going to be far away, no, I was still not out of the woods and there would be more painful changes for me and the kids to absorb. And now the kids had, Jesus H. Christ, a "step-mother" in Tiffany. Gag. She was NOT their mother, I was, I thought furiously. I'd have to find out if she was at all an adult, if the kids liked her, since she'd have control over MY kids for a number of weeks a year.

I snapped back to Reed and Rachel, who were gleefully dumping the contents of their suitcases on the floor.

"I brought you a present, Mommy!" Rachel was carefully hiding something behind her back.

"So did I!" Reed was rooting around in his pile of filthy clothes to find it.

"Ta da!" She proudly held out a ceramic jar covered in swirly black and red patterns. It was a touristy version of one of the ancient styles, but not too terribly hideous.

"Oh, Honey. That's lovely. Thank you so much! I'll put it on my desk at work right away." I gave her a hug.

Reed shyly held out a small box. Jewelry?!?

Inside it perched a thin gold ring with a tiny green stone set on it, a peridot it looked like. Simple, the way I liked my jewelry. It beat a big ruby any day of the week.

"Oh, that's darling! I love it." I slipped it on my pinkie finger and admired it, giving him a squeeze, too.

Both kids beamed.

"You guys are so sweet." My eyes were tearing up. Just when I thought I had ruined my life and theirs, they got me presents. And, come to think of it, their dad had bankrolled those gifts, so there was a tiny, tiny, reluctant spark of good feeling for him. Minute, fleeting, but there.

"You always bring us presents, so we wanted to get you one....." They both looked at me expectantly.

I got the hint. "I'll go get the ones I got you from Ecuador!" I ran to my bedroom closet where I had them stashed. Every time I went to those closets I thought things like I hid presents, their dad had hidden drugs.

I handed Reed the chess set and Rachel the dress and they both squealed in delight.

As I watched Reed set up the board and Rachel try on her dress, I could actually begin to feel a little hint of anticipation about moving from this house. Letting go of the place where we had all the fights, where he had stashed all the drugs, where his obsessive music playing and his chaotic messes drove us crazy. Dead rats. Kicked-down doors. Now I could get a place that was mine from the beginning, no baggage. I could axe the big lawn that was a bitch to take care of, the kids could even walk to school, the restaurants in Decatur were terrific... It didn't seem quite so bleak anymore. Hey, it occurred to me that even the kids might want to leave these memories behind, too. The school change would probably be the worst part, but that was simply inevitable after a divorce, and I'd explain the true nature of the family finances when the time came, when they were a bit older and could understand. In the long run even exchanging the overly entitled rich kids from their current school for some slightly more "normal" friends, from families that didn't go to London for spring break, would be good for them. We'd survive. Hell, maybe we'd thrive.

I grabbed a pile of dirty laundry and threw it down the stairs.

"Anybody hungry?"

Chapter 25

"Bexs? Are you there?"

THE END

About the Author

Rebecca Rollins, a pen name, spent most of her adult life writing academic books, five altogether. After retirement, she decided to forget the annoying detail of footnotes and bibliographies and try to write more creatively. Out the window of her study, just south of Santa Fe, New Mexico, was the daily inspiration of mountains, clouds, junipers, rabbits, birds, and even the occasional coyote walking by. Gifted with time as well as this setting of such natural beauty, then finding the perfect partner after many years of frustration in love, the words began to flow. Almost everything in the novel is based in "reality," of one sort or another. The authors' travels in Latin America, a painful divorce, the discovery of hidden talents, as well as learning of her twin who died in the womb all contribute to the tale. Rollins plans two other sequels, perhaps more.

Made in the USA
Columbia, SC
25 June 2022

62187437R00134